SEDENTARY SILENCE

ALEX H. SINGH

CONTENTS

About the Author

'A Dream is a glimpse of what you can have if you decide to walk down that path with no regrets...'

Alex H. Singh is a USA Today bestselling author who is Canadian, born and raised in Toronto, Ontario. He has established himself as an expert in the genres of thrillers, horror, and especially fantasy novels.

Alex's fascination with the world of literature started at a young age, and he has been honing his craft ever since. With a natural talent for storytelling, he began writing short stories and poems in his teenage years, and his passion for writing has only grown stronger since then.

Over the years, Alex has written and published many books that have captured the attention of readers around the world. His works are known for their gripping plots, well-developed characters, and immersive worlds that transport readers to another dimension.

Alex's love for the horror and fantasy genres is clear in his writing, as he weaves together spine-chilling tales of dark magic, mythical creatures, and supernatural forces. His ability to create a sense of suspense and tension has earned him a reputation as a master of the thriller genre.

With his USA Today bestselling status and his loyal following of readers, Alex H. Singh has become one of the most respected and sought-after authors in the industry. His dedication to his craft, combined with his passion for storytelling, has led to the creation of some of the most captivating books in recent years.

You can contact or follow Alex H. Singh, or simply see what he is writing next, at:

https://www.bookbub.com/authors/alex-h-singh

https://www.facebook.com/USATALEXHSINGH

To the Fearless Seekers of Sedentary Silence,

In the enigmatic shadows of horror, I, a USA TODAY BESTSELLING AUTHOR, welcome you to a realm unexplored. As you stand on the threshold of Sedentary Silence, you are about to embark on a journey where a secret cult casts its ominous shadow over a once-quiet town, and a deadly entity, thirsting for revenge, stalks its prey.

To those intrepid souls who are about to unravel the mysteries concealed within these pages, your courage precedes you. You are the first witnesses, the trailblazers of the chilling tale that unfolds here. May your journey be fraught with suspense, your nights haunted by the echoes of the unknown.

With a heart both heavy and elated, I extend my deepest gratitude to you, the future readers of Sedentary Silence. May the horror within these pages captivate your senses, the mysteries keep you on the edge, and the demonic entity send shivers down your spine.

Brace yourselves, for Sedentary Silence awaits.

With Trembling Anticipation,

Alex H. Singh

USA TODAY BESTSELLING AUTHOR

ALEX H. SINGH

USA Today Bestselling Author

One Pen, Boundless Worlds...

Content Warning: Sedentary Silence

Dear Reader,

Sedentary Silence contains explicit scenes of sexual assault, violence, and frightening content that may be distressing to some readers. The narrative explores dark themes and intense situations that could evoke strong emotional reactions.

Reader discretion is advised. If you find such content distressing or triggering, I recommend approaching this book with caution or choosing an alternative reading experience.

Your mental and emotional well-being is our utmost concern. If you ever feel overwhelmed or need support, consider reaching out to friends, family, or professional resources.

Thank you for your understanding.

Alex H. Singh

USA TODAY BESTSELLING AUTHOR

PROLOGUE

The shrill tone of the alarm pierced through the silence of the room. Daniela groaned under the duvet and reach out to the phone that was causing such a nuisance. Yet another morning when the alarm won the battle between man and machine. Daniela groaned again. She really had little a choice. She tossed back the covers and took a quick glance at her phone screen to get an idea of the time. 07:15a.m.

__Shit! __She exclaimed and jumped out of bed.

She was going to be late for work if she didn't hurry, struck like lightning by an acute sense of panic and getting ready in record time, so she wouldn't miss her train again. Her job didn't require her to be in so early, but that was exactly what she had been doing since she started working at Sunshine Media as assistant graphics designer. "Had been required to do" was actually the right phrase.

From the moment she walked through the doors of Sunshine Media just over two years ago, she knew it would not be the sunny job she had imagined. The walls were stark white, and the floors were slick black, and every person who worked there seemed to have a bone to pick with her or the other. When she had started out as an assistant, she had been beyond excited to be working in that capacity. It was supposed to be the start of something bigger—a much more promising career at the company—but things had changed in a short amount of time.

Bobby Barton had made it his life's work to make her life a living hell since the day they met. It took only one week for her to dread the mundane tasks that had once brought her joy. For every task she completed, for every move she made, Bobby made it his personal mission to put her down every chance he got. He would clip at her ideas during meetings and belittle her in front of coworkers.

She felt trapped—stuck in this never-ending cycle of abuse—and didn't know how much longer she could take it.

He liked to remind her that it would take years before the company would decide to hire her for a full-time role, if they ever decided to. He'd often say that if she ever expected to be hired, she needed to get herself up to his level of quality in work. While she respected his work ethic and skill, it wasn't as great as he made it out to be. Sure, he was good at what he did, but even she had done better when she worked in New York. Daniela dreaded coming into work. This morning was just another typical morning for her.

Daniela padded into her bathroom and reached for the cold metal handle of the sink's faucet. She wet her toothbrush bristles and quickly brushed her teeth before stepping into the shower. Water cascaded over her skin like a gentle rain, soothing at the same time. She knew she had little time before leaving for work, so she washed herself quickly and stepped out of the shower.

As she went back to her room, she glanced longingly at her huge porcelain bathtub across from the mirror, wishing she had time for a proper bath. Instead, Daniela threw on the first dress she could find in her closet, hoping it wouldn't be too wrinkled from being shoved between two sweaters.

Making sure not to wake up her aunt who lived with her, Daniela tiptoed towards the door of their home. She wished with all her might that Aunt Maureen would wake up early today and make breakfast for once, but stopped thinking about it when she remembered how busy and tiring last night was for them both.

Looking down at her phone screen again for the time: 7:32 AM. She shrugged into her coat, grabbed her bag, and headed out of the room, ready to face another day at work.

As she landed on the third step, Maureen was putting her coffee mug back on the tray. There were no telltale aromas of spices boiling or cereal popping. In fact, there was no cereal! In fact, there were no plates on the table, but someone had pulled out a chair and placed a plate with food on it. Sausage and eggs formed a circle around a hash brown patty that looked like they had taken it from a frozen dinner, but Daniela wasn't complaining. She sat down at the table.

"Morning, Aunty." Daniela said, the smile transmitting into her voice.

"Morning Sunshine." Maureen replied, walking towards the coffee maker. Daniela watched the older woman pour some coffee into another mug and hand it to her. "You don't sound that excited. It's morning though." She added.

"Is it really that obvious?" Daniela asked as she took the mug. She raised the mug to her lips and sipped the dark liquid.

"Huh-huh. What's the matter?"

She shook her head and looked out the window of the kitchen door that faced north east over a stretch of pasture land to where she could see a few rolling mountain tops. "Nothing I can't handle."

She adds, trying to convince herself as much as her aunt.

Maureen frowned and stared at Daniela for a moment, as though trying to read her mind through her eyes. "Then why do you sound this miserable every time you're leaving for work?"

Daniela sighs, "I've got to run, Aunt Maureen. I'll be late if I don't get out now. Have a great day!" She said with more than normal haste and ran out of the door before her aunt could continue with whatever line of dialogue she had begun with her niece.

Daniela paused at the corner and looked left, down a long street. She thought back to her conversation with her aunt as she walked down the street. Apparently, her frustration at her job was not so hidden as she thought. She kept walking, wondering how much longer it would be until she could turn around and run the other way.

She kicked a pile of leaves into the air and slid across them in large shuffling steps. The road was filled with leaves that told the story that September was ending. Although it had been hot for most of the summer, New York's short fall season brought brisk days with cool nights. Leaves yellowed and then turned red and orange before falling from branches to the ground below. This was a view that wasn't so common in New York. Her thoughts shifted to her life in New York. She knew better than to think about New York because she always ended in a down spiral, but she couldn't help herself. She missed New York and its crazy energy every day of her life.

In New York City, she had everything. Her life was like something out of a storybook for many. As the head Graphic Designer for Martin Media, she could travel internationally for her work and she was truly living the dream. Or so she thought...

A voice inside her mind reminded her of what she had to leave behind. Her boyfriend had betrayed her with their mutual friend, the company secretary.

The betrayal was deep–by not only cheating on her but doing so with someone she trusted. It felt like a double blow that made her question if there was any love at all or if it had all been a lie.

So, in order to start over and move past her heartache, she left it all behind and started a new life with her aunt and cousin. Despite fearing facing the future, she faced it bravely, knowing that she deserved better.

It was her fault. She had made the mistake of taking on the friend as a business partner because she thought they were friends. Their partnership at Daniela's own graphic-design firm had taken up all her time, so it was no wonder that she didn't notice what was going on with her fiancé. But after the breakup with him, she lost much more than just her fiancé and her dream man. She had lost her job at the high classed marketing agency because of their breakup, since one of them had to stay on board and it obviously wasn't him.

There was nothing to run to anymore, not even her old passion for design, which Daniela had given up when she met him and he took over most of their apartment in NY by filling it with furniture from his family's company—now ironically enough called Dragon Furnishings Inc. She would have to start completely over again. And fate appeared to present her with an opportunity: When her uncle passed away and left his whole estate behind for his stepchildren Daniela and Daniela, Daniela needed someone to look after things for her in Tisdale while she sorted out how to be on her own with no one but herself to lean on.

So Daniela picked up and left for Tisdale.

Tisdale was in beautiful northern Michigan. Once a tiny blip on the map, Tisdale had boomed with the railroad in 1875. Tisdale was just a small town now; peaceful and slow-moving, like most of northern Michigan. The population numbered around 1500 people and grew no larger than about 2000 during the summer. The college that provided employment for several locals, Ceder Villa University (CVU) sat just outside Tisdale's city limits, less than eight miles away. Students from all over the world came to learn for a year or two at CVU before graduating and moving into the real world. They stayed in nearby Ceder Villa Town and drove back and forth to school every day along roads as straight and flat as a sheet of paper. Such a busy little town for learning it was! All around Tisdale there wasn't much else except isolated farms tucked away amongst greenery, farmland nestled between hills that rolled out across the horizon like wrinkles on skin.

She was happy as she had her two best friends that kept her sane as she transitioned from NYC to life in Tisdale.

Kimbery was the light-skinned black Jamaican; people said she had dreads for days, and that wasn't an exaggeration. The woman had glorious hair, but Daniela was too self-conscious to really consider getting a hairstyle like hers.

She met Kimbery at the Tisdale College, where she took a refresher course when she had just arrived from New York. Kimbery worked for a radio station, Bardo Radio, as a radio host. It didn't surprise her when Kim told her where she worked. With the voice Kim had, like all the voices on the airwaves surrounding her in New York City, Daniela could not think of a job that would be a perfect fit for her. And not only did Kimbery have this vibrant, animated voice that drew you in and made you want to listen, taking any class with an open mind was always appealed to her because it kept your mind active and your imagination going.

And then there was Iris. Iris Dupuis was not your typical girl. There were many things about her that made her unique. She had been a holistic healer when Daniela had first met her, and she still followed the new age philosophy today. At 5 feet 5 inches, Iris had a petite frame, but was exceptionally curvy and attractive with beautiful brown eyes, short blonde hair with light pink highlights and big, generous lips that quirked up at one corner in a perpetual smile. In contrast to her feminine and outgoing personality, it was obvious from looking at her that she was of French descent. She often spoke at length about her background, always letting anyone listening know exactly what part of France she had come from.

When Iris travelled through the city, she always tried to see everything that was new. There was something about being in a crowded place that made her feel alive and unlike anything she had ever known. She loved those moments of wonder, these minor shocks, when you feel you are living for the first time in your life. Today it felt like summer had fallen into her lap: the air was warm, with a hint of nip to it; the sky shone bright blue and clear over the endless green as far as she could see; and people came at her from all angles, each one more unique than the next.

Daniela shook herself out of the daze; she had reached her destination. She took a quick look at the glass door to see what she looked like. Her hair was a little messy and there were streaks where she had wiped off some unseen spot or smudge on her forehead. Not like she ever did most times, anyway. She patted her hair down a little and tucked a stray strand into place. It was too late to change who she was.

Iris never grasped the fact that Daniela was one of those girls who simply didn't bother to make any effort to look beautiful. Her makeup was minimal and her clothes were never fashionable. She wore the same smock-like skirt from last year, weaved in a turquoise and yellow pattern. The skirt came to mid-thigh, hiding most of her legs, which Iris found odd for this climate because of the slight breeze coming in from the large window over their heads. They sat at an outdoor cafe on a warm Sunday afternoon, drinking lattes and eating pastries, when Daniela asked her if she ever felt fat. It didn't register until later that evening when Iris noticed how different Daniela looked without makeup, like she had no personality or sense of self-awareness. Daniela was one of those who took a bath, hurried into something in her closet (mostly inclined towards the hipster style), pack her hair into a messy bun or, at most, a ponytail, pull on her glasses and then head out. No time for additional make-up. Iris always found it annoying when they had to go anywhere together.

"Why must you be so wild and untamed?" Iris would scold.

"It is my nature," Daniela would retorted, lips set in a firm line.

"You may not value it, but you should - that Nicaraguan beauty runs strong in your veins. Just look at your skin! Light and almost sun kissed - a girl like you would make many turn green with envy if only they knew the real you. You need to take better care of yourself, Dani!"

"Leave me alone already!"

"Never! You have too much beauty not to be appreciated—why can't you see that? You are a beautiful young woman and I will make sure of that."

Daniela sighs heavily and submitted to Iris's lectures, hoping to avoid another campaign of self-beautification.

Daniela brought herself back to the present. The world of her favorite daydreams felt like another life. Every morning, before going into the building, she had to reassure herself continually so Bobby's talk wouldn't sting so much.

"I am smart, beautiful and amazing," she told herself through gritted teeth as she walked down the hall. "Nothing that man says would get to be me." Complex too. A voice in her head added at the end of the third chant, but she ignored it and repeated her everyday mantra once again. She was going to try really hard to not let him get to her today. Amen. Daniela walked into the office building with a confident smile plastered on her face, ready to do battle with another day.

Daniela walked into the office building with a smile plastered on her face. They always kept the double doors open in the morning, to air out the foyer and welcome everyone in. She had long ago learned not to let what others thought of as 'niceties' affect her. The place was clean enough, it wasn't dirtied any more than any other building of a similar size and age. The foundation was solid concrete and granite, and she enjoyed seeing how old things could stick around through the ages. It gave her hope that one day she might do the same thing. The janitor was doing his morning rounds when she got in.

George, dressed in woolen pants held up by suspenders and wearing a heavy coat that looked too sturdy for an indoor man, waved at her from across the room. His wiry hair was cut short with only a hint of grey in it; he probably kept it short for ease of maintenance. Still, patches of baldness were showing through; much like her own scalp beneath her dark brown hair pulled back into a ponytail.

With his baby-face and round, pudgy hands, he seemed more suited to take care of people than their buildings... Then again, Daniela was just as guilty of carrying out that idealistic falsehood. She wore blue jeans that hugged every curve of muscle like a second skin, just loose enough so they wouldn't inhibit movement or get caught on anything during fights if need be; and underneath those an orange sleeveless shirt with two large leather belts wrapping around her torso - one running from collarbone to hip and the other from waist to hip over top of it - giving her access to several pockets of varying sizes should she need them without having to go looking around for them in a hurry; such was life as a woman who carried concealed firearms most days of her working week. And like George's hair, hers was pulled back into complicated braids which did little to detract from how she looked. There were just a

few people she had to fake her smiles to and pretend she liked them...
And then there was Guy.

"Good morning, Daniela. How are you this morning?"

"Same old. You?"

"Hanging in there. It's a little chilly, though."

"True. I noticed it's been getting unbearably cold of late. A jacket or coat is no match for this frozen air we're breathing in."

"It's the end of September. That's how it gets around here - earlier sunsets and then the sun refuses to come until past 7:30 in the morning. It's like nature itself has given up."

"That's true. I noticed it got dark so early this week, it's like nightfall descended with no warning. I almost forgot it gets like this of the year - my memory fails me more each day! One would have thought after two years, I would know better by now."

"The weather is cruel sometimes. It wasn't this early last year, but here we are again."

"I have to get going now. Enjoy your day." She said and hurriedly headed on to the receptionist's desk before Bobby scolded her for her lateness once more.

"Enjoy yours," she heard him call back as she left to retrieve the mail, determined to get on with her daily routine and beat Bobby at his own game.

"Hi, Margie," Dani blurted out with a sigh as she stepped up to the receptionist's desk.

Margie looked away from the document and greeted Dani with a half-smile. "Hi Daniela, how was your night?" Her tone had an unfamiliar edge of excitement that caused Dani to pause for a moment before responding.

"It was... awesome. Until I woke up this morning." She thought, but refrained from speaking it aloud.

Margie smiled knowingly and asked about Bobby's mail. Dani instinctively reached for them when Margie handed her the envelope. But then something strange happened.

"I really don't think you'd be needing those anymore," she said with a knowing grin on her face.

Confusion flooded Dani's mind as she stared at the envelopes in her hands. "What do you mean?"

But Margie only shook her head and returned to work, offering no explanation. With one last smile, she wished Dani a great day.

Dani thought nothing of Margie's talk as she made her way to the coffeemaker. Usually she dropped off the mail first, then went to make coffee, but that would force her to see Bobby twice within minutes. She really wasn't looking forward to that this morning, so she was going to make just one trip and then deliver the mail and coffee at once. As the coffeemaker brewed the coffee beans, Dani opened up all the mails and stacked them on top of each other. Her job was just to open mails, not read them. She poured some coffee into a mug and headed out of the room, picking up speed as she neared Bobby's office. Something was off. She could sense it. But what? Dani set the mug and mails on the table next to her desk and started in on her work.

As she descended to the basement, a sweet aroma of fresh flowers permeated her senses. Daniela's eyes narrowed with suspicion as she made her way to the table and saw the source of the scent—a beautiful bouquet of roses. Checking for a card amongst the petals, she found an unfamiliar handwriting that read:

"Congratulations on your promotion, Dani,"

Bringing the card closer to her face, she became livid, balling her hands into fists. What promotion?! She thought angrily. Someone was playing a cruel joke on her and it wasn't at all amusing. With Bobby nowhere in sight, Daniela was determined to find the miscreant responsible and deliver swift justice—a bouquet shoved right up their behind.

Dani waited for the elevator to hit the top floor and then opened the door to her previous office. Her boss Jocelyn had moved her into a temporary office while they carefully dismantled Dani's old office and refurbished it for someone else. Jocelyn had short dirty blonde hair and was sporting a shot up cut that reached her shoulder blades when she first met her two years ago. Now she wore it shorter than that.

We were actually planning on coming over to your office. Former office, actually.

It was only when she heard the soft, dry voice of her boss that Jocelyn realized she wasn't alone. Margie, Guy and Aisha, co-worker, were standing around with smiling faces. Dani looked into Jocelyn's deep blue eyes to see if she could get answers to the questions brewing in her mind. Was this whole thing real? Was the flower and note not a prank of sorts set up by her friends to embarrass her?

A chorus of screams drowned out the entire office.

"Surprise and congrats!" they all shouted in unison.

Dani gaped, taken aback by the sudden outburst.

"I don't understand. What is going on?" she said, her voice trembling with confusion.

"Well, Daniela," Jocelyn started with a broad grin spread across her face, "I have promoted you to senior graphic designer. Congratulations! You deserve it!"

"But Bobby.... what about him?" Dani stammers.

"We'll discuss all of that later," Jocelyn cut her off sternly while taking a couple of steps back to assess the situation. "For now, move your things from the basement to Bobby's office and come see me in my office when you're done. And again, congratulations on your promotion!"

The corner of Jocelyn's lips curled up into a sly smile as her gaze shifted away before Dani could react or utter another word.

"Congrats," Guy chimed in and shook hands with an overwhelmed Dani.

Margie wrapped her arm around Dani's shoulder. "We must absolutely celebrate this momentous occasion sometime soon."

Dani suppressed a victorious smirk as she watched her colleagues depart the room. Could this really be true - that all her hard work had finally paid off and her career was about to take off? With a wave of doubt washing over her, Dani shook her head in disbelief, trying to clear away the thoughts that threatened to consume her. Just then, she noticed Aisha's piercing green eyes staring right at her.

"Congratulations, I'm thrilled for you. Absolutely thrilled." Aisha said curtly.

"Yes, thank you," Dani replied uncertainly. She had always felt uncomfortable around Aisha ever since they started working together. Her gaze seemed like the stare of a snake, making Dani suspicious if Aisha's seemingly pleasant attitude was just an act of false kindness.

"So thrilled you got promoted. Really, I am."

Dani felt the icy coldness in Aisha's voice and it made her belly flip with dread.

"Uh... thanks? I should probably start packing up my things now, if that's okay."

"Sure. Go ahead. Take your time," Aisha sneered mockingly.

Daniela trudged back down to the basement, a wave of confusion swamping her mind. What the hell was happening? This started out as a joke, but now it felt disturbingly real. If they promoted her, then where would that leave Bobby? Jocelyn had been so evasive when Dani had brought it up, merely murmuring something about talking later on. So many alarm bells were ringing; this whole situation seemed so wrong and off-kilter to her. With an anxious knot in her stomach, she punched in her cousin's number.

"Amelia Josie Diaz speaking," she said hesitantly, unsure if it was her cousin or not.

"Amelia, don't be so dramatic—you know it's me. What's going on?"

"You always like to jump right into business. So what is it?"

"It's a lot. Way too much, in fact. I got into work this morning and came across the news that someone had promoted me to a senior graphic designer role. It's crazy! But I can't help but wonder if this is all some kind of joke. Jocelyn knows about it, and I'm scared that she may be behind it."

"No way, it can't be true," Dani exclaimed as her face drained of color. "There has to be some kind of sick joke going on here. Bobby isn't even here yet, and this happens? What are the odds?"

"Take a deep breath," her cousin advised. "You know you have a tendency to overreact when things don't go your way. Go talk to Jocelyn and iron out the details before jumping to conclusions. I guarantee it's real."

Dani hesitated before reluctantly agreed. "Fine, but don't call your mum about this one. I don't think I could bring myself to deliver the news if it turns out to be a prank."

"Don't do..."Amelia cut off the call, leaving her with a feeling of dread. What had she gotten herself into? On one hand, she was thrilled to get the promotion, and it felt incredible to be acknowledged for her skills. But she couldn't help but feel something was off about this new situation. She remembered what Amelia had said—not to tell Aunt Maureen until she had things figured out, but that is because she knew her cousin was the one who would tell her instead.

"I'll kill Amelia." She gritted her teeth.

With a heavy heart, she put down her phone and went to find Jocelyn, knowing that her decision must surely have some consequences.

"Hi, Jocelyn." Daniela's voice was taut and strained, as if she had been holding back the words for far too long.

"Oh hi, Daniela." Jocelyn responded cautiously, her eyes narrowing behind her glasses. "So, how are you settling into your new position?"

"I don't know what to make of it," Daniela replied shakily. "It feels like some kind of cruel joke someone is playing on me. It all seems too surreal to be real."

Jocelyn sighed heavily in response. "It's no joke, Daniela. The promotion is as real as it gets."

Daniela's face tightened in anguish before she mustered up the courage to ask, "And Bobby? What happened to him?"

"I came in last night to do some work," Jocelyn began her story slowly. "And I found a note on my desk saying he was done with the company and he had quit saying nothing else. That was all."

Jocelyn cautiously handed over the delicate piece of paper that read Bobby's handwriting. How could he have vanished with no warning? A chill went down Jocelyn's spine as she read the plea for help.

"Without your help, I cannot do this because my hands are tied. You have studied with Bobby and you know everything there is to know about graphic design. You must take his place. No one else can do it better than you. Don't let me down."

She was shell-shocked that Bobby had left without a word, and asks in desperation if Jocelyn had tried calling him. "I even went to his house," she sighed, "but he's gone now. He isn't answering his calls, either."

Dani felt her stomach twist in dread, a ball of ice forming in the pit. Bobby had been inseparable from his phone so for him not to respond to Jocelyn's call; either there was something he didn't want to tell her, or something far more sinister was going on.

The thought of the rumor about a cult hiding away in Tisdale weighed on Dani's conscious like a boulder. It couldn't be true- no one had found any proof yet- but what if it was? What if this group of fanatics had taken Bobby? The thought of a group of people living in secrecy, with their own hidden agenda, sent shivers trickling down Dani's spine.

She turned around and saw Jocelyn standing there, excitement etched into her face. "Daniela?" She said, breaking Dani out of her thoughts. Dani quickly pushed aside the unease that had been building up inside her; she knew she needed a plan. She pulled out her phone and sent a message to her best friends. They hadn't hung out in ages and this was the perfect chance for them to reunite, however with her new promotion, she thought it was best to focus on the storm ahead, so she had a virtual hangout with her besties. The power of watching a movie is streaming together at each other's home.

CHAPTER ONE

"I just sent the deliverables to the client's email," Daniela said into the phone. "I'm waiting for them to send their feedback. From what I noticed, these guys like to take their time for some really weird reasons."

"How long?" Jocelyn asked through the slightly worn down cell-phone speaker.

"I really can't say," she responded as she looked at the blank screen of her laptop, "Unfortunately, these people like to take their time, which then ends up delaying the entire process. This project normally shouldn't last more than a month, but they've been dragging it on for the past three months. It gets tiring."

"Can you handle them?" Jocelyn exclaimed with frustration in her voice. Bobby had tried to work with the client before but could not get any actual progress out of them, and that had led to one of his frequent reprimands from Jocelyn.

"I'll manage," she scoffed. "I actually have been doing a lot of speaking with them and they have agreed to step up."

"How is your trip going?"

Jocelyn's face brighten, "It's been great. I should be back by the end of the week."

"Cool. We can't wait for you to come back."

"I can't wait either," she said, truthfully. "I hear you are doing quite the job back there."

Daniela smiled as the compliment softened her face and softened her tone. "It's a short time to assess what your work rate is like, but I am not disappointed. You do great work and you're excellent with the staff."

Daniela felt her face growing warm. She pursed her lips in dismay and turned away to keep her blush from showing. Jocelyn wasn't the type of person to dish out compliments, but when she did, it usually meant that she was particularly pleased with someone's work.

It felt good to be appreciated by her boss, especially as Jocelyn rarely complimented anyone for fear of losing their respect. You had to earn your right to be called a designer at Sunshine Media.; Dani knew this all too well.

Jocelyn continued speaking before Dani could think of something positive to said: "I'm not just saying this because I hired you or because I'm your manager, but I saw the work that you were doing at Martin Media. It was only a matter of time before the company hired you as a full-time designer. Now that Bobby has left, it was an open seat for you."

"You never mentioned that to me, Jocelyn. Full-time? With benefits?"

"Yes, as long as you keep up the quality of your work. There are still people waiting on new designs; we can't keep them waiting. And seeing as this is going to be a permanent position, I expect you to put even more effort into your work than ever before.

Jocelyn sighs, as if this was a conversation she had held before and one that she did not enjoy. "I know, but you worry too much. I've done all the digging I can and everything points to the fact that he skipped town.

Don't let it affect your work. Even if he returns, it won't affect your work. You would still hold your current position."

"It's not about the job," Dani said slowly, each word carefully constructed. "It's about Bobby." She paused, her face sad with the memory of him and his disappearance. "There's really not much else that you can do now, since you say you've already tried your best."

"Yes, I have," Jocelyn agreed. "Any other updates on the jobs at hand?"

Dani shook her head sadly. "None. We've covered all the grounds."

"Alright then. We'll speak later."

"Okay, bye."

She could try to get used to this. Running things... calling the shots... being the one in charge. But she didn't know when she would start easing into the tasks. It still felt a little off being the one giving orders and not receiving them. The fact that Jocelyn had been really magnanimous with her compliments today was an added advantage in making her feel like she had done something right. They had taken to telephone updates on the jobs at hand. Adjusting the name tag on her desk, Daniela read out loud what was inscribed on it.

—

Daniela Maria Savan,
Senior Graphic Designer

These reactions were about her new promotion and title. When she looked back now, a few weeks later, she wondered if she wouldn't have reacted as strongly if someone else had received that promotion. She could never be sure; however, her gut still told her that would have been the case.

Well, her intuition had been screaming at her since the day she accepted this promotion. The title on the name plate still didn't sit right with her. Two weeks into this job, she still couldn't understand why they had chosen her for the role. She worked hard, but nothing seemed to sway the decision-makers in a good way.

Two weeks into a new month, in a new job, Daniela could still feel the same sense of uncertainty as she had on the day of accepting this position. Bobby had been off the radar by now; he wasn't answering calls or responding to house visits by family or friends. Even his social media accounts were mute. It was as though he had vanished from existence. Daniela had an unsettling feeling that something ominous was going on.

It was odd that he would just leave his entire life behind. There had been no signs of distress, no warnings that he wanted to leave, but one day he just wasn't there and an envelope with a few boxes sat at the end of his desk. Everything he had was here, and he had just upped and outed. That unsettling feeling she got every once in a while came back to her. She still felt like something bad had happened to her predecessor. There was no explanation for all of this, and it baffled her all the time. A knock on her door bolted her back to the present.

While working as Bobby's assistant, the girl had been interning at the company for the better part of six months, but she was assigned to help her adjust to her new position.

"Good morning, Mam."

"Hi Patrice. And please, enough with the boss thing. I was Daniela before... I still am. Have a seat."

"Thank you." She replied and sat on the chair opposite Daniela. "You're a really cool person."

"Why, thank you. Why do you say so?"

"These past two weeks working alongside you have been truly remarkable. I've always known you to be kind, but I never expected your warmth to persist, especially after your well-deserved promotion. Knowing you received 'special training' from Bobby, I thought you might have changed."

Daniela leaned back in her office chair, her expression a blend of empathy and understanding. "I can't be the way Bobby was with anyone," she confessed. "I know firsthand what I went through working with him. But I have a feeling Bobby isn't the main reason you've come to my office. What can I assist you with, Patrice?"

Patrice nodded, taking a breath before speaking. "You're right, Daniela," she said. I came here with a clear and specific request. If the need ever arises, I was wondering if there might be an opportunity for me to work as your assistant. I believe it would be an incredible chance to learn from someone of your calibre. Your work ethic is exactly what I aspire to emulate. I've witnessed your dedication and expertise, and I'm eager to absorb as much as I can."

Daniela considered Patrice's proposal, her brow furrowing thoughtfully. "Your credentials are certainly impressive," she acknowledged. "I haven't entertained the idea of having an assistant before, as I've been accustomed to handling my workload solo. However, your suggestion has caught my attention. Since it's the second week of October, I'll take some time to reflect, and by next week, I'll provide you with a definitive response. In the meantime, I'd be open to having you work closely with me temporarily as we explore this possibility. How does that arrangement sound to you, Patrice?"

"Very. You're the best!" Patrice beamed with admiration.

Daniela, though appreciative, wanted to address business matters. "Thanks, I guess. What's the status with the tasks I assigned you yesterday?"

Patrice's face lost some of its sparkle as she replied, "I'm still working on them. I'm having a bit of trouble bringing the visuals together as you requested. It's not coming together as smoothly as I thought it would."

Daniela leaned forward in her chair, her tone confident and encouraged. "Here's what we're going to do. I'm not sure which application you're using, but I'd recommend trying to sketch for this task. And, Patrice, clear your mind of any preconceptions about what I might expect. Work on it as if it's your own project. I want to see your creativity shine through. There's a reason you're interning here, and I want you to prove it to me."

Patrice nodded, determination returned to her expression. "You got it, boss."

Daniela leaned back in her chair, fixing her intern with a steady gaze. "I expect it to be completed by the end of the workday."

Patrice saluted playfully. "Yes, ma'am," she affirmed, and with that, she exited Daniela's office, ready to tackle the challenge with renewed vigour.

Daniela couldn't suppress the genuine smile that crept across her face. Patrice had something special, a spark that reminded Daniela of her younger self. As she watched the intern leave her office with determination in her step, a thought crossed Daniela's mind. She had grown fond of Patrice, and if she ever considered having an assistant, the young woman might be the perfect candidate.

Having observed Patrice's dedication and talents closely, Daniela believed she had what it took to excel in the role. While Daniela couldn't see herself needing an assistant at the moment, she acknowledged that someday the time might come. That was one perk of her job—it provided her the freedom to make such decisions.

Daniela relished her new position as the Graphic Designer, and her colleagues, including Jocelyn, were equally delighted with her presence. However, there was one exception to the general jubilation—Aisha.

Aisha had made it her mission to pick up where Bobby had left off, and her demeanor had taken a considerably more hostile turn since the announcement of Daniela's promotion. However, Daniela paid little heed to Aisha's actions, convinced that they stemmed from nothing other than jealousy. Aisha had always harbored envy towards her, and it appeared this animosity would persist.

Previously, Daniela had pondered the reasons behind Aisha's jealousy and mean-spirited behavior. There seemed to be no justifiable cause for such envy. However, the recent promotion had provided a clear incentive. Who wouldn't be envious of a success story like hers? It wasn't every day that someone rose to prominence overnight because of their boss's unexpected departure.

Her thoughts then drifted to Bobby's unexplained disappearance. Despite passing time, Daniela couldn't shake the feeling that something had transpired with him. The note he had left sounded utterly unlike the Bobby she knew, and she couldn't reconcile it with his character. She revisited the days they had spent together in her mind, searching for any clues that might have shown his impending departure. As far as her recollection served her, there was no sign at all.

She replayed their last moments together in her mind, and the memory sent a chill down her spine. Bobby had become livid when he noticed she had injected some of her own creativity into the project they were working on together. She could never forget his words; each one cut through her like an arrow, piercing deep into her soul as he accused her of undermining his work. It was then that she fully realized how deep his resentment ran, and how it would ultimately lead to their parting.

She fumed at the memory of their last day together. Bobby's words still echoed in her mind as he had towered over her. *"You always try to make me look inferior! What did you think adding those changes would do? You're trying to take my place!"* His cruel accusation felt like a punch in the gut, and she recalled every detail of the too-familiar argument. She had just been trying to spruce up his lackluster design with her own touch, yet all Bobby could see was her attempt to oust him.

Daniela was stunned. She had been doing all the work, running errands for him, so why had he suddenly vanished without a word? She tried to convince herself she was overthinking things and nothing serious was happening, but her reassurances only faded away with each passing moment.

Her thoughts were becoming more frantic, and she wasn't making any progress. Glancing at the laptop clock, she couldn't believe it was already lunchtime. After spending hours at her desk, finishing one task after the other, her stomach rumbled with hunger and exhaustion. Still conflicted over what could have happened to her boss, Daniela took a break before getting back to work.

She hesitated as she saved her work one last time, fingertips hovering over the keyboard. She had to get out of here, but something was telling her to stay. What if someone got their hands on her laptop and changed the information she had worked so hard on? No, no way Aisha would do something like that... or would she? Daniela quickly threw the laptop into her desk drawer, securing it with a key from around her neck. As much as she wanted to trust her co-worker, she needed to be sure. With a sigh, she grabbed her lunch bag and marched out the door, ready to clear her head and think with no distractions.

"You're leaving already?" Margie questions as she approached the reception.

"Yep. I need a break from the hustle and bustle of work. Even I get over-whelmed sometimes," I replied.

"I understand completely," she said, nodding her head in agreement. "Oh, I have some mail for you. Would you like me to drop them off at your desk, or will you be collecting it when you get back?"

"I'll drop by after lunch," I answered.

"You really should hire an assistant. You've been working yourself too hard these past couple of days," she suggested, her brows furrowed in concern.

"That's true, but I'm not there yet. I'm still considering a few candidates for the role, so until then, I can manage." I gave her a smile before continued, "Alrighty then. See you later."

"Bye! Take care!" Margie waved goodbye as she watched me walk out.

Daniela sauntered towards Tisdale Park, her refuge from the world. She almost welcomed Bobby's harsh treatment - it gave her an excuse to come here and recharge, free of other people's chatter. Two blocks away from the office was her haven; when she had time to escape, this was where she would go. Bobby had broken her emotionally; other times, Daniela remained indifferent.

Five minutes later, she arrived at the park. It was eerily quiet - evidence of how modern-day society now lacks the traditional social gathering of parks; instead, everyone seemed to cling to screens and gadgets for enter-tainment. But Daniela was content with seeking alternative sources of joy. As she made her way to her usual bench on the grounds, she pondered that loss of connection between people and nature - an opinion which only strengthened as she settled down on the icy surface of her seat and looked up at the cloudy sky above. She'd grown up visiting the park often, but those days appeared to be over.

As Daniela sank into her cozy bench, the October breeze teased her hair. She gingerly tucked every lock back into place, careful not to let any escape. Beside her, she placed her lunch, that was tightly packed in her wicker basket. The bench she has chosen felt like a warm hug every time she stepped closer to it. Now and then, people of all ages filled the park. Daniela's gaze glimpsed an elderly couple walking hand in hand with their adorably tiny Chihuahua. The sight made her smile as a reminder that nature still had its own beauty, even when urbanization was on the rise. With that thought in mind, she opened up her basket and started enjoying her lunch.

Her mind raced, recalling the muted whispers that curled around Tisdale. Rumors of a dangerous cult that lurked in its shadows, hidden from view — so far out of sight that even the police couldn't locate them. She had mulled this over a thousand times in her head, but nothing seemed to make sense; there were no confirmations that this cult actually existed, yet it seemed too fantastical to be completely untrue... there had to be a grain of truth at the center of it all, she concluded as she pondered further.

Daniela had made a solemn vow to herself and the town—to uncover the truth, no matter what. She could feel it in her gut. This was something she had to do, or else she would be stuck in this small town forever.

After graduating from college with a refresher course in journalism, Daniela had set out to start up her own amateur news channel on a popular media sharing site. With one cameraman, two cameras, and a few other essential items, she was ready to go. Now the only thing missing was an audience. Little by little, they had been building up a loyal following, but it wasn't fast enough for Daniela.

Every Friday afternoon, they got together to look for interesting stories that were happening around town. Most of the time there would be something small-scale, like a kitten stuck in a tree—not exactly the newsworthy story that she wanted to cover for the rest of her life. But if she could find any leads about this cult story, that could change everything for the news channel.

Daniela had been trying her best to uncover the secrets of the cult. So far, she had made no progress - until a few weeks ago, when a student stood up and accused their professor of being a cult member. This announcement sent shockwaves through the town; everyone was curious and skeptical at once. Then suddenly, the police started an investigation into the allegations, and Daniela tried desperately to get in touch with the student.

The atmosphere around town was one of intrigue and speculation. Some people wrote it off as utter nonsense, while others were convinced that there was truth to it. As they waited for answers, people placed bets and engaged in conversations that filled the air.

But sadly, it was short-lived. By the next day, the student recanted her statement and said everything she said was a lie. The townspeople felt disappointed as they realized that someone had hidden whatever secret lay beneath the facade.

The Cult of Standish was born from the legend of Gregory Standish, an insidious Warlock whose family was feared for their pagan witchcraft. Tales of their unearthly powers and black magics spread like wildfire, and now followers of the cult have risen to honor Gregory's wicked legacy.

The rumors that swept through Tisdale were as chilling as they were terrifying. Whispers of a cult, with followers devoted to its every will. Dark and twisted rituals - from depraved sex acts, animal sacrifices and even rumored human ones - sent shivers down the spines of its citizens. Despite the fear, no one had any evidence to back up these claims. It was all just stories designed to shock and scare the youngsters at camps. But for her, it was an opportunity; one she would not let pass by without a fight. With determination burning in her heart, she sets out to find the truth hidden within the shadows of this nefarious legend.

She analyzed the facts she knew so far: her boss had gone missing with no warning. She had come up with a few theories in her head, but none that she could substantiate without further investigation.

Was he abducted, or had he left of his own volition? Had someone ordered him to pack a suitcase, making it seem like he'd chosen to leave? Too many questions circled in her mind, and she was running out of time — there was still a truckload of work to finish. The farewell note only compounded the mystery; Jocelyn counted it as evidence he'd gone for good, but something about it seemed off.

The words echoed in her head as if Bobby were speaking them himself. If only she could read the note again and uncover what it hid beneath the lines... but how could she without arousing suspicion?

Daniela sighed and looked down at her sandwich. She was down to her last morsel, so she savored it as best she could. After taking a swig of water to help wash it all down, she absentmindedly reflected on the criticism that seemed to come from every direction. Maureen had chastised her for not properly hydrating while eating, but what did it matter? It didn't feel like anyone respected her opinion, anyway.

Stiff from sitting in one place for too long, Daniela got up and brushed off the crumbs before packing away her lunch bag. She hadn't even taken the time to enjoy her meal, being so consumed by other people's issues instead. This whole situation was beginning to take a toll on her; she was losing sleep over it already, and now felt the start of a headache coming on.

As she started walking back towards the office building, she reminded herself once more - she needed to slow down and be mindful; putting other people's problems above hers would only leave her feeling drained. But there was still only twenty minutes left of lunch - if she ran, maybe she'd make it back in time.

Daniela rummaged her hands over her neck to soothe the pain in her muscles. But that was not all that ached. Something else nagged at her heart. She absent-mindedly clawed around her throat a second time and suddenly, she realized her locket had vanished! Fear seized her as she raced back to the bench where she lunched. But there was no sign of it? Daniela cursed herself for being careless. Resigning to defeat, she wheeled around dejectedly and trudged back to work with a heavy heart.

CHAPTER TWO

As Daniela opened the door to The Butterstick, a wave of heavenly aromas embraced her and welcomed her in. Her senses filled with a symphony of scents; delicate notes from the freshly baked goods, intense earthy richness from the ground coffee beans, and a creamy, buttery sweetness that engulfed them all. She closed her eyes for a couple of seconds and inhaled deeply, savoring the warm, doughy aroma that seemed to transport her to a place beyond time or space. Every time she entered The Butterstick, she stopped by the door and wanting to stay forever in this heaven on earth.

The Butterstick was a small but popular bakery in Tisdale, owned by the quaint elderly couple of Greta and Jake Martin. Since first arriving in the town, she had made frequent trips to this quaint cafe, so much so that she had developed a certain fondness for the owners. It was here that she had met her new boss, Jocelyn, and pitched her idea for a job. Naturally, it seemed only fitting that Heath and she would meet each Friday morning at The Butterstick - their weekly brunch spot where they'd discuss plans for their upcoming news channel segment "Eye on Tisdale."

Daniela surveyed the noisy room, her gaze swiftly landing on her usual corner. As it had been every day since they started going out together, Heath was there, nursing a neon green soda. He was always punctual, and she prayed he continued that streak. She hoped she wouldn't have to wait for him to show up after such a long day. Taking off her coat, she draped it over one arm and made her way towards him.

"You beat me here again?" she said with an affectionate smile as she took a seat across from him.

"Hey, Heath," she said when she reached him.

Heath rose to his full 6 feet four inches height, and gave her a tight embrace, much too close a proximity to Daniela's liking. He always made her feel small with his sheer size.

Unlike most jocks, Heath Bryan was an exception to the nerd-jock divide. He was an amazing computer genius, yet remarkably strong and muscular in the same breath. Not to mention that he had a knack for looking effortlessly good; from his glasses to his sexy haircut - it was no wonder why so many girls were head over heels for him. Yet the lucky ladies never got their way because all of Heath's attention was on only one person—Kimbery—who showed no signs of reciprocation.

Daniela knew about his secret love but promised herself not to meddle.

"Hey, my favorite cameraman! How are you doing?"

"Your one and only. And pretty good. Did everything go alright at work today? You sound exhausted."

"It was hellish! I can barely keep my eyes open. Stressful and tiring doesn't cover it. I feel like I could just rest my head right here on this table and drift off to sleep."

"Why didn't you call me? I would've come running to pick you up and take you home if you needed it."

"My house is not an option. I doubt we'll receive the privacy or gravity that this situation requires." Daniela hesitated. She wasn't sure if Heath was aware of Amelia's infatuation with him, considering the fact she had never taken her adoring eyes away from him. But somehow, he seemed oblivious to her affections. A smirk crept up on Daniela's lips as the hilarity of the entire affair dawned upon her: Amelia's unrequited love for a man who couldn't take his eyes off Kimbery, yet she didn't even show the slightest interest in him!

"What's funny?" Heath prompted; his deep blue eyes fixed on her.

Daniela's lips twitched at the corners. "Not funny really, just a little. Many people would say I should have called to reschedule for some other time, but here you are saying you could have come to my place. You need to find someone who can occupy most of your time, my friend. Maybe it's time you find yourself a girlfriend?"

Heath sighs exasperatedly and Daniela instantly regretted bringing up the topic. "For one, if I found someone, she won't stop me from deciding to come to you for work. Second," he said, pausing for emphasis as he stared pointedly into her eyes. "You're not helping matters either."

"Kimbery?" Daniela whispers, fully aware of where the conversation was heading and the potential for things to get nasty between them if they continued down this path. Her tired mind couldn't handle what she knew was about to come out of his mouth, and she sure didn't feel like dealing with it now.

"Let's not do this, Heath," she whispered, her exhaustion clear in her voice. "I'm drained and famished and just not ready to talk about this right now."

"Come on, Daniela, why won't you help me out? Couldn't you just say a few kind words about me to Kimbery? She listens to you, and I know she would take your advice. Even though from what I can tell, she's single right now."

The desperation was clear in Heath's voice as he pleaded with Daniela. She bit her lip, trying to keep her emotions in check. "You and I both know that I'm the last person who should give anyone relationship tips, especially after my last one went so horribly wrong. All I can tell you is that Kimbery is... busy with her work right now. Probably too busy for any relationship at all."

Daniela turned away, not wanting Heath to see the guilt that crossed her face. For there was an entirely different reason: she refused to make a case for him to Kimbery - despite how much it broke her heart to do it. The truth of the matter was that Kimbery was more than content being alone; determined to stay focused on her career instead of settling down into a romance. No matter how sincere his feelings may be, nothing could stop Heath from being rejected.

"I'm not just upset," she blurted out, her voice trembling. "I'm devastated! That locket was the only keepsake I had left from my grandmama, and now it's gone." Heath could see the tears welling up in her eyes as she spoke. He knew how much it meant to her. "It's been a week already. Are you sure you didn't lend it to Amelia or someone or something?" he probed gently.

"I can't believe I didn't find it! It must have gone missing when I left for work that day. I know I had it with me then," she exclaimed, annoyance lacing her voice as her eyes darted around the room in frustration.

"I hope you find it soon," he replied sympathetically.

"Me too. Anyway, if I'm going to contribute anything of substance to this meeting, I need to grab something to eat. Did you already get yourself something?"

"Yeah, I ate a while ago. You took so long to show up," he said, his mouth forming into a slight frown.

She huffed lightly and headed towards the sales counter of the small cafe. She would probably have taken just as long to arrive if she was on time - tidying up her desk to prepare for the weekend had been unexpectedly tedious, and every time she thought she could see the light at the end of the tunnel, more tasks appeared out of nowhere.

Daniela inched forward in line as an elderly woman weaved her way behind the man she was supposed to be standing behind. She inwardly groaned, now having to wait for yet another person to be served before making her order. The bakery was unusually crowded for a Friday; although there were often more people on the weekend, it had never been this full mid-week.

The first customer stepped out with his order and Daniela could move closer, but then something else happened. A wave of pressure flooded her bladder, and she clenched her thighs together in vain, hoping it would wane or even subside completely. But it didn't. She wasn't sure how long she would have to stay in the queue before it was finally her turn, but she desperately hoped that she could hold out until then. If she left for the bathroom now, she wasn't certain that she'd be able to get back into the same spot once she returned. The sensation intensified and panic set in. Just hold on a little longer, she whispered to herself.

At that precise moment, her phone vibrated against her butt and Daniela fished it out from her back pocket. Checking the display, she saw it was her aunt calling. Her mind instantly made up; she knew that this decision had been taken out of her hands; there was no way to take a call while surrounded by such a loud cacophony of voices in the bakery. She hastily mumbled some excuse about needing to get back home and stamped out of the line.

"I'll be right back, ma'am. I just need to take this call." She said to the woman before her, not daring to meet her gaze.

"Sure." the woman replies and shifted her eyes back to the counter.

Daniela slipped away from the line of customers and crept towards the stairs that led up to the bathroom area. She could feel their disapproving stares as she left them behind. Reaching the banister, she leaned against it for support and lifted her phone to her ear.

"Hi Aunty..." Daniela said into the phone as she made her way up the rickety steps.

"Hello, sweetheart. I just wanted to remind you to get some bread and milk on your way back home. I assume you'll still be at The Butterstick bakery?" Maureen's voice was like warm honey on a summer day; gentle yet insistent.

Daniela sighed in resignation. "Yes, Aunty, I'm still at The Butterstick bakery, and yes, I remember I should get some bread and milk - though you have reminded me twice since I left home today! You really don't have to keep reminding me every ten seconds."

A small chuckle escaped Maureen's lips as she spoke again. "Oh Daniela, I haven't been calling you every ten seconds! I just want to make sure you forget nothing on your errands today! You've been so busy lately it wouldn't surprise me if something slipped your mind! But if it helps put your mind at ease, then stop by the grocery store after The Butterstick bakery," she said with a comforting smile in her voice.

Daniela bit her lip before replying; it was all she could do not to groan aloud. With every passing second, she felt the pressure in her bladder grow stronger and more urgent until one thought pushed its way through: Please don't said 'one more thing'.

And yet these were almost Maureen's exact next words: "One more thing..."

Daniela closed her eyes tightly and prayed for strength. Was there nothing sacred anymore? Nothing too insignificant to escape Maureen's watchful eye? "What is it Aunty? Please tell me quickly!" She begged through gritted teeth.

Maureen chuckled again and answered without missing a beat: "Please check in on Amelia at work on your way back - your cousin recently started working part time at the ice-cream parlor across from The Butterstick during her lecture free periods. Amelia convinced your mother to let her work there while she attends Tisdale College for Nursing... but being so busy herself of late, your aunt needs someone else to look out for young Amelia! So please check in on her when you have a moment!"

Daniela couldn't help but laugh out loud; she didn't see any reason she had to check on Amelia when she already had so much on her plate, but Maureen apparently felt differently about that matter. "Alright, Aunty," Daniela conceded with mild exasperation. "I promise I won't forget now... Okay?"

"Yes," Maureen said one last time before disconnecting the call. "Thank you."

The moment she ended the call, she sprinted towards the bathroom, desperate to relieve herself before she peed her pants. When she arrived, she heard humming and the vigorous scrubbing of a brush coming from within.

Daniela pushed opened the door and saw an older woman tidying up the stall. "Sorry to bother you. I didn't know you were still cleaning this late. I really have to go now, though." She crossed her legs and fidgeted as she tried to hold in her pee.

The cleaner smiled kindly at her. "You can't use this one now, not yet at least. You can head down to the basement employee washroom for now if you need to quickly. Just make sure you hurry back here once I'm done here."

Her heart racing, Daniela thanked her profusely before rushing down the stairs with dread in her stomach. Working in the basement was something that brought back unpleasant memories, and these cold, sterile walls seemed to amplify them even more so now. A lone strand of cobweb brushed against her face as she descended further into the darkness below, sending shivers down her spine - if she wasn't creeped out before, this did it for her. Regardless, she slowly made her way down and hurriedly used the facilities before returning upstairs.

Dani crept into the room, her eyes scanning for anything out of the ordinary. The rotting wood and molding around her suggested to her that this place was long abandoned. She cautiously stepped over the barrels, which had decayed and watched as the thin film of dust danced in the light coming from a single dangling bulb. Even the air seemed stale and humid, permeating through every breath she took.

It was then that Dani noticed something else lingering in the atmosphere - an errant strand of cobwebs hanging from the ceiling. She felt her stomach drop, but knew she was here now and there was no turning back.

"I hate this place," she whispered under her breath as she rushed into the bathroom. After doing her business, she tried to flush the toilet but found the handle stuck with rust. She jiggled it multiple times before it finally yielded to her touch, sending up a gurgling sound and releasing murky brown water that reeked of rotten fish and algae. Daniela clamped her mouth shut as a wave of nausea washed over her.

Daniela tried to stifle a gag as she held her breath, wading through the musty smell of the bathroom. A distant yelp echoed in the basement, followed by a series of agitated cries. She shivered at the sound; grateful to hear people nearby, but ashamed of her own curiosity that had brought her here. Daniela slunk back into the shadows, sliding behind crates and tarpaulins, concealing herself from view.

Bracing her ears against the deafening music above, she attempted to make out what was being said in the depths of the basement. Trying to make out what was being said in the depths of the basement, she strained against the noise and recognized two familiar voices — Jake and Greta engaged in a heated exchange. Jake's face flushed red as he kept his arms crossed tightly over his chest with clenched fists. His mouth clamped shut and barely contained his rage as Greta spoke contritely, pleading for something that he wouldn't grant. Her expression was one of tension and worry, not anger.

Daniela feverishly attempted to make sense of the heated argument unfolding before her. She strained her ears to listen to every word. According to her findings; Daniela racked her brain for a plausible answer. If it wasn't the mob, as there were no mafiosos in town, then that left only one option -the mysterious cult lurking around. Daniela observed Greta's statement, noting how scared Jake looked afterwards. She couldn't help but feel a rush of emotion and an urge to assist the couple with their concerning problem. Though they barely knew each other, they had welcomed her warmly when she first arrived in town, unlike others who watched from afar and refused to communicate with the City Girl.

Greta uttered something incomprehensible before storming up the stairs, leaving Jake behind, his face pale with panic.

She turned around and watched as Jake trudged back up the stairs with a forlorn look on his face. Once he was out of sight, Daniela wasted no time in fleeing her hiding spot. Quickly, she went to retrieve her phone from her pocket. She had to take some pictures of what she'd just seen before leaving this place. But when she went to switch it on, she saw that missed Amelia's call. She wondered why her cousin would try to reach her there, when she'd clearly told her that she was going to be just nearby at the ice cream parlor. It was only after multiple attempts did she realize that there was no network reception down in the basement. With all haste, she took a couple of snapshots of the area before rushing back upstairs.

Upon getting back into the bakery, Daniela noticed Heath was not alone. Amelia was already sitting beside him and, judging by their conversation, it seemed like she'd arrived a while ago. That explained why Amelia had been trying to contact her earlier. All the shock of the day had killed whatever hunger pangs she may have felt earlier and she simply didn't bother to join the queue now, even though it wasn't too long.

"Ahh, so here you are," Heath said as Daniela approached them at their table.

"Where were you? I've been calling you all day." Amelia added in reproach.

"I'm sorry," Daniela apologized. "My phone must have been in silent mode and I guess I didn't hear it ringing. Anyway, what are you doing here instead of work?" A quizzical expression crossed her face as she gave Amelia an inquiring stare.

It was obvious Amelia had powerful feelings for Heath, though whether they extended to love or even infatuation remained a mystery to Daniela. She didn't want Amelia playing with fire.

"I thought I'd pop in during break and check on both of you," said Daniela, trying to sound casual. "Plus, Mum would have called to you to monitor me, so I saved her the trouble."

"Hmn... I could have sworn you had another reason for coming," Daniela trailed off as Jake ambled towards them. As soon as she laid eyes on him, a chill bubbled down her spine and she felt something was terribly wrong with him. Standing now just a few feet away from them, he seemed ready to break down any second.

"Good day, my dears," he said in a voice that didn't quite sound genuine. "Is there anything I can get for you?"

Heath replied promptly, "Yes, please! I'm hungry again; a croissant will do."

"Same here," chimed Amelia, "though I'll also have some black forest cake and a soda."

Daniela followed suit with an order matching Amelia's. She couldn't help but stare at the old man; he seemed to have aged indeterminably since she last saw him in the basement.

"Your orders will be ready shortly," he muttered blandly as he turned to leave.

Daniela knew she had to talk to him alone if there was any possibility of helping him. There must be something amiss beyond all his awkward smiles and forced affability.

"Umm, Jake," Danny murmurs cautiously, "can I join you? I need to complete the project regarding 'The Butterstick' logo re-design."

"Sure thing," he replied without hesitation, and gestured for her to follow him. As they walked away, Daniela could not help but feel unsettled - there was more than met the eye.

"I just wanted to make sure of the details. The colors should be yellow, blue and a bit of white, correct?"

"Yes," Jake replied as he moved away.

"And regarding the logo, I think you have seen the draft sent to you?"

"Yes, I have."

Daniela stepped forward and clutched his arm tenderly. "Are you all right?" Her question seemed to make him even more worried than he already was.

"Everything is wonderful." He responded quickly, looking around the bakery with obvious fear in his expression.

"No, it isn't. Something is obviously wrong here and I know it. Tell me now, Jake. You can tell me anything." She pressed on gently, peeking over her shoulder to see Greta heading their way.

"Daniela, why don't you come back and take your orders after conducting your business about the sign." He said hastily, as if trying to avoid her questioned.

She could only sigh in despair before making her way back to their table at the corner of the cafe. There, she whispered everything that had happened downstairs into Heath and Amelia's ears, insisting that there was something very wrong in town.

Amelia gasped sharply at this revelation while looking around warily. "That can't be true! There has been no sign of something like this happening since Tisdale was founded, according to what I've seen!

"I'm not too sure, but I could feel it deep down inside my gut. Here... I took some pictures in the basement just now. Have a look." Daniela continued uneasily, showing them the photos on her cell phone.

Heath and Amelia studied the picture closely, scrutinizing details Daniela had overlooked in her haste.

"What's that?" Amelia asked, her sharp gaze catching an anomaly in the photograph. It was barely visible to the naked eye, but her corrective contact lenses enabled her to detect a strange hexagonal symbol with a glyph of a dagger dripping blood from its blade. Someone inscribed the image onto the wall next to the storage room using what seemed to be invisible ink, but it was still just noticeable enough for her phone camera to capture it.

Daniela's heart raced; she hadn't seen this when taking the photo. This symbol was familiar...it seemed to appear whenever someone went missing or a tragedy was about to befall someone. It could have simply been a coincidence or even kids playing around, yet she couldn't shake off an eerie premonition that this wasn't a mere chance.

Lost as they were in their conversation; they didn't notice Jake approaching until he placed their orders at each spot with a warm welcome. Amelie asked him about his job at The Parlor and Jake replied happily while the mood lightened for a moment as they forgot the oddity of the photo.

"Well, it's been quite the night." She replied with a smile and immediately noticed that Jake's face had gone red. Heath and Daniela equally noticed this and followed his gaze to her phone. It appeared he had seen something on the screen that had startled him.

"Are you alright?" Heath inquired cautiously.

Jake exhaled sharply in response before uttering a single word: "Fine." His voice shook ever so slightly as he stepped back from the table. "If you'll excuse me, I need to go." He rapidly marched away but paused abruptly halfway to the kitchen.

Grabbing hold of his chest, his eyes rolled back as he dropped to the floor with a loud thud, barely missing hitting his head. Greta, who was just some distance from their table, rushed to his side immediately, alongside some other patrons present in the bakery. It was obvious by his grasp of his chest that he was having a heart attack and Amelia joined them too, trying desperately to get him to relax and lessen his symptoms, even if only momentarily. However, nothing seemed to work; all the while, Jake kept gazing at Daniela, almost like they were the only two people in the room.

Soon enough his lips moved ever so slightly as though he was trying to say something - she strained her ears harder to make out what he was mouthing - and soon enough she could make out what he uttered - possibly his last words before closing his eyes and passing on.

"Marked by Standish," murmured Jake, his voice so soft and fragile it was barely a whisper. Greta tried desperately to bring him back into the light, tugging at his shirt and calling out for him to open his eyes once more. But it was too late; Daniela felt an icy chill seep through her heart as she watched the paramedics rush in from the ambulance, franticly trying to revive him - all of their efforts futile against death's unrelenting embrace. He was gone.

And still she heard those words echoing like a funeral dirge inside her head; "Marked by Standish". His last whispered plea hung heavily in the air like a thick fog, begged her to find out what his cryptic message meant.

CHAPTER THREE

The cobalt blue Chevrolet crept along through the deserted darkness, the headlights barely cutting through the fog. Rod drove into a large clearing, hidden from view, that was known as the spot to go for couples ready to take their relationships further. He adjusted his rearview mirror and glanced over at Becca in anticipation. She silently acknowledged him with a knowing smile.

An eerie silence loomed between them as Rod set the parking brake and shut off the engine. The stars shone brightly above like glittering ornaments on a Christmas tree, just like he remembered from his childhood. An inviting breeze blew softly over the couple's faces as they rolled up their windows.

Becca had been expecting this moment all night; it was why he hadn't yet taken her home. The air felt heavy with mutual desire, thickening with anticipation of what could come next — but after all, tonight wasn't any ordinary night.

Rod Dailish and Becca Danvers had raced away from the restaurant, a sense of anticipation building between them. They had met just a month ago when she had given one of his colleagues, Christie, a ride to her office; it was fate. The minute she saw his attractive figure donning a navy pinstriped suit, Becca felt an inexplicable connection that she just couldn't ignore.

"Are you sure you don't want me to drop you off at your place?" She asked him as they took their seats in the car.

He flashed her a mischievous smile. "I'm sure," he said, his voice low and husky. Giving directions, he led them to an abandoned park by the lake in no time.

The headlights illuminated the dark night, casting shadows on the secluded spot where they took their third date. Becca stepped out of the car and made her way towards Rod, who already stood waiting for her with his hands stuffed deep into his pockets. Without wasting a single moment, he pulled her closer and planted a soft kiss on her forehead.

She wrapped her arms around him and looked up into his eyes. "So here we are," she whispered, feeling her heart skip a beat.

As they sat in the secluded love garden, Becca couldn't help but thank her lucky stars that she had helped Christie that day. If it weren't for that chance meeting, she would never have met Rod and wouldn't be in this moment right now. The anticipation of what was to come sent shivers down her spine. They had been on three dates, and tonight was the night it was going to happen. The moment their bodies would become one.

The garden was a well-known spot for couples looking to make out in privacy. Bushes and shrubberies that were meticulously maintained surrounded the enormous expanse of land. There were benches scattered throughout the area, each providing a perfect view of the surroundings. It was on a cliff with an absolutely breathtaking view of the city below and the endless sky above, which made it even more special for them.

Rod gazed into her eyes as he wrapped his arms around her, pulling her closer to him, feeling her warmth against his skin. "Are you ready?" he whispered seductively into her ear.

Becca could feel her heart racing at the sound of his voice and simply nodded, unable to form any coherent words. As the night went on, they lost themselves in each other's embrace until they reached their pinnacle.

Afterwards, they lay there wrapped in each other's arms, overlooking the dazzling lights of the city below. Rod's hand intertwined with hers as they stared up at the star-filled sky together.

"That meal was extraordinary!" Rod exclaimed.

Becca smiled, the same seductive smile that charmed him when they had first met. Her gaze signaling to move beyond the small talk. She didn't have to say a word; he leaned in eagerly, their lips locked in a passionate embrace.

In a swift moment, she was pulled into his embrace, her feet dangling off the seat as she straddled him. His kisses moved from her mouth down the length of her neck and Becca squirmed at his touch, as though an electric current ran through her veins. She wanted to feel his skin against hers and wasted no time in fumbling with his buttons, pulling them open one by one. He felt as if he were melting inside her kiss, tasting of grapes after their dinner of wine.

The passionate intensity between them was reaching fever pitch, both struggling to release each other's clothing. Finally free, Becca gasped as his warm skin touched hers, sending shockwaves throughout her entire body.

Their laughter echoed within the car as Becca tore off her shirt and Rod's eyes roamed over her body. He moved closer to her, his fingers running lightly over her bra-clad chest, then down along her thighs. She wanted him to touch her more. She pulled up her skirt, baring more of herself to him, and his gaze followed hungrily.

He was fumbling with the clasps of her bra when Becca covered his chest with her hands, caressing him, feeling the warmth radiating from beneath his clothes. Finally, free of its confinement, she felt her breasts spill out.

Rod circled around them with the pad of his fingers and pleasure began to coursing through her veins in spurts. His mouth covered one nipple, and he drew circles around them until they were hardened peaks.

Becca felt a rush of chill air from the air conditioning unit against her skin as his hand travelled higher still, tracing what seemed like an eternity on the edge of panties before pushing them aside. His finger found its way inside her and she gasped in surprised delight. He pushed further, pushing forth wave after wave of pleasure that had Becca panting against his neck. Her grip tightened on his arm as she felt release for the first time.

Rod dragged out his hand from under Becca and cupped both of her breasts gently with both hands as he looked deeply into her eyes.

Rod stiffened as a distant ringing cut through the passionate air, and his hand froze when he recognized the tone. It was Becca's phone, chirping from somewhere in the car. At that moment, they both looked up and met each other's gaze. Without having to exchange any words, they ignored the persistent call and dive back into their own world of desire.

He quickly pulled her back down and started kissing her again with a deep passion. His hands roamed over her body as he fondled her breasts, eager to get them back to where they were before interruption. She arched against him, pushing her chest closer to him, thrusting towards him with growing need. Rod increased his intensity as he felt her moans escape from deep within, responding with even more force.

Just then, the same phone started ringing again - once, twice and then another phone joined in. This second sound was Rod's; they both had received calls at precisely the same time. Annoyed by this disturbance, Becca lifted herself off him and sat back on his lap.

"We should probably answer them," she said, gesturing towards the phones and moved over to the passenger's seat beside him. But despite their efforts to respond to the urgency of the calls, all they could do was sit there in silence as their phones kept on ringing without ceasing.

"We don't seem to have much of a choice," he said, his lips tightened with anger. Someone had ruined the perfect night they had planned together. Both of them grabbed their phones simultaneously.

"Let's shut off these blasted things after this," Rod barks and glanced at his phone's display. The caller ID was unidentified and marked as "unknown number". His fury was on full display now.

"Just great! Interrupted by an anonymous call," he muttered, scowling.

"That's strange. My call is from an unknown number too," Becca remarked in disbelief as she handed him her phone for confirmation. Rod took it from her and saw that she was right.

As Becca received the phone back, something caught her attention—a muffled sound coming from outside the car, near the bushes. In any other situation, she would have written it off as an animal rustling about, or maybe even a gust of wind. But after receiving two mysterious calls back-to-back, her anxiety levels were too high for such logic.

"Rod, I think I just heard something," she cautiously began and waited for his response.

Rod turned to look at her and asked skeptically, "What?"

Becca felt her heart racing, but pushed forward with determination in her voice. "I'm not sure what it was. Can you please go out there and check? It'd be better to be safe than sorry." She punctuated her words with a beguiling smile before added, "Check and then we can forget whoever is calling and get back to our evening."

He nodded in agreement and stepped out of the car into the crisp night air.

Rod scoffed, trying to suppress the heat that was rising in his throat. He grabbed his shirt from the back seat and carelessly tossed it over his head, feeling its fabric slither over his bare skin like a serpent. With every passing second, he felt the time slipping away. His body yearned for respite, so did his mind, so did his soul–whatever the sound she heard was, it had better not be a distraction from his much-needed escape.

He pressed the central locking button on his side of the car and unlocked the doors. He thought he should have told her to forget about checking on the mysterious noise she heard, but reality proved otherwise. She was making herself paranoid about the coincidence of those calls, and he had no other choice than to step out of the car and investigate.

The night air greeted him with an icy embrace as he stepped out and shut the door behind him. Rod quickly swept the area with a quick glance. Everything seemed fine from where he stood - just one squirrel running past him, nothing else moved. The temperature remained warm, as it had been when they had arrived here earlier on. He was certain that nobody came close to their vehicle while they were inside it, so there was no reason for them to worry.

Not willing to take any chances, he flicked his phone's flashlight to light up the surrounding shadows. It illuminated every corner of their surroundings- everything seemed peaceful apart from the lone creature scurrying away in search of food or shelter. Unconvinced yet relieved, Rod tried to do one last checkup before returning to his car.

He felt a jolt of dread as he turned away from the area and trudged back to his car. To Becca. He could make out her silhouette standing outside the car, curious why he had taken so long. As he got closer, something glinted in the corner of his eye and made him stop in his tracks. Taking out his camera, he shone it on the side of the car, moving closer as it illuminated a disturbing sight. His once beautiful spray paint was now scratched with a symbol; one he knew too well: Standish.

Rod's heart thudded hard in his chest. This was a sign belonging to the notorious cult that had recently been terrorizing their town; the cult of Standish. The tales of this organization had spread like wildfire after the University incident and all of Rod's fears came crashing down upon him at the sight of this symbol. He recalled how he had been receiving threatening letters and calls from an unknown person for months now but had since done everything he could to avoid them. Now, every worrisome piece clicked into place and Rod was grateful for Becca's persistence in getting him to go out tonight—if she hadn't, then this chilling warning would've gone undetected. So much for a quiet evening.

The distant rumblings of the phone calls echoing throughout the deserted parking lot caused a chill to run up Rod's spine. He had seen the carving on his car, and he knew he was in trouble. How were they able to track him down and even get Becca's number? In a hurry, he got back into his car and met Becca, who asked, "What took so long?"

Thoughts raced through his mind as he lied, said, "I had to be sure there was nothing out there. Let's leave this place now." Becca wanted to know what happened, so she paused before asked, "What did you see out there? Is everything alright?"

He tried to make light of the situation, pretending it was probably just some horny teenagers playing pranks. "Yeah, everything is fine.", he said, trying to sound casual, but inside he was panicking. He didn't want to explain the threats or the letters or even the mark on his car. Trying to conceal his fear, he quickly added, "It's nothing. I just feel we should leave." His plan worked and Becca agreed, buttoning her shirt in preparation. She hadn't wanted to tell him at first that she had been feeling uneasy since they arrived.

Rod turned the key in the ignition and started the car; however, a strange noise emanated from the engine each time he attempted to start it up again. Undeterred by the malfunctioning engine, Rod drove away from the loitering shadows of danger.

"Hey, what's going on?" Becca asked with a sense of worry in her voice.

"I'm not sure. I heard a strange sound coming from the engine, and now it's stopped working. That was never there when we parked this car, or ever since I got it. Let me look." He stepped out of the car as he spoke and reached for his phone torchlight to get the bonnet open. Active 2: Someone had cut the chords in the engine, which he noticed as the light scanned through. Panic struck him like a storm as sweat covered Rod's forehead. He then scanned the body of the car, and within less than an hour, he found the tires had been slashed. Now fear overwhelmed him, and he desperately yelled at Becca, "Get out of the car right now! Take your things and leave!"

She poked her head out through the window and said in confusion,

"What?"

His scream reverberated through their surroundings, "GRAB YOUR STUFF AND GET OUT OF THE CAR NOW!"

Becca heard the sternness in his voice and triggered her senses. Something was definitely wrong with the environment they were in. Rod wouldn't ask her to exit the car like that if this wasn't serious. She quickly tidied herself up, buttoning her shirt as she emerged from the car.

She ran towards Rod, who seemed frozen, his unblinking eyes gazing into nothingness. His stormy face betrayed the man she had just shared dinner with, and something inside her trembled, too.

"What's the problem?" Becca asked, trying to keep a grasp of composure.

Rod's adamance grew even more intense as he explained that someone had maliciously slashed his tires, marked his car, and tampered with his chords. He further urged them to leave immediately without calling the police, leaving Becca no choice but to oblige.

They started walking away from the car before Becca noticed her phone had lost its reception bar, dropping from five to zero. "Strange," she exclaimed, reaching out for Rod's phone instead as an alternative. To her surprise, Rod also encountered this issue; both their phones had been rendered useless within mere minutes of being there. A chill raced down Becca's spine as the realization hit her - their only ways of communication have gone offline. Rod could feel it too - a rising fear cloaking him in a blanket of goosebumps.

Rod and Becca stopped in their tracks, hearing a menacing whisper coming from the bushes nearby. The noises were low at first, but quickly morphed into an ominous crescendo, and Rod knew it was all his fault. He should have taken the threats seriously; why didn't he trust his gut?

The fear washed over them like a tidal wave as Rod draped his arm protectively around Becca's shoulder. But before he could fully register anything else, a sharp pain jolted through him. His grip on Becca loosened, and he crumpled to the ground. She screamed in terror, whirling around to see three cloaked figures standing behind them in the shadows.

Becca tried to run away, her heart pounding in her ears. But her attempt was short-lived; she stumbled on her own leg and slammed to the ground. Her ankle lit up with fiery pain and she screamed out again in agony as she attempted to stand back up. Before she could even move an inch, rough hands grabbed her and pinned her arms behind her.

Becca lay in a panicked state, unable to process what was happening; all that registered was the pain Rod was enduring. She had no way of knowing that her presence had put them both in danger.

Her body trembled as she watched one of the cloaked figures drive a knife into Rod's spine. His pained scream echoed through the room, piercing Becca's heart. Her assailant leaned close and whispers menacingly into Rod's ear, "You should have answered us when we came calling. We dislike being ignored." And with another twist of the blade, he pulled away and let out a sinister laugh.

In vain, Becca attempted to free herself from the other figure's grasp as his hands crept up her legs toward her skirt. With each movement, his touch seared her skin and sent chills down to her core. Powerless and afraid, Becca held her breath as he explored further up her thighs.

Apparently, the worst of her ordeal wasn't over yet. His grip tightened around her neck like a vice, suspending her almost a foot above the ground with ease. Rebecca struggled helplessly as she felt her breath being sucked out of her throat, clawing at his hands in vain to get free. The strength and cruelty of his grasp sent shivers through her body that soon gave way to trembling fear and deep-seated terror.

She was thrown against the car's hood with such force that an audible gasp escaped her lips as hot pain radiated through her already bruised ankle and entire being. Becca whimpered like a wounded animal, trying desperately to muffle her cries with muffled sobs.

"What is the name of the girl you had an appointment with a few days back?" he asked menacingly, his tone low and controlled. A man's voice — no woman would have possessed the strength to do this to her.

Her throat felt clogged with fear and despair — she could barely whisper. "I... I don't know," she stuttered weakly before he tightened his grip around her neck again, squeezing mercilessly. She let out a faint whimper as another hand compressed her tender ankle.

His description of the girl he sought after made Becca realize whom he meant—skinny, blonde hair, beautiful lips, perfect body, young & nubile–she knew exactly who it was. But in the face of his wrathful rage, she just couldn't seem to make words come out of her mouth, even when faced with physical pain and suffering beyond measure.

He repeated his question more insistently this time: "How do we find her? What is her name?" He forced the words out between gritted teeth as though speaking was just as painful as experiencing his wrathful presence herself.

Rebecca opened her mouth then closed it again as tears streamed down from her reddened eyes while she shook her head feverishly, no longer able suppress these emotions any longer - but all that came out were small sobs and pleas for mercy. Suddenly realizing that there was no escape from him now or ever unless she uttered the name he sought after, she hung her head in defeat and whispered meekly: "I know her.... Please stop hurting me...I know her... Her name is..."

"Her name is Rachel...Rachel Chambers of Ceder Villa University, I swear! Please stop hurting me!!" Becca begged, tears streaming down her face. The pressure around her throat and ankle suddenly released and a flood of relief washed over her, yet the pain in her leg was still excruciating. Mucus dripped from her nose into her mouth, making it difficult to breathe or talk.

The figure snapped their fingers at Rod and his assailant, showing they had gotten all they wanted. Becca was lifted off the car and carefully placed inside. The other cloaked figure followed suit, with Rod beside her. As the door closed shut, Becca knew these abductors didn't plan to release them anytime soon.

Without warning, the car engine roar to life and started moving. The cloaked figures stood outside waving goodbye as the car sped up forward at break-neck speed. Rod felt dread weighing him down as he realized that if he didn't gain control of the situation fast, they were both going to plunge headfirst off a cliff face; meeting certain death. The bleakness of their situation hit him like a ton of bricks, and he resigned himself to what looked like an inevitable fate.

Rod frantically slammed the brakes, his knuckles turning white from the effort. Despite the pain, he felt nothing in return. The unyielding black metal mocked him despite all his effort. His heart sunk into his stomach as he realized the brake had given out, and nothing else in the car worked either. He tried to change gears, but that too was met with silence. Knowing his fate was sealed, Rod watched helplessly as the car tumbled forward over the edge of the cliff and down towards its impending doom.

A flurry of figures stood on the edge of the abyss, watching intently as it sunk deeper and deeper towards its untimely death. Yet, one figure differed from its kin; instead of cruel joy, an air of pensive apprehension hung about their cloaked figure. They were not present during their comrades' malicious revelry when they extracted what they sought from their victims. With trembling fingers, they drew a cell phone from within their robes and dialed a number, waiting for someone to answer on the other end.

"It is done," they said after a moment's pause, "We have found our sacrificial lamb and her knowledge." A deeper voice hummed through the handset before they replied, "We will take her once she has finished classes this evening." A pause followed before they granted their response, "The pleasure is ours, Dark Priest," and ended the call shortly thereafter.

CHAPTER FOUR

Daniela lay on the sofa restlessly, flipping through TV stations in search of something to ease her boredom. She had been stuck at home since the night before when she first felt her cold coming on, and it had grown worse as the day went on. Her Aunt had gone out of town with her cousin Amelia to visit some relatives a few towns away, leaving Daniela alone with no one to pamper her through her illness. Not being able to be a part of the Halloween celebrations she so loved deflated her spirit even more and left her feeling frustrated and disappointed.

Just then, Daniela heard chattering outside on the front porch and felt a spark of joy ignite within her heart. It must be Kimbery and Iris, she thought with delight, as they had called to let her know they would come over today. They walked into the living room armed with soups, medicine and ginger ale - just what she needed!

"Oh, hi you two!" Daniela said, attempting a weak smile. "I'm so glad you're here. You do not know how much I need someone to pamper me right now."

Kimbery and Iris smiled knowingly before setting up their offerings for their sick friend.

"Don't worry," Kimbery said reassuringly, as she handed Daniela a bowl of soup. "We'll take care of you until you get better."

"Hey, guys!" Daniela said with a voice heavy from her blocked nose.

Her friends Iris and Kimbery had just walked in, each of them carrying jars and bottles, which they set down on the table next to the remote. As Kimbery sat beside her on the couch, she exclaimed.

"You look like you haven't slept in days, Dani. You really need to take it easy or else this stress will kill you."

Daniela slowly wrapped her blanket around herself and said, "What can I do? It's not like there's anything I can do about it."

Iris shrugged her shoulders before asked, "When are your aunt and Amelia coming back?"

"Tomorrow...or maybe the day after," was Daniela's response.

Without hesitating, Iris picked up one jar on the table and handed it to Daniela, said, "Here, have some of this." She then looked at Kimbery. "Do you think you could grab us a spoon?". After fetching a spoon from the kitchen, Kimbery returned to the living room.

"Take a spoonful of this," Iris said, pointing to jar one. "And two spoonsful of that," she added while pointing at jar two before continued: "Drink some soup and ginger ale afterwards; that should help you feel better."

Daniela took the spoon from Kimbery but eyeing the jars suspiciously; all she could see was something greenish and slimy looking in one and murky liquid in another - both smelled horrible too. She instinctively closed her eyes as she gulped down the concoction, letting none of it touch her taste buds. When finished, she slammed down the spoon onto the jar and eagerly grabbed one bottle of ginger ale nearby for relief.

Attempting to change the topic, Daniela asked, "So what's been happening around town? Nothing much recent, right?"

Kimbery tried to brush off her question by said "Not really..." but Iris who added "Well, they are all pretty upset about Jake's death, though quickly cut that off."

Kimbery sighed as she said solemnly, "It's really heartbreaking. I've known Jake for forever. His death hit me hard, too."

Daniela nodded gravely in agreement and continued, her eyes welling up with tears. "You can't imagine what it was like to witness him taking his last breath...and I only knew him for a short while, but he was always so kind. It's just such a tragedy."

Iris contemplated for a moment before speaking, her voice solemn and quiet. "I did not know about his heart disease. I wonder what could have possibly caused the attack? But then there's Greta...I feel like she isn't as upset as you would expect she would be. Something just doesn't add up for me."

Kimbery furrowed her brows, perplexed by Iris's observation, "How do you know she isn't feeling anything at all? Jake was her husband of so many years, after all."

Daniela shook her head in confusion, lowering her gaze to the floor. Honestly, I don't know either. Lately, I've had this intuitive feeling that won't go away. Like my old boss disappearing without explanation? It feels like something is off here and I can't shake this nagging feeling deep inside of me.

Iris smiled sympathetically and responded with understanding in her voice, "Your intuition isn't crazy—it's actually a good thing to still be connected to your essence like that! Too many people go through life not being aware of their own intuitions and inner guidance system, so it's great that you're still able to tap into yours."

Kimbery nodded slowly in acknowledgment before added thoughtfully, "That makes sense; I remember reading something about how intuition and holistic healing are related. Interesting connection indeed."

Iris rolled her eyes and glanced back at Daniela. "You still taking those anxiety pills? What're they called...Relaxal?"

Daniela smiled, feeling a wave of warmth wash over her as she was reminded of the many secrets she shared with Iris. "Yeah. Not as often as before, though. Why do you ask?"

"It's just a theory I'm working on, but it could explain why you've been so intuitive lately. It's one of the side effects of Relaxal - precognition. And it makes sense if you think about it; you always know what's right and wrong, how to spot a lie from a truth." Her friend gave her a knowing look as if it were obvious, and for once, Iris' spiritual ways like Kimbery, did not put Daniela off whose glazed eyes revealed her boredom with the topic.

"Right," Daniela said with a laugh, trying to lighten the mood. "So, Kimbery, how's work at the radio station?"

"Work's been awesome!" She beamed in response. "I'm loving every bit."

"Great! Oh," Daniela said, thinking twice before she spoke any further. "Actually...I had something I wanted to ask you; if that's alright."

Kimbery nodded encouragingly. "Sure thing. What is it?"

Daniela sighs softly before she continues. "It...it is Heath."

The corners of Kimbery's mouth curled down in confusion as she replied, "What about him?"

"Do you know he likes you?" She felt her heart rate increase as everything came out in one breath, followed by an awkward silence afterwards. "I mean...if you're interested...in him..."

But then Kimbery let out a loud laugh that made Iris turn around with a scowl on her face - which only made them both laugh harder - breaking the tension filled moment between them. Taking a deep breath, Kimbery shook her head in response to Daniela's question when she finally composed herself again. "Not in the least bit," she said firmly. "Heath is really not my type, and he needs to learn to move on."

"Well, he apparently hasn't. He really does like you, and even though I would not chime in, I honestly think you should give him a chance. A trial run, at the very least."

Kimbery opened her mouth to reply when Iris shushed them both.

"Guys, please keep it down a notch. I can hardly hear anything over your chatter, and I really want to catch this news report."

The two girls silently obeyed, turning their heads towards the TV set with rapt attention. Their eyes widened as the headline scrolled along the bottom of the screen—a couple had been found dead inside their car on Make-Out Hill. The scene behind the reporter was one of despair— yellow police tape surrounding an overturned car that had plummeted off the Cliffside, ending its deadly descent in a raging fireball of pain and suffering.

The voice of the reporter emanated through the somber room as he began his story: "It is indeed a tragic day here at Make-Out Hill where a couple has been confirmed dead following a harrowing car accident. There has been much speculation about what may have caused such a tragedy; one theory being that in the heat of the moment, they started their engine and somehow lost control of the vehicle before sending it hurtling off the Cliffside below. The bodies were badly burnt from fire that erupted after impact. The victims' identities remain unknown for now, but we will keep you updated as more details arise."

Ian Winters reporting for The News Network.

Kimbery's hands flew up to her lips in shock as she whispered-yelled, "Oh my goodness! What a horrible way to die—I can't even fathom it!"

Iris nodded sorrowfully in agreement before casting her gaze towards Daniela. "I know," she said sadly before letting out a long yawn. "Suddenly I feel oddly fatigued...are there any sedatives in our medicine cabinet?"

"It is quite normal to feel drowsiness after consuming such medication," Kimbery said as Iris nodded in agreement.

"I will come see you off," Daniela asserted and was about rising from the sofa when Kimbery interjected, "No need to bother. We will take our leave ourselves."

Kimbery and Iris slid out of the room, allowing in a faint glow of light from the morning sun outside. The door creaked softly behind them, leaving Daniela alone with her thoughts. She leaned back onto the cushions, feeling more drained than before.

A part of Daniela missed the locket she had lost a few weeks ago during one of her soul-searching travels post break-up. A wise Buddhist monk in Thailand who blessed it had gifted it to her; claiming it would help guide her towards salvation. His words had provided solace in what felt like an eternity of pain and despair. Yet now that it was gone, she felt incomplete, like an integral piece of her soul was missing.

Sighing heavily, Daniela forced herself to relinquish those thoughts and succumb to her medication's gentle embrace. Her eyes shuttered close as peace enveloped her body.

The thumping bass from the speakers shook the hall with an electricity that seemed to bring everyone in it alive. The room was alight with activity, as students pulsed and vibrated around Rachel. In her corner, she let out a deep sigh, both of relief and exhaustion; it had been twenty minutes since her feet had stopped moving, transitioning from party-goer to spectator during that time. She had taken a break from her rigorous studying and come to one of the Halloween parties her classmates were hosting - the first actual break she'd taken in months.

Rachel remembered how much thought she had put into picking out the perfect costume for this very night-she had wanted to make sure her schoolwork would not overshadow this holiday. But then reality struck like a ton of bricks and reminded her about her upcoming midterm exam she hadn't even started studying for. Groaning inwardly, Rachel already knew who would win the battle between books and fun this time, too, so she began making her way out of the building.

Just then, an Elvis Presley impersonator stepped in front of her, blocking Rachel's path.

"Leaving so soon? I was going to ask you for a dance!" he said with a wink.

"Yeah," Rachel replied with a small smile. "Some things just came up."

"Are you sure it has nothing to do with school again?" asked the impersonator, raising his eyebrows skeptically.

"Nah, it's not even close to school work ," Rachel lied, hoped her voice didn't give away her guilt. "I just remembered I have some stuff I need to take care of."

"Stay a little longer," he said with a twinkle in his eye. "Can't it wait?"

For a few moments, Rachel hesitated - on one hand, there was the promise of pure blissful fun and forgetfulness she craved; but there were hours upon hours of study waiting for her back at home. The temptation was great...but alas, eventually Rachel smiled wryly and shook her head.

"No, it can't. I'll see you around." She said hastily, dashing away from her classmates and out the door before another one of them could corner her again.

Desperately hoping to flag down a cab, she walked some distance from the house. For ten minutes, not a single cab was in sight. With no other choice, she figured that her soberness would be enough to carry her to the bus station safely, cutting through the park on the way.

Lugging her body in her chosen costume, she started strolling toward the park. Her chunky black boots made a clomping sound with each step, and her tight leather pants creaked as they hugged her curves. Although she had opted to go for a Goth look for the party, she hadn't gone all the way—she had kept parts of herself intact like her signature dark red lipstick and strawberry blonde short locks. Chuckling aloud at this realization, she focused instead on making it to the bus station without getting blisters on her feet or being attacked by any unknown forces in the night.

The two dark figures seemed to appear from nowhere, their slimy cloaks covering them from head to toe. Rachel couldn't make out any facial features through those hoods, but she had an uneasy feeling that they were watching her.

"What do you think you're doing out here? How dare you walk around so carelessly," one of them croaked in a deep voice.

Rachel felt a shiver go down her spine as she started walking faster, her heart racing with fear. But the figures kept up the same pace, tracking her like shadows. She could feel them waiting and watching eagerly for any wrong move she made.

For the first time, Rachel noticed how silent it was here; not even the birds chirping or people talking. There wasn't a soul in sight. It was almost like something was lurking in the air, making everyone flee from this place.

The masked man was growing aroused just from watching Rachel's hips swaying. His thoughts drifted away as he fantasized about caressing her smooth skin and tasting her lips. He knew these feelings of lust were forbidden by his cult, but he was gradually getting to where he stopped caring about it. Little did he know Rachel didn't even belong to his group.

Finally, Rachel dialed someone on her cellphone and spoke hurriedly into it before making it into the park. The cloaked figures quickly backed away from her before vanishing into oblivion. When she stepped into the park, she was shocked at the emptiness. She expected there would be teens running amok, but there was no one.

The chilly evening air put off the local kids, leaving the park vacant and eerie. Rachel walked on while speaking into her phone in a low voice. It was as if she was having a conversation with someone, though no one else was present. This had become her defense mechanism; it kept people away from her and made her feel safe in situations like these.

As she continued to walk, Rachel heard something snapping behind her and paused mid-sentence. Fear filled her as she looked around for any sort of sign of what had caused the sound. Her hand trembled as she brought the phone back up to her ear, asking whoever was on the other line to wait for just a moment while she investigated.

The night seemed to stretch on endlessly, every noise setting off alarms in Rachel's head as she tried desperately to stay calm. She cautiously ventured forward, trying not to let fear take over.

Using the scant moonlight, she cautiously scanned her surroundings but could make out nothing. She was about to return to her phone call when a shrill bark echoed through the air. Startled, Rachel dropped her phone, and it clattered to the ground. A pug in a bat costume charged out from behind one bush with a branch clamped in its jaws. Behind him was Anna, a dog walker whom Rachel recognized. So that's Mr. Biggles, she thought as he barked at her again.

"Hi, Mr. Biggles," she said, trying to forget the shock and her shattered phone for a moment - the pup looked so cute in its costume.

"I'm really sorry Mr. Biggles startled you," Anna apologized before racing off after the now runaway pug.

Rachel shook her head as she bent down to pick up her phone and the battery and back cover that had scattered all over. As she went about collecting them, a glimmer near the water fountain prompted her attention, and she moved closer to survey it. The moonlight had hit off something metal, which caused it to reflect in the darkness. It was a silver locket with hints of gold and an inscription hand-engraved on its surface. Rachel collected the locket along with her phone parts and read the inscription, which was written in Sanskrit - Peace, Serenity & Sanctuary.

Being a language major, she was desperate to make sense of the strange Sanskrit inscription etched in the cold metal locket. Rachel wore the pendant around her neck, enclosing it with her warm palms. She knew that returning it to local authorities or placing an ad stating she had found the locket in the park would be the right thing to do, but she couldn't help feeling a little attached to it as if its presence brought a sense of tranquility. After all, she had grown up being told that what goes around comes around and that stealing someone else's belongings can have dire consequences. The owner was probably frantic with worry, so she had no other choice than to return it.

Suddenly, another noise came from behind, and Rachel quickly turned around. She immediately recognized Mr. Biggles peeking through the bushes with his big green eyes and scruffy fur coat. Relief replaced her previous unease before she noticed a mysterious figure standing beside him, dressed in all black like a monk with two small eyeholes where their eyes should be visible. A shiver ran down her spine as the figure stood still, saying nothing but constantly watching her every move.

"Can I help you?" Rachel asked nervously, taking a few steps back and keeping her gaze on the figure. It stood opposite her, observing in awe for what felt like many minutes until finally, Rachel started walking away at a quicker pace while repeatedly turning back to see if the figure followed her. He didn't move a muscle, and when Rachel finally put some distance between them, she slammed into something else and watched as her phone clattered onto the floor for the second time that night.

Rachel raised her head and a surge of fear surged through her body as she saw two figures standing before her, both wearing all black. They were tall and imposing; one had their hands firmly pressed over her mouth. Rachel desperately tried to scream, but the sound seemed to vanish in the air.

The two masked men forcefully began dragging Rachel towards the centre of the park, and as they tried to pull open a concealed door, Rachel seized her chance to escape. Her feet felt heavy beneath her, weighed down by her uncomfortable shoes, but desperation drove her on. Time was not on her side - if only she could take off the shoes!

But there was no time. Instead, she ran frantically, trying to put as much distance between herself and them. But before she could register what was happening, Rachel stumbled forward as the heel of her right shoe gave out from underneath her. The concrete pavement sped towards her face and everything went dark. Pain seared through her head and ankle where it had contacted the fountain wall.

Rachel felt a searing heat, a sticky warmth that dripped from her face. The metallic, coppery scent of blood was unmistakable. As the blood ran down her face and splashed onto the locket in her palm, she realized that she had been cut. Desperately, Rachel tried to escape her captors' confinement around the water fountain. With her last effort, she scrambled desperately onto her feet, using the cold concrete as support, and when their eyes met, they both lunged for her simultaneously.

Gripping onto the edge with an iron grip, she fought hard against their efforts to pull her away. But it was no use as her palms grew slippery and her fingers gave way one by one. Just then, a sharp pain pierced through Rachel's fingernail as it broke off from its root and a deafening scream escaped into the night air. Then suddenly, and with such force, like a bag of potatoes, Rachel found herself thrown on the ground in front of them as they watched her writhe in agony.

The shorter figure stepped closer towards Rachel with a malicious sneer across his lips, but before he could come any nearer, she mustered all the strength she had left to lash out with a single kick right at his shinbone like lightning. He yelped in pain and stumbled back in shock at her unexpected resistance.

The man broke away, screaming in agony. He stumbled backwards while his partner strode forward menacingly. Suddenly, the hurt man regained his force and lunged toward Rachel with a vicious hatred, aiming his shoe square at her belly. Fiery pain lanced throughout her body as he connected with her tender skin. He kicked again, and she felt an iron taste in her mouth as the coppery flavor of blood filled it. Rachel gasped for air and curled up on the ground to endure.

What had she done? Who were these men that wanted her so badly? Like some long lost friend, they treated her like they knew her secret desires, but she did not know who they were. Rachel closed her eyes tight and muttered a silent prayer to God for deliverance from this misery. Before she could steady herself to open them again, a thunderous blow landed on the left side of her face, followed by another just as loud on the other side. Rachel's shriek died out in her throat as an unexpected shock took over her entire being. Then one last kick sent her into unconsciousness as she fell against the unforgiving concrete pavement below. Her attacker leaned over to check for signs of life before trying to remove her tightly clasped leather pants.

"For God's sake, give me a hand here!" the smaller man shouted to his partner, who was standing at a distance, looking on as he hit the girl. His companion trudged over and help pull her pants down with great effort. Wondering how women could squeeze themselves into such tight pants. Without damaging it, they eventually took them off her frail body.

The two masked men wasted no time as their hands quickly roamed over the unconscious girl's body. His partner eagerly mounted her, not caring or even noticing that she was still a tight fit for him. They both wanted only release, not an ounce of love or compassion for the young woman underneath them.

With no remorse, he continued to efficiently thrust into her as if it was an Olympic sport he was determined to win. When his partner had finally reached climax, they dragged their sated bodies off of her and immediately dressed themselves.

The taller man tugged on his leather pants and adjusted his t-shirt, pulling it down around his midsection before focusing on his companion. The shorter one followed suit and together, they grabbed under the girl's arms and hoisted her up from the ground. Dragging her limp body between them, they made their way towards the open trapdoor on the floor beneath them. The taller one jumped in first and waited for the shorter one to shove the lifeless form of the girl down with him before jumping after her himself.

With a deafening thud, the heavy trap door swung shut, enclosing all three in total darkness and cutting them off from civilization above them. Meanwhile, outside in the dead of night, a glimmering locket laid at the bottom of a fountain, quietly telling its tale of the unfortunate girl who had lost her battle with malevolent forces—demonic or otherwise—that had taken her down into its depths.

Daniela shot up from her spot on the sofa, trembling with fear. Her stomach churned with bile and she stumbled out of the room, desperate to reach the marbled bathroom across the hall. A few moments later, a sound of retching broke the eerie silence that shrouds the house.

Daniela cautiously stood up, washing her face with cold water to soothe her racing heart. She glanced at her reflection in the mirror above the sink, only to see something that made her blood run cold - a bright red handprint smeared across her forehead. She reached up to touch it and was immediately met with its sticky wet texture. Just then, the mirror shattered into a thousand pieces as if someone had thrown a stone at it. The sudden sound sent chills down Daniela's spine and caused her to snap awake.

She scrambled off the sofa and stumbled towards the door, only to find it opening just as she arrived there. Maureen and Amelia walked in with their bags, each giving her puzzled looks. "You look terrible, Dani," Amelia whispered. Maureen furrowed her brows in worry before piping in, "Did we wake you? We weren't supposed to be here until tomorrow."

"Yes," Daniela croaked out weakly, still trying to catch her breath from what could have been nothing more than an awful nightmare. But it had felt so real when she was dreaming - almost too real for comfort. Maureen gave Daniela's shoulder a gentle squeeze before heading off towards the kitchen. Amelia lingered by Daniela's side for a while longer before said, "Why do you look like you just saw a ghost? You look really pale."

Daniela took a few moments to process those words before nodding weakly and finally responding, "I do?" Amelia smiled softly before turning around to grab Daniela, a warmer blanket and some water for her parched throat. As she watched them fuss around her, taking care of things she never asked for or expected, she couldn't help but feel an overwhelming sense of love sweeping through her.

As Daniela pondered, her dream played out in her mind as if it were reality. She felt the feverish heat that had taken over her body and the warmth of the blood from her dream pressed against her thoughts. She remembered what the mirror had shown - a reflection that shattered into pieces like an omen of something dark ahead. Confusion and doubt clouded her mind as she struggled to make sense of it all. - what did any of this mean?

CHAPTER FIVE

Daniela labored to sit up, her body too weak to hold her weight. She had tried on her jeans moments before, but had fallen back into the bed in defeat. Her fever had been unexplainable, and she dreaded going to work; an additional responsibility that came with the job which she had accepted without forethought. Worry lined her face—since the night prior, she hadn't been able to shake off the feeling of unease that lingered from the nightmare where blood seeped from her forehead as if it were alive.

The false awakening was something she was familiar with from the articles written about it. The fear she was feeling was getting more intense by the second, although she could not pinpoint what sat heavy on her heart.

Finally, after much effort, Daniela pulled up her jeans and somehow stood. She felt rushed and anxious, being aware that November had just started and she didn't want to be late for work. She grabbed her handbag and laptop bag and quickly made way out of the room. She would have breakfast at a later time when she wasn't so busy at work. On her way out of the house, Daniela adjusted her scarf around her neck only to hear someone call out her name behind her. When she turned around, Kimbery stood there, smiling in greeting.

"I figured I'd find you awake," Kimbery murmurs as she swept Dani into a long, tight embrace. When they parted, Kimbery turned Dani away from the busy street, so they could speak without obstructing pedestrian traffic.

"Where else would I be on the first day of the month? Not in bed, that's for sure," Dani shot back with her usual spark.

"That's why I'm here," Kimbery smiled mysteriously. "Almighty Dani needs a reminder to relax every once in a while."

Dani scowled at the nickname her friend had given her, though her eyes sparkled with amusement. "What did you do?"

"Oh, nothing much," Kimbery mocked innocently. "Just called your office and asked for a sick day."

Dani felt tears of relief well up behind her eyes; if it weren't for Kimbery's timely intervention, she would have forced herself to go into work despite feeling under the weather. She was too responsible to skip out - or ask anyone for help.

"How did you arrange it?" Dani asked cautiously, wiping away tears with the back of her hand.

"Well . . ." Kimbery started slowly, mischief twinkling in her eyes, "I had to pretend to be you and call your boss. But you don't need to thank me; it was my pleasure!"

A soft laugh escaped Dani's lips as she planted a kiss on her friend's cheek in gratitude. "Thanks all the same," she replied fondly.

"So," Kimbery changed the topic suddenly with an excited glint in her eye, "are you up for an adventure? It's not like I called in sick for you just so we can do this, but I thought it might break your boredom since you're stuck at home."

The mere mention of the word adventure stirred something inside Dani; she loved the thrills and excitement that came with any mission.

She eyed her friend skeptically before responding in amusement: "An adventure, huh? What did you have in mind?"

"So, it's like this. I need help to find some new recordings for the radio show and Adam suggested some callers from the past that wanted to talk about The Cult of Standish. Thought you'd be into it since you love the cult and all... and are kind of a wannabe journalist."

Daniela's eyes lit up. "You wouldn't believe how interested I am! Let's do this," she said excitedly, but then paused before continued. "But first... there's one thing I have to do."

Kimbery groaned inwardly. She knew what was coming next.

"I want to go back to the park one last time, see if I can find my locket." Daniela revealed. "It's been gone for weeks now, but I still feel incomplete without it. It means so much to me–if I can just go there again and still can't find it, then I'm willing to accept it's gone for good."

Kimbery sighed heavily as she heard her friend's words; searching for something lost for so long seemed like a fruitless endeavor, but she had no other choice than to agree. "Fine," she finally responded.

They both walked briskly towards the park, talking about anything and everything, though they both had an elephant in the room. Daniela wanted to ask Kimbery to reconsider her stance on the Heath situation, but she couldn't bring herself to start such a conversation. It was becoming more and more difficult for her to stay on the sidelines regarding their relationship because there wasn't one anymore. Kimbery continued chatting animatedly about her job, while Daniela responded when necessary. She had little to say since she'd been stuck at home with her fever.

When they arrived at the park, Daniela took Kimbery to the spot where she had last seen the gold locket. They split up and started searching around the pool frantically for ten minutes, with no positive results. Kimbery made her way over to the fountain to quench her thirst and rest for a bit. Though deep down inside she knew that this search was futile, she couldn't bring herself to vocalize it and break her friend's hope. She bent over the concrete basin of the fountain in order to scoop some cool water into cupped hands when something shiny caught her eye at the bottom of the pool - a glimmering gold chain!

"Dani!" she called out loudly, "I found it! The locket is here!" Kimbery exclaimed as she pulled out the golden trinket from its aquatic prison and leaned against the hard concrete wall, waiting for her relieved friend.

Daniela sprinted through the park, her chest aching from the ever-growing sense of dread as the search yielded no results. A tiny spark of hope flaring to life at Kimbery's words gave her a renewed burst of energy and, without pause, she snagged the locket from the small girl's hands and threw it around her neck.

The moment the chain settled on her skin, an unbearable fire seared through her chest. She collapsed onto the metal door beneath her, clawing desperately at her chest to quell the agonizing pain. Her teeth gritted together as she tried to muffle her cries of anguish, tears streaming down her face.

Her vision was fading fast when she heard Kimbery's voice from some-where far away, "Are you alright? What's wrong? Oh, no! Please don't die!" Daniela worked hard to focus on the sound and with every ounce of strength left in her body, she gasped out, "Help me...please...help me..."

Rachel jolted up from her deep slumber as a paralyzing pain spread through her body. She felt like she had been beaten and battered all over. Though disoriented, she tried to get up, only to be sent right back down from the sheer agony that coursed through her veins. With her head spinning, Rachel's vision swam with confusion as she lay on the cold floor of what looked like an abandoned warehouse.

She wanted to call out for help, but when she tried to speak, blood sput-tered from her lips instead of words. Clutching the wall beside her to prop herself up, Rachel wiped away the sticky crimson liquid from her mouth and surveyed her surroundings further. Her eyes honed in on the bright red color coating her legs, a reminder of the trauma she had gone through. Every inch of her body hurt; not just physically, but something much deeper inside her—inside her very sense of being.

Rachel struggled to piece together the night's events, flooding into her mind like a broken record. She remembered leaving the party and traversing the park just moments before somebody or something had come after her... Thrusting and pushing against every ounce of strength she possessed. For what felt like an eternity, Rachel fought against the masked figure until eventually they had both fallen into a murky pond. Even then, Rachel refused to give up and kicked at him before everything went dark. Tears welled up in Rebecca's eyes as flashes of being brutally struck in the stomach came rushing back to her.

She surveyed the dark, dank room with her one good eye, struggling to make out the scant shadows that loomed above her in the dim light. Her left eye was swollen shut, its bruised skin a tender reminder of the attack she had suffered earlier. With great difficulty, she righted herself and stumbled towards a door that seemed to be the only salvation from this place. And then she noticed it: a ladder leading upwards. She tried to call out for help, but her throat felt as if it was on fire, and her voice came out as a mere whisper. In desperation, she took a deep breath and shouts again, "Help me! Please!" But no response came.

Kimbery rushed to Daniela's side as she collapsed onto the ground, her eyes wide with confusion and pain. She bent down to help her up and noticed a mysterious trap door in the ground, curiosity tugging at her, yet overriding that was her concern for her friend.

The throbbing sensation in Daniela's chest slowly ebbed away, enough for her to heave herself into a sitting position. This unexplainable turn of events baffled her; nothing like this had ever happened to her before now.

"What did you say?" she croaked out, barely able to make out Kimbery's words over the ringing in her ears.

"Are you alright?," Kimbery asked with genuine worry in her voice.

Daniela spoke quietly, still trying to process what had just occurred. "Yeah. I think so. I do not know what happened back there. I just felt this hot pain in my chest like something was slicing through it."

"You're probably still not feeling well and you most likely got overexcited about finding the locket. You should probably go home and rest." Kimbery said, pulling her up gently while Daniela stayed silent, pondering on the strange sensations she faced moments ago.

"I was excited to find the locket, but this pain," she shook her head in disbelief, "this pain is nothing I've ever felt before. It felt like something else entirely, not the locket."

"Fine. Just go home and rest," Kimbery adamantly implored, her forehead creasing with worry as she silently tried to urged Daniela to concede.

"No," she replied with determination that could not be rivaled. "I still want to pick up the tape recordings from Bardo Radio, they should answer some of my questions about the cult". She paused for a moment before pleaded with Kimbery one last time: "Please?".

"Fine." She agreed and walked away, Daniela not too far behind.

As the two of them left the park, Kimbery thought she heard something. It was like a faint voice emerging from the shadows, calling for help. She stopped mid-stride and concentrated hard to ear it again and while searching for its source. Then, suddenly, there was another cry for help—this time more distinct and accompanied by words.

"Help! Somebody please help me. My little baby monster is out of control," said a small voice.

Kimbery's heart raced as her eyes searched frantically toward the sound. That was when she spotted a little girl fending off an energetic puppy at her feet. Kimbery took a deep breath as she relaxed into her normal state and followed her friend without another word.

The clock chipped at 3:00 a.m., echoing in the deserted park. Rachel lay motionless, her soft breathing barely audible in the quiet night air that had settled over the grounds. The trap door creaked open and streams of moonlight cascaded down, illuminating Rachel's sleeping countenance. Two masked men descended upon the scene, their leather boots clambering against the ladder rungs as they proceeded into the underground chamber. They paused for a moment to look upon the young girl, surveying every inch of her body to ensure nothing was amiss after the eventful evening prior.

The shorter man pulled a handkerchief from his pocket and cautiously placed it over Rachel's nose, having doused it with chloroform before arriving. His companion cast him an accusatory glance; they both knew what would happen should their victim become conscious during transport—any misgivings would be reported directly to the Dark Priest, and neither wanted to bear the wrath of such a man. Collectively, they hoisted up Rachel's limp frame and made haste towards an undiscovered part of the park, often overlooked by even its most frequent visitors. A secret garden belonging to a member of the cult - its location remained unbeknownst to all except those who were initiated into its mysteries. Fenced off from public view, in plain sight yet hidden from curious observers, here was where clandestine meetings would occur and sacrifices be offered without fear of prying eyes. Before them laid out seats and a stage setup ready for use, and soon enough Rachel joined its ranks as one more silent witness to secrets best left unknown.

The two men harshly dragged her towards the dense shrubbery and tore off her clothes. The shorter one felt his gut clench as he stared at her vulnerable beauty, asleep on the ground. Despite his best efforts, he couldn't ignore the fierce surge of arousal that shot through him. He looked away guiltily, knowing that the Dark Priest was expecting them to deliver a pure sacrifice for the ritual.

They yanked out a water hose from their knapsacks and washed away all evidence of the rape. They took extra care to make sure there wasn't even a trace of blood left, in order to ensure that she would be suitable for the ritual. It was a good thing they had to do this cleansing - otherwise, they wouldn't have been able to bathe her without raising suspicions.

When they were done with the lengthy process, they pulled out a white dress from the taller man's sack and dressed Rachel in it. After tying her up securely, they carried her to the stage, where an ominous-looking stone table was set in the middle. As they awaited for the ceremoniously late Dark Priest, their nerves jolted as something moved behind them...

Daniela thrashed around her blankets, trying in vain to drift off into sleep. She had gone through the entire repertoire—counting sheep, counting numbers backwards, staring at the ceiling. 4-7-8 breathing wasn't helping either. Groaning, she turned over and glared at the clock on her nightstand—already 1 AM.

She couldn't help but think about the tapes from Bardo Radio that she'd received from Adam. According to some voices on the recordings, entire villages had vanished because of their refusal to join a Salem-based cult led by a malevolent warlock who was determined to create a new order and seize power for himself. As if that weren't bad enough, other accounts hinted human sacrifices were being made to an obscure god to bring this powerful witch deity back from the dead. It was all so bizarre, but it gave her chills.

Insomnia plagued Daniela. She opened her eyes to clutch a locket, which had been a gift from Amelia. The clock on the bedside table showed it was 3:28AM, just two minutes remaining until the witching hour. It felt like some unseen force was taking over her mind, and she shook her head in frustration. Daniela put on her flip-flops and made her way downstairs to the kitchen.

The light from the kitchen illuminated the hallway, and when she arrived at her destination, she saw Amelia sitting on the island. Her friend was studying a medical research book and sipping a cup of tea. Daniela quietly pulled out a chair and took a seat beside her companion.

"You haven't slept?" Amelia asked with concern in her voice, glancing up from her book.

Daniela nodded in reply before asking why Amelia wasn't doing the same. "I've got these crazy midterms to prepare for," her friend answered. "I have a lot to cover."

"I shouldn't disturb you then," Daniela offered as she stood up from the chair, but Amelia quickly interjected. "No, it's fine; I was about taking a break before you came in."

Feeling relieved, Daniela smiled, then suggested making some tea while they chatted about school and work. She busied herself preparing two drinks before coming back to join Amelia on the kitchen island.

The clatters of horses' hooves and the sinister laughter of cloaked figures filled the air as they marched forward, towards their destination. Rachel was bound in between them, her mouth gagged, and her vision blurred by a haze caused by chloroform.

They arrived at a large hall that had been hastily transformed into an altar for sacrifice. Two cloaked figures stepped forward to bring Rachel up to the make-shift alter on the stage. Then, after a few moments, the dark priest made his appearance. He wore completely black clothes and held a small black bag in his hand. As he strolled closer, he nodded towards the two cloaked figures, who bowed in respect before turning away, revealing their masks.

The priest set his bag down and started emptying its contents — two knives and a curved knife and a small axe — onto the table. He murmured to the two figures. "Well done. You have served us well."

"Thank you, dark priest," said the taller one as he eyed the peculiar weapons before him. "Umm...where are the others?"

"There are no others," came the reply from the priest. "This sacrifice had to be done as soon as possible, so no formal invite was given to other members." With that being said, they both stepped back and allowed him to take over.

He let out a low hum before picking up the curved knife off of the table and wiping it across his robe with reverence. Bowing his head, he raised his hands in the air and started chanting in an increasingly growing tempo. A deep rumbling voice echoed throughout the chamber as it reverberated off of every wall and pillar.

Rachel could hear this weaving chant inside her head even through her daze caused by chloroform, and she gradually regained consciousness more and more with each passing second. She tried to move her body but discovered that it was bound to whatever she lied upon. Despite being unable to free herself, she opened her eyes just enough to see what surrounded her: above her was a man holding a knife while chanting with eyes closed. Fear clawed its way up from within when Rachel realized that this strange scene was real and not just some nightmare.

She thrashed around, desperately attempting to break the binds that held her in place. Her eyes darted left and right as she shifted her head, and for a moment, she noticed two people standing on the lower ground. They were dressed in black garbs identical to those of her abductors, but deliverance was not at hand. For Rachel recognized them—one of them had been an acquaintance from her high school and the other was the older brother of a close friend. What did they want with her?

Rachel quickly returned her gaze to the man who had yet held his blade menacingly before her. It was obvious–no matter what these strangers desired, it wouldn't mean escape or freedom for her. She was going to die here. A muffled sob escaped her throat, stifled by the gag strapped around her face.

As if oblivious to Rachel's anguish, her captor began his incantations and soon he paused, staring down at the young woman, almost as if surprised to see that she was conscious. He whispered, though there could be no mistaking the coldness of his words: "Hello, Rachel. Don't worry; you will go to a better place... Your death is important; it is a great honor you have been chosen as the lamb for this sacrifice which will bring life back into our god."

Rachel shook her head back-and-forth in vehement refusal.–she had no desire for any such honor. All she wanted was to go home and forget all of this had ever happened.

"Shhh... don't worry, my child. I promise you that this is a sacrifice for the greater good. It will resurrect our beloved god, Gregory Standish. He is the author and finisher of all," he murmured in her ear, gripping her tightly as he raised the knife high above his head.

In one swift motion, he plunged the blade deep into her chest with such force that it thudded against the bones and ripped through her tear-filled eyes. Rachel desperately attempted to scream as the searing pain pierced her whole body.

However, the tight gag muffled any sound she tried to make and silenced her agony. The crimson liquid started dripping from her wounds and flooding her vision until finally eventually blurring it away completely. Her voice was lost and soon after, so was her hearing, followed by the sight of the man who had just taken her life. In those last conscious moments before death finally engulfed her, Rachel felt an incredible surge of hatred course through every inch of her being—more intense than ever before.

The priest pulled out the bloody blade and swiftly slit open her throat to ensure she was dead. He knew it wasn't necessary, but he also wanted to ensure that when Rachel arrives at another realm in death, there would be no room left for her to speak ill of their god Standish's name —silence served as a sign of utmost respect here. After wiping off the blade onto a small rag on the slab, he gestured towards two men standing nearby and said: "Dispose of it...bury it somewhere she would never be found." With a heavy heart, they obeyed his orders and took away Rachel's lifeless body.

The two men trudged towards the still body lying on the ground. In the growing darkness of night, death was hard to distinguish, and she seemed almost peaceful in her sleep. They knew they would have to transport her to the graveyard where no one could ever find her amongst the other bodies, and she'd be left alone in the cold enveloping silence. As if it was premeditated, neither of them uttered a word while picking her up and departing, letting their sombre memories drift away with the wind like dust.

It was nearly 5AM and Daniela longed to yawn as her eyes were heavy with exhaustion. She felt a chill creep through the room, one that she couldn't explain, but it felt like a presence was looming near. Amelia was oblivious to the sensation, instead chattering away as if nothing was wrong.

"Wow! We have been up for quite some time now," Amelia exclaimed.

Daniela had no energy to respond other than said, "We sure were. Gotta get some sleep now."

"Good night cuz," Amelia said cheerfully, not realizing what she said.

"It's actually already morning." Daniela replied in a low monotone voice and strolled away towards her bedroom, still feeling the mysterious malevolence that followed her.

CHAPTER SIX

Daniela slumped in front of the MacBook, her gaze flicking over the website, scanning for the changes needed to finish the project. The Mayoral campaign site was one of the company's important projects; an assignment she had taken on after her predecessor abruptly vanished months ago.

Abandoned by her mentor and under immense pressure—the website was due to be published before the end of November—Daniela had been working on it for close to four hours now. It was 1:28 PM, and hunger pangs had gnawed at her stomach. But she had forced away thoughts of food, chugging endless cups of black coffee instead. She hadn't even eaten breakfast today. So when her eyes finally landed on the clock, Daniela decided she'd gotten too hungry to proceed with any sort of efficiency and shut down her computer.

She rose from her desk chair and stumbled towards The Butterstick—still faintly dreaming of a hot lunch to fill her rumbling belly—but there was another purpose beneath that primal need: finding out how Greta was doing since Jake's sudden passing. Maybe talking would help them heal together.

Surprising though it was, The Butterstick seemed the same as ever without Jake around; Greta had done such an amazing job running the place that nobody would really have noticed the change. Daniela was walking towards her favorite spot when she caught sight of Iris at a table, looking lost in thought, barely touching a plate of food before her - very unlike her friend. She changed direction and made her way over to her, pulling out a chair and tapping her shoulder softly.

"A penny for your thoughts?" Daniela asked as she sat down.

Iris seemed surprised to see her, but smiled weakly. "Oh hi, Dani. I didn't see you coming."

"That's because you were somewhere else," Daniela said with an understanding smile. "What's the matter?"

"Well, it's..." Iris hesitated. "I don't know if it's worth discussing."

Daniela refused to accept this answer and urged her on: "If it could make you lost in thought like that, I think it definitely is worth discussing". Out of the corner of her eye, she saw one of the waiters making their way over to them; a girl wearing a yellow top with The Butterstick logo embossed across it and a pair of black jeans.

"Good afternoon, Daniela. Hi Iris," the waitress said proudly, flaunting the pad and pen in hand. Her aura suggested she was new here, probably fresh from college or something similar. Iris simply nodded in response while Daniela greeted her warmly and gave her ordered: "Hi Patrice, I'll have a triple decker BLT sandwich with fries please."

"Triple decker BLT with fries coming right up," she replied, before turning away to attend another customer. As soon as Patrice was out of earshot, Daniela turned back to Iris and prompted her once more: "So you were saying?"

"I feel a dread like nothing I've ever known," Iris gasps. "A palpable evil lingers in the air and it's intensifying every day. I can't put my finger on what it is, but it's there..just hovering over us."

"Are you on Relaxal? That could be the source of your feeling," Daniela suggested cautiously.

Iris shook her head vehemently. "This isn't something that drugs can fix. Trust me. I'm not off any pharmaceuticals as of now."

Daniela nodded slowly, unsure of how to help her friend with her fear. All she knew was that when Iris had strongly held apprehensions, they were usually justified. She smiled reassuringly. "We don't know what we're dealing with yet and that's okay. I believe you, though; if you've got a bad feeling, then things might not turn out so great," she said as she stood up from her chair and headed towards Greta's office door. "But ah—Greta had been missing since Jake passed away, so I wanted to check on her myself while I was here."

She reached up to knock on the entranceway and peeked inside before entering, seeing Greta seated at an old oak table with a stack of books sprawled across it. Daniela tapped lightly on the door frame and pushed it slightly further open.

"Hi Greta," Daniela called out softly, walking into the office and standing in front of the desk.

Greta peered up from the book and acknowledged Daniela with a nod. "Come in," she whispered, gesturing for Daniela to take a seat by one armchair beside her desk.

Daniela waved her hand dismissively and smilingly refused the offer as she readied herself to explain her intentions for being there.

"No thanks," she replied kindly, "I just came here to check in on you and see how you're coping without Jake here...I haven't been here since he left us."

Greta gave a sad smile of acknowledgement and closed the book she had been pouring through moments ago.

"It's all right," she breathed after a momentary pause, "It hasn't been easy, but I'm doing my best to manage."

Daniela nodded sympathetically in understanding before speaking once more.

"I'm so sorry for your loss," she said sorrowfully, "I hope everything will be okay."

Greta sighed sadly in response before reaching out for Daniela's hand briefly, as if to comfort her too, before letting go again and returning to her book.

"Thank you, darling. I really appreciate your checking in on me."

"Umm, I should probably go now. I still need to finish up lunch before I have to get back to the office."

"Understood. Maybe we can catch up some other time."

Daniela bowed her head ever so slightly and began making her way back to her table where her lunch had been set down by Patrice, who was seated across from Iris, whose gaze was fixed directly ahead as if she was in a trance. Daniela perched herself down in the chair and reached for one fry.

"So... did you see her?" Iris finally spoke up after several moments of silence between them.

"Hmn-hmn."

"And? What do you think? Any change? How is she doing?"

Daniela began picking apart a strip of fry with her fingers, not wanting to give away too much information, just in case someone else was to overhear their conversation. "Well, she looks fine on the surface level, says she's fine. But then again, I couldn't help but remember what we talked about the other day; that something about her seemed off." She paused for a moment and looked up at the clock above the counter—realizing how much time had passed since she first sat down for lunch - before continued, "I don't know what it is exactly, but it's as if nothing has changed despite everything that he put her through."

She hurriedly gobbled the rest of her lunch and glanced back up at the clock before standing from her chair and said, "Either way, I'll be late to work if I don't get going soon–there's still so much more work that needs to be done for today. See ya."

Daniela leaned back in her chair, still attempting to complete the website. She had traded out her Mac for the laptop that her predecessor used to begin the project. From what she observed so far, there weren't too many corrections needed; most of them being attributed to the programmer and not her own work. She was simply performing these last-minute checks before signing off, as everything looked intact.

Focusing on the screen, Daniela continued inspecting every inch of the website. Just a few moments into her exploration, she spotted an anomaly in a single pixel. Daniela would have never noticed this if it hadn't been for a specialized website creator program she got from her friend's laptop - a program she had gained earlier because of her passion for perfect picture quality. Now, this program was helping her out with the Mayoral Campaign's website - something that held great significance to her.

What was this distortion? It is probably just an inconsistency in the system. Sometimes certain pixels would appear distorted, but clicking on them usually solved the issue. With that thought in mind, Daniela hovered over the pixel and clicked - but nothing happened. When she realized she wasn't brought to another page anymore, curiosity got the best of her and she clicked again–only this time, the pixel redirected her to another URL.

Daniela felt her heart plummet. How could I have been so careless? She scolded herself, desperately feeling for the power button to force-start the laptop. Then suddenly, something on the screen caught her eye - an insignia of some sort. Her curiosity momentarily killed off the fear and dread that had infiltrated her senses. She peered at the URL again to make sure she hadn't misread it.

She couldn't believe what she was seeing...an .onion domain—that meant this was part of the dark web! What kind of site would embed itself into a Mayoral campaign website? She wondered, her thoughts blurry with confusion.

It took some moments, but eventually, the page loaded and Daniela saw the insignia more clearly. The panic surged back in all its glory at what she saw—the sign of the Cult of Standish! She frantically scrolled through the page and gasped when she realized exactly where she was—a restricted area of a site intended only for members of the cult! This was enough evidence for Daniela to be certain; they existed! But it wasn't enough for her story to be credible...she needed more than just a website to prove it. She needed actual people, names, faces - someone who could testify against them.

That's when an idea clicked inside her head. If she could gather evidence of them recruiting someone, then she would have all she needed to prove their existence.

Daniela nervously scurried away from her laptop as she heard the approaching footsteps in her office. She quickly closed it and plastered a false smile on her face, awaiting the person who breezed into her room moments later.

A wave of relief swept over her when she recognized that it was only Jocelyn, her boss. "Hello there," she said, "I just came to let you know I'd be leaving a bit early. I don't want you running around looking for me when I'm gone."

Daniela's heart raced even more if that were possible, expecting Jocelyn to discover something suspicious about her current behavior. "Oh? Is anything the matter?" Daniela asked.

"Not at all. I just have some errands to run." Jocelyn replied with an intensity in her voice which made Daniela feel exposed, like she had been caught doing something wrong. The air around them felt heavy and repressed with silence as their eyes locked together, before Jocelyn interrupted the moment with further questions. "Are you alright?"

Daniela swallowed hard before responding shakily, "Hmn?" Her body shook as fear coursed through it while her mind raced between excuses as to why she was so jittery.

"I asked if everything is fine. You seem a bit jumpy, a lot spooked, in fact." Jocelyn continued observing Daniela intently yet wearing an expression of concern upon her face.

Knowing that she couldn't lie, Daniela took a deep breath and released it slowly in attempt to calm herself down before speaking again. "Yeah, I'm fine," she spoke quietly but firmly in rebuttal to the accusations of nervousness that had been directed towards her earlier. "I guess it's because I just got back from the Butterstick. I saw Greta and it was sad seeing her without Jake by her side - still trying to come to terms with his passing"

Jocelyn nodded sympathetically and spoke softly yet thoughtfully: "I do understand the feeling. Jake was a great man but that's life for you. Some are destined to live and others to die," pausing briefly as she took a deep breath before continued "Don't let it get to you too much."

Her words were calming yet sorrowful at once, bringing light to the darkness of death yet conveying comfort in the knowledge that this sentiment was shared between them both. mustering up a faint smile amidst the tears threatened to spill down her cheeks, Daniela offered up a muffled thank-you in response before watching Jocelyn leave with one final comment: "See you around". Nodding in agreement, Daniela confirmed "Yeah - see you tomorrow."

The instant that the door shut behind her, Daniela immediately turned back towards her laptop; no doubt distracted by what lay beyond.

The sunset washed out the deserted graveyard with a supernatural golden hue. Hugo, the janitor made his way through the cemetery grounds, checking for any intruders or vandals that had snuck into the cemetery. He was determined to make sure everything was in order before he left.

He arrived at the far end of the graveyard, where no mortal soul had ventured. This was where the girl had been buried by her cult followers after they killed her in their sickening rituals. The grave was nothing more than an unmarked mound of dirt, void of any inscriptions or adornments. Hugo shook his head as he thought about it, wondering why anyone would do such horrible things to another human being.

He grabbed his potted flowers and a can filled with water and marched towards the grave. The cultists had asked him to plant some colorful blooms on the grave so it wouldn't look too different from its neighboring graves. As Hugo began planting the flowers around the edges of the grave, something strange happened - as soon as his fingertips came in contact with soil, each plant started wilting away one by one like they were cursed!

Stunned by this sight, Hugo looked up from his task, disbelief etched upon his face.

Hugo felt his stomach lurch, unable to process the bizarre phenomena unfolding before him. He had to record this moment in time for others to witness the strange event he was witnessing too. This proved similar to the tale of that taco seller who had stumbled across a clandestine cult and been written off as insane when he divulged their secrets.

Making sure to take notice of every detail around him, he carefully placed another flower on the ground and immediately seized his phone to capture enough evidence to back up his claims. When he watched the recording back, Hugo decided that the only way to prove himself was by sending the video directly to the Dark Priest. Cursing under his breath as soon as he realized that his phone's signal wasn't functioning, Hugo tried every tactics he could think of, all in vain. It had been happening for weeks now; at random moments throughout the day his network would drop out entirely and never return for what seemed like forever.

Just as Hugo dropped his phone in frustration and reached out for it once more, a chilling mist began to roll in from all directions, covering the graveyard rapidly within seconds so that not an inch of vision remained. Hugo's ears picked up a distant noise punctuating the thick silence yet before he could trace its source, his phone vibrated with an incoming call. With an involuntary gasp of fear, Hugo dropped it again but quickly collected himself on realizing how ridiculous it was to be scared of fog; after all, it was just a mist. Kneeling down with trembling hands, he frantically searched the ground for his phone.

Hugo heard his phone ringing faintly in the air, he strained to follow the sound until it led him right up to the grave that he had been tending moments ago. He crawled closer to the grave and knelt on all fours, dread starting to build inside of him as he gazed upon the empty hole that should have housed a body. All around him flowers wilted from the soil, an unexplainable force killing them off with no mercy. His heart raced as he realized that his phone was still ringing from within the hollow graveyard plot, and for a moment he debated turning tail and running away. Yet something kept him rooted in place, and so Hugo stretched out one arm towards the mysterious source of sound, determined to retrieve his phone from whatever cursed power dwelled here.

As his fingers grazed against the cold circle of metal, he saw his cellphone come alive on its own accord. The video camera switched on by itself, pointing right at him – unless he looked behind himself, something unfathomable filled his vision. Something that never should have been there. For just a few minutes beforehand, Hugo had been alone in this cemetery – alone, yet now a faceless figure stood behind him, watching Hugo's every move.

He peered through the phone screen, gazing at the terrifying figure. Her skin was so deformed that he would not have recognized her as a person if it weren't for the hooded cloak draped around her body. But her neck... Hugo felt his stomach tighten when he saw where her neck should have been. Instead, there was an immense gash revealing a web of pipes and wires, almost as if she were some sort of machine. Tears of blood trickled from her empty eyes, like a broken doll in need of repair. She seemed to be staring straight back at him, yet something about her gaze made him feel like he was just a speck of dust fading away into nothingness.

A cold sweat rapidly ensued, as his breathing started to become heavier. He couldn't take his eyes off her, but he knew what he saw wasn't real. The image must surely be an illusion– one he wished with all his might would disappear– but before he could process his thoughts any further, he heard the sound of a shovel whizzing past his ear and thudding against his neck. Hugo fell backwards into the grave as death slowly engulfed him, his head severed from his body.

Daniela had been sitting by her work laptop for hours, her eyes strained and body cramping. She knew something was going to happen, she just didn't know when. In the meantime, she opened her MacBook and started doing other jobs. Suddenly there was a chime from the laptop, an incoming communication. Quickly turning to it, Daniela saw a notification in a forum chat with only three people in it. Two of them had already sent messages.

She looked closely at the usernames but couldn't figure out who they were. The message read that there would be a meeting at Tisdale Cemetery to find out what happened to "the body". Her mind reeled as she tried to think of what body they could be referring to.

Her gut told her this could be big – a news story she couldn't pass up. She grabbed her phone off the table and dialed Heath's number, still staring at the computer screen. She needed him by her side for this one.

Heath answers on the second ring, "What are you doing now?" she asked frantically.

"Well, hello to you too, Dani. I had an amazing day. Trust yours went well too?" he said sarcastically.

"I'm sorry. Hi Heath. Listen, don't go home yet - come pick me up at work instead."

"What's going on?" Heath asked with a hint of curiosity in his voice.

"We're on the verge of something big," she said breathlessly.

"Can't this wait?"

"No, it can't, Heath. Enough of your cynicism; get down here right now! You need to take the camera with you since this is of the utmost importance, so don't go home first. I'll see you in fifteen."

Heath hung up, and Daniela suddenly felt a wave of excitement overwhelm her. She shut down her laptop and quickly packed up her things before briskly exiting the office into the lobby to wait for him.

True to his word, he showed up in less than fifteen minutes and they drove off together towards the cemetery. On the way there she filled him in on all the details she had uncovered so far. When they reached their destination, Heath parked his car in the lot and looked at her in disbelief before uttering:

"I think maybe you shouldn't keep this solely between us two."

"That's why we're here," she replied determinedly. "To get some solid proof which would help our case with the police or whoever else needs convincing."

He was quiet for a few moments more before continued: "Think about it; if we're going to tell them anything, we really do need hard evidence first. Let's go see what happens during this meeting."

They grabbed their equipment from inside the car and rushed through the misty air up to the location described in the message, finding an appropriate spot to hide nearby where they could observe without being seen. With their camera at the ready, they waited patiently for someone to show up.

CHAPTER SEVEN

Daniela sat across from Heath, their backs pressed against the cold stone wall of a mausoleum. Heath was fidgeting nervously, his eyes darting around the dark cemetery. Daniela spoke in hushed tones, trying to calm him down.

"Seriously, Heath, we just need to be a little more patient. Just a little more. Something is going to happen soon. I can feel it in my bones. Just trust me, Heath."

Heath breathed out a deep sigh, "Run me through everything that you saw again."

"I already did, Heath." She replied curtly. Heath shot her a look that stopped her from saying anything further.

"Fine." She begrudgingly continued, "I was scouring the website when I got a message alert. The two of them were talking about 'a body' and a meeting."

"Their exact words?"

"I don't remember, but they were discussing checking on 'the body' and seeing if all was good. They said they'd meet here to check things out and from their conversation, '. So you see they would have to come?"

"I guess so," Heath replied uneasily and slumped back onto the ground.

Suddenly a beep pierced through the quiet of the cemetery startling both of them. Daniela turned to him with an intense glare like she was going to rip his head off.

Heath immediately knew why he had received that text; he had left his phone's sound on a loud profile. He shot her an apologetic look and quickly silenced his device.

Knowing very well what this could lead to, Heath kept his gaze low avoiding eye contact with Daniela. Beyond the fact that it was inappropriate for his phone to be so loud, he felt guilty too. Daniela wasn't aware of the texts he had been receiving lately or who they were from.

Lately, Heath and Amelia had become more than just passing acquaintances. They talked often and he was almost certain that their bond had grown into something deeper--but how would Daniela take it? He had recently been lecturing her about Kimbery and the thought of him having feelings for her younger cousin felt like a betrayal.

He opened up his phone to answer the text from a moment ago but hesitated, hoping to find a way to tell Dani without making things awkward between them. His mind raced as he glanced out towards the entrance of the cemetery again, feeling strangely on edge.

Daniela knew there was something going on with Heath; she could sense it in the air. Ever since he read that mysterious notification on his phone, he seemed jumpy and secretive. It made her uncomfortable, and her intuition told her there was something off... could Heath be involved with the cult somehow? She shook away the thought, convinced that it wasn't possible.

But still, what was he hiding from her? Her gut told her that this time something bigger than Jake's involvement with the cult was at play. But deep down she didn't believe it--Heath certainly wasn't the type.

If he was, she was certain the cult had already taken her life. Or perhaps they wanted to keep him close to her so they would know every detail of her progress. Who better to corrupt all the evidence she collected than an insider? She risked a glimpse at Heath and noticed he was still distressed - but less so than before. No, Heath definitely wasn't one of them; she could feel it in her gut as much as sense him keeping something from her. It started soon after the text came in.

The conclusion was obvious; the message came from someone she knew or else Heath wouldn't be so anxious. It must have been Kimbery! Daniela's heart glowed warmly; were Heath and Kim finally an item? She respected their desire to wait until they were sure before announcing it, even if it meant being patient.

Daniela felt beyond elated for them both, hoping that their future together would be filled with happiness. If they desired privacy before releasing the news, then she would honor their wishes.

The night sky glowed ominously over the graveyard, and the two men were shrouded in its penetrating silence. Vandel Zen had been seated on a small boulder since the crack of dawn, anxiously awaiting his companion's arrival as he filled his lungs with long, deep breaths. He knew that Craig was never late for anything, so why today?

As if responding to his inner turmoil, an aged black SUV appeared at the cemetery entrance, leaving a trail of dirt in its wake. It came to an abrupt halt and Vandel's eyes narrowed with suspicion as he watched for any signs of movement from inside. Five minutes passed and finally Craig emerged, but it wasn't enough time to quell Vandel's boiling rage. He despised waiting, especially when there was important business to attend to.

Vandel stomped heavily across the dried grass and gravel that dug into the bottom of his shoes. His mission was clear - Hugo instructed them to cover up Rachel's fresh grave before anyone noticed. The caretaker may have been good at his job, but everyone knew that he could be quite lazy. Vandel was counting on Craig's punctuality this time and he refused to budge until it was done. He pulled out his cell phone to call Craig and all he heard was the service tone on the other end.

"Why in the world are you late?" Vandel yelled through gritted teeth, "We have more important things to do than cult business! How much longer must

"Goddammit! No signal!" Vandel bellowed in frustration, fists clenched and veins bulging. He was sure something shady was going on here; his crime from months ago coming back to haunt him. But of course, the priest couldn't have known about Rachel. There had to be another explanation. With a purposeful stride, he circled around his SUV, smacking his phone every few seconds in a desperate attempt for reception, until he finally disappeared from their view.

Daniela shot up like a bullet, breaking the silence of the night air.

"What do you think you're doing?!" Heath whispers harshly as he grabbed her arm and yanked her back down.

"He's gone. I need to see where he goes." She said determinedly and started getting up again.

"Wait a minute! He might not be alone. What if someone sees you?" Even in the dim light, Heath's eyes were wide with anxiety, his voice trembling with fear.

"Someone has to make sure he leaves!" Daniela pleaded and before her companion could react she darted away into the darkness.

Heath struck out after her, cautioned her once more to "Be careful down here". She nodded weakly before watching him disappear into the night, already missing his comforted presence.

Alone, Daniela felt a chill run down her spine. Her heart began pounding wildly as reality set in - they were really close to uncovering who or what was behind this whole thing now...and it scared the hell out of her. What had they gotten themselves into?

As she crouched in the dense foliage, Daniela's heart thudded so loudly that she worried her enemies would hear it. As if on cue, a chilling wind swept through and raised goosebumps on her flesh. She had never felt so vulnerable. Suddenly, an ominous intuition took hold of her - a premonition of something gruesomely catastrophic that was about to happen. Her senses were heightened, but the fear had turned into ice-cold resolve.

Unaware of Daniela's growing panic, Heath stood amidst the shrubbery, keeping his eyes peeled for any signs of danger. Vandel fiddled with his phone, hoping to get some cell service. With bated breath, they waited for a sign of what to do next.

"Help me!"

The voice was hushed but unmistakable, and it reverberated through the cemetery like a death knell. Heath ducked lower into the bushes as all color drained from his face- he had not imagined it after all! And what's worse? What if it was Daniela who needed help? He gnawed at his lip, feeling utterly helpless.

"Daniela!" screamed Heath in his head as he tried to piece together all scenarios in his mind. It was a trap - he knew it in his gut! Should he risk everything to go out there or stay put? In a flash of decisive courage, Vandel sprinted towards the source of the distress call with Heath hot on his heels.

Vandel's feet trudged on, as he prayed that he was going the right way. He thought he detected a faint flicker of color from the corner of his vision and had to stop in his tracks. He quickly turned to face the source, but all there was an illusion. His breath hitched; it must have been a bird or some other insignificant creature, he concluded. Just then, a firm grip clamped onto his shoulder and Vandel's body cringed under its weight. He knew it. His entire journey had been one giant setup and Craig had deceived him. His heart sunk into his abdomen and his mind raced with dread.

Daniela held her breath, every fiber of her being screaming at her to stay put. But no, she had to be the hero and now she was pinned down on the dusty floor, praying that Vandel wouldn't spot her. She hadn't expected it to be this hard, trying to help someone in need. A small sigh escaped her lips as she tried to calm herself. She could feel a bead of sweat trickle down her face and silently cursed herself for not being more prepared.

Suddenly, there was a rustling in the bushes and Daniela's breath caught in her throat. Vandel had heard too. She waited with bated breath, straining to hear footsteps or any indication that he was coming closer. Silence enveloped the small clearing like a shroud; even the cicadas that had been so incessant before were eerily quiet now.

"What the fuck, Craig?" The voice came from just beyond the thicket, causing Daniela's heart to race faster.

"You almost shit your pants, Vandel. You should have seen your face when you turned around," the man called Craig replied amusedly. Daniela peered through the leaves and saw two men standing on the other side; one she recognized as Vandel while the other must have been Craig.

"That was not funny, Craig. Not funny at all."

"What you scared of the dead? It was hilarious man."

"I thought the priest sent me here to have me killed or something. Especially when you didn't show up."

"Oh come on, man, you're just paranoid. The priest can't do anything like that."

Daniela listened intently as they spoke. So there was a priest involved in this mess too? She made a mental note to dig deeper into their motives once she emerged from hiding.

Daniela was frozen in place, her ears attuned to the conversation between Vandel and Craig. She had to be careful, especially with rumors of a dark priest abounding.

"What took you so long?" Vandel questions.

"I got a flat, and the cell phone didn't work." Craig replies.

"No reception," Vandel murmurs, "I tried to reach you too."

"Where were you going?"

"Someone was screaming for help. I wanted to check it out."

Before he could finish his sentence, a distant shuddering cry for help reached Daniela's ears. A jolt ran through her body as the familiar voice traveled closer before quickly vanishing again, leaving a chill in its wake.

Vandel started, cutting himself off mid-word. "That's the voice."

"Damn, I thought you were hallucinating," Craig mutters. "Let's split up and search around this area; there should be a graveyard somewhere nearby. We'll meet back here in ten minutes." With that, Craig turned on his heel and marched away while Vandel moved in the opposite direction.

Daniela stealthily stood, straightening from her crouching position as she readied herself to follow Vandel. She couldn't shake the feeling that the voice had come from this very spot twice already. She prayed that Heath would join Craig on the other side. Taking one last deep breath, she followed the path that Vandel had taken.

Vandel sped forward, dragging Daniela along with him. Moments before they arrived at their destination, his foot stumbled against something on the ground. It immediately emitted a bright light from its surface. Daniela shot behind the closest tree and peered around cautiously to survey if anyone else was in the area. To her relief, it seemed like Vandel was alone.

He bent over to pick up the phone, yet before he had time to register what he was holding, a video began playing on the screen of the mysterious device. The sight made him freeze in terror; his fingers trembling and losing strength by the second, causing the phone to slip out of his grip.

Slowly, his gaze shifted towards Rachel's grave where a headless corpse hung precariously over the empty pit. His complexion went pale and a cold sweat spread across his face as bile rose in his throat- followed by dry retching as he struggled to keep nausea down.

Daniela edged closer while Vandel hunched over dizzily. Her ankle caught upon a dead branch that snapped loudly under her weight. Shit! she swore under her breath before slowly shifting back into her original location.

Vandel's head flinched towards the sound of rustling leaves, the shock pulling him out of his daydream. His eyes zoned in on the silhouette of a young girl standing beside a tall tree, mere feet away from Hugo's now decapitated body. Vandel knew who was responsible for the man's death in that moment, and she was staring right at him. He immediately pulled out his forty calibre Glock, closed one eye and aimed it at her.

"What th-" Daniela tried to scream in terror, but the shock held her still, frozen to the spot.

She watched helplessly as he fired a shot that hit nothing but air. Heart pounding against her chest, Daniela finally found her legs again and sprinted away from Vandel with all her might–even though every step felt like wading through quicksand. Her lungs burned and thighs ached as if they were on fire, but she kept running until a large mausoleum came into view. Without thinking twice, she ducked inside and weaved between the rows of tombs until she reached a stone casket of which she could hide behind.

Hot tears coursed down her cheeks as soon as she crouched down. A terrifying reality had set in; where is Heath? Is he okay? She had no phone on her to call him and all hope seemed lost until she heard heavy footsteps entering the mausoleum – footsteps that were nearing her adopted hiding spot by the second. Closing her eyes tight, Daniela clamped a hand over her mouth to stifle her cries; what have I gotten myself into?

Vandel trudged along the length of the mausoleum, desperately seeking out the perpetrator who had disappeared here moments ago. He knew in his mind that it must surely be her. No one else could possibly be responsible for the gruesome fate Hugo had met with.

As he ambled towards the exit, his eyes caught sight of a light brown footprint in the damp mud. Stopping dead in his tracks, Vandel wheeled around and shut the door tightly back behind him. This should be fun, he thought to himself sinisterly. She was nothing more than a caged rabbit now.

"Hello there," he said in an acidic tone that Daniela could feel from her hiding place, even though she couldn't see him yet. Her tears began to flow once again and she shivered at his words as they echoed down the tomb-like structure.

"Come out, come out wherever you are," Vandel continued to sing mockingly, "I promise to be gentle. It'd be so quick, you won't even feel a thing."

Daniela's heart pounded relentlessly against her chest as a strange feeling crept up onto her skin; something was about to happen. As quietly as possible, trying not to alert him of her presence by the sound of her thumping pulse, Daniela sobbed into her trembling hands.

Suddenly, a loud gunshot and a shrill cry split through the stillness that surrounded them like a sharp blade slicing through butter. Daniela jumped out of her skin and screamed in terror before quickly clapping her hands over mouth. Taking in several deep breaths, she attempted to steady herself before cautiously turning towards the source of the sound.

Standing before her with blood trickling freely down from between his eyebrows, inexplicably propped up by leaning against the wall, was Vandel with an intense look of shock written on his face. His body went limp shortly after as he sank to the ground without uttering another word or making further noise.

Heath heard the gunshot and immediately Craig sprang into action, yanking out his pistol and sprinting after Vandel.

"No!" Heath screamed with anguish as he watched the man disappear from view, knowing that there was nothing more for him to do. He whirled around and ran from the cemetery, frantically patting his pockets in search of a cell phone.

Miraculously, he found a signal bar and frantically dialed the police.

"Someone help me! A friend is in trouble at Ceder Villa Cemetery," Heath exclaimed feverishly. "Two men have guns and they have been shooting..."

The dispatcher's voice came on the line: "Calm down, sir. We'll be there shortly."

Craig followed the heavy steps imprinted in the mud, sprinting into the mausoleum. His body tensed up as he saw two lifeless bodies on the floor. He raised his gun towards her with a determined look on his face.

"Who the hell are you?" Craig bellowed, staring at her through narrowed eyes. "Tell me why you killed Hugo and Vandel. Who sent you?"

"I-I swear I don't know anything about them! Please, believe me! I didn't do this." She replied through sobs, her hands shaking uncontrollably.

"Then who did!?" Craig shouted, saliva flying from his mouth. He stepped closer to her, towering over her small frame.

"I don't know! I really don't know! Please, it wasn't me!" she said frantically.

Craig seethed with rage and clenched his fist tightly around the butt of the gun. "You will pay for this, bitch!" he said darkly and went to press down on the trigger.

Daniela watched as every movement felt like time had been frozen in place; an icy chill lingered in the air and a thick cloud of mist formed at their feet. Suddenly, an invisible force seemed to grip Craig's hand, preventing him from pulling the trigger. A yelp escaped his throat and the gun dropped out of his hands as if it were magnetically repelled from his grasp. Blood began to ooze from a gash on his forehead as his knees buckled beneath him.

The man, his face as blank as a sheet of paper, opened his mouth like he was searching for words but not a single sound escaped. He stared unblinkingly at Daniela as if he saw right through her to something behind her. It took what seemed like an eternity before she realized that he wasn't looking straight ahead, but past her. But no matter how much she tried to make sense of the situation, nothing made any sense and there was nothing she could do to help him.

Daniela felt her stomach drop and her heart thump painfully in her chest. She attempted to move away from this strange room, away from this bizarre scene, but it was like someone had fastened an invisible weight to her feet and she couldn't take one step forward. Even when a raw cry left her lips and spread through her chest like wildfire, she still couldn't break free from whatever had stolen over her body.

A grotesquely disfigured hand emerged slowly from her chest, followed by a figure – the silhouette of a girl with no throat and a gaping hole where her heart should have been. Daniela wanted to scream until she dropped to the floor below, yet inexplicably none of those actions came to fruition.

The figure moved nearer Craig with an eerie sneer on its lips, and whispered icily: "Did you miss me?" Its fingertips crawled down his chest until they reached his zipper. He desperately wanted to protest but his body remained immovable under its spell.

Craig stood petrified as the creature continued tracing circles around his fly, all the while studying him intently with those hollow eyes.

The malevolent being languidly unbuttoned his trousers and let them fall to the ground. He exposed his soiled, unwashed underwear. The figure beside him reached in and started to satisfy his desires. Craig may have felt aroused if not for the sight of what was happening—only fear shot through him. In that instant he realized this must have been how Rachel felt when he and Vandel had forced themselves upon her. He wanted to apologize, to tell her that he wished he could take it back, but no words would come forth from his silent throat. Tears pooled in the corners of his eyes as they ran down his face.

A hand emerged from within Craig's underwear drenched in blood. It trailed long intestine strings in its grasp. Daniela tried to scream but her voice failed her. She couldn't believe what she was seeing, icy terror coursing through her veins like a heavy presence weighing down on her chest. Her hands hit her thigh as some part of her conscious returned.

A lump in her pocket made her remember that she still had her phone with her all along. With a trembling hand she snatched it out of her pocket and clicked pictures with horror-stricken eyes as the figure raised their finger with a razorblade nail and made one clean slice through Craig's neck. A stream of blood gushed out of the wound and Craig's body crumpled to the floor—Daniela released an ear-splitting shriek because of the morbid event before her.

Frantically now, she took more photographs but quickly realized that they weren't clear enough for any sort of evidence or exoneration against these killings. Just then the perpetrator turned around and began walking towards her—Daniela stumbled backwards as she hastily tried to take clear photos.

Daniela's hands trembled as she frantically switched on her camera flash. The sudden illumination of the chamber caused an eerie, yet imposing figure to pause its tracks around her. Taking advantage of this fortunate moment, she took pictures rapidly and backpedaled towards the exit; casting one last gaze of terror upon the beast before finally making her escape.

Outside, a cold gust of wind welcomed her arrival. Darkness engulfed Daniela as she ran into the night, barrel rolling through open graves and murky fog until a shadowed building stood before her - the old, church just beyond the cemetery. She felt like she had been running for hours and her legs were about to give up at any second but her fear kept propelling her forward.

When she reached the steps of the church, Daniela collapsed breathless atop them. All she could see was a blur of black and white before hearing a voice calling out in concern,"Holy Mary! Are you alright child?"

With every ounce of strength left in her fragile body, Daniela crawled towards the nun but soon felt herself fading away and collapsing in exhaustion. The last thing she heard before slipping into unconsciousness was the nun's cry echoing throughout the graveyard.

CHAPTER EIGHT

Bright, searing white lights flooded into Daniela's eyes, nearly blinding her as she opened them. Before she could adjust to the brightness, she immediately shut her eyes tight and pondered where she was. She knew she was nowhere near home, these lights were too dazzling for her own bedroom. Gradually, Daniela opened her eyelids a fraction of an inch and allowed them to get used to the light before opening them all the way.

As she surveyed the room, Daniela noticed that the entire area was paraded in lifeless white hues. There was a certain clinical atmosphere that made her uneasy; it wasn't until she tried shifting her hand to wipe her face that Daniela realized there was an IV line connected to her arm. A hospital? How had she even arrived here? As much as she tried hard to remember what had transpired beforehand, nothing emerged from the thick fog that had settled over her mind.

Suddenly, the image of two empty eyes shrouded by blood-stained skin floated through Daniela's brain and caused her to bolt upright with a loud shriek. An ear-piercing alarm blared throughout the area as Daniela felt her heart hammering wildly within her chest and her breathing becoming labored and irregular. Two figures suddenly raced into the room and a voice broke into Daniela's mind effectively shaking away her silent musings:

"She's hyperventilating! Her heartbeat is skyrocketing," said a female sharply.

"Daniela, can you hear me?" a deep, gruff voice echoed inside her head. "We are here to take most excellent care of you, but we need your help in doing so. If you can understand me, try to relax, dear."

The same image crossed Daniela's mind again, this time showing the entire body. The sight caused her heart to beat faster and more wildly than ever before. She desperately tried to scream out loud, but no sound emerged from her tight throat. Her brain pulsed with agony as her chest heaved with labored breathing. Suddenly she felt a sharp prick in her arm that vanished just moments later. Gradually, her heartbeat began to slow until it steadied itself and her eyes drifted shut.

Amelia carefully navigated her way through the sea of white coats and nurses that flooded in and out of her cousin's room. She had been waiting with Kimbery and Iris since Heath had called them to inform them of the incident. While they were gathering, Amelia had met a nun who had come with Heath and a striking police detective by the name of Liam. In any other circumstance, Amelia would have definitely flirted with the handsome man, however this was not the time or place for such distraction; Daniela needed Amelia to keep her head on straight.

If only Amelia's mother hadn't left for a trip to check up on a relative. Since she'd gotten the call from Heath alerting her to what had happened, Amelia had tried desperately to reach her mother but to no avail. Without help from home, it was now up to Amelia to take care of her beloved cousin. Fortunately, she knew all the nurses and doctors at the hospital since she volunteered there every week as part of one of her college courses so at least that shouldn't be too hard to deal with.

"Heath?" A voice sounded right next to Amelia, breaking into her thoughts. She looked up and saw that Detective Liam was done speaking with the nun.

"Here, sir," Heath answers, reluctantly getting up.

"Heath, come with me. We need to talk." Liam motioned for him to follow as he strode down the hall. "What really happened at that cemetery?" The detective's voice echoed off the walls. His eyebrows were raised, anticipation in his eyes.

"Officer I already told the other officers what went on. Daniela and I host an online show together; her being the anchor and me as the cameraman. Our current story centers around a supposed cult living in town called 'The Standish Cult.' We decided it would be necessary to document things at the cemetery because it was rumored to be eerie and potentially linked to this cult," Heath replied, an uneasiness settling over him. His eyes darted away from Liam's penetrating gaze, avoiding any more questions on the matter.

"And then what?" Liam inquired, frustrated by the lack of answers provided.

Heath shook his head slowly, not wanting to divulge any further information about their horrific experience that night. His life relied on keeping his mouth shut; if only they hadn't discovered what was living inside that cemetery, he wouldn't have been put in such a dangerous situation now standing across from Liam. He couldn't risk getting himself and Daniela killed for a news story that would likely be silenced even if they got it out there.

"Listen, I'm not sure what those strangers were up to," Heath said, his voice trembling with fear. "They could have been mischievous or on a more serious mission like theft. When we heard them coming our way and saw them in the vicinity where we were hidden, we couldn't resist splitting up. Then the gunshot and then I dialed 911."

Liam intently listened as Heath spoke, scribbling something every once in awhile on his notepad without uttering a single word.

"I can see that you believe Daniela might be somehow involved in the murder of those two men," Heath concluded, his gaze honed on the observer's face. "But I swear she had nothing to do with it. She would never commit such an act. If you think perhaps she was defending herself against something or someone—then you must forget that thought because Daniela isn't one to take that kind of drastic action no matter the circumstances."

Liam nodded slowly as he jotted down some final notes before looking up again and speaking in a steady voice, "I will take all of this into account whilst noting how adamant you are regarding Miss Savan's innocence. Right now, there are no charges against either you or Miss Savan but keep in mind that I may ask for your assistance and presence at some point during the investigation process, so until then try not to leave town too far away

"All right, detective," Heath said curtly and spun around, not wasting another breath on the man. He had already divulged too much information, and he knew it. Anyone could have easily pinned the murders on him, citing his obsession with crime books and movies as evidence of motive and technique. The less Heath spoke, the better for him and Daniela. As Heath strode away from the detective, the air around him grew colder, and a sickening sense of dread crept up his spine.

Daniela woke with a throbbing headache that felt like an invisible vise squeezing her skull. The ache in her chest was even worse, as if a serrated saw had cut it open. Groggily her eyes opened to take in the small, private room she'd been placed in; it lacked any comforting amenities, save for a beat-up bible resting on the windowsill and a glass of water on the table beside her bed.

As she stretched out an arm to reach for the glass, it slipped from her hand and shattered on the floor, sending shards up beside her bed.

Daniela's gaze fell upon thin lines of blood drawn upon her arm, and the scattered pieces of glinting glass reflecting the light from outside.

The sound echoed down the hall and Liam heard it, running towards Daniela's room without hesitation. He stopped short when he saw the girl sitting amongst the mess of broken glass and bloodied water. He asked if she was alright but received no response. Her forehead creased ever so slightly as if deep in thought or concentration; he stepped around the bed and firmly grabbed her shoulders, shaking gently in an effort to bring her back into reality. But still, his words went unanswered.

Daniela's head started to spin in circles, her gaze transfixed on the pool of blood which was steadily thinning as water ran over and through it. It stirred something deep within her memories that scared her but she could not place it. Thoughts danced around her skull like a tornado, until finally a vision of death flashed across her mind's eye; a man's guts being clutched by contorted fingers of a demonic entity.

With a loud cry, Daniela fell to her knees and mumbled strange incoherencies, unaware that Liam had been shaking her. Desperate for security she grabbed him tightly in an embrace and refused to let go, tears streaming down her face all the while.

It was only when Iris came bursting into the room with Amelia and the others that Daniela released Liam. "Dani? What happened detective?" Iris asked with hysteria bubbling in her voice.

"That's what I'm here to find out, Miss Savan. Can you hear me?" Liam said softly, his voice cutting through the sobs of the frightened woman. It was a perfect opportunity to question her while she was still in shock, and he needed answers. Nothing at the scene made any sense, no matter how many times he replayed it his head; there had been bodies and they had found the gun, but nothing else could explain the pile of guts on floor or even the victim's slit throat.

He steadied his gaze towards Daniela and spoke more sternly this time. "My name is Detective Liam McGregor and I'm the one in charge of this case. What happened at the cemetery, Miss? I need you to help me understand this so we can wrap things up quickly. What happened to those two men?"

Daniela uttered between her tears and stutters, "She..she..she killed them. It killed them. It was horrible...Oh my God! Oh my God! She ripped his.... Oh God."

Liam tried to keep her calm with gentle words, "Calm down, Daniela. You're safe now. Just tell us what happened. Alright?" His eyes glanced up to see all four of her friends looking intently at him with concern, yet none of them attempted to move closer or comforted her. He seemed to have their trust that he could handle this situation alone.

With horror in her voice she continued amidst hysterical sobs, "It was too horrible for words...Oh God, it was terrible!"

Liam redirected her attention back to him with assurance in his voice, "I know, dear. It's fine now". He leaned in slightly as he gently coaxed her for more details, "Just take your time and told us what happened.

"It was a...a creature. It seemed like a girl but its appearances were ghastly, a fiend. I watched as it sprung from nowhere when the man entered the tomb. I didn't see how it killed the first one until the gunshot rang out. Its eyes locked in on me and with a gut-wrenching rip, it mercilessly tore my companion limb from limb right in front of me!" screams escaped her lips before she could choke them back down, her hysteria slowly starting to abate.

"How did you manage to escape from her?" Liam inquired, his eyes narrowing slightly beneath his furrowed brows as he observed the change in her demeanor.

She hesitated as if searching for an answer, before finally speaking: "I had grabbed my camera, hoping that if I had any proof then no one would call me crazy. In a desperate attempt to get something visible on film I flicked on the flash and - thank god - it startled her enough for me to make my escape. But I don't recall anything after running into the church; who found me here?"

As she glanced around at her friends with sunken eyes, all they could do was stare back at her silently and sympathetically. "Hi guys," she whispered and as she turned back to him, Liam realized a transformation had taken place - gone was the scared woman; now stood curiosity in its stead.

He cleared his throat and announced, "Detective Liam McGregor, ma'am. I am the detective assigned to this case." He noted with satisfaction how quickly any fear faded away the moment he identified himself as police. "You have nothing to worry about," he added reassuringly and proceeded to lay her back onto the bed gently. "Now let me fetch the nurse so we can get you cleaned up."

Striding out of the room, Liam sensed that there was something childlike and genuine about the girl. He had to admit she'd seemed honest, but the entire story didn't quite add up. No matter what he did, this whole paranormal business never made his job any easier.

Reaching the nurses' station just in time, Liam watched as one of them - the same who had attended to her earlier - returned from taking care of another patient. Leaning against the countertop, he called to her.

"Hey there. I just left Miss Savan's room, and she ended up cutting herself with a glass; shards and water are everywhere. Could you please get somebody to clean it up and dress her wound?"

"Sure thing," the nurse nodded. "Anything else?"

"Actually," Liam said, just as she was turning away from him, "do you have any idea what happened to her phone?"

The woman shook her head. "I'm afraid not; when she arrived here we found she had nothing on her except for the clothes she was wearing. Probably fell out at the church when she collapsed."

"Ah, okay. Thanks."

"No problem," came her reply before she hurried along to Daniela's room.

He gestured for the tall, lanky officer in blue stood closest to him. "Robson," Liam called urgently. The man spun around immediately. "We need to take advantage of this chance; Miss Savan's phone is still at church. Go down there and collect it for me; report back as soon as you have it."

"Yes sir!" Robson saluted crisply before marching off.

Liam wheeled around and began his return march to the young girl's room. He was certain that the mess had been cleared up by now, though he couldn't be sure about what was left of the phone--perhaps it could answer all their queries and explain the bizarre situation. 'd have to wait and see.

When Liam re-entered Daniela's chamber, he saw that the nurse had already taken care of the wound on her wrist; meanwhile, the janitor had done a splendid job disposing of the debris. The only person remaining in the room besides Daniela was her cousin Amelia, who sat alongside her on the bed.

"Thank you so much for coming," Amelia said with gratitude.

"There's nothing to thank me for yet; you're all free to go as soon as I say so, but don't leave town until I contact you again," Liam replied, turning away from them to make his exit.

However, before he could take one step forward, a new outburst interrupted him. Liam spun back around and caught sight of Daniela slipping back into hysterics.

"Please, save him! Save him! Detective, save the officer!" she pleaded amidst fresh tears streaming down her face.

"Oh lord..." Amelia mumbles under her breath in despair. How was she supposed to take care of this vulnerable girl if episodes like these kept occurring? Would they ever find a way to restore Daniela's mental state or would she be doomed to suffer?

"Dani?" Iris inquired nervously.

"Save him! Somebody save him! Save Officer Robson... Somebody please!" She continued her desperate cries.

The sudden outburst took aback Liam. How had she possibly known about Robson and why did she preach about saving him? He hadn't even mentioned officer Robson in her presence, let alone being outside the building. She frantically fought against his grasp but he held firm, whispering soothing words as he brushed her hair away from her face.

"Officer Robson will be alright. I promise you nothing will happen to him," he attempted to reassured her, though that seemed futile.

"No! You don't understand!" Daniela screeched in a desperate tone. "He's going to die! She'll kill him if he gets there!" Her sentence ended abruptly when a rancid smell began to seep into her nostrils. Peering around at their unfamiliar surroundings, she noticed they had been transported to a rickety balcony of old building, surrounded by barren land. Nothing looked familiar; where were they? The voices of Liam and her family asking what was wrong with her started to fade out of her consciousness.

As the eerie sound drew nearer, Daniela spin around like a top. Her heart leapt at the sudden presence of a long staircase spiraling down into an abyss of darkness. As she carefully shuffled to the edge of the balcony, her eyes briefly scanned the stained-glass window of Mary and Jesus. Daniela's heart raced with familiarity as she remembered this scene from her past,

"I know this place." Her voice echoed in the cold air as if it belonged nowhere else.

Liam quickly snapped out of his trance and whipped out his notepad. He felt drawn by a mysterious force to take notes on what was happening before him. His instincts proved correct when Kimbery lashed out, "What do you think your doing?"

Without missing a beat Iris butted in, "Something has taken control over her body and mind," alluding to the state which Daniela had suddenly found herself in. She was lost in time, unaware of the worry etched on their faces.

Daniela continued her tale regardless, "I see him now..." her voice trailed off as if consumed by some inner power. Before them, their minds were painted with visions of an officer saying his goodbyes to a nun before surveying the church grounds.

A piercing ring echoed in the distance, catching Officer Robson's attention. He instantly began to scan his surroundings, eyes wide and seeking, but all he could see was silence. As if guided by a strange force, the officer's gaze shifted up and right towards where Daniela stood — transfixed with fear.

The man seemed to float toward her as he stepped closer, and she involuntarily stepped back in reaction. Her heart raced faster than it ever had before, threatening to burst out of her chest as he neared her. The air around them thickened and became dense as time passed slowly, like tar trapping everyone in place. But then suddenly, he veered away from her and approached the balcony with haste.

Perplexed yet relieved, Daniela exhaled endlessly while watching the man bend over and pick an object off the ground — only to realize it was her phone! With confusion painted on her face, she slowly crept closer to him while still trying to process what was happening. Yet strangely enough, no matter how close she stepped or how much she waved her hand in front of his face, the officer didn't bat an eye at her presence.

He fished out his own phone from his pocket with one swift motion and started dialing a number without shifting a single muscle in his body. She desperately wanted to get a glimpse of who he was calling, but even when standing right next to him she couldn't make out the name displayed on the screen. After a couple of seconds, the person on the other end picked up their call.

"What the bloody hell is this?" Officer Robson barks into his phone, face ablaze with anger. Daniela inched closer to him, her eyes wide with curiosity as she desperately tried to listen in on the conversation.

"Yes sir..." he continued sternly. "The reports are true...Two of our men have been murdered and there is a witness." His voice trailed off as his mind began to process the implications of what this meant for their entire organization.

Daniela felt a wave of nausea wash over her and her stomach churned with dread. She knew this feeling all too well, the horrible premonition that something bad was about to happen.

She watched intently as Robson gingerly reached for the girl's phone and swiped the screen to unlock it before navigating to her photo gallery. The photos were distorted and only hints of a figure were visible on the phone screen. He then proceeded to zoom in until he could make out the pair of eyes in the photograph. Suddenly, they blinked!

Robson gasped and leapt back in shock before quickly recovering from the surprise. Drawing conclusions in his head, he deduced that in her state of panic, the girl had possibly pressed on the video button instead of snap a photograph. All remained silent as Robson stared at the phone pictures, his facial expression unwavering as he contemplated his next move.

His phone suddenly buzzed, cutting through the stillness like a knife. Robson glanced at it briefly before sliding his finger across the screen.

"Hello?" Officer Robson shouts, his voice crackling and distorted by the static that filled the line. He waited for a response, but all he could hear was the deafening sound of the static. He cursed under his breath and hung up.

"It's not just your network," Daniela whispers behind him, her voice steady and urgent. But Robson didn't hear her words. He was already running down the stairs to his car, barely noticing the alarm blaring in the distance.

Daniela raced to the nearest window and looking outside saw Robson's car already running with someone hidden in the backseat. She felt as though she had been punched in the gut—all at once she felt sadness, anger, and dread course through her veins.

"Please," she begged desperately as Officer Robson drove away, "You have to find him or she'll kill him." She yelled in desperation, her voice echoing throughout the room.

Liam watched horrified as Daniela's emotions transformed from scared and gentle to fierce and angry. She had such honesty in her eyes, Liam felt a sting of pain in her plea for him to find Robson. He didn't understand why, but his gut told him something was amiss here, and this feeling had never failed him before.

"I'll go look for him, Miss," he said to Daniela then turned to Iris who still remained composed. "Get a nurse to take care of her; I'll be back soon."

Fastening on the siren of his car, Liam drove like a madman all the way to the church. To his relief, there was no traffic or any other disruption that could have delayed his journey. From afar, he saw the police car still intact with Robson seated by its wheel. The young woman must have been hallucinating after all. He then proceeded towards the car, although fear struck his core at what he might find when he got there.

As Liam approached closer, he felt nauseous - it seemed like the figure in front of him hardly resembled Officer Robson. He gulped as he neared the car; nothing else around was damaged or burnt save for the charred corpse of Rick still sitting at the vehicle's wheel with a melted cellphone in hand. With relief mixed with shock, Liam pulled up some distance away before walking towards Robson's body. It was an unpleasant sight which would remain etched into his memory forever.

How did she know? It was unfathomable, as if the universe had conspired to betray her. He had been with her all along, watching her every move as he narrated the things she saw and felt. She had not once left his sight, yet the phone in his hand could only belong to Daniela. The realization hit her like a ton of bricks. How could she have known?

"I can't take this anymore, I must be going mad." Daniela's voice trembled as she mumbled in despair to her cousin Amelia. After the detective left, the two of them had calmed down somewhat but stress still weighed heavily on their shoulders. The nurse had only come into the room to make sure both of them were fine before heading off again. Iris went to get some soothing herbs to ease Daniela's frayed nerves, Heath left to fetch some food for the two of them and Kimbery went off to get a change of clothes for both girls.

Amelia stood up from her chair and ran her fingertips through her cousin's hair, trying to soothe her. "Don't worry Dani, it's just the emotional shock from everything that's happened, that's all. Iris said some people become psychic vessels after they've gone through some-thing traumatic like this. Everything will be alright by tomorrow love. Don't you fret now."

"I don't think so Amelia," Daniela replied weakly, shaking her head.

A voice came from outside the room then, calling out in shock, "Oh my God! Daniela!"

Amelia looked towards doorway with surprise before recognizing the person who had entered - it was her mother Maureen accompanied by a nurse. "Amelia, I got your voicemail and rushed here immediately. I also tried calling Daniela but the phone just kept ringing until it went to voicemail."

Daniela slowly raised her head and glanced at her aunt with tired eyes before uttering quietly, "Aunty."

Maureen gasps in alarm at seeing her condition before asked in concern, "What happened? Nurse...is she alright?"

The nurse nodded silently before replied reassuringly, "Yes ma'am, she'll be able to return home tomorrow provided we keep an eye on her for a bit more. She's still in shock due to what has occurred."

Maureen asked hesitantly, not wanting to leave her niece in that burdened state, "Are you sure?"

"Yes ma'am," the nurse replied calmly; although there was no mistaking the anxiousness lurking beneath his composure.

Irritation flashed across Daniela's face as she finally spoke up fiercely, "No...the nurse is wrong! I'm seeing things happen beforehand which is not normal!"

The nurse's offer of explanation had Daniela contemplating in silence. Though it seemed farfetched, it was better than the alternative that she was going crazy.

"Alright people, it's time to say your goodbyes," Jane said firmly, a hint of authority in her voice.

"No, we'd be staying the night. Our friends have gone to get clothes and something to eat, Jane," Amelia retorts.

"Amelia, you and your mother need to go and get some rest. You've done enough for today. I know how hard you work at school and then again when you come here to volunteer. The least I can do is take care of your cousin," Jane replied, her voice softening as empathy swept through her being towards the young family before her.

"I..." Amelia started to argue but Jane quickly cut her off.

"No arguments. Visiting hours are actually over." Her brown eyes glanced at the clock on the wall before returned their gaze towards them all. "I only let you stay so long because you're one of us now."

Maureen stepped away from where she had been standing and began walking towards the door with Amelia close behind her. "Thank you for understanding ma'am," Maureen voiced her gratitude as they stopped at the entrance. "We'll be back first thing tomorrow."

Jane nodded her response and turned on her heel to leave them alone for their goodbye. "But Mother..." Amelia started again but Maureen silenced her with one stern look.

"No buts, Amelia. We'll call your friends on the way home." She looked towards Daniela then, who was sitting on the bed with wide eyes full of fear and uncertainty - normal emotions for someone suffering from shock as she was doing since having premonitions about events yet to come true. "Daniela?"

"Yes Aunty," she answered hesitantly, not wanting them to leave her alone here with all these unknowns surrounding her life now.

"We have to take our leave now," Maureen smiled gently at her niece before continued, "We'll be back here first thing tomorrow, okay?"

Daniela gave them a small nod in affirmation and watched them leave as an ominous feeling lingered in the air.

"Fine, mother." Amelia said and stepped off the bed. She leaned down to press a gentle kiss on Daniela's scrunched forehead and then her right cheek before straightening back up. "Be strong, Dani. You'll be through this night with the blink of an eye."

"I will, Amelia. I'm sure of it."

"May strength fill your being, my beloved child. May the loving grace of our Lord be with you"

"Amen, aunty." She whispered with a weak smile plastered across her face as her aunt and cousin exited her hospital room.

The oppressive emptiness that filled Daniela's heart after they left was immense and she curled herself in a fetal position with her back facing the cold window as if that could somehow keep away any lurking fears she had been trying to ignore throughout the day. The light from her medical care equipment shone harshly in the dark room and soothed her anxieties for the time being, allowing her to rest with relative ease.

Just as sleepiness started to creep into her bones, something out of the corner of her eye caused Daniela to sit up in shock with wide eyes; there was a figure looming outside her window looking in towards her direction with such hate and fear that Daniela felt like it would leak inside the room like slime if she looked any longer.

Her mouth opened involuntarily as if she wanted to scream but nothing but silence followed; the figure reached out towards the window but immediately pulled its hand back as though it had been terribly burned before letting out a high-pitched shriek and glaring even more intensely at the windowsill causing Daniela to turn to look in which direction it was looking at before it finally ran away. Sitting next to were these figures feet had been prior was an old bible and although Daniela did not know what purpose it served for this creature, it had miraculously repelled whatever it was.

CHAPTER NINE

Daniela continued to massage her temples, the cool November air blowing in through the open window like a balm for her pounding head. She had been dealing with an unbearable amount of stress lately, the kind she had never before experienced. Everyone--whispers, stares and snickers--seemed to think she was crazy for knowing what was going to happen next.

The news about her psychic abilities seemed to have spread like wildfire throughout the town, each day adding more untruths to the speculation. She had tried her best to discredit all the rumors but there were far too many people for her to talk to. Besides, she had almost lost her will as it is...all she wanted now was to forget the past few weeks and everything she had endured.

Unable to stand it anymore, Daniela leaped from her desk chair and slammed her fists against the wall in frustration. Tears stung her eyes as memories of that time replayed in her mind, oppressive and unyielding.

The eerie silence that hung over the town was misleading. The Cult of Standish was not just a myth, it was real and had taken hold of the community's core. Only a select few knew the truth, including myself,

Heath, and Amelia. I couldn't bring myself to reveal it yet, not until I had devised a plan.

What shocked me even more was discovering that Heath and Amelia were secretly dating. My curiosity piqued when I accidentally glanced at their messages on Amelia's phone while playing a game. The texts revealed the pair's forbidden relationship, one they desperately tried to keep under wraps. It all made sense now: the messages that almost blew their cover at the cemetery were not from Kimbery after all, but my cousin.

I still hadn't gathered enough courage to confront them about the truth. Every moment spent in their presence felt like walking on eggshells. The danger lurking around us seemed too great to speak openly about anything anymore.

Every ounce of conviction within her was devoted to finding proof that the cult actually existed. Uncovering evidence that could be presented to the police seemed far more consequential than using it for a feature on her show. The claims were too outrageous not to be backed up with proof.

She had to make sure she had enough evidence before revealing her bombshell to Detective Liam who appeared to be a reasonable man. She didn't want him witnessing that peculiar look of pity from everyone else when they assumed something was seriously wrong with her, like her boss Jocelyn - who had been treating her better than usual ever since she returned to work and introduced the new routine of checking up on her every morning and when leaving for the day.

This scavenger hunt for evidence became paramount if she wanted to avoid added scrutiny and being deemed as insane. Everyone kept an analytical eye on her, so she had to get her hands on tangible facts without having them dismissed as circumstantial.

The thought of her boss hovering around her, sparkling with a superiority complex had been scratching at Joyce's brain until finally she had to confront her and insist that she was more than capable of getting the job done without extra supervision. How Joyce had heard about her foreshadowing abilities, Daniela did not know, but unlike every other person who had come by to offer their condolences and sympathy since her promotion, Joyce had refused to give any ground on the matter.

A sharp knock on Daniela's office door snapped her out of her thoughts. Rolling her eyes and sighing heavily, she asked whoever it was to enter. She silently prayed in her heart it wasn't one of those sympathy visits again - she had already suffered through entirely too many of them for one day. The look of surprise that crept onto Daniela's face when Aisha walked in with a stack of files tucked under her arm couldn't be hidden. It had been months since the woman had paid her a visit.

The look in Aisha's green eyes as they settled upon Daniela appeared almost... concerned? Gone was the resentment and envy she so often saw gleaming deep within their depths; replaced instead by something akin to emotions Daniela could not quite grasp. Aisha opened her mouth to speak, before quickly closing it again - apparently thinking better of whatever it was she intended to say. For a brief moment, the slightest trace of what seemed like a smirk tugged at Daniela's lips; the best thing that had happened to her all day.

"Good afternoon," Daniela greeted softly, offering the other woman a polite smile.

"Hmn," Aisha replied through her nose, barely making eye contact before falling silent once more.

"Yes? Is there something you need - something I can help you with?"

She could not help but notice how sharply Aisha responded denying needing anything from her before abruptly dropping the files onto the table with an uncharacteristic thud. "No," came her curt reply, though it seemed like it took everything in her not to asked after Daniela's wellbeing.

"They are?" Curiosity shone in Daniela's eyes as she motioned toward the files.

"Files that were mistakenly dropped on my desk. They belonged to Bobby before he left so they should go to you."

Daniela glanced up from the stack of documents on her desk as Aisha spoke in a hushed tone, though she still managed to convey authority and duty in her demeanor. The Aisha she knew was struggling to find her way back and Daniela wished her best for finding the right path once again. She nodded solemnly in response, and without acknowledging her gratitude, Aisha quickly turned on her heels and vacated the room leaving Daniela alone in the silence of her office again. Just as she was about to stand up and do a victory dance due to being rid of the pestering nuisance, her phone rang suddenly.

"Hello?" she said apprehensively into the receiver.

"Hi. It's Maria. From the hospital?" came an unfamiliar voice on the other end of the line.

"Oh hi Nurse Maria. Good afternoon." replied Daniela politely, with a hint of surprise in her voice as if someone had unexpectedly disrupted a soliloquy from her end.

"Good afternoon, Miss Savan. I just wanted to remind you of your follow up exam today," continued Nurse Maria firmly yet sympathetically, as if she completely understood what Daniela was going through at that moment and wanted to make sure she didn't miss the appointment.

"Oh right. I almost forgot," responded Daniela with a sigh of resignation, knowing deep within that despite never actually wanting to go ahead with it, this follow-up check-up at the hospital might be something necessary for her recovery after all - even if only mental or emotional instead of physical. "Please try to come down to the hospital. It's just routine check to be sure you're doing better," added Nurse Maria gently but insistently reminded Daniela of why she should try and attend the appointment despite not really seeing any need of it herself.

"I know," agreed Daniela reluctantly as she checked her watch which showed the time ticking nearer and nearer to the end of her working hours for the day. "Luckily, I'm at the end of my working hours so I'll drive down as soon as I can. Is that alright?" She tried asked assertively yet hopefully, hoped there would be some flexibility in their schedule for any changes that might arise since it wasn't really necessary for her to be there as far as she was concerned anyway.

"Yes ma'am," replied Nurse Marie firmly but also kindly, seemingly understanding and respecting Daniela's point of view too while still conveying how important attending this appointment was for her own wellbeing "Have a wonderful evening."

"You too Nurse Maria," sighed out Daniela before finally ending their call with a bit more assurance than when it began but still feeling somewhat perturbed by it all at the same time nonetheless.

In an attempt to deflect these anxious thoughts from her mind - one which often troubled her whenever she had an upcoming medical appointment - Daniela started tidying up mess on her table; picking up files that Aisha had brought earlier off the floor and then piling them atop another with a clink against the wooden surface echoing throughout the room all around after which she decided it would be better if she just drove down now rather than wait

Daniela placed the files on her table and bent over to pick up the small, silver key that had clattered onto the floor - it looked very much like the ones used in all the 'privileged' staff lockers. She inspected both sides of the key and noticed Bobby's locker number etched into back of it. Daniela knew his terrible habit of forgetting his keys; this must be the spare one - she was sure of it!

A wave of anticipation swept through her body as she stood from her chair. Half-running, Daniela entered the locker room and pushed open the door, quickly scanning the area to ensure she was alone. She then proceeded forward until she located Bobby's locker. After spinning the combination, Daniela pulled down on the metal handle and revealed a coat, bag and group of assorted keys nestled inside - they were familiar items that she'd seen countless times since starting work at the firm.

Taking a moment to inhale, Daniela noted the stale air that filled Bobby's locker - laced with hints of dust and something else... A mixture of excitement and nervousness blossomed within her as she searched for something more than what met her eye. Something good was going to come out of this, she just knew it.

Daniela's forehead creased in deep worry as she contemplated the strange circumstances surrounding Bobby's disappearance. It was bizarre enough that no one could explain his vanishing; more unsettling still was the fact that he had seemingly done so without taking anything of his own, not even his coat and house keys. Something was definitely wrong here. A person who quit their job and decided to leave town would never do it without packing at least some of their belongings, particularly items such as these which were essential for everyday life.

Holding the keys tightly in her hands, Daniela locked the locker with a clang and leaned against its frame. Even the newest recruit on the force would have known there was something off about this whole situation; it was just too suspicious and unbelievable to be dismissed as coincidence. But now her thoughts shifted to the mysterious pixel she'd found on the website earlier - could it be linked to Bobby's whereabouts? All the pieces were slowly fitting together in her mind but before she could make any real sense of it all, a distant sound interrupted her contemplation: the faint sound of someone panting over the phone.

Realizing it was Heath calling her back, Daniela quickly picked up, trying to ignore the thought of how her personal life might soon become intertwined between him and Amelia given their recent dating relationship.

"Dani," Heath said, still breathless into the receiver.

"Heath, are you alright?" She asked with trepidation growing within her. "Why? You seem out of breath."

"It's probably just your imagination," he replied, confusion laced through his words.

"What's up? Amelia mentioned you had an appointment at the hospital - have you already gone?"

"Amelia....Oh," Daniela murmurs in surprise while inwardly cringing; why hadn't that thought crossed her mind before? Despite feeling embarrassed and exposed she pushed onward, "What?"

"Well, I was about to go and investigate something after work...but then I got really caught up in it." Daniela explained breathlessly as she described the events that had occurred earlier that day. "Bobby's apartment seemed like the right place to start our search. What do you think?"

Heath's voice grew tight with worry, his words coming out as a warning. "But what about your appointment at the hospital? You can't keep putting your health on the backburner."

"Oh please, not this again! Can't you stop mothering me like my mum?" Her tone held an edge of exasperation.

"No, Daniela - I'm not going to let you push this aside today. You need to go for your checkup now, and then meet me at the hospital. We'll drive down to Bobby's from there," Heath insisted sternly.

Daniela paused for a moment before reluctantly responding. "Alright, fine. I guess I'll see you at the hospital." She said harshly before ending the call.

Daniela sat in the sterile waiting room, clutching her aunt's rosary like a lifeline. She could feel each bead sliding through her fingers as she recited her prayers. The click of her beads against the wooden pew was deafening in the silent space.

A sudden voice jolted her out of her trance and she quickly pocketed the rosary before walking towards the nurse. Despite being hopeful about good results, Daniela couldn't shake off the lingering fear that lingered around the edges of her mind.

"Hi again, Daniela."

"Hi. What do they say?" she asked, nodding towards the folder in the nurse's hands.

"Clean bill of health?"

"It says here that you've been feeling much better? No headaches, sickness and what not?"

"Yes, well except of course when I get really, really stressed out."

"Well, the prognosis seems to be much better. There's nothing to be alarmed of. I'd advise that you try as much as possible to relax a lot since stress triggers the headaches."

"Sure will."

"Alright dear. That would be all for now. Just make sure to check in for your next appointment is all."

"Thanks Maria." Daniela said and headed out briskly towards Heath's direction. As soon as she caught sight of his unruly hair, she picked up pace to match his hurried steps.

"Hey." She blurted out breathlessly.

"He-hey. How'd it go?" he asked anxiously.

"Pretty good, mum," she teased with a grin before added "The nurse cleared me up for usual rest and no stress advice."

"Which, I'm sure you won't keep to," Heath sighed exasperatedly. "I can't help but be worried about you, me and Amelia especially. We all care about you, you know that? So please stop stressing yourself and answer me - are you ready?"

"Yes," Daniela nodded before a voice from behind called her name. She spun around to see the police detective working on her case - Liam. He had come when she was admitted to the hospital but since then they hadn't seen each other except for work related purposes. This time, however, she allowed herself to actually take him in; he looked quite handsome now that she thought of it.

"Sorry I startled you," Liam apologized.

"It's alright," Daniela replied and felt an almost unnoticeable tap on her shoulder from Heath as he left them alone. She slipped him the key to Bobby's apartment as a silent sign of gratitude before speaking again. "How are you doing?"

"Pretty great," Liam answers after a few moments of silence. He seemed to really want to ask something else but kept hesitating whether or not should do it. "And how are you? You got your check-up and were given a clean bill of health, didn't you?"

She nodded happily, thankful for the best news today. "My doctor says I'm in perfect condition."

"You're quite strong person," Liam comments admiringly with a smile. "Have there been any new developments in the case? Anything new we could have missed?"

"We still don't know anything more than what we knew weeks ago," he said sadly before glancing at his watch nervously and back at Daniela with a shy expression on his face. "...Do you have plans for tonight? Would you like to go out to dinner with me - maybe Butterstick?"

"Oh!" Daniela said, taken aback by Liam's request. She felt her heart racing as she considered the possibility of going on a date with this handsome detective. His gaze penetrated her soul and left no doubt that he was attracted to her. The thought made her feel alive in ways she had forgotten existed.

Even though Heath had been nothing but helpful since they met, she knew it wouldn't be appropriate for them to all go out on a date. After quickly composing an inconspicuous text message to him, Daniela waited for his reply. He responded almost immediately, which confirmed to her that he had seen something beyond what met the eye. Her cheeks burned with curiosity and anticipation as she reread his words before quickly typing back a brief response.

She looked up at Liam and smiled. "I'm ready when you are," she said cheerfully. Even though part of her still felt uncertain about leaving the safety of her home, the drive to discover more about this mysterious man clouded her judgment.

"What happened to Dani? Why isn't she coming with us?" Amelia inquired, her voice frantic with curiosity. She had been standing in the parking lot with Heath for the last few minutes, waiting for Daniela who had gone off talking to some handsome detective that Heath had mentioned seeing earlier. In reality, Amelia was happy that Dani couldn't make it; this meant that there was now a slight chance of her going too - if she knew how to play her cards right with Heath.

"She said something about going to the Butterstick with Liam." Heath replied nonchalantly, as he started the car's ignition.

Amelia raised her eyebrows in disbelief. "You're kidding me! Who goes out on a date at such an odd hour?"

"Maybe it's not a date," he retorted skeptically. "It might be just work related."

"Yeah, whatever you say." Amelia sighs, still not convinced that the dinner was anything short of a romantic one.

With a wave of his hand, Heath offered to drop Amelia home. "Come on, let's go."

"Wait! To Bobby's apartment?" She blurted out, still trying to hastily put her seatbelt on. She wanted to accompany him more than ever before; if only she could convince him.

"No way!" He growled through gritted teeth, shaking his head firmly. "I can't take you there with me. It's too dangerous; look what happened with Dani."

"Wait! That's exactly why you should have someone else accompanying you; someone who can call for help if needed be. If you hadn't called the police back then, God knows what would have become of Dani. Please! I really want to help." She pleaded desperately.

Heath let out a heavy sigh and glanced into her determined eyes before finally relenting. "Alright then. Get ready; we leave in five minutes!"

Heath groans in frustration and smacked the steering wheel. Amelia could be quite tenacious, but he knew she must be right this time. With a resigned sigh, he muttered, "Just make sure you stay close behind me."

"Yes!" She hollered victoriously, planting an exuberant kiss on his cheek.

"You won't believe this but ever since I've been in town, this is the first time that I'm trying the salmon." Daniela said while she savored the flavor of the morsel in her mouth.

The drive down to The Butterstick had been nothing like she had expected. In her mind, it was going to be more of a question and answer type of night. But they actually conversed on the way there - and quite comfortably at that.

"So what do you think?" Liam asked eagerly as he bent forward, his eyes wide like a child expecting their parents' approval.

"It's absolutely delicious. I think I may have found my new favorite here."

"If you hadn't had the salmon in all this time, then what did you usually get when you come here? Please don't tell me it's just the BLT." He said with a smirk. Daniela grinned somewhat shyly and diverted her gaze from him. "Oh seriously?"

"It's really nice." She replied defensively, attempting to hide her embarrassment at being caught in such a mundane habit.

"You seem like you tend not to take risks. You should try something new every once in a while; you never know how life could surprise you otherwise."

Daniela felt her heart beating rapidly against her rib cage at his words; but she quickly forced herself to maintain composure. It was strange how deep an impression this man made on her, someone whom she had met only hours ago - yet she couldn't help feeling drawn to him almost immediately. Come on Daniela, focus! Put your poker face back on!

"So why did you bring me here then? Is this some kind of ploy to make me reveal something?" She asked jokingly, wanting to break the tension and relieve some of the confusion that seemed to flood her mind whenever he was around

"Well," Liam said as he placed his cutlery on top of each other. "Because I think you're an amazing person and I'd like to get to know you better."

Daniela smiled coyly, her cheeks flushing with delight. "Cheesy much?"

Liam let out a hearty laugh. "I know it sounds over the top but that's how it is. And believe me, if I was a poet, it would be much more graceful. But on a more serious note, that's why I want to get to know you better."

"Okay then. What else do you want to know about me?" Daniela asked eagerly, unknowingly leaning in closer across the table while absentmindedly playing with her hair. As soon as she became aware of her unintentional flirtation, she quickly sat back up and focused her attention back onto the plate of food before them both.

"What don't I know? Where are you from?" He replied inquisitively, observant enough to have noticed the sudden shift in her mood when she began talking about coming from New York City.

She sighed heavily before starting to explained, "I used to live in New York before coming here, where I worked as a graphics designer. The Big Apple was my home for many years."

Liam noted his concern and hesitation in her voice, and watching her glazed eyes struggle with emotion pained him deeply. Despite the fact that he felt so uncomfortable seeing her hurting, he wanted desperately to understand what had happened for her to leave such a beautiful place behind.

"So what made you come down here then? You had such a successful life there," He asked curiously.

A subtle grin crossed Daniela's face as she softly spoke, "Let's just say there was nothing for me in New York anymore."

"I had it all until my world came crumbling down. That bastard fiancé of mine cheated on me with the company secretary, and I got fired from the marketing agency. That's when my misery began, so I moved here after my uncle passed away. The rest, as they say, is history."

Liam ran a hand through his hair as he looked at Daniela apologetically. He could tell she was still healing from her breakup and he couldn't help but feel bad for her. He wished he could do something to make things better for her, but what did he really know about this? All he knew was that he didn't want to miss out on getting to know her.

As soon as Liam uttered these words, Daniela felt a sudden inexplicable uneasiness in her stomach. She gazed up at him cautiously while pushing away the morsel of salmon in her mouth. Why was he being so nice to her? Since the traumatizing incident with her ex-fiancé, she had turned into a skeptic when it came to men. But deep down inside, she yearned for companionship and a chance at love again.

Trying to push those thoughts aside, Daniela shook her head helplessly and asked if Liam was alright after seeing the worried look on his face. But before Liam could answered, she muttered "Are you getting those feelings again?". In an instant, Liam shot out of his chair and was by her side, understanding that she was referring to the panic attacks she used to get ever since that nightmarish incident occurred.

He grabbed onto her hands tightly and reassured her softly, "Hey there...It's okay, I'm here for you." As he looked into her eyes, Daniela felt odd warmth in the pit of her stomach - something she hadn't felt in a long time.

Using his arms as a support, Liam carefully guided Daniela off the chair and slowly made their way towards the stairs that led to the bathroom.

As he shooed away people who were blocking his path, Liam groaned in frustration when they realized that the bathroom was occupied.

"There's another one at the basement," Daniela spoke up weakly before a wave of nausea hit her and she was consumed with pain from another headache. Too weak to walk, she leaned on him heavily as they trudged down the steps that would lead them to the dreaded basement.

The room they entered had an eerie vibe - Daniela could see her own breath in the air as lights flickered on and off. Loud cries echoed throughout the place, making it harder for her to think clearly. Then a drop of blood landed on her arm and when she looked up, she saw traces of blood splatter across the ceiling. Her thoughts raced as tears filled her eyes, yet none seemed to flow down her cheeks. As if in slow motion, the door started to open revealing a figure waiting right at its frame. Suddenly, a voice called out her name, snapping her back to reality and she stared back into Liam's worried face with vacant eyes and a heavy heart.

She knew what the vision meant but did not know if Liam will understand.

"It's happening again," she whispered, her eyes transfixed on something unseen. Her voice trembled with a sense of dread that pierced me to my very core. "It's happening here. Someone at the Butterstick is going to die. Someone... right above us." She trailed off, and for a moment silence hung heavy in the air between us.

I could feel my blood run cold as I gazed upon her haunted expression. It was then that I knew, beyond a shadow of a doubt, that she had seen something. Something evil, lurking just around the corner.

CHAPTER TEN

H eath shut off the engine of his car and drove cautiously
towards Bobby's luxurious building - one of the most expen-
sive in town. He felt a slight twinge of envy, thinking about
how much money it must have taken for Bobby to live here. He
glanced over at Amelia who was sitting quietly beside him, her eyes wide
with anticipation. Daniela would never know if they snuck a peek
inside; Heath had kept it from her deliberately. After all, she had warned
him more than once not to venture anywhere near Bobby's place.

Heath stepped out of the car with a sense of dread pervading
throughout his body. "Shall we?" Amelia asked, her voice hushed and
restrained. "Oh shut up." Heath croaked hoarsely,. "Let's go."

The two made their way gingerly to the apartment door, standing in
suspense as Heath turned the knob. What greeted them was a sight of
sheer chaos - shards of glass were strewn across the floor, remnants of
furniture that had been upturned lay next to magazine papers and
clumps of dirt.

"Watch your step," Heath advised as they both inched further into the
living room.

"This whole place is a total mess," Amelia observed in awe as she surveyed her surroundings.

"Yeah," he murmured apprehensively, feeling his heart leap up his chest with each step forward. "Just be careful."

Amelia's mouth opened, ready to respond back to Heath, but it quickly shut. Her gaze shifted to the wall behind him and her brow furrowed in recognition. The strange symbol was just as she remembered it from Daniela's phone at The ButterStick.

"It's a sigil," she said and stepped closer to the symbol etched into the stone wall. "We saw this same thing on Dani's phone. Don't you remember?"

Heath thought for a moment before slowly nodding his head. "I do."

Amelia traced her fingers along the edges of the mark, feeling the bumpy texture of its surface. An eerie sensation washed over her, like this symbol had always been meant for her to find in that moment. It felt strangely familiar yet somehow distant and distant all at once.

Daniela's eyes widened with fear as she spoke to Liam, her voice shaking. "We need to leave now, Liam. Something evil is coming and I'm terrified." She sensed the demonic figure heading straight for them. It was a feeling that had been brewing inside her since they walked into the restaurant.

Liam couldn't help but roll his eyes as he listened to Daniela ramble about ghostly apparitions. He didn't believe in the supernatural, not one bit. But he knew his girlfriend well enough to realize when something was truly bothering her.

"Dani," he tried to reason with her, "let's just stay here and face whatever it is together. I promise you, nothing will happen."

But Daniela wasn't having any of it. Panic was beginning to consume her and Liam knew he had to act quickly before things escalated further. He rushed over to her and held her tightly. "I'm here for you," he whispered soothingly into her ear, "just breathe and focus on me."

After several moments, Daniela began to calm down. Her breaths were still ragged but the hysteria had subsided somewhat. Liam knew that this was their moment to act.

"I need you to tell me everything," he said gently, holding Daniela's hands in his own. "Every detail of what you saw and felt."

Daniela's eyebrows furrowed as she studied him, her lips parted before the faintest of whispers emerged from them. "Yes," she whispered with a hint of hesitation, still seeming unsure but not wanting to deny him.

With that prompt, Daniela focussed intently on the vision that had brought them here and started relaying all the details she could remember.

"Amelia! What in the world are you doing?" he bellowed, rushing towards her by the coffee table in the living room. His intuition told him that inviting her to this task was a grave mistake and seeing her perform these antics only validated his suspicions.

"About to listen to Bobby's voicemail obviously," She retorted, pressing play with great anticipation.

"Oh for goodness' sakes, Amelia. So, the man can know some people have been here snooping around when he gets back!?"

"If Heath - if he gets back... For all we know, if these buildings are as mysterious as they claim to be, there could be surveillance cameras watching us right... now! Why not just go on and find out the juicy stuff?" She inquired nonchalantly. "They always have juicy information in voicemails."

Heath couldn't help but wonder how she had acquired such knowledge and asked curiously, "You know all this how?"

"TV dude," Amelia scoffed with eyes rolling. "TV - don't you watch police procedurals?"

The recording began: Bobby, I won't say this again. If you don't embrace your destiny, you won't like what will come for you. You know what to do...

Instantly, Amelia squealed in excitement. "That's it! That had to be one of those cult people! The Sigil proves everything - the cult certainly had a hand in all of this!"

Heath couldn't believe that she might actually be right this time and admitted reluctantly "We should check around the house again. Do a more thorough search around."

Amelia questions hesitantly, "What exactly are we looking for?"

Heath contemplated for a moment before responding confidently. "The same thing that we have been searching for all along – anything that can link us to Bobby and why he's disappeared; Anything that can link us to Bobby and the cult most especially."

"Let's check the room first then?" Amelia suggested eagerly.

But Heath wanted to cover more grounds faster so he proposed firmly: "No, separately."

"Fine. I'll take the bedroom. You can do this area."

"Be careful, Amelia." He said in a serious voice, feeling anxious for her safety.

"I always am!" She replied with enthusiasm and marched off to the bedroom.

Heath sat quietly watching her as she moved away, her spirit filling up the whole room. But right now his mind was tinged with worry; he just wanted them out of there as soon as possible. After what seemed like ages, he dragged himself away from the chair and made his way to the kitchen. As he opened up the refrigerator, Heath found it stocked to the fullest; almost like the guy had gone grocery shopping only to leave immediately after that. Even the garbage bin near the door which led to the backyard was full - an unlikely thing for such a person whom Daniela described as not one to lift a finger if it could be avoided, no matter how much money was lost in doing so.

Amelia gasped on seeing how her bedroom was turned upside down — bed covers inside out, shreds of magazine paper strewn across the floor, clothes carelessly flung around - all of it making her stomach clench in disgust. Just then, a noise came from within the closet, making her scream in surprise.

"Babe, are you okay?" called Heath running into the room, worriedly looking around for danger or a weapon.

"I heard something from that closet over there," She replied in a quavering voice while pointing towards it apprehensively.

"Let me check it out for you." He said protectively and started walking towards it, but Amelia stopped him with a firm hand on his arm.

"No. Let me handle this," she declared firmly and prepared herself for whatever was about to come out when she opened the closet door.

Suddenly they both let out frightened screams at seeing a ball of fur launch itself from inside when Amelia opened the door - obviously scared by their presence - revealing a small brown cat cowering against far wall of the closet.

A brown Bengal cat, fur trimmed with pristine black stripes, stood before them and eyed them suspiciously. Amelia's heart beamed as she stared into the cat's emerald eyes; her love for cats unexplainable. She bent over and fingered the name tag that hung around the cat's neck – Robyn Tuggles – and smiled.

"This is strange. No one in their right mind would leave their car unattended to and just go out of town like that. Definitely not Bobby." Heath finally said after an extended period of silence.

Amelia nodded in agreement and then almost gasped when a thought dawned on her. "That I agree with. But what about the cat? He must have been alone for so long already."

Heath clenched his teeth, trying his best not to snapped at Amelia. He ruffled the short strands of hair atop his head and shifted his weight to his left leg, rolling his eyes at Amelia's proposal. "For Christ's sake Amelia, are you insane? You want to take that home? What would you say if anyone recognizes him?"

"Yes, Heath," Amelia cooed, batting her eyelashes harmlessly. Taking out her phone, she added smugly, "I'm texting Mother now to tell her I'm bringing my friend's pet home because he's leaving town for some urgent issue. Oops...sent."

Heath groaned in exasperation, realizing he had no means of changing her mind. "Amelia, taking the cat home may not be the most suitable option here. What do you plan on doing if it turns out someone does actually recognize him? Let's just drop it off somewhere and make our way back."

But Amelia had already made up her mind and there was nothing more Heath could do than reluctantly oblige.

"It's already too late, Heath," I said, letting out a sigh of defeat. "Mum sent a text back saying the cat would be good for everyone. Boom – there you have it."

Heath grumbled in frustration as he buried his face in his hands. "Oh shoot!"

Daniela's eyelids slowly fluttered shut and her breathing steadied. Focusing deeply, she began to make her way down the pathways of her subconscious until she found herself back in the dingy basement again with Liam at her side.

"I'm here," she said firmly, loud enough for him to hear.

"Okay Dani, talk me through it." His voice was low but confident.

"Your gun is out and in your right hand. It's a...a 9mm Beretta. Semi-automatic." She felt a thrill as his eyes widened in surprise - he knew that she was knowledgeable when it came to firearms.

"Wow." He whispered to himself, unable to contain his astonishment. "The gun is...ash and you have seven...no eight rounds in it."

There was no way she could have known those details – her visions rarely provided such specific information.

He slowly exhaled and ran his hand through his hair before resuming their conversation. "Okay, what time is this?"

"It's...its 10:39 PM," She replied hesitantly, feeling a wave of relief pass over her as soon as the words had left her mouth. She snapped out of her trance before asked, "Did you get everything?"

He tapped on his phone before replied, "Yeah I recorded everything. So it's 8:10 now - we still have plenty of time between now and 10 to secure the whole place. Let me just make a few calls for backup and I'll be right back - don't worry alright?"

Daniela only nodded before watching him leave The ButterStick to get help.

Daniela slumped onto the table, her eyes drooping in exhaustion. The fatigue had taken its toll on her; her body wanted to sleep despite the knowledge that the thing would seize such a vulnerable state upon within her. Steeling herself against the lure of slumber, she opened her eyes, only to find Liam peering down at her with an expression of concern.

"You looked so tired. I didn't want to wake you." he said softly.

"It felt like I'd been asleep for mere seconds."

"It was much longer. I managed to call in backup and they have all arrived as plainclothes detectives seated at different tables around the restaurant; hopefully we can catch this guy without any hassle."

"I hope so, but do they know what we are up against? What do they actually know?"

He sighed heavily before answered, "I couldn't tell them everything, but they do know there is a perp here so they should be prepared for anything."

She nodded before turning away from him, towards the live band playing songs of different artistes throughout the room - currently being 'Stay With Me' by Sam Smith. Hours dragged by without any sign of suspicious activity occurring inside the restaurant - yet Daniela still sat in fear and worry, occasionally glancing in Liam's direction as if searching for reassurance in his gaze. He wondered how much trouble he had gotten himself into simply by believing in her words; after all, she knew nothing of his gun, and had no way of proving its existence. It was almost time...

He gawked in awe as the minute hand on the grand clock passed the 34 mark and ticked onwards to 35. In that instant, the whole room went dark - like a curtain had been pulled over the atmosphere inside the restaurant. Daniela spun around abruptly and collided into Greta, who was almost reaching her table when the lights went out.

"I'm so sorry, I should have watched where I was going," Daniela apologized, but Greta paid her no attention. All she could think about was preserving her business; death had already taken her husband here and she wouldn't let any other rumors ruin it.

"Yes, I apologize for the power outage. It must be due to that ongoing blackouts all around us. Can someone please come and help me turn on the generator?" Greta said with a hint of distress in her voice.

Liam flipped on his small torchlight and glanced at his watch: "Three more minutes till she arrives." He spoke softly to Daniela.

"I'll go with you Ms.Greta." Daniela uttered before Liam could attempt to stop her.

Greta nodded gratefully; "Thank you, dear." And with that they both made their way down towards basement quietly until they got there. "Where is the switch?" Greta asked looking around then pointed to wall on right side - "Right there".

Moving forward Daniela felt chills running up her spine, something felt wrong; as if some kind of strong force was trying to pull them away from what they were doing. With an extra push not to give into fear they both reached over to find a thin metal box near the corner of the room. Turning it slowly, Greta breathed out in relief as light flooded back into the restaurant and welcomed them back home.

Daniela's heart raced as she stood before the wall, her fists clenched. She knew that sigil had been there recently—before it had been carelessly painted over. Taking a deep breath to calm her nerves, she stepped forward and pulled down on the heavy lever. Just then, a presence materialized behind her back and Daniela spun around quickly to find Greta staring back at her.

"You did it," Greta said with appreciation in her voice. "Thank you, dear."

Daniela smiled hesitantly as she made her way up the stairs. As they ascended, loud arguments drifted from above. Feeling an adrenaline surge through her veins, Daniela took the stairs two at a time, eager to see what was happening. When they reached the top, Liam came thundering down the stairs.

"Liam!" She exclaimed, letting out a breath of relief. "What in the world is going on up there?"

"One of the patrons got into a fight with another patron," Liam replied calmly.

"Nothing serious." He cast his gaze over Daniela to make sure she was alright before continued. "I'll be up soon to handle this. I won't condone such behavior in my restaurant." With those words Greta left them and proceeded to the dining area.

Just then, Daniela felt a wave of nausea hit her and the lights began flickering off and on again like a broken flashlight. Her vision blurred and she fell faint; but before her body could hit the ground, Liam reflexively went on his knees and caught her. Frantically dialing numbers on his phone he tried desperately to call for help upstairs when suddenly Daniela's eyes fluttered open.

"Dammit!" Liam cursed under his breath, dropping to the floor with Daniela in his arms. He carefully laid her limp body down and cautiously crept up the stairs, only to be blocked by the entrance slamming shut right after a gunshot had echoed from the dining area. Shrieks pierced through the basement, and he froze on the spot, torn between helping those upstairs or comforting Daniela who had woke up screaming at this point.

He quickly chose the latter and brushed a strand of hair away from her forehead. "Are you okay?" he asked anxiously, his gaze still glued to hers. As soon as her eyes followed his, they shot towards the ceiling, where three drops of blood slowly dripped onto his face – an eerie reminder of what was going on upstairs.

The door suddenly creaked open, casting a dark silhouette of a woman against the light. Before either of them could make out any of her features, she had disappeared again like some kind of a ghostly apparition.

Daniela let out a shaky whisper. "Did you see that?"

With no time for words, Liam sprang off the floor and grabbed his gun from its holster, motioning for her to follow him with a swift nod. On their way up the stairs, something made Daniela reach into her pocket and grab her phone - only to realize that she had missed Heath's call multiple times earlier. Anxiety flooded her chest as they moved closer and closer to the living room... It was happening.

As he stepped on the last stair, Liam whipped his head around to the corner and pointed his gun directly at the woman who had cast a long shadow. Daniela spun around towards him just as Liam was lowering his weapon. Greta stood against the wall under the dim lightbulb that illuminated only her and no one else. Her eyes were wide open and a gaping wound was present in its place where her heart used to be. On a plate, right next to her, lay Greta's bloody heart, with droplets of crimson spilling onto the floor.

Daniela screamed in terror, averting her gaze from all the gore before her. But as she looked away, something else caught her eye - two empty hollows staring back at her with an insuppressible rage. Before she could utter another sound, someone yanked her hair from behind and pulled her back down into the basement. Daniela missed a step as she plummeted down the stairs, the door slamming shut behind her.

"Dani!" Liam shouts and started racing toward the entrance. He hadn't made it more than a few feet when he felt something grab him by the collar and hurl him across the room into a counter.

"Aaaarg!!" he cried out in pain as his back collided with the pointed corner of the counter. His gun clattered onto the ground and he fell right on top of something soft - flesh. With trembling hands, Liam moved along the surface to find a face, and gasped when he did. Everywhere around him lay unconscious bodies of his officers and restaurant patrons.

"Shit! Shit!! Shit!!!" he whispered under his breath as he tried to stand, wincing from the sharp ache in his back. A loud screeching sound pierced through the air, reverberating off the walls until it felt like Liam's ears were being torn off. He blinked rapidly and touched his fingertips to his ears, only to find them slick with blood. Struggling to keep conscious, he could just make out a figure emerging from the darkness, its eyes empty and cold and its skin already starting to decay. Liam stared into the abyss for what felt like an eternity before everything went

Daniela screamed in agony as she tentatively prodded her tender, horribly swollen ankle. The searing pain was excruciating and she feared the worst; a broken bone. With a shuddering gasp, Daniela raised her hand to her forehead; a deep gash oozing blood over her face. A matching gash graced her ankle as well.

The thing was still out there somewhere, and if it found her, who knew what would become of her? Driven by sheer desperation, Daniela forced herself to ignore the pain and crawled on her stomach away from the spot where she had fallen down the stairs. She could feel her skin bruise beneath her as she moved forward but it was not enough to stop her. Until eventually, she could take refuge behind an oil barrel located near the generator switch.

Daniela cautiously poked her head over the top of the barrel and scoured the basement for any sign of the creature that had tormented her. Then her gaze fell upon a gruesome sight: a trail of blood leading straight from where she had initially landed to where she now hid, right behind the barrel.

"Oh God!" Daniela said softly under her breath. In order to remain unseen, she needed to eliminate any trace of evidence that might give away her presence. Lowering herself back down, she crawled around desperately searching for something with which to clean up the trail. Her eyes lit up when they finally settled on an apron lying discarded on the floor nearby. Quickly snatching it up, Daniela scrambled as fast as she could back into hiding - only for a fresh wave of pain to hit as more blood leaked out from between her fingers clutching at the wound on her ankle. She had lost so much already; this was not good. Wincing and biting down hard on her lip to stifle another scream, Daniela managed to wrap the apron tightly around her ankle in search of relief.

Daniela scrunched against the cavernous barrel, peering into the darkness for an escape route. And then she saw it: a small frame of light at the back of the dank basement. She crawled flat on her stomach, her skin stinging with each movement made towards the beckoning patch of light. As Daniela neared the end of her perilous journey, the cool air brushed against her face and she felt a small pang of hope stirring from within. Her ankle injury temporarily forgotten, she hastened towards her freedom--

Suddenly, there was a sound. A jolt went through Daniela's body as the door to the basement opened and in stepped faint yet distinct footsteps. An icy chill ran down her spine as she scrambled up the stairs as quickly and stealthy as she could. The moment she felt the fresh air outside, Daniela sprinted away from the restaurant without turning back; all that mattered now was putting distance between her and whoever was pursuing her.

Her chest heaving from exhaustion and adrenaline coursing through her veins, Daniela pulled out her phone with shaky hands and called Heath's number--only to hear his voicemail prompt. Tears blurred her vision as desperation and relief mixed together within her.

"Heath!" She screamed between sobs. She repeated his name over and over, frantically dialing his number with trembling fingers. The ringing seemed to go on forever, taunting her. "I'm...somewhere around The Butterstick...Oh God! Heath, I need you now more than ever! Please come meet me at the radio station. Please, I can't stay there! Please, please, I beg you." Tears raced down her face as desperation clawed at her insides.

"Thank you for listening to my show, night crawlers. I hope you enjoyed it as much as I did and don't forget to tune in again tomorrow! I love you all, cheerios!" Kimbery said with a chuckle before turning up the music. Setting down the headphones, she stood from her chair and stretched out her stiff limbs before sitting down again and taking one last look around the studio. It had been yet another successful show; her audience was growing more and more with passing of each day, something she hadn't anticipated when she first started this adventure.

Just as she was settling back into her chair, a loud pounding startled her. Frowning suspiciously, Kimbery removed her headphones and cautiously made her way over toward the door. When she opened it, a sight of pure terror met her eyes. Her friend Daniela stood in front of her, badly cut up and bleeding profusely. Without wasting any time, Kimbery hauled Daniela inside and quickly cleared off the small cushion sofa for her to sit on.

"What happened?" Kimbery asked gently, trying not to sound too alarmed or scared even though she already knew what the answer might be.

"She's after me," Daniela replied between ragged breaths. "She's killed Greta and everyone at Butterstick and now she's after me. Oh God...I don't know what I'm going to do." Her voice grew louder and more frantic with each word that left her mouth until eventually it became strained with desperation.

Kimbery could feel the fear radiating from Daniela's body like an aura, so thick that it almost made it difficult to breath.

"I heard you loud and clear, Dani, but I need you to tell me everything one more time. Greta, Butterstick and... was it Oh God? Just tell me so that I can figure this out, okay?" Kimbery urged her friend, searching for the right way to help Daniela out of her distress.

Daniela made an attempt to speak, though her words got stuck in her throat. Suddenly, her phone burst into a shrill melody. She quickly fished it from her pocket and pressed the Answer button without looking at the Caller ID.

"Heath!" she cried into the receiver, praying it would be him at the other end of the line.

But there was no response.

Daniela's heart raced faster as she listened to the deafening silence on the other side. Not even a breath could be heard – until suddenly a menacing screech split through the heavy air. In an instant, Daniela flung the phone away and rose up to face Kimbery with wide eyes of terror.

"She found me," whispered Daniela, desperately clinging onto every ounce of hope that could possibly grant her reprieve from her predicament.

Kimbery wrapped her arms around Daniela in an effort to console her fear-stricken friend. "Hush now," she said soothingly. "You're just in shock. Let me call the police from here and they'll come handle this person you're talking about."

"She's... no... person." A wave of panic ran through Daniela as she spoke those words, feeling as if there was nobody who could save her from this force of evil that had been unleashed upon her.

Kimbery pulled away slightly so that she could look into Daniela's eyes. "Shhh, don't worry my dear," she said warmly, brushing away a lone tear trickling down Daniela's cheek. "Anyone that can have this effect is indeed terrifying – but give me some minutes while I use the radio in the office."

"No! No!! You can't leave me here," begged Daniela frantically, gripping Kimbery's arm tightly as if refusing to let go would keep her friend by her side for longer.

"I'll be just close by. The office is right here. You see?" Kimbery said, pointing to the sheet of glass that partitioned the studio and the office. "I'll watch you from there, okay? I'll need to be quick, so go ahead," she added, her voice filled with urgency.

Daniela nodded before sinking into the sofa, resigned to her fate with a heavy sigh. Kimbery quickly strode out of the studio and into the office, dialing at once as she clutched onto the radio. Daniela instantly sat up straight and watched her friend's silhouette through the glass, her eyes wide with trepidation. She was beginning to feel a presence in the room and whipped around frantically, searching around for any signs of life besides herself - but no one was there.

A chill ran through her body for what seemed like an eternity, intensifying as a ghostly mist crept in from nowhere and enveloped her surroundings in an eerie fog. Fearful and overwhelmed by her dread, Daniela limped towards the glass panel that separated them and bashed on it repeatedly with both her fists - though regardless of how loud she shouted or thundered against it, Kimbery was oblivious to her distress calls. Letting out a desperate sigh of relief when Kimbery stayed bent over and continued talking on the phone, Daniela knew that help had finally arrived.

Kimbery whirled around to check on her friend, only for the entire room to be shrouded in a thick fog. Her eyes widened in terror as the radio slipped from her fingers and clattered to the floor. There stood a mysterious figure behind Daniela, almost like it had come out of nowhere. Kimbery squinted, trying to make out the shape in front of her friend, was that a face?

Before she could move or question who it was, Daniela disappeared into the fog and with her, the ghostly presence disappeared too. Fear gripping her chest, Kimbery sprinted out of office and towards the studio. As she yanked open the door, more fog swept out of the room and into the lobby. "Dani!" She screamed desperately as she stumbled into the dense mist. Her voice echoed throughout the room yet there was no sign of Daniela anywhere.

Then suddenly Kimbery noticed something lying close by; Dani's phone on the ground near the sofa she was sat on earlier. She picked up the device and switched on its torchlight. With every step she took, her breath came out in white trails which made her realize how cold it had become inside. Again, she shouted out Daniela's name but there was still nothing to hear but silence. As she began to carefully search through what little of the room she could make out in this eerie atmosphere, something hard yet soft at the same time met her touch - what felt like a body!

She swiftly spun round to find Daniela standing right behind her looking crazed - not moving one bit or uttering a word - like time itself had stopped for her. With trembling hands, Kimbery directed the light onto Daniela's face only to be met with an equally frightened pair of wide-eyed expressions.

"Why on earth didn't you answer when I called you?!" Kimbery screamed at Daniela.

Still, her best friend remained silent and still. Kimbery's heart began to race faster than a train; fear gripped her being. She sprinted towards Daniela and put her hand close to her nose, desperate to see if she could detect the gentle rise and fall of breath. In that moment, chillingly cold air escaped Daniela's nostrils. Kimbery shielded herself from the intense coldness as she exhaled a sigh of relief.

Suddenly, she heard a gruff voice outside calling out. "Police! Please open the door, ma'am."

Kimbery felt like all hope had been sucked out of her. Finally help had arrived, but was it already too late? Collapsing against her best friend in defeat, she waited for whatever outcome fate had in store.

CHAPTER ELEVEN

Daniela lay on her bed, oblivious to the white world outside. The snow had been pouring non-stop since the second week of December, and yet the town was not bustling with Christmas cheer like it used to be; ever since the incident at The Butter-Stick two weeks ago, the whole town had been thrown into a state of mourning over Greta's loss. Daniela herself had been battling her own demons for days, ever since she'd been discharged from the hospital.

The doctors had told them that Daniela was in shock and trying to block out something terrible that happened at The Butterstick. Every time someone came to visit – Iris and Kimbery with their concerned looks, Heath and Amelia with their worry, or Maureen with her prayers – Daniela heard them but could not respond. Maureen often told the others that she was going to the nearby Church to pray for a fast recovery for her niece. Even Jocelyn, who'd come visiting at the house only a few days ago, ordered a non-responsive Daniela to take as much time as she needed to recover.

But still Daniela lay motionless on her bed, staring vacantly up at the ceiling, unaware of anything around her. What terrors lurked in her mind, no one could tell.

A burning sensation in her heart told Daniela that she had been through enough. Hospital walls were a reminder of pain and suffering that was slowly healing but still, had not disappeared. Still, the only thing she could do was remain quiet- silence being her only weapon.

Liam felt responsible for what happened to her; he often reached out his hand to hers and each time, his heart broke knowing that she wouldn't feel it. Nevertheless, he continued visiting her both at home and hospital, trying his best to render help and company. He couldn't understand why she was so unresponsive to everyone around her. If only he could have been there to protect her before any of this happened.

The thing which troubled him most was Daniela's carefree attitude towards her own safety. After collapsing, she would put herself at risk once again? Most recently, when she discharged herself from the hospital without doctor's permission or supervision- it made Liam anxious; too anxious for words. It wasn't long since they first met and yet, he already felt something strong for her. He couldn't bring himself to let her endanger herself any longer. That conversation needed to happen.

Fear and anxiety pounded through Liam's veins as he raced to Maureen's house. He had not expected what greeted him when arrived: a mere shell of his beloved sister, Daniela. Where there was usually joy and mirth, now only dejection and void remained. Maureen had warned him of the changes she'd noticed in her niece, but he never imagined this.

Daniela sat unmoving in the chair, her eyes clouded with turmoil, refusing to even acknowledge his presence. He knew that Maureen thought work would help her find her way back from whatever place she had been taken off to—it had worked for him in the past. With a gentle kiss to her hand, he mumbled a goodbye and looked over his shoulder one last time; out of the corner of his eye, he swore he saw the hint of a smile upon her face.

Determination suddenly filled his chest as Liam rushed out to join Maureen in the kitchen. It was clear to him that it was time for drastic action if they wanted any hope of helping Daniela break free from whatever had stumbled upon them both on this day. An idea forming in his mind, so outrageous it could hardly be called normal— he would throw a "Welcome Back" party for her! When Liam explained his plan to Maureen, she agreed wholeheartedly without hesitation.

With hope in their hearts, they parted ways until the next time they could check on her. But before leaving, Liam paused at the door and whispers softly into the air: "Take care of yourself, Daniela. We are really worried about you. I know you can hear me...I'll check on you soon."

"How is she, Liam?" Maureen asked with a concerned expression.

Liam heaved a deep sigh as he dragged himself into the room. "Still in the same state. She just stares at the ceiling like Leonardo DaVinci painted a masterpiece up there or something."

Maureen frowned. "That's so unlike Dani. When she does talk, she doesn't stop going on and on about getting back to work right away."

An idea struck him then, one his heart had been begging to suggest for hours now. His nerves began to flare up, but he decided to take the plunge anyway. "I was actually thinking of something Maureen... not that I'm trying to disturb you or anything..."

She waved her hand in an impatient gesture. "Go ahead with it already."

"Right... well, I thought maybe we could arrange a small welcome back celebration for Daniela? You know, just our way of telling her how much we love and care about her even while she was sick and convalescing? A little gathering might do her a world of good."

Maureen seemed deep in thought as she mulled over his suggestion. After what felt like eternity, she gave him a firm nod and declared, "Yes, this is actually a brilliant idea! We should do something to lift her spirits and nothing better than a party can do that! I'll text Amelia and get this organized right away - thank you, Liam."

A spark of disappointment lit up in his chest when Maureen didn't even consider his offer for help. But he pushed aside this feeling of rejection and reminded himself that at least he had done something positive for

Daniela's recovery by suggesting this plan. He gave Maureen a curt nod and said,"I'll be waiting for your update then."

He grabbed his keys and wallet from the kitchen island, but before he could make an exit, a fur ball brushed up against him. Startled, Liam looked down to find a wild-looking Bengal cat staring up at him with large, sapphire blue eyes. His heart skipped a beat as the silky brown tabby curled up in his lap and began purring energetically. Liam couldn't help but smile; cats had always been his favorite furry companions.

"Aren't you a pretty thing?" Liam whispers, running his hands over her spotted underbelly. He noticed the collar around her neck, noting the name 'Robyn Tuggles.' "Well hello there, Robyn," he said fondly.

Maureen was watching with delight; she too was a feline lover. "Your cat is quite a beauty, ma'am," Liam comments.

"Oh thank you! She's actually not mine...we're taking care of her for Amelia's friend." Maureen explained.

"I see," Liam replied thoughtfully. Taking one last look at the roly-poly furball in his arms, he said goodbye to Robyn and handed her off to Maureen. "All in good time," he said to her reassuringly. "She'll be back to normal soon."

Maureen gave him a grateful nod as she cradled the felines softly in her arms. "I hope so," she replied solemnly.

As Daniela sank back into the office chair, she furiously clicked through the open laptop screen, her blue eyes widening at every new connection she made. Despite the fact that she was engrossed in this client's work, her real purpose there was to dig into the mysterious website of the mayoral campaign. She had to finish the job first- anything less than perfect would have catastrophic consequences for her career.

It had been a surprise when Jocelyn called and asked Daniela over the next morning without an argument from her aunt. Upon waking up, Daniela rushed down to the office and discovered the most challenging task available; this was her opportunity to prove that despite past incidents, she could function like a regular person.

With the job done and mock ups sent for approval, it was time to delve into the hidden cult website. All she needed was proof; one person on the website would be enough to take them down. As she clicked through page after page of strange symbols, photos and videos, something caught her eye- it seemed too coincidental not to investigate further.

Daniela rubbed her temples as she felt a headache coming on again. She pushed herself away from the over-worked desk and headed downstairs to get some water.

The office was quiet and dark, not even the sounds of typing came from any of the cubicles or near her workstation. There was just an uneasy stillness that hung about the place in thick air.

Downstairs Daniela could feel her headache dissipating as she drank down a glassful of icy cold water. It refreshed her and made her feel a little more human. She grabbed another glass of water, a bottle of aspirin, then walked back upstairs taking a seat at one of the gathering tables near the stage. A few minutes later Aisha reached the basement stairs, turned towards the hall where she knew there was another set of stairs that lead to this level, and began walking towards them. Then she heard what sounded like footsteps above her head so she stopped and listened carefully. The steps continue for several seconds but then they suddenly stopped. Aisha figured it must be someone like herself who had headed to get a drink of water during a break when nobody else was around to disturb them.

Aisha quickly descended to the basement, her heart pounding in her ears, trying to figure out why Daniela would be here. She had heard rumors of a monster living in the depths of the basement, but she never thought anything of it until now. As she reached the bottom of the stairs, Daniela was standing in front of the water fountain with her back to Aisha.

She seemed off, hunched over and her hand tightly clenched. Her long black hair cascaded down her face covering it as droplets of blood streamed down where tears should have been. Aisha was too scared to move closer, but couldn't help but inch forward as curiosity got the best of her.

As she moved closer without a response from Daniela, Aisha started to feel quite uneasy and scared. The damp musty smell emanating from Daniela filled up the room and made her skin crawl - much like wet soil. Suddenly, Daniela snapped around, revealing sharp teeth of all shapes and sizes that were bared at Aisha as one earplug slipped out from her earpiece.

Aisha gasped in shock as she saw that although her face seemed grotesquely deformed, it returned to normal when she turned around. The cup of water dropped spilling all over them as Aisha tried to grab her shoulder.

"Ahh!!" Daniela screamed, her eyes wide and startled. Aisha had walked by the entrance way so quietly that it had taken her off guard. She gulped, trying to calm down her racing heartbeats, and continued nervously, "I-I'm really sorry for being...for being so jumpy and absent minded."

Aisha gave a slight shake of her head in apology, "It's my fault. I should have been more careful not to startle you like that. Again, I apologize."

Daniela didn't said much more after that; she just quickly bent over to help clean up the mess on the floor they had both made before a sharp sting shot through her hand. She pulled her hand back away from the cleaning supplies and in an instant, it was coated in a crimson red liquid. Her forehead scrunched in confusion as she looked at it more closely - there was a tiny cut from what looked like paper right in the middle of her palm – almost as if it had cut itself when handling some of the office supplies earlier

She felt Aisha's eyes on her; worry welled up within them and pooled around their edges. Before Aisha could voice out any protests, Daniela spoke first, "It's alright," she said with finality, "it's just a small cut. Nothing to worry about." Trying to reassured both herself and Aisha - though mostly the latter - she forced a smile onto her face while inside she was screaming in pain.

"If you say so," Aisha mutters hesitantly but left nonetheless with one last worried glance towards Daniela before heading back upstairs to her desk.

The moment she was alone again Daniela let out a sigh of relief and winced as pain surged through her arm once again. That's when she remembered the First Aid kit that sat atop the old fridge in the corner collecting dust like cobwebs along its walls – how did anyone manage to keep their food cold with such an ancient machine? But it seemed harmless enough so without hesitation, Daniela grabbed hold of it and returned to tending to her wound.

She frantically rummaged through the First Aid box, her fingers trembling as she grabbed the paper wrapping of the band aid and tore it with her teeth. She dipped two fingers in the bottle of methylated spirit and carefully rolled a cotton ball between them before pressing it over the cut on her palm. Wincing at the searing pain, she brushed away the clotted blood to get a closer look. The gashes were deep, four straight lines that could only have been created by nails. Confused, Daniela raised her hands up to inspect her own fingernails but saw nothing at first. Upon further inspection, she found small traces of dried blood underneath her middle and index nails. Her brows furrowed, feeling a strange sense of déjà vu wash over her as she realized what had happened.

She couldn't remember cutting herself and yet here she was with these painful gashes on her palm. But there wasn't time for her to dwell on this any longer; she had to get out of there - now. Reassuring Jocelyn that she would be back soon for some much needed R & R time, Daniela hurriedly left the office and made her way to the mall.

As soon as she stepped inside the newly renovated building, Daniela felt overwhelmed by the sheer number of people crowding around her from all sides. Everywhere she turned, elbows poked into her ribs or arms brushed against hers. Despite being constantly bombarded by unfamiliar faces, Daniela pushed forward until she came to stand in front of one of the two story high buildings. This was Tisdale's only shopping centre that everyone seemed to flock into every day; everyone except for Daniela who rarely came here for shopping.

As she leisurely strolled down the street, admiring store displays, out of the corner of her eye, a black leather mini skirt caught her attention. It was paired with a silk button-down man-style shirt which looked more dazzling as she stared at it for longer. She couldn't resist the urge to try on the outfit and stormed into the store.

Daniela stepped into the changing room, stripped off her clothes and peeled off her underwear to reveal an array of scars and bruises scattered all over her body. As she tugged on the skirt, muffled moans of pleasure echoed throughout the space. Daniela groaned as anger began to swell within her – why did people choose to have sex in places like these? Shaking her head in annoyance, Daniela continued to get dressed and eventually walked out of the stall.

A small mirror hung outside the changing room. Daniela shifted around until she saw herself in full effect. The skirt clung tightly against her long legs which had rarely been exposed to sunlight. Suddenly, Daniela saw a reflection of a young woman wearing a sales girl's uniform emerge from one of the stalls next to her – zipping up her dress hurriedly. Another eye roll later, Daniela marched back inside the room to change back into her own clothes when she heard a voice coming from the stall behind hers.

"I did it again, dude. Left another girl in my wake." He boasted to the other boys, puffing out his chest with pride as he reveled in their admiration.

Daniela had heard it all before; the insufferable boasting of these immature boys who thought they were invincible. They would always brag about their 'conquests' and play acts of machismo with each other. The only thing she felt for them was a sort of pity and sometimes a feeling of revulsion.

"Dude, I can't believe I scored her. It was like the campus girl that went missing right? Yeah, she was mine. The Dark Priest is gonna recognize me soon, man. If you want to be somebody, keep your eyes on me 'cause I'm close to the top now!" A shiver ran down Daniela's spine as she paused to listen to him boast with such arrogance about his latest victim.

Glancing up at the mirror, she noticed her reflection for the first time and took in the details of the beautiful blonde-haired girl staring back at her. She felt an eerie familiarity with this girl, like she had seen her somewhere before but couldn't quite remember where. Her heart raced as the girl in the reflection began to move towards her, almost as if it were trying to reach out for help. She stepped away from the mirror slowly, fear sweeping through her body.

The reflection advanced ever closer as Daniela stepped away, her heart racing in terror. The once normal face of the girl in the mirror began to contort and twist as the fluorescent lights above flickered an ominous cacophony. Daniela watched in disbelief as the transformation took place, unable to comprehend what she was witnessing.

Her eyes darted around frantically for her phone so she could call someone for help, but it was nowhere to be found. She turned back to the demonic figure in the glass and froze as a hoarse voice spoke.

"Get comfortable watching everything that is about to happen," the creature hissed, dressed identically to what Daniela was wearing. "This...this is your prison. I am now in charge of your life."

Desperately trying to scream for help, Daniela opened her mouth, only to find no sound would escape from within her throat. In complete frustration, she pounded at the walls with her fists yet still no sounds were heard. Closing her eyes tightly, hoping it would all just be a terrible nightmare she'd wake up from soon enough, when she opened them again she was standing at the front of the store - or so she believed.

Miraculously finding her way out of the darkness, Daniela sighed with relief only for it to turn into confusion when she looked down at herself; she was still wearing the same clothes from before! She made a frantic dash back into the changing room only to find no one there. "I'm actually out here!" Daniela cried desperately as she spun around and came face-to-face with her reflection in the mirror - instead of her own image however, it was that of the young blonde's from earlier staring back at her. A gasp escaped her parted lips.

The demon with Daniela's face twisted her lips into a smirk and sauntered out of the mirror, leaving the young woman looking on in terror and disbelief. As soon as she had gone, Daniela sprinted after her, panic rising in her chest.

She watched the imposter knock on the changing room where the boy had been only moments before. The girl wanted so desperately to shout out to him - warn him not to open the door. Warn him to run away as quickly as he could. But her voice seemed lost and soundless in her throat.

The young man opened the curtain with a sordid smirk, presuming it was his fling returning for another round. His expression grew even more lecherous when he realized it was some other attractive youth that stood at the entrance. He looked her up and down, observing her body clad in a mini skirt and lascivious top that revealed three buttons too many at the neckline.

"What can I do you for?" he questioned, eyes still scanning her hungrily from head to toe.

"Could you please help me with my zipper? It seems to be stuck," She offered in a beguiling voice, gesturing towards the side of her dress with delicate hands.

"Sure... Come on inside." He replied promptly, opening the curtain wider for her to enter.

The deceptive creature stepped through the doorway, swaying gracefully on high heels as she moved further into the room. Once she had gone sufficiently far enough into the changing room, she spun around wantonly until she faced him again. Her lips curled into an inviting smile as she raised two fingers to stroke his arm lightly in a sensation-seeking touch.

"You're quite handsome," She cooed appreciatively, and gave his bicep a playful pinch, "I bet you look better without these clothes."

He paused briefly before responding in an arrogant tone, "Wanna see?" His eyes met hers challengingly as he lifted one hand to gesture towards himself suggestively.

Daniela felt a jolt of excitement as she saw that the man she had been observing was aroused. She allowed herself to savor the moment, knowing that the real Daniela watched on helplessly from within her body. Suddenly, he pulled her shirt over her head and tossed if aside. His eyes were wide in wonderment as they roamed her body.

Instantly, his hands circled around her chest and began fondling her breasts. He didn't stop there, pushing forward to press his lips against hers. With every movement, he seemed more impassioned, his grip tightening as he started to undo the buttons of her blouse.

"Careful," Daniela managed, between gasps for air. "I haven't paid for this yet."

He chuckles softly, a deep throaty sound that sent chills through her body despite its menacing tone. "Oh that shouldn't be a problem." His fingers worked quickly until there was nothing holding back her bra any longer and he pushed his face into her exposed flesh.

All at once, desperation filled Daniela and she scrambled around the bedroom for something -- anything -- that would disrupt this obscene scene taking place in front of her. She grabbed a chair with both hands and slammed it against the wall multiple times; however, no matter how hard she tried, no sound came out of the mirror reflecting all that happened before her eyes.

She sobbed quietly then louder as humiliation bubbled up inside her -- what had been done to her was not something she would have ever allowed someone who wasn't especially close to do while she still held control of herself. But now, even that control had been taken away from her. Tears streamed down as she watched the man slip his hand brazenly under her skirt.

As Daniela collapsed to the ground in tears, her gaze shifted to the looming mirror behind her. In its reflection, she saw herself but it was not her. The figure before her had to be the diabolical force that was destroying her townspeople.

Daniela reached out and shoved him onto the only chair in the room, stripping him of his boxers and leaving his rigid manhood exposed. She stepped out of her panties, pushing him back into the cushion as she settled atop him. Her moans echoed through the room as he entered her, their eyes locked the whole time. Though she stared at him intently, he couldn't understand why she wasn't enjoying this like all the other women he'd been with. He averted his gaze from hers and let himself get lost in pleasure instead. But then something caught his eye in the mirror - a girl The Cult of Cavendish had paid him to spy on; Rachel.

He jolted in surprise and spun around to find no one there besides Daniela standing before him fully clothed, looking at him quizzically. He quickly checked himself, confused when he also found himself fully dressed. Before he could ask what was going on, she thrust both hands forward and grabbed his face tightly with her claw-like fingers. Staring directly into his eyes she spoke: "What did you do? What did you see?"

"All men are like you, boy. Nothing but a plague," She hissed, her claw-like fingers slowly crawling down his chest. "The thing with diseases," she continued, leaning in close to him "is that they all have to die eventually."

Daniela abruptly felt her cold lips brush against his own. Just as he started to melt into the kiss, an intense pain shot through his tongue as she bit down hard and tore it out of his mouth. He fell back from the force of her jaws and screamed in agony, the blood gushing from his wound as he stumbled against the wall.

Struggling to stand, Daniela peered at his stomach and gasped in horror; once muscly abs were now fast disappearing before his eyes. It was like watching himself wilt away like a leaf. He gaped at Daniela in shock, who merely grinned wickedly before turning on her heel and strutting out of the changing room.

Passing by the girl who had been having sex earlier, Daniela couldn't help but offer some advice. "Next time," she said sternly, "think twice before fucking someone - You never know who might be HIV positive". And with those words still ringing in her ears, the girl watched in awe as Daniela cast one final glance over her shoulder before exiting the store in style.

The girl stared at Daniela's retreating back, dumbfounded and fearful. She had never entertained the idea that this complete stranger had suggested; but when she paused to contemplate it, it made sense. With a determined expression, she stormed away from her desk and quickly strode to the changing room. As Daniela patiently waited outside, an ear-piercing scream bellowed from inside the room. It was clear to her that the girl had seen the wreckage in there.

Her spirit soared within her as something unfamiliar washed over her. This time, satisfaction and glee flowed through her for what lay ahead of him. She felt different...powerful. As she regally adorned her new attire, she no longer felt like herself - yet it no longer mattered; she felt liberated. Suddenly, words I will never fear again echoed in her mind.

CHAPTER TWELVE

As the bright yellow cab pulled up to the white picket fence that surrounded Daniela's home, she stepped out, adorned in a new leather skirt and a shirt dress. Her turquoise heels clicked against the pavement as she made her way towards the door. A sense of excitement and self-indulgence filled her as she thought about her recent shopping spree. But a faint sound of giggling coming from inside the house suddenly interrupted her thoughts.

Frowning, Daniela cautiously opened the door and crept inside, her heart racing with suspicion. And then all at once, a chorus of voices shouts, "Surprise!" She jumped, startled by the suddenness of it all, but as she looked around the living room, she couldn't help but smile. Her whole family, friends, and even some not-so-friendly acquaintances were gathered together to celebrate her birthday.

Iris, Heath, Kimbery, Liam, Amelia, and Jocelyn stood beaming at her, while behind them stood Aisha, Margie, and even George with grins plastered on their faces. Overwhelmed and touched by their gesture, Daniela felt a swell of warmth in her chest as she realized that despite all the hardships life had thrown at her recently, she still had people who cared for her deeply. And for that moment, she forgot all about the incident that had been on her mind earlier. All that mattered was this unexpected but much-needed reminder of love and friendship.

"Today is not my birthday." Daniela stated, her voice hollow and distant. She sat in the middle of the living room, surrounded by her loved ones who had gathered to lift her spirits during these trying times. Her aunt smiled warmly at her, knowing that she was struggling with the sickness that had befallen her.

But as Amelia and Kimbery commented on her outfit, Daniela felt a surge of anger rise within her. "I just wanted to try something new," she snapped defensively. Her friends exchanged glances, wondering why she was being so defensive about her appearance.

As the party continued, Daniela stood apart from the rest, feeling disconnected and lost. Even Jocelyn's compliment couldn't distract her from the turmoil within. But then another voice caught her attention.

"What's wrong with you?" Heath whispers, noticing her tense demeanor. "You've been through a lot, babe. It's okay to let your guard down."

But before Daniela could respond, Kimbery announced it was time to start the party. As she hit play on the music and everyone began dancing and chatting, Daniela remained rooted in place. She couldn't shake off the weight of everything that had happened lately.

"You look beautiful," Jocelyn said again, this time with sincerity in her tone.

"Thanks," Daniela murmurs, finally allowing herself to relax a little.

But as she turned away, she couldn't ignore the sinister whispers of doubt and fear that still lingered in her mind.

They were all dressed to the nines, and even the house seemed to be in on it with its lavish decorations. Daniela couldn't help but feel like she had missed something. She did a quick mental check of the date and realized it wasn't even close to any special occasion.

Suddenly, Liam appeared at her side, interrupting her thoughts. "Sorry to bother you, ma'am," he said to Jocelyn, "but I need to speak with Daniela."

"No problem," Jocelyn replied with a dismissive wave. "I'll catch you later, kid."

Liam turned back to Daniela with a serious expression. "Let's find somewhere private to talk, okay?"

She nodded, feeling a sense of nervousness wash over her as they walked away from the party crowd towards a chaise lounge by a window. They sat down and stared at each other in silence for a few moments before Liam spoke.

"There's something about you that always calms me," he began quietly. "It feels like I can actually trust you."

Daniela felt a flutter in her chest at his words, realizing that she was starting to develop feelings for him. "I could say the same about you," she replied softly.

A small smile tugged at the corners of Liam's lips as he continued. "And if I may say so, you look absolutely beautiful tonight."

Daniela blushed and looked away, trying to hide her growing smile. "Thank you."

"But seriously," Liam said with a teasing glint in his eye, "you should dress like this more often."

"Maybe I'll get a sexy nurse costume," she joked back.

Liam chuckled. "That would definitely be interesting. But all jokes aside, you have amazing legs."

"And you are quite the handsome detective," Daniela counters, flicking her hair back and lightly touching his arm.

Without realizing it, she found herself gazing up at him through her lashes. Liam couldn't help but feel a tightening in his chest at her gaze.

"Thank you," he said sincerely. "But seriously, I think you're truly beautiful."

A small grin spread across Daniela's face as she tilted her head, looking at him with playful eyes. "Is this you trying to flirt with me, Mr. Detective?"

Liam's smile widened. "Would that be such a bad thing?"

Daniela's response was cut short as a sudden movement behind them caught her off guard. A cat leapt onto Liam's lap, causing her to startle. "Oh my God!" she exclaimed, glaring at the feline intruder.

Liam chuckled and playfully scolded the cat, Robyn Tuggles, for his surprise appearances. Daniela couldn't hide her irritation at the unwanted addition to their meeting.

"You brought a cat?" Her annoyance was evident in her tone.

"No, he's been here before I arrived. Didn't you know?" Liam replied casually.

"No, I had no idea." Daniela's irritation turned into confusion. "Whose cat is this?"

"It belongs to Amelia. She asked Maureen to take care of it while she's away. Want to pet him?" Liam offered, pushing the cat towards her.

"No thanks, get that thing away from me!" Daniela cried out, shuddering at the thought of touching the cat.

"What's the problem?" Liam asked, concerned by her sudden change in demeanor.

"Nothing, I...I'm allergic to cats," she lied. In reality, she loved cats and had never been allergic to them. But there was something about this one that made her uncomfortable, she couldn't quite put her finger on it.

"I'm so sorry," Liam apologized immediately and released the cat back onto the couch. Just then, his phone rang and he excused himself to answer it.

"What's going on?" Daniela asked as he spoke on the phone.

"There's an incident at the shopping mall in town. I have to go." Liam sighed with disappointment.

"It's okay, work comes first," Daniela reassured him with a forced smile as he hurriedly left. As soon as he was gone, she let out a sigh of relief and shuddered again at the thought of being near that strange cat. Something about it just didn't sit right with her.

He leaned in to plant a kiss on her cheek, but recoiled at the coldness he felt. She noticed his hesitation and whispered a goodbye, still taken aback by the unexpected gesture. She couldn't help but think about how much she liked him. "I'll call you later," he promised as he left. She smiled and watched him go, anticipating their next encounter. He couldn't get her out of his mind, knowing there was more to her than meets the eye. But for now, they both needed to keep their feelings at bay, lest they cross another boundary and risk everything.

Daniela's voice trembled with emotion as she spoke, her gratitude overflowing for the gesture her friends had shown her. She couldn't believe how lucky she was to have such amazing people in her life. "I truly have no words to express how grateful I am. Thank you from the bottom of my heart for making me feel so loved and cherished." Her smile widened, radiating genuine happiness.

Amelia and Maureen exchanged a knowing look, both feeling touched by Daniela's words. They were glad they could bring some joy into her life. And when Daniela burst out laughing, they couldn't help but join in.

"You're welcome," they both said in unison, causing Daniela to laughed even harder.

Her laughter died down as she remembered something important. "Oh, I should thank Jocelyn and the others at work tomorrow. But right now, I just want to say thank you to Amelia and Aunt Maureen for throwing this wonderful party."

"It was our pleasure, my dear," Maureen replied warmly. "Now go rest in your room while we clean up."

"Okay, aunty." Daniela started to leave when a thought crossed her mind. "Amelia?"

"Yeah?" Amelia replied playfully.

"Please make sure that cat stays far away from my bedroom." The tone in Daniela's voice made everyone in the room pause.

Amelia couldn't resist teasing her cousin a little. "Yes, your highness."

Daniela rolled her eyes at the sarcasm but then added seriously, "I'm not kidding, Amelia."

"Fine, I'll keep an eye on the cat," Amelia promised before heading upstairs to her own room. As she closed the door behind her, she couldn't help but wonder why Daniela seemed so adamant about keeping the cat away from her room. It was strange and slightly unsettling.

Daniela thrashed about in her bed, tangled in her sheets as she fought against the oppressive weight of her dreams. She had finally managed to fall into a fitful sleep after hours of tossing and turning, but it offered no solace.

Disoriented and anxious, she bolted upright and fumbled for her phone to check the time - 2:45am. The room was shrouded in darkness, amplifying her sense of unease. Desperate for distraction, she stumbled out of bed and shuffled towards the bathroom.

Flicking on the light switch, Daniela winced at her own reflection in the mirror. She looked exhausted and on edge; dark circles under her eyes, hair unkempt and damp from sweat. Splashing water onto her face, she tried to calm her racing thoughts.

But even as she dried off with a towel, she heard a familiar car engine pull up outside their townhouse. Dread seeped into her bones as she peeked out the window and caught sight of Marve Brittle's lecherous figure stepping out of his car. Her blood ran cold.

"Why is he here? What does he want?" Daniela murmurs to herself, heart pounding in fear and disgust at the thought of encountering him. She had always avoided him like the plague - everyone knew he was a slimy creep.

But now, in the dead of night, he seemed to have found his way to their street. To her house. And Daniela couldn't shake off the feeling that it was somehow connected to her unsettling dream. Her stomach churned with dread as she waited, frozen in place with dread and anticipation for what would come next.

Daniela watched in exasperation as Marve stumbled across the lawn, headed towards her house. She knew exactly what was going to happen - he would knock on her door, refuse to leave until someone answered, and then stumble back to his own home. It was a cycle that had become all too familiar. Frustrated, she sank to the floor as the lightbulb flickered above her, accompanied by the bone-cracking sounds emanating from her body. The air grew cold and an eerie wind whipped around her, causing her hair to fly wildly.

In the mirror before her, she saw Rachel's bloodied face staring back at her with bloodshot eyes. Daniela's jaw dropped in shock as she ran her fingers over her face, feeling the grit of soil beneath them. Her reflection morphed back into her own just as Marve reached for her front door. Without hesitation, she flung it open and faced him with a determined look. "Not tonight, Marve," she said firmly. But as soon as he raised his hand to knock, Daniela's reflection changed once again, mirroring Rachel's disheveled appearance. Panic rising within her, Daniela backed away from the mirror and fled out of the house, leaving behind a confused Marve standing at her doorstep.

"What do you want?" Daniela snapped, her voice dripping with hostility.

Marve stumbled drunkenly towards her, surprised that she had opened the door. Before he could enter, Daniela's grip on his arm stopped him. Her grasp was strong for a girl.

Stunned, Marve tried to move past her but was pulled back with such force that he fell to the floor. As he struggled to get up, Daniela stared hard at him. He could see the anger in her eyes as he stumbled out of her sight and made his way to his own house.

He fumbled with his key, still confused by Daniela's behavior, before finally managing to open the door. But as he stepped inside and looked back at the girl's house, he saw Daniela standing in front of him, now in his own home.

"It was very rude of you to walk away from our conversation, Marve," she said coldly.

Marve glanced back and forth between her and her own house, realizing that it was impossible for her to have followed him so quickly.

Before he could even process this thought, Daniela grabbed him by the neck and threw him against the wall. As she did, he watched in terror as she transformed into a demonic creature with bloodshot eyes and a dislocated shoulder - Rachel.

Panicked and desperate for help, Marve reached for the phone and dialed 911.

"Hello?" he cried into the receiver. "Help!" he yelled as fear seeped through every word.

As Marve tried to speak, Rachel was upon him. In one swift motion, she twisted his wrist and disconnected the call. He cried out in pain, pleading for mercy. But Rachel was on a mission – to make him pay for what he had done.

Ignoring his cries, she grabbed him by the throat with one hand and lifted him effortlessly off the ground. With a forceful blow, she slammed him against the wall, causing it to slowly unfold and reveal a dark void behind it. Desperate hands reached out and pulled Marve into the darkness as he screamed and struggled.

But his screams were silenced as another hand covered his mouth, muffling any noise he could make. The more he fought against the unseen forces, the faster he was pulled into the void like sinking sand. And just as quickly as it appeared, the wall reassembled itself, trapping Marve inside.

With a sinister smile on her face, Rachel lifted her finger and with one swift movement, the final brick snapped back into place. Leaving Marve trapped in his own personal hell, she chuckled to herself as she made her way back home. Justice had been served.

Amelia jolted awake, a gust of cold wind blowing through her room. She turned to see her window, which she distinctly remembers closing before bed, now wide open with Robyn Tuggles perched on the sill. The Bengal cat was fixated on something outside, meowing louder than Amelia had ever heard.

"Robyn, what is it?" Amelia sighed as she got out of bed and slipped on her house slippers. She made her way to the window and reached out to pet the cat, who immediately jumped at her touch.

"Why are you so jumpy?" she asked with a chuckle, peering down at what had captured the cat's attention.

Sitting on the wooden swing in front of the house was Daniela, Amelia's cousin. It was late, and yet there she was, swinging back and forth aimlessly. Amelia checked the clock and frowned. Why was Daniela sitting out there all alone?

She quickly threw on her dressing gown and made her way downstairs, shivering as the cold seeped into her bones. A light mist had creeped into the house through the open front door. As she stepped outside, she saw Daniela's back facing her as she swung.

"Hey," Amelia called out, wrapping her arms around herself for warmth. "What are you doing out here in the middle of the night?"

Daniela didn't respond, just kept swinging silently. The only sounds were the chirping of crickets and the creaking of the old swing set.

Amelia walked closer until she could see Daniela's face - or what was left of it. She screamed in horror at the sight of her cousin's mutilated features before realizing it was just a nightmare. But then why was Daniela still sitting there on the swing?

The rusty chains of the swing creaked as Rachel pushed herself back and forth, her bloodied face twisted into a sinister smile. She had been waiting for Amelia, knowing she would come. As Amelia approached, her hand reaching out to touch Rachel's shoulder, a police car screeched up to the house next door. Two officers emerged and Liam joined them, leaving Daniela alone with Amelia.

"Is everything alright?" Liam asked, his eyes flickering between the two girls.

Daniela slowly rose from the swing, her features shifting from Rachel's face to her own. She looked bewildered and disoriented, not understanding how she had ended up outside on the swing when she had last been watching Marve through her bathroom window.

"Everything should be fine," Amelia interjected smoothly. "I just came out because I saw Dani here."

"Dani?" Liam's brow furrowed in confusion.

"I just needed some fresh air. I was feeling nauseous," Daniela replied, trying to act normal and avoid raising any suspicion from Liam and Amelia.

Liam's expression turned serious. "We received a call about Marve's house and came to check it out."

"And?" Amelia prompted.

"There was nothing there. No sign of Marve or anyone else. Just evidence of a struggle," Liam explained. "Did you two notice anything strange while you were outside?"

"No," they both reply in unison, shaking their heads.

"I did see something," Daniela spoke up, pointing to a beat-up car parked nearby. "That's Marve's car." The tense silence that followed made it clear that this was something worth looking into further.

Liam's eyes scanned the darkening sky as he thanked Daniela and Amelia for their cooperation. "Be careful, both of you," he warned, his voice laced with concern. "Stay indoors from now on. We don't know what this Marve guy is capable of."

The two women nodded in agreement before tapping each other and hurrying inside, eager to escape the chilly night air. Liam watched them go, making sure they were safely inside before turning back to the task at hand.

He combed the area for any clues or leads, but after a fruitless thirty minutes, he was forced to call in backup and set up a perimeter around Daniela's home. There was something off about her behavior when he had questioned her earlier. Had she been withholding information? Or was she simply surprised by the mention of Marve?

Liam shook his head, frustrated by all the unknowns. But one thing was certain - he wouldn't rest until this case was solved and his community was safe once more.

The faint light of dawn danced across Daniela's face, stirring her from sleep. She sat up in bed and stared at the ceiling, unmotivated to start her day. She knew she would be late for work, but it didn't matter to her. She was going to take things at her own pace.

As she swung her feet over the edge of the bed, Daniela noticed bright red stains on her white sheets, right where she had been lying. Panic set in as she searched her body for any injuries, but found none. Just as she started to remove her shirt to investigate further, a loud banging on the door made her jump. Frantically, she threw a duvet over the bloodstains before answering.

"Good morning," she greeted Amelia with exhaustion in her voice.

Amelia brushed past her into the room without responding. Daniela's bed was still unmade, which was highly unusual for her neat and organized roommate. And come to think of it, Daniela hadn't been wearing her glasses lately.

"You don't even look like you've showered yet! You're going to be late. Oh, speaking of being late, I might be a bit delayed coming home today. I have a...a date with Heath after work."

"What? A date? Since when?" Daniela questions, taken aback by this news.

"I didn't tell you? Well, now you know. Anyways, I'll see you later." With that, Amelia swept out of the room.

Daniela stood there in shock for a moment before quickly getting ready for work. But as she rushed around the apartment, thoughts raced through her mind - Why wasn't Amelia acting like herself? And why was blood mysteriously appearing on her sheets? Something wasn't right.

Amelia closed the door to her room and headed to the bathroom, leaving Daniela alone. Standing before the mirror, Amelia couldn't help but feel a shiver run down her spine. The reflection staring back at her seemed almost alive, as if it was fighting to break free.

"I'll find a way to rid myself of you," she muttered, determined to be rid of whatever this entity was. "You are just a figment of my imagination."

But as she left the bathroom and went to pick out her outfit for the day, the figure in the mirror laughed mockingly. It was not going anywhere; Rachel had no intention of leaving Daniela's mind. She reveled in the control she had over her host, relishing in the fear and uncertainty that she caused.

"You need me, Daniela," Rachel whispers through the looking glass, sending chills down Amelia's spine. "And I'm not going anywhere."

CHAPTER THIRTEEN

The frigid wind bit at Daniela's exposed skin as she emerged from the grocery store, her arms laden with bags. She pulled her parka tighter, determined to make it to her car without succumbing to the bitter cold. As she trudged towards the nearby park, she couldn't help but take in the picturesque scene around her - Tisdale covered in a blanket of snow, its streets eerily peaceful despite the recent string of murders.

But instead of finding solace in the holiday cheer that surrounded her, Daniela felt only anger and resentment. How could everyone act as if nothing had happened? The police may have increased their presence and things may seem quieter, but the fact remained that a killer was on the loose.

And yet, there were still Christmas carols blaring from every corner, and cheerful carolers making their rounds. It made Daniela sick to her stomach. She hated how normal everything seemed, how unaffected by the tragedy that had struck their town.

She reached the park and took a deep breath before sitting down on a bench. "I can't believe everyone is just going about their business like nothing happened," she muttered to herself.

"Excuse me?" A voice startled her, and Daniela turned to see an elderly woman standing nearby.

"I said," Daniela repeated louder, trying to control her rising frustration, "how can everyone be so jolly when there's a murderer out there?"

The woman's eyes widened in surprise before narrowing with suspicion. "Now dear, don't go spreading rumors. The police have everything under control."

Daniela scoffs. "Right. I'm sure they do." She stood up abruptly and walked away, unable to stand the delusion of those around her any longer.

As she made her way back home, all Daniela could think about was how much she despised this holiday season and all those who celebrated it with such blissful ignorance.

As Daniela hopped into her aunt's beat-up Volkswagen, she couldn't help but feel a sense of loneliness. Heath, the perfect "get-to-church" ride, had gone home for the holidays in the next town. She overheard him telling Amelia that he would try to sneak away from his family and drive back down to Tisdale for a day or so. Even Iris, her friend and co-worker, had hitched a ride with him to see her family. That left Daniela alone with Kimbery, who had gotten two weeks off from their job at the radio station. The holiday season was in full swing and Christmas songs flooded the radio, but Daniela didn't want to hear any of it.

The drive home was quiet as she navigated through the snowy roads. She resisted the urge to turn on the radio and instead focused on driving safely. By the time she arrived at her house, she was covered head to toe in snow from her walk to the car.

Shaking off the snow, Daniela kicked off her boots and quickly went inside to put away the groceries. As she sighed, she realized there was still so much work to do for the huge holiday feast happening that day. Her aunt Maureen had invited Liam, which meant everything had to be extra special. Daniela wasn't sure why, but her aunt seemed to really like Liam and had even invited him to join their family feast. It must mean she approved of him.

As Daniela rummaged through the bag for the jar of sundried tomatoes, her gaze was drawn to the brown fur of the Bengal cat they were currently cat-sitting. She chuckled as she saw him tugging at a roll of her aunt's knitting yarn, his mischievous nature on full display. Unable to resist, she set down the jar and knelt down to pet the soft creature. The cat purred contentedly under her touch, bringing a smile to Daniela's face.

"Why hello there, little troublemaker," she said playfully, scratching behind his ears. It suddenly occurred to her that this was the first time she had truly acknowledged the cat's presence in their home. Her mind raced with thoughts of why she had never paid attention to him before.

Before she could dwell on it any longer, she remembered that Kimbery would be ready and waiting for her as she was her ride to church, so she had to hurry and get ready and then leave to meet her at the agreed coffee shop. Hurriedly, she made her way upstairs to get ready. As she pulled on her blue Sunday dress and leggings, she couldn't help but feel a pang of nostalgia for simpler times when she didn't have to worry about her memory lapses.

With one last glance at herself in the mirror, Daniela braided her hair and put on another pair of black boots. She grabbed a pair of mittens and smiled determinedly at her reflection. "It'll be fine," she reassured herself.

But deep down, she couldn't shake off the feeling that something was wrong with her. She hoped that things would return to normal soon.

Her phone rang out loud, startling her from her thoughts. The jarring ringtone echoed through the empty room, a stark contrast to the peaceful morning light that filtered in through the windows. Kimbery would be ready soon and if she wanted to make it to their meet-up at the coffee shop on time, she had to leave immediately. Grabbing her leather purse, she hastily stuffed her phone, wallet, and a small scented candle inside before slinging it over her shoulder. She quickly made her way to the coat rack and snatched her warm wool coat and patterned scarf from their hangers. As she bounced down the stairs, her feet padded softly against the carpeted steps.

She stopped by the bottom of the stairs and bent down to greet the fluffy orange cat that had been sitting patiently by the steps. Its soft purring filled the space as she scratched behind its ears.

"Goodbye, Robyn," she said with a smile before standing up and heading out the door.

Amelia stared in surprise at her cousin's retreating back as she headed out the door. What had just happened? She had just entered the kitchen when she heard Dani coming down the stairs but was frozen in place when she saw her cousin petting the supposedly allergic-to cats. Confusion clouded Amelia's mind as she tried to make sense of it all. And why did she leave without her glasses or rosary, something she always carried?

It dawned on Amelia that this wasn't like Daniela at all. It had been a long time since she last saw her with a rosary wrapped around her wrist. The pieces of this strange puzzle were starting to come together, but Amelia still couldn't make sense of it all.

"Something's not right here," Amelia mumbled to herself as she tried to come up with an explanation for her cousin's sudden change in behavior. But no matter how hard she tried, nothing seemed to make sense. It was as if someone else had taken over Daniela's body and mind.

The air felt heavy with unease as Amelia couldn't shake off the feeling that something sinister was lurking beneath the surface.

A sense of unease washed over Daniela as she sat in her darkened room, pondering the strange occurrences that had been happening lately. She knew she needed to talk to someone, but who? Her mother was too preoccupied with running errands and her friends were no help. A flicker of headlights outside caught her attention and she saw Liam's patrol car drive by. An idea sparked in her mind - Liam would be the perfect person to confide in. Not only was he a cop, he seemed to have a soft spot for Daniela. She quickly dialed her mother's number, making up an excuse about needing to pick something up from work before hanging up and heading out to meet with Liam.

Meanwhile, Amelia paced back and forth in her living room, her mind racing with worry for Daniela. She couldn't shake off the feeling that something was seriously wrong. As she stood by the window, gazing out into the night, she made a decision. She would go to church alone and then return home with her mother after picking up Daniela's car from work.

"Hey Mum," Amelia said as soon as her mother answered the phone.

"Amelia, where are you?" Maureen's voice sounded concerned.

"I'm at home, Mama. When are you coming back to prepare for Mass?"

"Soon. I just finished all my errands."

"Oh okay. Umm, mum? You can go on ahead to church without me. I'll meet you there later." Amelia lied smoothly.

"Why? We agreed you'd ride with me."

"Yeah but I've got to pick up something from work." she continued confidently, hoped her acting skills were convincing enough. "Daniela's brought back the car and has just left to meet Kim. I'll ride back home with you."

"Just don't be late, Amelia."

"Yes, Mum." She ended the call with a deep sigh, her mind already racing with plans on how to help Daniela. She prayed for guidance and a solution as she waited for Liam's arrival.

After what felt like an eternity, Liam finally knocked on the door. Amelia quickly opened it, relief flooding through her at the sight of him.

"Hey Liam," she said, trying to keep her voice steady.

"Amelia." Liam looked slightly surprised but smiled warmly at her. "Is everything okay?"

"No," Amelia blurted out, unable to contain her worry any longer. "It's Daniela, something is seriously wrong with her."

Daniela stood shivering outside the deserted coffee shop, her teeth rattling in her head like a prisoner's chains. The winter air pierced through her thin jacket, freezing her to the core as she waited for Kimbery to pick her up. The temperature had plummeted since she left earlier and yet, despite the bitter cold, she remained rooted in the snow. She welcomed the icy kiss of each delicate snowflake that landed on her flushed cheeks, finding solace in their gentle touch amidst the harshness of the night.

But as she closed her eyes and took a deep breath, savoring the momentary peace, her ears were suddenly assaulted by the distant sound of Christmas carolers. Daniela's heart seized in panic, her pulse racing as dread washed over her. Why must they disturb this moment? Why couldn't they just be quiet?

The carolers grew louder with each step, their joyful voices ringing out into the silent night. How had she not noticed them approaching? Daniela could feel a pressure building inside her head, a sharp pain stabbing at the right side of her skull. It felt like something was clawing its way out of her body, desperate to escape.

Her legs trembled as she struggled to remain standing, a wave of nausea threatening to overwhelm her. "Shut up...shut up!" She muttered under her breath, clenching her fists in frustration. But the carolers continued on with their cheerful song, oblivious to Daniela's distress.

"Please...just shut up!" She cried out louder this time, but it was no use. One of the carolers finally heard her plea and turned to look in her direction. Daniela saw recognition flash across the old woman's face before she quickly turned away. But it was too late - Daniela knew that she had been seen and there was no going back now.

As the young lady's voice pierced through the air in a shrill scream, the woman's eyes widened in fear. She could see something was terribly wrong with this girl, her face contorting with an unusual pulsating vein that seemed to throb with a life of its own. Despite her growing concern, the woman continued singing with her peers, keeping an eye on the troubled girl. The closer she got, the more she could see the girl's unsteady balance and obvious distress.

"Is everything alright?" she asked cautiously, noticing the girl's head bowed in agony.

The answer came as a whispered reply, barely audible over the deafening sound of the group's singing. "I'm just feeling a bit sick is all," Daniela confessed.

Concern etched on her face, the woman offered to call for help, but before she could even finish her sentence, Daniela's anger erupted. She was tired of the constant questions and prying eyes, wanting nothing more than to escape this suffocating environment. Just as the nosy woman was about to speak again, a loud car engine revving caught their attention.

Without hesitation, Daniela recognized Kimbery's voice shouting out to her. "Hop in!" she heard Kimbery call out.

Relief washed over Daniela as she scrambled towards the car, grateful for a way out of this suffocating situation.

The woman's heart raced as she watched Daniela frantically rush into the car and fumble with the seatbelt. In a panic, she moved closer to the car, her mind racing with worry. What was wrong with this girl? She needed help, and fast.

But as she approached the car, fear struck her like a bolt of lightning when she locked eyes with Daniela. The girl's normally warm brown eyes were now a blazing red, filled with both hatred and seething anger. It was as if some otherworldly force possessed her.

The woman stumbled back in terror, unable to tear her gaze away from Daniela's intense stare. Every fiber of her being was overwhelmed with a deep sense of dread. She had encountered something truly terrifying.

As the car sped off, leaving a trail of dust in its wake, the woman remained frozen in shock. Her face drained of color, she could barely move as she tried to process what had just happened. With shaking hands, she clutched onto her chest, trying to calm her pounding heart.

It wasn't until the car disappeared completely from view that the woman could finally take a shaky step backwards. She knew she would never forget this encounter, for it felt like staring into the eyes of pure evil.

Feeling numb and shaken to her core, the woman slowly made her way home, unable to shake off the haunting image of Daniela's intense glare burned into her memory forever.

As they drove to church, Kimbery couldn't help but glance at Daniela, her keen eyes trying to decipher the quiet woman beside her. This was not the lively and talkative friend she knew. For the entire five minutes of their ride, Daniela had remained silent, her gaze fixed on the passing scenery outside the window. It was as if something was weighing heavily on her mind.

Finally, Kimbery decided to speak up. "You've been awfully quiet today. Is everything alright?" she asked with genuine concern.

Daniela's response was a mumbled thank you for driving her to church, before falling silent once again.

A sense of unease crept over Kimbery. Something was definitely off with her friend, but she pushed aside her curiosity and gave Daniela the space she deserved. After all, she had been through a tumultuous few weeks and needed time to heal.

As they approached the church, Kimbery pulled over and turned off the car engine. "Do you mind walking from here? Parking might be difficult closer to the church and I don't want us to miss Mass," she offered.

"It's fine. A walk would be nice," Daniela replied softly.

With that settled, they both stepped out of the car and began their journey towards the church. The crisp air surrounded them, adding a tinge of chill to the already tense atmosphere between them.

"Shall we?" Kimbery gestured towards the entrance of the church.

Daniela nodded and followed closely behind her friend, both lost in their own thoughts as they walked towards salvation.

As Daniela stepped further away from the car, a feeling of unease settled in her stomach. She couldn't pinpoint why, but something about going to confession today made her skin crawl. But she had come this far and nothing would stop her from entering the church. Despite the sharp pain in her abdomen, she clenched her fists and continued walking with determination. Her friend Kimbery finally noticed her discomfort and asked if she was alright. Daniela assured her, though her voice was strained and her head throbbed with a growing migraine.

Finally reaching the church, Daniela's aunt Maureen greeted them with cheerful excitement for Christmas. But as Maureen touched Daniela's hand, she flinched and looked at her niece with suspicion.

"Are you okay?" Maureen asked, concern evident in her tone.

Daniela forced a smile and nodded before turning to enter the church. This confessional was important to her - no one else would understand the pain she carried inside. As they greeted other family members outside the church, Daniela felt the weight of their expectations weighing on her. She needed to get this off her chest before the ceremony began.

"Merry Christmas, Aunt Maureen," Kimbery chimed in cheerfully.

But Daniela's response was quiet and subdued, causing Maureen to question if she was feeling less than festive.

"Not quite feeling the holiday spirit yet, Daniela?" Maureen prodded, placing a hand on her niece's shoulder.

Daniela swallowed hard and managed another forced smile before whispering, "I'm fine."

But deep down, she knew that wasn't true. And as they walked into the church together, Daniela couldn't shake the feeling that this confession would be more difficult than she ever imagined.

A shiver ran down Daniela's spine as her aunt touched her hand. "Don't give me that," she scolded, feeling the icy coldness of Daniela's skin and the rapid thumping of her pulse. "Your hands are ice cold and your pulse is racing so fast, I would have thought your heart was running a marathon."

Kimbery chimed in, her tone apologetic. "She has been awfully quiet since I picked her up."

"I'm seriously fine, guys," Daniela insisted, trying to dismiss their concern. "I'm just feeling a bit lightheaded. I was so late doing all the shopping; I didn't get a chance to grab something to eat. And besides, I brought the wrong pair of gloves and as you can see it's quite chilly out here. So stop worrying and let's get inside before I get any colder."

Her Aunt and Kimbery followed behind her, but Daniela couldn't shake off the feeling that they were still concerned. She quickened her pace, eager to escape their worried gazes. The grounds of the church fair spread out before them, bustling with people and filled with the scents of delicious food and sweet treats.

As they made their way through the crowd, Daniela could hear her aunt greeting some familiar faces. She was grateful for the distraction, knowing that Maureen would have kept asking her questions about her well-being. Someone tapped her shoulder and she turned to see Kimbery looking at her with pity in her eyes.

"I'm seriously fine, Kim," Daniela reiterated with more conviction this time.

"Yeah, I believe you," Kim replied unconvincingly.

"Right. You can go on ahead. I'll join you soon."

"I'll find us seats then."

"Thanks," Daniela said with a small smile before heading towards the confessional booth, needing a moment alone to gather her thoughts and calm her racing heart.

As she made her way to the box, Daniela noticed the abundance of people in the church today. It was a rare sight, considering that usually only a handful of faithful congregated for Sunday service. But it seemed that Christmas had drawn in more worshippers than normal. She couldn't help but wonder why people only turned to God during festive periods and not throughout the year. Did they not feel the need for His presence in their lives until it was time for celebrations?

She kneeled before entering the confessional box, taking a deep breath and silently reciting a prayer for forgiveness. "Come Holy Spirit into my soul," she whispered, "Enlighten my mind so that I may recognize my sins and grant me the grace to confess them fully, humbly, and with a contrite heart. Help me to firmly resolve not to commit them again." She then turned her thoughts to Blessed Mary, asked for her intercession through the Passion of her son.

Finally, she prayed for all the angels and saints to pray for her, a sinner, to repent from her wrongdoings and unite her heart with theirs in eternal love. With a final amen, she entered the confessional box and waited for someone to join her on the other side of the wooden wall.

After only a brief moment, Daniela heard the door on the other side open and saw the faint figure of a man sit down. The barrier between them concealed most of his features, but she could tell he was quite young by his voice.

"In the name of the Father, the Son, and the Holy Spirit," he began as they both made the sign of the cross.

Daniela's hands trembled as she made the sign of the cross, her eyes darting around the confessional. "It's been a year since my last confession, Father," she began, her voice shaking. "I've been going through...a lot in the past few months. It's becoming too much to bear."

"The Lord will give you strength, my child. Speak your heart."

Gulping, Daniela took a deep breath before pouring out her fears. "It all started when I got curious about the Cult of Standish. My friend and I wanted to find out more about it, just for fun. But then things took a dark turn...the cult turned out to be real."

Father Michael's brow furrowed in concern, but he urged her to continue.

"At one of their meetings, I saw...something. A girl, or something that looked like a girl. But there was an air of darkness around her, a feeling of pure evil that I could sense even from a distance." Daniela closed her eyes, trying to push away the memory.

"She killed two men in front of me, Father. In the most gruesome way imaginable. And then...then she struck again at the Butterstick and killed Greta." A shudder wracked Daniela's body as she remembered the old woman's severed heart on a plate.

"I know it was her. No one else would have such cruelty in their heart." She took a moment to steady herself before continued. "I tried to look away, but all I could see were those hate-filled eyes staring back at me. And then...her demonic hands grabbed my hair and pulled me away. I barely escaped with my life."

The gentle voice of the priest cut through the silence, filled with genuine concern for Daniela. "My dear, you've been through so much," he said, his hand resting lightly on her shoulder. "How have you been coping with everything that has been happening?"

Tears welled up in Daniela's eyes, despite her efforts to hold them back. They spilled over onto her cheeks, leaving a trail of mucus as she struggled to compose herself. "I...I don't know anymore," she admitted, her voice barely above a whisper. "It feels like my life is spinning out of control." She sniffed and reached for a tissue from her purse, wiping away the evidence of her tears.

"It's okay, my child," the priest reassured her. "You can trust me with your troubles."

Daniela nodded gratefully as she tried to gather her thoughts. "I'm not myself lately," she confessed. "I keep losing time, hours just disappear without me knowing what happened. It's overwhelming and I don't know how to handle it. I thought maybe only a priest could understand."

The priest's kind expression never faltered. "You can confide in me and I will keep it between us," he promised.

"Thank you, father," Daniela said, offering a small smile through her tears. She took a deep breath before continuing, feeling a sense of relief wash over her as she shared her struggles with someone else. "I should probably go before mass starts. But I feel better now that I've talked to someone about this."

"I'm glad you do," the priest said warmly. "Before you go, perhaps say ten Hail Marys and make an Act of Contrition."

"My God, I am sorry for my sins with all my heart," Daniela recited with sincerity. "Please help me to do penance and be better, and guide me away from temptation and sin. Amen."

The words of the priest echoed through the church, a solemn and powerful declaration. As he spoke, the scent of incense filled the air, mingling with the hushed whispers of the congregation. Daniela knelt in the confessional box, her heart pounding as she waited for absolution. The weight of her sins hung heavy on her shoulders, but she knew that this moment could bring peace and forgiveness.

Finally, the priest spoke those sacred words and she felt a sense of relief flood over her. She exited the box with a lightness in her step, a physical manifestation of the spiritual burden lifted from her soul. Looking around the crowded church, she spotted her friend Kimbery sitting in the back row and her aunt a few rows ahead. Daniela made her way to Kimbery's side, their hands clasping in silent support.

"Hi," she whispered to her friend.

"Hi," Kimbery replied softly. "Your aunt wanted to sit with her friends up front. She said Amelia had some errands to run but she'll join us soon."

"Okay," Daniela nodded, taking in the full pews and tired faces around them. "Looks like everyone is feeling the Christmas rush."

"And exhaustion," Kimbery added with a small smile. "I'm sure if it weren't for the holiday, many wouldn't have made it to Mass today."

"I was thinking the same thing earlier," Daniela chuckled softly. "So what did I miss?"

"A whole lot," Maureen replies. "Father Christopher Jackson is conducting the mass."

Daniela's gaze shifted to the heavyset man in the black robe standing at the altar. The dim lighting in the church cast shadows on his features, adding an air of mystery to his appearance. His sandy brown hair had clearly been recently trimmed, and his deep-set eyes seemed to hold secrets within their depths. As she watched him, Daniela couldn't help but wonder why he had stayed with her and missed the entrance procession.

"The Lord be with you," the priest began.

"And with you," responded the congregation in unison.

Daniela listened as Father Jackson delivered a heartfelt sermon about the true meaning of Christmas and how we must always trust in God's plan, even in times of sorrow and hardship. Her attention was drawn back to the priest as he asked everyone to pray for Jake and Greta, a couple who had recently passed away.

As the whole congregation bowed their heads in prayer, Daniela found herself unable to close her eyes like everyone else. Instead, she continued to stare at Father Jackson from her seat in the back row. There was something about him that intrigued her, something that no one else seemed to notice. Perhaps it was just a gut feeling, but she couldn't shake the feeling that there was more to this priest than met the eye.

A voice in her head started to scream at her, a relentless barrage of accusations and revelations that made her blood boil with rage. The man who claimed to be a messenger of God was nothing but a fraud, preying on the blind faith of the townspeople. Daniela's breath grew uneven as the vicious thoughts consumed her mind, drowning out any sense of reason.

A loud thud against the window beside the priest jolted her out of her trance. She turned to him, only to find him paralyzed with fear as well. But before she could react, another thud sounded from the other side of the stained glass window, followed by flickering lights and extinguishing candles. Panic spread through the congregation like wildfire as they scrambled for safety.

Kimbery turned to check on Daniela, but she was already fixated on the right side of the church, straining her eyes to see what had caused the noise. As Maureen shouted from the front, asking if everyone was okay, Kimbery could only nod, too afraid to speak.

With trembling hands, she reached for her phone and quickly sent a text to Amelia, warning her to stay away from the church. But before she hit send, she added that something sinister was happening inside and cursed under her breath as yet another thud shook the very foundations of their supposed sanctuary.

Christopher Jackson's hand trembled as he reached for the stained window, ready to let in some fresh air. But his movements froze when he saw the lifeless crow lying on the crimson-red snow just outside. Its neck was twisted at an unnatural angle, blood staining the pure white snow beneath it.

Before anyone could react, a loud thud echoed through the church, halting all conversation and movement. The sudden chaos erupting inside the church drowned the priest's voice out. Candles flickered and died, leaving only dim moonlight to illuminate the panicked faces of the congregation.

"The lights...priest?" A trembling voice rang out from the back of the church.

But before the priest could offer an explanation, a deafening roar filled the air as lightning struck the old church building. The ground shook violently, shattering windows and sending shards of glass flying through the air. Black clouds swirled above the church, a dark omen of what was to come.

As if sensing their terror, a swarm of crows descended upon the church like a plague, their beady eyes glinting with malice as they pecked at terrified parishioners.

Screams filled the air as people trampled over one another in a desperate attempt to escape. And yet, amidst the chaos and fear, something sinister stirred within the darkness of the church, hungry for more chaos and destruction.

At the altar, the crows descended upon the priest with ferocious intensity, their razor-sharp beaks tearing into his flesh as he screamed in agony. The doors slammed shut, trapping the terrified onlookers inside as they frantically tried to escape the madness. Kimbery flung herself to the ground, desperately swatting at the vicious birds as one of them aimlessly pecked at her eyes, while Maureen cowered in a corner, shielding herself with her purse.

Amidst the chaos and terror, Daniela remained eerily calm and unfazed. The birds avoided her completely, sensing a powerful force emanating from her. She watched in silent determination as the priest struggled against the onslaught of feathered attackers, but they were relentless and showed no signs of backing down. Daniela fought with every ounce of strength she had left, willing her body and mind to resist the dark entity that threatened to consume her.

But it was a losing battle. Sweat poured down her face in torrents, drenching her clothes despite the chilly air in the church. She gritted her teeth and clenched her fists, repeating a mantra of defiance repeatedly. However, the demon within her was too strong, its malevolent presence overwhelming her weakened defenses. With a final burst of resistance, Daniela's body succumbed to its control, standing tall beside the screaming priest as he writhed in torment before her.

The birds stopped pecking and prodding at him momentarily, giving the priest a brief reprieve. He wheezed and gasped for air, his heart racing with fear and adrenaline. When he turned to look beside him, he realized that a young girl had been standing there all along. As he tried to rush towards her to protect her, the birds began attacking him again, their sharp beaks and claws viciously lashing out. Panic rising in his chest, he was about to plead with the girl to run when he noticed something strange - the birds were avoiding her completely. With each step he took closer to her, the attacks from the birds lessened until they were no longer a threat at all. Standing next to her, none of the birds dared to come near them.

Puzzled and trembling, the priest looked up at the girl as she leaned down and whispered in his ear, "Today is the day you will experience sacrifice for your people, Dark Priest."

His body froze in terror as he processed her words. Suddenly, he turned to get a better look at her face and was met with shock and horror. This was not the innocent girl he thought she was, but wore the same clothes as before, this time with an eerily familiar face - that of Rachel, the Virgin Sacrifice who had been taken before him just moments ago.

Kimbery scrambled away from the floor, sending the crow flying with a shriek. She spun frantically, searching for Daniela amidst the chaos. A flash of fabric caught her eye at the front of the church, but that couldn't be right - Daniela was just here at the back. Despite her blurred vision and injuries, Kimbery crawled towards the front, determined to capture proof on her phone.

Meanwhile, Rachel's eyes burned with rage as she glared at the priest who had destroyed her life. He couldn't believe his eyes - she was supposed to be dead, buried and forgotten. But there she stood in front of him, flesh and blood, ready for revenge.

"You took everything from me," Rachel snarled through gritted teeth. "Now it's my turn to take something from you."

Before the priest could even process her words, Rachel plunged her claw-like nails into his spine, paralyzing him instantly. A wicked grin spread across her face as she watched him crumple to the floor, her features contorting into a demonic form. With one swift movement, she reached past the holy water font and snatched up the very knife he had used to sacrifice her. Raising him up effortlessly with one hand, she sliced open his neck in a single merciless stroke, reveling in his screams of pain as blood gushed out onto the sacred ground below.

Amelia and Liam cautiously parked the car a safe distance away from the abandoned church, their eyes drawn to the swarm of crows circling above it. "What's going on?" Amelia asked, gripping the steering wheel.

Liam's face was grim as he observed the birds flying in and out of a broken window. "Stay in the car," he ordered, quickly making his way to the trunk of his car.

Thankful for always keeping an extra can of aerosol for cleaning his gun, Liam grabbed it along with a lighter before heading towards the church. As he approached the front door, he could hear faint howls and screams coming from inside. He tried pushing and shoving at the door, but it wouldn't budge. So he ran to the side entrance and attempted to open it, with no luck.

Meanwhile, Kimbery had been recording everything on her phone in a daze. But suddenly, she saw the priest fall into a bowl of holy water, followed by another person screaming and jumping back in terror. The crows seemed to be reacting to this as well, swirling around the priest's body before abruptly swarming towards the doors.

Just as Liam kicked open one of the doors, the birds came crashing into him unexpectedly, causing him to fall to the ground.

As Kimbery's eyes fluttered open, her mind raced with a single thought: Daniela. She quickly scanned the room, heart pounding in her chest, until she spotted her friend lying motionless against the back wall. Her face was covered in cuts and her wrists bore angry burns.

But there was no time to worry about that now. Maureen, still lying face down on the floor, seemed too paralyzed with fear to move. Kimbery whispered to her that it was over, hoping to snap her out of it. As if responding to some unspoken signal, people all around them suddenly shot up from the ground and began running towards the exit in a frenzied panic. They pushed and shoved, trampling anyone unfortunate enough to be deemed too slow.

Maureen finally got up once she was certain the worst of the stampede had passed. But there were still injured people scattered on the floor, crying out in pain and shock at what had just happened in their peaceful church. Without hesitation, Maureen took it upon herself to check on each person, offering comfort and reassurance.

Meanwhile, Amelia burst into the church and helped Liam to his feet. She had seen the sudden exodus of crows from the front of the building and knew it was safe to enter. As she pulled Liam up, they both heard a blood-curdling scream from inside. Without a second thought, they raced towards the sound and found Maureen frozen in horror at the altar where Father Christopher's lifeless body lay slumped over the bowl of holy water. The sight caused their hearts to plummet with dread and grief for their fallen leader.

CHAPTER FOURTEEN

melia's heart raced as she guided her mother away from the lifeless body of the priest. Liam rushed to Daniela's side, frantically trying to awaken her. She gasped for air, flailing wildly and mistaking Liam for a swarm of birds. As she realized her mistake, relief flooded her face and she pulled him into a tight embrace.

A smile tugged at Kimbery's lips as she watched Daniela cling to Liam. It was clear that he was the one who would help her forget the past traumas inflicted by her previous partner. She reached for her phone to call for help, but it stubbornly refused to respond. A shiver ran down her spine as she realized the once-safe church now felt hostile and unsettling.

Hours later, after the ambulance had come and gone, Kimbery took Liam aside and recounted the events that had unfolded. Caught up in their conversation, they didn't notice Father Thom praying with Maureen until he spoke of an imminent evil lurking among them.

Liam's grip on Daniela tightened as she whispered her desire to leave. Without hesitation, he led her towards the exit. As they passed Father Thom, they overheard him warning Maureen of a looming danger.

"We have to go," Daniela pleaded, fear evident in her voice.

"Right now," Liam agreed firmly, taking her hand and leading her out of the church.

As they stepped outside into the night, a feeling of dread settled over them. Something dark and malevolent lingered in the shadows, waiting for its next victim. And they knew they needed to get far away from this cursed place before it was too late.

The news of the church chaos spread like wildfire, with people from all over flocking to the scene even hours later. Even Iris and Heath, who had originally planned to be out of town, decided to change their plans and rush back. As Kimbery sighed in resignation, she made her way to the deserted radio station, knowing that at least here she could be alone without feeling lonely amidst the holiday crowds. She had tried calling Daniela to join her, but all she received was a constant stream of voice-mails. It seemed she would have to brave this Christmas as a lone ranger. "Looks like it's just you and me against the world again," she muttered to herself as she settled into the familiar booth, ready to face whatever may come on this tumultuous day.

Amelia stood in front of her cousin's door, her hand hovering over the doorbell. She couldn't bear to see Daniela's cold and uninterested face, but she couldn't avoid this confrontation any longer. Ever since the disaster at Mass, their family had been fractured. Sleepless nights and haunting memories plagued Amelia's mother, while everyone else in the community mourned the "unfortunate death" of Father Christopher.

But there was one person who seemed to have emerged unscathed from that fateful day - Daniela. Her once caring and empathetic nature had been replaced by a distant and apathetic demeanor. She no longer showed any interest in anyone else's well-being, leaving Amelia to shoulder the burden of comforting their grief-stricken aunt, Maureen.

As Amelia finally pressed the doorbell, she could feel her heart racing with apprehension. The sound of footsteps approaching on the other side made her tense up even more. "What do you want?" Daniela's voice was sharp and dismissive as always.

"I just...I wanted to talk," Amelia replied tentatively.

Daniela let out a tired sigh and opened the door wider for Amelia to enter. As she stepped into the familiar living room, she couldn't help but notice how different it felt now. There was a heaviness in the air, a sense of loss that seemed to linger long after the tragedy had passed.

"How can you be so unaffected by everything that happened?" Amelia blurted out, unable to contain her frustration any longer.

Daniela's expression remained unchanged as she took a seat on the couch. "I'm not unaffected," she said quietly. "I just choose not to dwell on it like everyone else."

Amelia stared at her cousin in disbelief. How could she be so callous? But then again, maybe Daniela was just trying to protect herself from the pain.

"I wish you could understand how hard it is for the rest of us," Amelia said, her voice filled with emotion.

Daniela finally looked up at her. "I do understand. But I have my way of coping."

Amelia realized that she would never truly know what was going on inside Daniela's mind. But she also knew that she couldn't keep shouldering everyone else's pain. It was time for her to take care of herself too.

The entire household seemed to be walking on eggshells around Daniela, and even the typically fearless Robyn Tuggles would cower and hide at the mere sight of her. It was unsettling. Amelia had tried talking to Liam about it, but he could only conclude that Daniela was in denial, living in a fantasy world where everything was fine despite her traumatic experiences. Even as Amelia gathered the courage to knock on Daniela's door, she couldn't help but wonder if her friend would snap and attack her. But she quickly pushed those paranoid thoughts away. After all,

Daniela was just going through a rough time and this behavior was expected.

With a deep breath, Amelia knocked on the door three times before waiting nervously for a response. "What?" came Daniela's sharp reply from inside.

"Hey, it's me," Amelia answers in a gentle tone. "I need a favor. Could you please keep my mom company while I run some errands? She's cooking Christmas dinner and I don't want her to be alone with her thoughts."

There was a long pause before Daniela grunted and reluctantly agreed. "Fine," she said curtly.

Amelia couldn't help but feel a sense of relief wash over her as she thanked Daniela and hurried off. She knew that having someone like Daniela by her mother's side would provide much-needed comfort during such a difficult time. And maybe, just maybe, spending time with someone else would also help Daniela heal from her own pain.

Amelia's heart raced as she heard the reluctant agreement from her grumpy cousin. Without hesitation, she turned on her heels and sprinted down the stairs to the safety of her mother's presence in the kitchen. Her chest heaved with anxiety and adrenaline as she desperately tried to escape before her cousin could change her mind.

She planted a quick kiss on her mother's cheek, barely registering the warmth of the shawl being draped over her neck. "I have to go, Mom," she said breathlessly. "I convinced Dani to come help with cooking."

Her mother nodded absentmindedly, focused on mixing the batter in front of her.

"Please take care of yourself while I'm gone," Amelia pleaded, already inching towards the door.

"Hmmn," was all her mother replies.

Knowing time was running out, Amelia promised to pick up some of her mother's favorite pumpkin pie on her way back. "I love you, Mom," she said with a sense of urgency.

"I appreciate that," came the soft reply from behind.

As Amelia heard the door to Daniela's room slam shut, she knew it was now or never. With one last goodbye and a hurried exit, she bolted out of the house at full speed, leaving behind any thoughts of staying for longer than absolutely necessary.

A thick block of ice, measuring four centimeters in height, was stubbornly lodged at the bottom of the door, effectively sealing the radio station shut. Kimbery let out an exasperated sigh. She should have known that the heavy snowfall overnight would cause problems like this. But it hadn't crossed her mind to bring a pickaxe with her on her journey. Her frustration turned into desperation as she tugged and pulled at the unyielding handle of the door.

Twenty minutes later, panting and exhausted, she managed to wedge the door open just enough for her to squeeze through. Inside the office building, she removed her glove and flicked on the lights and heater, grateful for the warmth that enveloped her. Collapsing into one of the chairs in the lobby, she closed her eyes for a brief moment before her ringing phone jolted her back to reality.

"Iris." Kimbery answers wearily.

"Hey Kim, what's up?" Iris's voice came through the speaker.

"Nothing much."

"Are you close by? I'm picking up food and wanted to know if you want anything."

Kimbery considered for a moment before replied, "Yeah, sure. Fries and wings sound good. And if they have hot chocolate, make it extra spicy."

"No problem," Iris said with a laugh. "Where should I meet you?"

"At the station. I couldn't bear another minute in that frozen house. I'll be waiting for you guys."

Iris chuckled again. "We'll be there soon. Heath went to get Amelia."

"What's going on between those two anyway? They seem closer than usual," Kimbery asked curiously.

"Oh, are you jealous?" Iris teases.

Kimbery rolled her eyes. "Jealous? Of what? Don't be ridiculous."

Kimbery's heart sank as the words spilled from her phone, each one a sharp dagger piercing her chest. She could feel the heat rushing to her face, burning with anger and betrayal. How could Heath have moved on so quickly? And with Amelia, of all people?

But she couldn't dwell on her own feelings for long - the detective's call demanded her attention. She wrapped her arms around herself, trying in vain to ward off the cold that seeped through her skin and into her bones despite the heater. She braced herself for the worst as she answered, steeling her voice to sound calm.

"Detective Liam," she said, forcing out the words through gritted teeth.

"Liam's fine, Kimbery. Hi," came his reply, seemingly oblivious to the turmoil she was experiencing.

The small talk was like salt in an open wound, but she played along, mustering up a strained "Hi" in return. But when he asked about the pictures from Mass and mentioned his device, she couldn't hold back any longer.

"No," she snapped, "I haven't been able to get anything off of my damn phone! And now I have to deal with this cursed android. You just had to remind me of my misery."

He chuckled lightly at her frustration before said, "You sound like an iPhone snob."

"I am a snob when it comes to this!" she exclaimed, unable to control the bitterness in her tone.

Silence stretched between them as they both took a moment to regain their composure. At last, Liam spoke again.

"Anyway, I've got this device that I think might help. We'll copy all your media and sift through everything to see what images you might have caught."

Despite herself, a spark of hope flickered inside Kimbery. Maybe there was still a chance to find some answers amidst all this chaos. But as she waited for Liam to arrive, she couldn't shake off the feeling of being betrayed by those closest to her. Her Christmas had been shattered into a million pieces, and she didn't know if they could ever be put back together again.

The sound of bustling city streets and distant cars hummed in the background as Kimbery spoke into her phone. She was currently at Bardo Radio, a building just a short distance from The ButterStick, or what used to be The Butterstick. Her words were met with excitement on the other end of the line.

"Oh great! I'm within walking distance from there. I'll be right along," came a voice filled with anticipation.

"Thanks," Kimbery replied gratefully. "No, thank you for sharing. See you soon."

As she hung up the phone, Kimbery sank into her chair, her mind flooded with memories of the incident at the church. It had been chaotic and sudden, leaving everyone wondering what could have caused it all. The swarm of birds attacking without warning, it was like something out of a horror movie.

A soft knock on the door broke her from her thoughts. Without hesitation, Kimbery jumped up and swung open the door to reveal a smiling Iris holding a bag of takeout against her chest.

Behind her stood Amelia and Heath, both looking relieved to see Kimbery safe. In her peripheral vision, she saw Liam pulling into the driveway.

"You're a lifesaver, Iris love," Kimbery said as she hugged her friend tightly before ushering them inside. "Come on in guys, it's freezing out there." She closed the door behind Liam and led them to the mini dining area.

As they settled in, Liam wasted no time in getting down to business. "Where's your sim card?" he asked pointedly, causing Kimbery to pause mid-sip of water.

"You just got here, dude."

"The earlier the better," Liam replied coolly.

Heath looked up from the takeout bag he was rummaging through and gave a wary glance to Liam and Kimbery. "Sim? What's going on?"

"We're trying to retrieve pictures from my sim card," said Liam, pulling out a USB sim card reader and his laptop. "They were taken at the church before my phone was destroyed."

"How is that possible?" Amelia asked, rubbing her chin in thought.

"It's worth a shot," said Kimbery, handing her sim card over to Liam.

Liam quickly inserted the sim into the card reader and connected it to his laptop. His hands shook with anticipation as he searched for any pictures from the night at the church. But after multiple attempts, there was nothing. He tried searching for pictures from the day before and after with no luck. It was a dead end.

"Any success?" Kimbery asked anxiously.

"No, I can't..." Liam was cut off by a loud notification beep coming from Iris's side of the room.

"Looks like you've got mail, Kim," Iris chimed in, still tapping away on Kimbery's phone.

"I couldn't find anything," finished Liam as Kimbery made her way over to Iris. He closed his laptop and watched as Kimbery scrolled through her mailbox.

"I don't understand your obsession with these games," she teased Iris. "Out of all the options, you chose Candy Crush. People stopped playing that ages ago."

"Hey now, mind your own business," retorted Iris playfully.

"That's my phone, damn it! And my private business." she spat back, angrily scrolling through her unread messages. Five notifications lit up her inbox, but only one caught her eye - the one she received after Mass. It was an ominous message, informing her that her iCloud file had been shared with another one of her email addresses.

"Guys, something was automatically uploaded and shared to my iCloud. A video from the night at Mass." Kimbery's voice trembled as she spoke, panic rising in her chest.

The others crowded around her as she clicked on the file. Gasps and curses filled the air as they watched in horror. The 1 minute and 38 second video showed a flock of monstrous crows attacking the congregation during Mass. Everyone was screaming and running for cover as the birds swooped down, scratching and pecking at their faces.

Kimbery stumbled away from the group, face pale with shock. She connected her phone to the main computer in the studio, which was linked to multiple screens around the room. As soon as she hit play, all the screens came to life, displaying the terrifying footage in high definition.

Iris's hands flew to her mouth in disbelief as she watched the chaos unfold. She had heard about the incident, but seeing it firsthand was a whole other level of terror. The priest was shown swatting desperately at the birds, trying to protect himself and his parishioners. But what caught everyone's attention was the mysterious figure lurking behind him, a sinister smirk on their face as they controlled the swarm of killer birds.

The group huddled around the small screen, watching the video with horrified fascination. Kimbery's whispered revelation of Daniela's attire sent shockwaves through them all. Gasps and wide-eyed stares followed as they saw the figure standing behind the priest, a figure that appeared to be Daniela but was distorted in some unfathomable way.

As they continued to watch, a sickening realization set in. The transformation of Daniela's face, from tanned and familiar to ghostly pale and unrecognizable, was only the beginning. In one swift motion, she drew a knife and plunged it into the priest's neck, blood spurting out in a gruesome display.

Kimbery was the first to react, running to the nearest waste bin to empty her stomach as she retched uncontrollably. Amelia could only watch in horror as Daniela continued her brutal act, her blonde hair stained with blood and hiding a face that belonged in nightmares.

The room was filled with screams and cries as they witnessed a cold-blooded murder unfold before their eyes. Even though Amelia tried to look away, her gaze was drawn back to the screen as she saw the priest's head snap back from the force of the attack.

And then, something even more inexplicable happened. The headless body dropped into a bowl of holy water on the table, sending splashes of blessed liquid across the room. Daniela's hand, coated in holy water and blood, revealed burns that mirrored those Amelia had noticed on her cousin's hand just days before.

Silence hung heavy in the air after the video ended. No one dared speak for fear of breaking whatever trance they were caught in. The reality of what they had just watched slowly sunk in, leaving them shaken and speechless.

Amelia finally broke the tense silence. Her voice quavered slightly as she spoke, her eyes haunted with fear. "I believe Daniela's claims that some entity possessed her. The same thing that killed those men in the cemetery." She paused, swallowing hard before continued. "She said it was something grotesque, like a demon. And now, standing here with this monstrous creature in front of us, I can't help but see the truth in her words."

Heath, his usually confident demeanor now shaken, spoke up. "I think it's high time I tell you all everything." He took a deep breath before plunging on, ignoring any objections from the others. "Daniela and I have reason to believe that the Cult of Standish is real. In fact, we know it's real." He glanced around at his friends' stunned expressions before continued. "We stumbled upon their website and learned about a meeting that would be held at the cemetery. We went there for proof for our show." He faltered, his eyes filled with remorse and regret. "But then we heard someone talking about disposing of a body...and a cry for help coming from inside the cemetery. Dani and I split up to investigate and...that's when we found out about the killings."

As he finished his explanation, Heath's gaze met Liam's in silent under-standing. This was all too much for anyone to handle, especially for Liam who had developed feelings for Daniela. Was it harder to accept that the girl he cared for was being tormented by a demonic entity or that the cult he thought was just a myth turned out to be terrifyingly real? With a heavy heart, Liam sank back into his chair with a defeated sigh, unsure of what steps to take next in this dangerous and harrowing situation.

"I can't even begin to comprehend this." Iris said, her voice trembling as she stared at the video of Daniela's possession. "But I have an idea, a risky one, but it might be our only hope. We need to test how far gone her possession truly is. And there's only one thing that might reveal the truth - Holy Water."

Liam sat upright, his eyes widening in shock. "What are you suggesting?"

"We have dinner plans at Maureen's later tonight," Iris continued, her words coming out in a rush of desperation. "We can slip some Holy Water into Daniela's food and see how she reacts. If the demon has a strong hold on her, it will become evident. But if not, she'll just make an excuse and leave the table claiming to feel unwell."

The group exchanged uneasy glances, but the urgency of the situation outweighed their fear.

"Are you certain this is our best course of action?" Kimbery asked.

"I'm positive," Iris replied with unwavering conviction. "We have no other choice."

Liam took charge, mapping out their plan. "Amelia, Heath, go to the church and retrieve some Holy Water. Kimbery and I will go to the police station and try to identify the blonde girl in the video. We need to find out who she was before she became possessed."

"But why do we need to focus on her?" Amelia questions.

"We need answers," Liam explained softly. "If we can uncover the identity of this girl, we may also uncover the reasons behind this demonic possession and the murders it has caused."

The group nodded in agreement, steeling themselves for what lay ahead as they prepared for their dangerous mission to save Daniela's soul and bring an end to the terror that had gripped their town.

With a heavy sigh, Amelia finally resigned to Liam's decision. She knew she couldn't change his mind, no matter how hard she tried. So instead, she turned her focus to the task at hand.

"Iris, I need you to go keep Daniela occupied," Liam instructed. "Amelia says she's alone with Maureen. I'm sure Amelia is worried sick about her mother, even if she doesn't say it."

"Of course," Iris replied without hesitation.

Amelia felt a rush of gratitude towards Liam for taking charge and handling the situation. Her mind had been spinning ever since they started discussing everything that had happened. Now, with Iris looking after Daniela, she could find some peace of mind, albeit temporary. All Amelia could do was hope and pray that things would be resolved soon.

Iris stood in front of the door, her heart pounding with fear and anticipation. She said a silent prayer, not for herself but for her friend Maureen. She was afraid to go inside, afraid that she would find Maureen hurt by the demon they were about to confront. But she had promised to be here, and so she knocked on the door with a trembling hand.

The door opened after what felt like eternity, and Maureen stood in front of her with a wide grin.

"Iris! My darling. Merry Christmas." Her warm embrace dispelled Iris's fears momentarily.

"Merry Christmas, Maureen." Iris replied, letting out a sigh of relief.

"How are you doing?" Maureen asked, concern evident in her voice.

"Could be better. But I can't complain," Iris replied with a forced smile.

"Come on in, love. I'm so glad you came." Maureen stepped aside to let Iris enter.

As she hung her coat on the hanger, Iris couldn't help but inhale deeply. The scent of home-cooked holiday food filled the air and calmed her nerves.

"I can't wait to bury my fingers into everything, Maureen. The whole place smells divine," Iris said with genuine enthusiasm as she followed Maureen into the kitchen.

"Oh, Dani is around somewhere," Maureen said as she checked on the dishes cooking on the stove.

"Daniela!" She called out, and a young girl with dark hair popped her head out from behind the counter.

"Hi Dani." Iris greeted her cautiously.

"Hi," Daniela replied coolly before disappearing back into the kitchen.

The tension between them was palpable. They were both here for one purpose- to confront the demon who had been haunting their lives. And now it was time to face it head-on.

Iris's heart sank as she looked at the person in front of her. This wasn't her friend, Daniela. The real Daniela would have been jumping with excitement, eager to hear all about Iris's trip. But this impostor merely said a half-hearted "hi" and sat nonchalantly on the couch. Iris had to stay strong, she couldn't let this thing take her friend away.

"We have a lot to catch up on," she said, trying to sound casual as she motioned for Daniela to join her in the living room.

As their mutual friend Maureen disappeared into the kitchen, Iris inspected this stranger in her friend's body. Something was off, and every word she wanted to say faded from her mind. She could only hope that the real Daniela was fighting to come back.

"What's new?" she asked, trying to break the awkward silence.

"Nothing," came the flat response.

"Nothing? After all this time apart? Come on, girl, don't leave me hanging."

"There's nothing. I've been stuck here."

Iris quickly shifted gears, hoping to get some answers. "I heard the detective has a crush on you. And you conveniently forgot to mention it."

"Yeah, he does," Daniela replied monotonously.

"Now spill the details. Is he finally 'the one'?"

"He's alright. Maybe. I don't know. I want to take things slow...there's just too much on my mind right now." A dark shadow crossed Daniela's face before she stared blankly ahead again. Iris didn't know what was going on, but she knew something wasn't right with her friend.

Iris paced back and forth, frustration building with each passing moment. Daniela seemed more interested in her phone than the missing persons case they were supposed to be working on. But just as Iris was about to voice her annoyance, the sound of the front door creaking open filled the air. Her heart leaped at the sound of Amelia's voice, accompanied by Heath's. Finally, some progress.

Amelia made a conscious effort to avoid Daniela and Iris as she entered the house with Heath. She couldn't face them knowing what they had planned. In secret, she and Heath had obtained Holy Water from the church and spiked the pumpkin pie in the fridge with it. And as she closed the door, she caught sight of her mother digging through the pantry with determination. Hurriedly, Amelia retrieved the bottle from her purse and added Holy Water to the soup and tomato sauce. They couldn't risk everything on just one dish.

With their plan in motion, all that was left was to wait.

Kimbery slumped into Liam's chair with exhaustion, rubbing her tired eyes. Hours at the police station had yielded no results in their search for missing persons. Every lead ended in disappointment - either the girl they found wasn't who they were looking for or the pictures provided were nowhere close to resembling the victim.

"Any luck?" Liam asked wearily, eyes still glued to his computer screen.

"Not yet," Kimbery sighed, leaning back in her chair. "This is a never-ending maze."

Liam's heart ached with every item he picked up from his desk, trying to distract himself from the crushing reality that the girl he thought was worth waiting for was now possessed by an angry demon. His phone buzzed in his pocket, a message from Amelia tinged with urgency. Dinner was ready, but Liam couldn't bring himself to leave just yet.

"Liam!" Kimbery's voice broke through his thoughts.

He answered absentmindedly, unable to shake the image of his perfect girl now being controlled by a malevolent entity.

"I just spoke to Lindsey. She's pretty sure Rachel is the one who took over Dani's body."

"Pretty sure? That's not enough."

"I know, but I can feel it in my bones. Lindsey mentioned Rachel had a hair appointment before she disappeared and hasn't been seen since."

Amelia's text flashed on his screen again, a stark reminder that dinner was waiting and they needed to hurry.

"God, I am dreading the next few hours."

"Me too, Kim. Me too." Liam's voice trembled as the weight of their impending confrontation settled heavily on his shoulders.

The sweet scent of food lingered in the air, mingled with an unspoken tension that hung over the family. Maureen sat at the head of the dining table, flanked by her daughter Amelia and her son Heath. On the opposite end sat Daniela, her wild eyes fixated on the chicken as if she hadn't eaten in days.

"Shall someone say grace?" Maureen asked, breaking through the awkward silence. Before anyone could respond, Daniela reached out and tore into a piece of chicken with ferocity. She devoured it quickly and grabbed for another piece, tearing it apart with her bare hands. The others watched in shock as Daniela wolfed down the entire bowl of chicken without saying a word.

Maureen's mouth hung open in disbelief, but before she could scold her niece, Amelia's hand tightened around her wrist. "Don't," she mouthed to her mother, who reluctantly leaned back in her chair.

As they sat in awe, the lights above Daniela began to flicker on and off. Even Amelia's usually calm demeanor couldn't hide her fear as she held onto her mother's wrist tightly.

When Daniela demanded more food, Amelia quickly led her mother into the kitchen to get some. "What is happening? Why is she acting like this?" Maureen whispers to Amelia once they were alone.

"I don't know, Mum," Amelia replied with worry etched on her face. They both knew something was not right with Daniela, something dark and sinister. And they were about to find out just how deep it ran.

"Mum, you need to listen to me and go with the flow. You may not understand now, but you will soon. Just trust me, everything is fine," Amelia pleaded with her mother as she nervously paced around the kitchen.

But Maureen was not convinced. "Not like this, she's not! I want to have a word with that young lady," she spat back.

Amelia's heart raced as she tried to come up with a plan.

"Mother, please. We'll talk about it after dinner, okay? We have guests over," she said, hoped her mother would take the bait.

Reluctantly, Maureen carried out the tray of ribs while Amelia followed with potatoes and her mother's special basil veggie soup - Daniela's favorite meal. She hoped that her cousin would at least eat something.

But as soon as Daniela saw the food, she tore into it without using utensils and covered in BBQ sauce. The others at the table watched in shock and disgust as she continued to stuff her face without a care in the world. Even when Amelia tried to suggest getting dessert, everyone backed away from the table in fear.

Amelia could feel her anxiety rising as she realized there was no controlling Daniela's behavior. She exchanged panicked looks with Iris and Heath who also seemed on edge.

Desperate for some sense of normalcy, Amelia forced a smile and suggested getting pie for dessert. But as Maureen hesitated, Daniela reached for the bowl of soup causing everyone to quickly retreat from their seats.

In that moment, things were spiraling out of control and there was nothing they could do to stop it. All they could do was watch in terror as Daniela devoured everything in sight."

Maureen's throat closed up with unspoken protests as she reluctantly followed her daughter into the kitchen. Her heart shattered like broken glass as she left the dining area behind, the remnants of their disastrous dinner still littering the table. Her niece's behavior was that of a savage, a side of her she had never seen before. The kitchen felt suffocating, and as she turned to leave, the door slammed shut behind her, trapping her inside.

A familiar voice whispered in her ear, causing a cold shiver to run down her spine. "Go outside," it commanded. "Kimbery is waiting in the car. Go be with her."

Maureen's mouth was covered by a strong hand, its grip tight and stifling. She spun around to see Liam and Amelia standing behind her, their eyes pleading with her to comply. Confused and afraid, Maureen didn't dare ask questions. Taking her jacket from Amelia's outstretched hand, she hurried outside through the back door, not looking back as fear consumed her heart

Completely focused on her bowl of soup, Daniela was oblivious to the chaos erupting around her. The steaming liquid burned her throat as she gulped it down, trying to ignore the searing pain. Suddenly, the soup splashed onto her delicate red lace top, causing her to gasp and jerk back. With a loud clatter, the bowl crashed to the ground and shattered into countless shards. A sharp agony coursed through her body, causing her to shake uncontrollably and let out a piercing scream that seemed to echo with the voices of a dozen men.

The lights in the room exploded one by one as Daniela's screams grew louder and more ferocious. Plates flew off the table and smashed against the walls, while a frigid chill crept through the air, freezing everything in its path.

In a fit of manic strength, Daniela grabbed the table with both hands and flipped it over, barely missing trapping Iris and Heath underneath. The two cowered under the debris as they watched in horror as their friend continued to shriek, her voice now thundering like an army marching towards battle.

The Christmas tree, once adorned with sparkling ornaments and twinkling lights, now became a projectile hurtling towards them with deadly force. Pine needles littered the floor as the tree slammed into the wall, leaving behind a trail of destruction.

"Snap out of it!" Iris screamed at Daniela amidst the chaos, but another deafening shriek drowned her words out.

Frantically crawling away from their possessed friend, Heath and Iris could only watch in terror as their cozy holiday gathering turned into a nightmare before their very eyes.

Amelia stood frozen in terror, her eyes locked on the kitchen door where her cousin Daniela stood possessed by a dark and powerful force. The rage emanating from Daniela was unlike anything Amelia had ever witnessed, sending shivers down her spine.

As Daniela slowly made her way towards Amelia, panic set in and she tried to run but found herself rooted to the spot. Daniela's hand shot out and grasped Amelia's throat, lifting her off the ground effortlessly. With wide eyes, Amelia saw her feet dangling helplessly as she struggled for air.

A hoarse voice echoed through Daniela's mouth, accusing Amelia of betrayal and threatening death. A sudden gust of wind picked up, tossing objects around the room with violent force.

Liam rushed forward to rescue Amelia but a single glance from Daniela paralyzed him, his leg giving out with a sickening crack. Heath attempted to intervene as well, but Daniela's strength was too great and he couldn't break her hold on Amelia's neck.

Heath tried to intervene but was no match for Danielale's strength. She held onto Amelia's neck like a vice, ignoring Heath's attempts to pry her away.

A blood-curdling scream erupted from Daniela's throat and Amelia felt the pressure around her neck suddenly release. Daniela fell to the ground, writhing and screaming in agony. Behind her stood Iris, holding a shattered bottle that once contained holy water. In a panic, Amelia reached into her purse and grabbed two needles, plunging them into Daniela's back.

The screams turned into pitiful whimpers as Daniela fell unconscious to the ground. As Iris cried out in shock and confusion, Amelia couldn't help but wonder what other horrors awaited them in this battle against evil.

Amelia gasps for air, her breaths ragged and shallow as she collapses onto the ground. "Tranquilizers," she whispered through gritted teeth. "I injected her...with tranquilizers."

"Well, at least we know it works." Iris said grimly, her eyes fixed on the monstrous being now lying still. "But how do we rid ourselves of a Demon?" Her voice wavered with fear and desperation as Amelia crawled over to Liam to make sure he was okay.

Every second that passes feels like an eternity, the danger growing more palpable by the second. They're running out of options and time, and Iris knows that their lives hang in the balance.

Chapter Fifteen

Maureen's eyes were wide with shock and fear as she turned to her daughter Amelia, her voice trembling as she asked, "What just happened, Amelia?"

Amelia's usually calm demeanor was replaced by a sense of urgency as she replied, "Mum, I need you to take a deep breath and sit down. I'll make some tea and then I'll explain everything."

But Maureen refused to be placated, her emotions running high as she exclaimed, "Don't you dare tell me to calm down and have some tea! I want answers right now. How could Daniela be responsible for all of this? And you expect me to just sit and relax?"

Amelia took a deep breath before answered, "I know it's hard to believe, but Daniela has been possessed by some demonic force."

Maureen's hand flew to her mouth in shock. She stumbled backwards and sunk into the nearest chair, trying to process this new information. "What? How? When did this happen? Why?" Her questions tumbled out in a jumble of confusion and fear. Amelia placed a comforting hand on her mother's shoulder as she calmly repeated, "I told you to sit down and calm down. I'll explain everything."

The tremors of fear and shock shook through Maureen's body as she listened to Amelia recount the events that had unfolded in their small town. The mention of a cemetery incident, a real-life cult, and multiple deaths sent chills down her spine. She could feel her heart racing as she struggled to process it all.

She imagined the eerie silence that must have fallen over the cemetery when Heath and Daniela stumbled upon a body. The thought of those men being killed, possibly by the hands of this mysterious missing girl, only added to the dread in her chest.

"The hospital? For God's sake what is wrong with you children? Call them and tell them to take her to the church," Maureen pleaded, her voice quivering with fear. She knew that the church was the safest place to be in times like these.

As Amelia continued speaking, Maureen weakly stood up from her chair, feeling dizzy and disoriented. The weight of all these revelations was almost too much for her to bear. She stumbled towards the home phone, desperately trying to wrap her head around everything.

A part of her wanted to deny it all, to reject these seemingly unbelievable theories. But deep down, another part of her knew that something sinister was brewing in their town. Too many strange occurrences had been happening lately, too many unanswered questions.

With trembling fingers, she dialed Father Thom Sendry's number, hoping that he could make sense of it all. As she waited for him to answer, she prayed that he would have a solution before it was too late.

Liam's knuckles were white as he gripped the steering wheel, his mind a whirlwind of panic and confusion. It was Christmas Day, meant for joy and celebration, but he found himself driving through the snowy streets with a possessed woman in the backseat. His love interest, Daniela, lay unconscious between two other passengers - Iris and Heath - who were also grappling with this unexpected turn of events. Kimbery sat beside Liam in the front, her concerned gaze never leaving him.

As they approached the church after receiving a message from Amelia, Liam berated himself for not thinking of it sooner. Thankfully, Father Sendry had been briefed on their predicament by Maureen. With just two blocks left to go, the car suddenly jerked and came to a stop. Liam cursed under his breath as he tried to restart it, but all attempts failed.

"What's going on?" Iris asked anxiously.

"I have no idea," Liam replied through gritted teeth. "The car won't start. I'll check under the hood."

He stepped out into the biting cold, snowflakes falling gently onto his shoulders. As he opened the hood, a cloud of smoke billowed out - an alarming sight considering there was no reason for the engine to over-heat. He went to Kimbery's window to report his findings.

"The engine is overheated," he said, trying to keep his voice steady. "I don't know why."

"Can you fix it?" Kimbery asked with concern.

"I...I'm not sure," Liam stammers as he frantically searched for a solution. Panic rose in his chest as he realized they were running out of time to save Daniela from whatever demonic force had taken hold of her.

Liam struggled with the smoking engine as Heath approached. The snow he grabbed from the side of the road offered a glimmer of hope, but Liam's strained eyes couldn't see what was causing the car to over-heat. Suddenly, a movement behind him startled him.

"Let me see." Heath said, startling Liam even more.

"Come on, man! You scared the crap out of me." Liam replied, trying to calm his racing heart.

"I'm sorry. I took a mechanic course for fun in school. Turns out it wasn't such a waste after all." Heath explained, examining the engine.

"Thanks, man." Liam said gratefully.

As the two men delved into the hood of the car to locate the source of the smoke, Kimbery turned to Iris who was still seated in the back. Clutching a rosary tightly in her hand, she seemed calm for someone trapped in a car with a possessed girl. Kimbery didn't think she had that kind of strength and bravery within her. Even sitting up front, she was trembling at the thought of what could happen if Rachel took control again.

Iris pulled on her rosary, murmuring Hail Marys under her breath as she waited for Heath and Liam to work their magic on the car. She felt a sense of peace and calm wash over her. There was no use panicking in this situation. It wouldn't solve anything or bring Daniela back. Instead, she focused on maintaining a level head and hoping for the best. She knew Daniela would do the same for them if they were in this predicament.

Heath's heart raced as he peered down into the smoking engine one last time. But this time, he saw it - a small flicker of fire nestled between the chords. Without hesitation, he grabbed handfuls of snow and frantically tried to smother the flames. After the third scoop, the fire finally went out. But as he reached in to check for any further damage, something caught his hand and held it in a tight grip.

"Shit. I'm stuck," Heath grunted, panic rising in his chest.

"What's going on?" Liam asked, rushing over to help free his friend's trapped arm. They pulled and tugged with all their might until finally, Heath's hand was released, bringing with it a half-burnt photograph.

"What is that?" Liam asked, squinting at the image in confusion.

"It's...it's Amelia," Heath gasps, shocked by the unexpected discovery.

"But why would her photo be in your car?" Liam questions, studying the date stamp on the back of the picture.

"This doesn't make sense," Heath mutters, his mind racing.

"This photo was taken way before I even came into town."

"And yet here it is," Liam stated grimly. "Something is definitely not right."

Before they could contemplate any further, Heath's thoughts turned to Amelia. "She's in trouble," he said firmly, slamming the bonnet shut and sprinting towards his car.

Inside, Kimbery and Iris were unconscious while Daniela was nowhere to be found. The realization hit Heath like a punch to the gut - someone had taken Amelia and now they had Daniela too.

"We have to find them," Heath said urgently, determination burning in his eyes as he jumped into the driver's seat and peeled away from the scene with Liam by his side. Time was running out and they needed to save their friends before it was too late.

Amelia's phone rang and she answered eagerly, hoping it was her friend Heath. "Heath! Did you make it to the church?" she asked.

"Amelia, where did you leave your phone?!" Heath's voice sounded frantic.

"I was in the bathroom. Why are you so worked up?"

"Just listen to me, Daniela is missing and I have a bad feeling she's coming back for you."

Amelia's heart began to race with fear. "What do you mean? How did she go missing?"

"The car broke down and we found your picture burned in the engine. There's no time to explain, get out of there now."

Amelia hung up and rushed to her mother's room, panic rising in her chest. She grabbed a large trench coat and scarf for her mother and urged her to get ready to leave.

"What's going on?" Maureen asked, concern etched on her face.

"Heath just called. Daniela is missing and she could be dangerous when she gets here."

Amelia's hands shook as she grabbed the keys to her mother's car. They needed to get to safety, fast. The police station was their best bet, but Amelia knew it would be closed for Christmas. She sped down the snowy path towards the station, fear gripping her chest.

As they pulled into the driveway, a figure stood in their way. Daniela, Rachel's accomplice. Panic surged through Amelia as she crashed into the police parking wall. Her mother lay unconscious beside her and Amelia knew she had to act quickly. Without hesitation, she grabbed her purse and fled, leaving her mother behind.

The icy streets mirrored Amelia's racing thoughts as she sprinted towards the ice-cream shop where she worked. She fumbled with her keys and finally got the door open, adrenaline pumping through her veins.

With the alarm disabled and no one around, Amelia found sanctuary under a table in the backroom. She could only pray that Heath would find her message in time. Alone and vulnerable, Amelia waited in silence, listening for any sign of danger.

Suddenly, her phone lit up with a text from Heath, telling her he was on his way. Relief washed over her as she clung to her phone, knowing that someone was coming for her. But until then, she was on her own against Rachel and Daniela's wrathful vengeance.

Amelia's heart hammered against her chest like a caged animal, each beat echoing in her ears as she sat frozen behind the table. The suffocating silence only amplified the sound of her breath, a frantic gasping that sounded like a hurricane compared to the stillness around her.

Suddenly, a loud creak shattered the quiet and Amelia's body jolted in fear. She tried to brush it off as just the pipes or her imagination, but then she heard it again - closer this time.

As the backdoor began to shake violently, Amelia's phone screen illuminated with an incoming call. But she couldn't risk moving or making any noise that could draw Rachel's attention. She knew the deranged woman was prowling above her on the table, ready to strike with her sharp, claw-like nails. All it would take was one wrong move from Amelia and she would be torn apart.

Blood dripped onto the floor with a sickening plop, drawing Amelia's eyes down in horror as she realized Daniela was right above her on the desk. Every instinct screamed at her to run, but she remained frozen in terror under the table, completely unaware of Rachel's looming presence above her.

In that moment, Amelia's heart pounded in her chest as she heard another sound coming from the front door. Her breath caught in her throat and she prayed for whoever it was to be a savior. She hoped that the noise would distract Rachel, who hovered above her like a sinister shadow. With trembling fingers, Amelia traced a quick sign of the cross and mustered every ounce of courage to crawl out from under the desk.

As she emerged, she let out a sigh of relief but it quickly turned into terror when she saw there was no one on the table where Rachel had been moments ago. Panic rising in her chest, Amelia sprinted towards the front of the store and tears of joy streamed down her face when she saw Heath standing there. She ran into his arms, seeking safety and comfort.

"Where's Daniela?" he asked urgently.

"I don't know," Amelia replied, her voice shaking with fear. "I'm not sure. She was right on top of the table before you came."

Heath's brows furrowed in confusion and concern. "I really don't understand, Amelia. Why is she after you? And who is this Rachel person?"

Amelia's body stiffened at the mention of Rachel's name, her eyes betraying her fear and guilt.

"I don't know," she said defensively, but her expression gave away her deception.

"Now is not the time for lies," Heath stated sternly. "What did you do?"

Tears continued to stream down Amelia's face as she confessed through sobs. "I swear I haven't done anything wrong... or at least I didn't think so until a few days ago." She took a deep breath before continued. "It was about a year after my dad passed away when money became extremely tight for my mom and me. Even though I was working at the hospital, we were barely making ends meet."

Her voice trembled as she recounted the events that led to this dangerous situation. "I was working one day when a man approached me. I had never seen him before. He offered to make a sizable donation for my help. All he wanted was information on where certain drugs were kept in the hospital."

Amelia's confession hung heavy in the air, her fear and guilt consuming her. She didn't know what else to say or do except cling onto Heath, hoping he would protect her from the consequences of her desperate actions.

Heath's eyes flashed with anger as he interrupted Amelia, grabbing her by the shoulders and shaking her violently. "What drugs?" he demanded.

Tears streamed down Amelia's face as she confessed, her voice trembling. "Anaesthetics...sleeping aides...I didn't know if it was illegal to give that information. But I needed the money for myself and my mom."

Heath's grip tightened, his voice low and menacing. "That's how you were recruited into the Cult of Standish. And now your cousin is possessed because of it."

Amelia's heart dropped as Heath whispers in her ear, his words dripping with accusation. "It's your fault."

She couldn't believe what she was hearing. "What did you say?"

"It's your entire fault," Heath repeated, a smug smile playing on his lips.

Amelia took a step back in shock, but Heath followed, his hands still gripping her shoulders tightly. "The drugs you told them about were used to sedate Rachel. They allowed for her to be raped, scarified."

As the truth sank in, Amelia felt sick to her stomach. How could she have been so blind? How could she have unknowingly contributed to such horror?

But before she could fully process her guilt, Heath continued to taunt her, his voice rising to a yell. He shook her even harder, his fingers digging into her skin. "Your fault!" he screamed in her face.

Amelia stumbled backwards, fear and regret consuming her as she realized the magnitude of her actions. She had unknowingly played a part in Rachel's suffering, and now it was too late to undo it.

Amelia felt a pair of hands grab her from behind, pinching into her arms with a vice-like grip. She struggled against the unseen force until she could turn around and come face-to-face with Rachel's twisted and contorted visage. A primal fear rose within her as she spun around in search of Heath, only to find him gone. With dawning horror, Amelia realized that it had been Rachel all along, manipulating events and playing them like puppets.

Before she could even react, Rachel lunged forward and grabbed Amelia by the throat, lifting her effortlessly off the ground. An insane grin spread across Rachel's face as she lifted her other hand, revealing razor-sharp claws that glinted in the dim light. With a vicious swipe, she slashed at Amelia's exposed shoulder, causing blood to gush out in a painful torrent. The searing agony caused Amelia to scream in terror and pain as Rachel dropped her to the ground like a rag doll.

Gasping for air and clutching her bleeding shoulder, Amelia finally realized the true extent of the danger she was in. "This...this can't be happening," she gasped out in disbelief.

"Oh but it is," Rachel sneers, her eyes glowing with an unholy light. "I want you to feel every ounce of pain and suffering that your drugs have allowed them to inflict on me."

With superhuman strength, Amelia forced herself to her feet and stumbled towards the door, desperate to escape this nightmare. But the relentless pursuit of Rachel continued as she pushed open the heavy door and ran barefoot into the freezing night. Her shoulder throbbed painfully with each step, but she didn't care as long as she could put distance between herself and Rachel.

But just when she thought she might make it out alive, there was a sharp crack followed by an intense spike of pain shooting through her ankle. Amelia's balance faltered and she fell hard onto the icy pavement, hitting her head with a sickening thud. As her vision blurred and darkness closed in, she realized that Rachel had used some sort of supernatural power to trip her up.

As she lay there in agony and fear, Amelia could only pray for someone to come and save her from this living nightmare. But deep down, she knew that this was far from over and that Rachel's twisted games were only just beginning.

Father Thom's heart raced as he watched Amelia's desperate struggle to reach safety. He sped down the road like a madman, his mind reeling with Liam's shocking revelation. This was the same evil that had claimed Father Christopher's life and now it threatened the lives of his congregation.

Slamming on the brakes, he leapt out of the car and sprinted towards her.

Amelia's tears flowed uncontrollably as she saw Father Thom approach, pointing frantically behind her. His eyes followed her trembling finger and his blood ran cold at the sight of Daniela staggering towards them, covered in cuts and scratches, her nails digging into her own flesh. The intense hatred emanating from her eyes chilled him to his core.

"God help us!" Heath cried out as he and Liam rushed to Amelia's side. They had left the church as soon as Father Thom did, dropping off the others at the police station before racing to this very spot to assist their priest.

"Take her to the prayer chapel at the station," Father Thom commanded without hesitation. "You all must stay there until I give further instruction."

Gently lifting Amelia onto her feet, they winced at her pained cries. As they hurried away, Liam couldn't resist stealing a glance back at his beloved Rachel, only to be met with a searing glare of anger. Fearing for their safety, Father Thom brandished his crucifix and strode towards Daniela with determined steps. When he stood mere feet from her, he made the sign of the cross over himself, ready to confront the demonic force within her.

"I command you, unclean spirit! Reveal yourself and your minions who dare attack this holy vessel of God. Speak to me and only me! Tell me your name and your vile mission!"

A wicked grin spreads across Daniela's face before her features contort into the twisted visage of Rachel. "Is this what you wanted? The real me?" she taunts.

"I want to speak to the demon using this servant of God as a puppet! Why do you use her for such destruction?" the priest cries out in desperation.

"Because we are linked. I can control her body and bury her soul, using it as my vessel to carry out my bidding," Rachel replied in a chilling, raspy voice.

"In the name of Jesus, I demand that you vacate this body immediately!" Father Thom commands.

Rachel cackles with bitter amusement. She strides towards the priest and snatches his cross from his trembling hand. "Do you think this trinket has any power over me?" she sneered before pressing it against her forehead. In an instant, smoke billows out from under the cross as Rachel screams in agony. Her body begins to melt, pooling into a grotesque mixture of water and blood on the floor.

With a shock, Father Thom whirls around, searching for Rachel. But before he can fully comprehend what is happening, he feels a freezing grip close around his ankle. He winces in pain as the icy hand solidifies, trapping him in place. As he falls to the ground, he sees blood-stained footprints leading off into the snowy night, heading towards the police station.

Chapter Sixteen

As Liam and Heath burst through the creaky door of the police station, Amelia clung to them tightly, her broken ankle sending waves of searing pain with each step. Her piercing cries echoed through the corridors, reaching even the farthest rooms.

Maureen was sitting in the office Liam had put Kimbery and herself in when she heard her daughter's screams. Panic seized her heart as she recognized Amelia's voice and she broke away from Kimbery's comforting hug, rushing towards the source of the screams. A cry escaped her throat when she saw her daughter's battered form.

"What happened to my baby girl?" Maureen wailed, tears streaming down her face.

"It was Daniela," Heath replied grimly. "Or rather, Rachel - the girl who possessed Daniela. She tried to kill Amelia."

Maureen's confusion only deepened at this revelation. "Why? Why would this girl want to hurt my daughter? What have we done wrong?"

Amelia watched her mother's grief-stricken state with a heavy heart. She longed to tell everyone the truth about her involvement in the town's infamous cult, how she had been an unwilling participant. But the intense pain in her chest kept her from speaking.

"Don't worry Maureen," Liam said sternly, placing a comforted hand on her shoulder. "We'll figure this out and stop Rachel once and for all."

The sound of heavy footsteps echoed through the station, drawing concerned looks from the officers. Liam was back, with three others in tow. They all had a sense of urgency, but their faces were etched with worry.

It had been a chaotic night already, with Liam and the sudden influx of frightened people. But no one dared to ask questions, not when it was just the few officers left on duty. However, with an injured girl, Detective Blake knew there was no avoiding explanations now. He led Officer Huntley and Joy to join Liam.

"Care to tell us what's going on, Liam?" Blake asked sternly.

"We need to get this girl to the hospital."

Liam's face darkened as he hesitated before responding.

"There's too much going on for me to explain right now. Just know that someone...or something...is after us. It's not safe for Amelia or any of us to go to the hospital." Before he could elaborate, the lights in the station flickered

erratically.

"Damn it!" Liam cursed, his eyes scanning the room.

"Everyone, we have to move fast. Head to the chapel and stay there until it's safe."

The other officers wasted no time, scrambling towards the hallway. But Detective Blake remained rooted in place, holding out a hand to stop Liam.

"Liam," he demanded firmly. "What exactly is happening?"

"Listen, detective. This is bigger than you or your badge. We'll explain everything, but right now we need to get to safety before it's too late,"

Heath growled, his eyes filled with urgency and fear as he pulled Detective Blake aside.

But Blake was determined to know the truth. He couldn't just let this go. "I'm not leaving until I have answers," he asserted, even as Liam tried to coax him towards the backdoor.

As they made their way down the dimly lit hallway, every creak and rustle sent shivers down their spines. It felt like an eternity until they finally reached the halfway point, but then a loud sound echoed through the corridor - someone had activated the building's public address system.

"Daniela..." Liam whispers, his voice trembling with fear. But suddenly her demand rang out through the speakers: "Hand that girl over to me or I will take you all down."

Detective Blake's blood boiled at the audacity of someone threatening law enforcement in their own station. Despite Liam's insistent pleas for them to keep moving, Blake refused to budge.

"Liam, go on ahead. I'll stay and find out who is behind this and what their agenda is," Blake commands, calling Officer Huntley to join him.

"Fucking listen to me, Blake!" Liam cried out in frustration.

"This is not something to play hero with. Let's just get to the chapel and figure things out from there."

But Detective Blake was determined to get to the bottom of this threat once and for all. He wouldn't back down no matter what dangers awaited him.

Blake's heart pounded, fear and adrenaline coursing through his body as he and Huntley frantically ran through the dark, deserted streets. Liam's warning echoed in his mind, the words sending chills down his spine. This wasn't just any criminal they were after - it was a supernatural being. Blake couldn't deny the terror that gripped him at the thought.

Suddenly, they came to a stop, and Blake could see the outline of a figure in front of them. His instincts screamed at him to turn and run, but he forced himself to stay rooted to the spot. Liam's urgent voice broke through the silence, pleading with him to listen, but Blake knew they couldn't waste any more time. He had to see for himself what they were dealing with.

With a deep breath, Blake pushed past Huntley and approached the figure cautiously. As he got closer, he could see Liam's gun and rosary clutched tightly in his hand. The realization hit him like a ton of bricks - Liam believed in this supernatural threat. And if someone as rational and level-headed as Liam was scared, then there must be some truth to it.

Tension hung thick in the air as they continued their search, each step bringing them closer to danger. Every shadow seemed to hide a lurking evil waiting to pounce on them. But they pressed on, determined to find Daniela before it was too late.

Time seemed to stand still as they made their way towards the chapel where Amelia and Maureen were waiting for them. The only sounds were their own hurried footsteps and Liam's constant prayers under his breath.

Finally, they reached the safety of the chapel, relief flooding over them as they reunited with their team. But Liam's remorseful expression caught Blake's attention once again. He couldn't help but wonder how much more danger they would face before this night was which is why he decided Huntly and himself would take first watch.

Heath had to hold back tears as Amelia's pained cries filled the air as she was lifted up. Despite everything she had already endured, she somehow managed to stay conscious. As they entered the chapel with Officer Joy by their side, Iris and Kimbery rushed over to help them settle Amelia on a pew for some much-needed rest.

Maureen couldn't contain her emotions as she saw her daughter's injured state, tears streaming down her face. "Oh my dear child, what has happened to you?!" she exclaimed in a hushed voice. "I don't understand any of this. Please, someone explain it to me," she pleaded, turning to Heath for answers.

"It's going to be okay," Heath reassured her.

"I demand an explanation! What is going on? I want to know every-thing, every single detail," Maureen demanded, desperation lacing her words.

"I wish I could tell you. It all started when Daniela stumbled upon a hidden website during her project. We discovered that the cult we thought was just a rumor is actually real. And since then, we've been in constant danger," Heath explained.

"Oh my God," Maureen breathed out in shock and disbelief. The severity of the situation finally sinking in as she processed the information.

The dim lights in the hallway flickered intermittently as Blake and Huntley made their way back to the station. The air was thick with a pungent stench, causing both men to struggle for breath as they entered the building. The smell of dried blood and dirt hung heavy in the air, seeping into every crevice and permeating their senses.

Huntley pulled out his flashlight, the beam cutting through the dark-ness like a knife, as they neared the station. He quickly did a sweep of the room, but there was no one in sight. A sudden cracking noise from behind him made him spin around, his heart racing. He signaled to Blake, who was checking closets, that he would be back and cautiously approached the cracked window.

As he stood there staring at it, the crack began to widen and spread on its own before abruptly stopping. A chill ran down Huntley's spine as he realized something supernatural was happening here. He turned at the sound of movement behind him and saw an outline of a girl standing just a few feet away, her features blurred and indistinct.

"Hello?" Huntley called out, but received no response. "Are you injured?"

Still met with silence, he tried again. "Do you need help?"

But the figure remained motionless, almost ethereal in her stillness. Huntley felt a wave of fear wash over him as he slowly approached her, calling out once more. Despite his proximity, she did not move or respond in any way. It was like she was frozen in time.

Huntley couldn't shake off the feeling of unease as he stood facing this mysterious girl who seemed to defy all logic and reason.

Detective Blake's heart raced as a ghostly voice echoed through the empty station. Against his better judgement, he followed the sound, leaving the safety of the closets he had been searching. As he approached, he could feel an eerie chill creeping up his spine.

Both Blake and Officer Huntley stood on opposite sides of the deserted station, their guns drawn and ready for whatever lay ahead. But nothing could have prepared them for what they saw next.

A figure stood before them, unmoving and unresponsive to their commands. The dim light from Blake's flashlight revealed a face that sent shivers down his spine: Daniela. But this was not the Daniela they knew - her eyes were black as midnight, half of her face covered in blood and raw, pink patches of skin peeking through the wrinkled flesh.

As if sensing their fear, Daniela's hands transformed into claw-like appendages, dripping with fresh blood onto the floor. A primal instinct took over Blake as he cautiously approached her, gun still aimed at her.

But it was too late. Liam had been right all along - this was no ordinary person. This was something else entirely. And now Blake and Huntley were caught in its grasp.

With a sinking feeling in his gut, Blake knew they were in serious danger. He should have listened to Liam's warnings instead of foolishly dragging himself and his officer into this nightmare. But it was too late to turn back now. All he could do was pray that they would make it out alive.

"Get down!" the man yells, his voice laced with urgency as he pulled his companion to the ground. Shards of glass rained down on them from the shattered window above, glinting in the dim light like deadly snowflakes. A sharp pain erupted in the man's shoulder as a piece of glass embedded itself into his skin. With a grunt, he raised his gun, scanning for their unknown attacker but she had disappeared without a trace.

"Let's get out of here!" he barked, grabbing his companion's arm and pulling him to his feet. Blood dripped from the wound on his shoulder, staining his shirt with a deep red. They stumbled towards the exit, adrenaline coursing through their veins as they made their escape from the chaotic scene. "We need to regroup with the others," he panted, trying to catch his breath. "Fuck!"

In the distance, a sharp gunshot pierced through the air and Liam's body immediately drenched in beads of sweat. Panic set in as he sprinted down the hallway, his heart racing with each step. In the midst of it all, he thought he heard someone call his name, but when he stopped to listen, there was only silence. Confused, he scanned his surroundings, trying to make sense of what was happening.

Then, like a whisper carried by the wind, he heard it again - a voice calling out to him. It sounded like Daniela at first, but then it changed into someone else's voice. Still unsure of where it was coming from, Liam stood frozen in the middle of the hallway. His eyes darted back and forth, searching for any sign of the source.

Little did he know, just above him hung Daniela - completely hidden from view. She had been waiting for this moment, hanging upside down on the ceiling like a predator ready to pounce on its prey. As Liam continued to search frantically for the source of the voice, she silently watched and waited for the perfect opportunity to strike.

Wiping the sweat off her brow for what felt like the hundredth time, Iris frantically tried to staunch the flow of blood from Amelia's injury. The once vibrant teenager now lay pale and lifeless on a makeshift bed in the church, while her mother Maureen wept silently beside her. Iris knew that if she didn't act quickly, they would both be lost. She turned to Officer Joy, her voice shaky with desperation.

"Where's the first aid kit?" she asked urgently.

"In the kitchen," he replied, gesturing down the hall.

Without hesitation, Iris sprang into action. "Heath, keep pressure on the wound," she commanded before rushing off to retrieve the kit.

"I don't think that's a good idea, ma'am," Officer Joy protested. "You should stay here and make do with what you have."

"I'll be fine," Iris said stubbornly. "Just take care of everyone here."

As she turned to leave, Kimbery offered to accompany her. But Iris knew that risking one life was enough, and she needed someone to stay and help Heath and Maureen in case something went wrong. With a quick goodbye and a silent prayer, Iris rushed towards the kitchen.

The hallway was dimly lit and eerily quiet. She could hear her own rapid heartbeat as she fumbled for the light switch. Finally finding it, she scanned the room frantically for the first aid kit. There it was, on the counter by the sink. As she grabbed it and turned to leave, a loud crash jolted her heart into overdrive.

She slowly made her way back to the main room, her mind racing with fear and worry for those inside. Before opening the door, she took a deep breath and steeled herself for what might lie ahead. She couldn't afford to lose anyone else today. With trembling hands, she slowly opened the door and stepped inside, ready to face whatever challenges lay ahead.

The hallway was suffocatingly dark and eerily silent as she cautiously made her way back into the station. An unshakable feeling of dread clawed at her insides, urging her to turn back, but she gritted her teeth and pushed on. Turning a corner, she came face to face with Liam, who was frantically searching for something. A sudden movement caught her eye above him, and her heart stopped when she saw Daniela twisted and contorted on the ceiling, glaring down at Liam like a predator ready to strike.

"Liam!" she screamed, striding towards him with determined steps. She tried to act as if she hadn't noticed Daniela above him.

"What are you doing here? Why did you leave the safety of the chapel?" she demanded, coming to a stop in front of him.

"Amelia is badly injured. I need medical supplies to save her," he replied urgently.

"It's too dangerous for you here. You have to go back and wait. I'll get the supplies for you," Iris insisted.

Before Liam could protest further, she took one step closer and embraced him tightly. "Daniela is lurking on the ceiling above you," she whispered into his ear.

"Oh my God, Liam!" Blake's voice echoed down the hallway as he and Huntley approached. Relief washed over them when they saw Liam and Iris together in the corridor.

"What happened?" Liam asked, pointing his gun at Blake's bleeding shoulder.

"It's a long story. I got hurt by that thing," Blake explained through gritted teeth.

"Iris, take Blake to the chapel. Huntley and I will get the supplies," Liam orders, already making his way towards the medical room with Huntley close behind. The tension in the air was thick as they all knew their lives were hanging by a thread in this hellish nightmare they couldn't escape from.

Without warning, Rachel pounced on Huntley like a wild animal, catching everyone off guard. Her claws dug into his neck, drawing blood as she raked them across his skin. Iris grabbed Blake's arm and they ran as fast as they could, the sounds of guttural gurgling and spattering blood echoing in their ears.

Rachel stood triumphantly over Huntley's writhing body, her finger inserted into the deep gash on his neck. She licked the blood off her finger sensually, her eyes locked onto Liam with a seductive gaze.

"Humans..." she sneered. "So useless... a sack of shit!" Her voice rose in anger as she straightened up and focused on Liam. "Give me Amelia and I will spare your pathetic lives."

"Why? Why do you want her?" Liam asked calmly, though fear pulsed through his veins. "Why are you killing all these innocent people?"

"Innocent people?" Rachel scoffs. "This lot? They are far from innocent. No one is innocent. These people deserve every single thing that is coming to them. And more!" She bellowed, her rage palpable.

Suddenly, something caught Rachel's eye - a glinting object approaching at a steady pace. Turning to face it, she saw Kimbery wielding a silver cross. Grinning wickedly, Rachel turned back to Liam, but kept a wary eye on Kimbery.

"We need to get supplies," Kimbery said calmly. "The detective and Amelia are badly injured. I'll stay here while you go retrieve what we need."

"But..." Liam started to protest.

"Go!" Kimbery commanded, holding out the cross as protection against Rachel's demonic strength.

Rachel's eyes burned with a cruel intensity as she stood before Kimbery, brandishing the cross. But Kimbery refused to show any fear in the face of this being. She knew these creatures fed on fear and she was determined not to give it what it wanted. After a few tense minutes, Liam returned from the kitchen with a medical bag in hand. Together, they slowly backed away toward the door leading to the chapel. With each step, Rachel's piercing scream seemed to echo through the air, causing the windows to shudder and crack under its force. Holding tightly onto each other's hands, Liam and Kimbery rushed into the safety of the chapel and slammed the door shut behind them.

As they caught their breaths, Liam turned to Iris and handed her the medical bag. "Is everyone okay?" he asked, his voice full of concern.

Maureen nodded, her eyes wide with shock. "Is Daniela alright?" she asked, worry etched across her features. "It's not her fault, you know."

Liam gave a solemn nod. "I understand," he replied, knowing that there was no use blaming anyone for what had just happened. They were all in this together now, facing an unknown enemy that seemed to be growing stronger by the minute.

Countless hours ticked by as they huddled in the shadows of the chapel, hearts racing with fear and anticipation. The hallway echoed with sinister sounds, but no one dared to move from their hiding spot. Only Liam risked a glance, his eyes met with the lifeless body of Huntley, lying in a pool of his own blood.

Maureen leaned against the cold pew, exhaustion and worry etched into her face. She clutched her rosary tightly, mumbling prayers for Amelia and all those trapped in the chapel. Her mind couldn't help but drift to Daniela, and the unimaginable horrors she must be facing. Suddenly, Maureen's gaze was drawn to the window. Two dark eyes stared back at her through the glass, hands pressed against it and a long tongue licking at the surface. With a loud cry, Maureen jolted everyone out of their thoughts.

"Come out and play with me, Liam," Rachel taunted from outside. "You can't hide forever."

"What the hell is that?" Joy whispers, his voice trembling with fear.

Before Liam could respond, a pungent smell filled their nostrils - something burning. As they watched in horror, Daniela appeared outside, her presence illuminated by a raging fire surrounding the chapel. An evil grin spread across Rachel's lips as she watched them cower like mice before a cat.

Liam's mind raced as he surveyed the burning chapel. They had to escape before it was too late. Every exit was engulfed in flames, except for the front door. "We need to move, now!" he shouted over the roar of the fire.

Panic set in as everyone scrambled to find anything they could use for protection. Liam and Heath picked up Amelia, who was unconscious from smoke inhalation. They made their way towards the front door, with Iris and Maureen following closely behind.

But as they reached the hallway, a glimmer of light caught Liam's eye. The door to the service stairway was slightly ajar, despite being locked earlier. "We have to split up," he said urgently.

"No! We can't leave anyone behind," Iris protested.

"We have no choice. Someone needs to check that door. Iris, go with Heath and help him carry Amelia out through the front door. Maureen and Blake, you go with them. Kimbery, Officer Huntley, and I will check the stairway door. Whoever gets out first, call for help."

Tears streamed down Maureen's face as she prayed fervently while they made their way to the front door. With trembling hands, Heath pushed it open and they were met with fresh air.

"We made it," he whispered in relief.

But their moment of reprieve was short-lived as they heard a loud crash from behind them. Turning around, they saw that the chapel entrance had collapsed into a raging inferno.

"God be with us," Maureen sobs as they ran for their lives. Their footsteps echoed loudly in the empty corridor as they sprinted towards safety. Finally reaching outside, they gasped for air and looked back at their burning sanctuary.

"We're free," Heath said quietly, tears streaming down his face. But their ordeal was far from over as sirens wailed in the distance and they realized the gravity of what had just happened.

Liam sprinted down the hallway, his heart pounding in his chest as he led the group towards the stairway. The others could barely keep up, their footsteps echoing off the walls. Adrenaline surged through Liam's veins as they reached the door, desperately trying to pry it open. He could feel the danger and urgency radiating from the others as Kimbery kept watch behind them.

Just when Liam thought they might have a chance at escape, a pair of skeletal hands burst out of the door, grabbing onto Huntley's arms with a sickening crunch. Before anyone could react, they were dragged into the darkness beyond and the doors slammed shut with a finality that sent chills down Liam's spine.

A pool of crimson liquid oozed out from under the doors, staining the floor and walls. This time, Kimbery's scream echoed through the hallway as she realized they were trapped with whatever lurked on the other side of that door.

Liam's hands grip Kimbery's tightly, his heart racing as they sprint towards the open front door. A sense of dread fills him, knowing that this exit was far too easy for Rachel – she never did anything without a twisted motive. Just as he turns to warn Kimbery, his eyes catch sight of her horrified expression as she stares through the doorway. He turns to see Rachel, with Amelia at her mercy and Daniela kneeling by her side.

Rachel yanks Amelia up by her hair, causing her to scream in pain as her twisted face contorts with malevolent intent. Liam knows that Rachel wants Amelia dead and there is nothing that will stop her from getting what she wants. And the thought that she brought Amelia here just to make sure Liam witnesses her brutal demise sends chills down his spine. She wants to punish Daniela too, and losing Liam is the only way she can think of hurting her. Despite inhabiting Daniela's body, it is clear that Rachel is still in control, giving orders and relishing in the terror she is creating.

As Rachel raises a finger to make cruel incisions on Amelia's face, she hears a familiar voice – Father Thom, the man she had trapped in an ice prison not long ago. A wicked smile crosses her lips at the impressive display of his escape. She knows sparring with him will be entertaining, but first, she must finish off Amelia and send a warning to anyone who dares cross her path.

Rachel released her iron grip on Amelia's hair, causing the girl to collapse onto the ground like a lifeless doll. She watched as Amelia frantically crawled away, but Rachel remained motionless. No matter how far she ran, Rachel knew she would always find her. With a satisfied smirk on her face, Rachel turned to face the trembling Priest. Her eyes glinted with amusement, wondering what tricks he had up his sleeves to combat her demonic powers. As she spoke, her features shifted back into her human form.

"Let's see what you and your God can do," she taunted Father Thom.

He held out his bible in his shaking hand and began reciting passages from the book of Luke. As he read, Rachel started to hyperventilate, her veins bulging under her skin. Her once beautiful face contorted grotesquely, revealing her true demonic nature.

As Thom continued to chant prayers and verses, a ferocious gust of wind whipped through the hallway, knocking everyone off balance. The flames surrounding them grew stronger and more intense, trapping Amelia, Liam, Kimbery, and Thom within their fiery prison. The lights flickered wildly and the entire building shook as if in the grasp of an earthquake.

With unwavering conviction, Thom made the sign of the cross over himself and bravely addressed the demon possessing Daniela. "Father, I beseech your holy name and call upon the power of Christ to cast out this unclean spirit tormenting this innocent child," he declared with authority.

As he spoke these words, Rachel let out blood-curdling screams and thrashed about in agony. But Thom persisted, commanding all satanic and demonic forces to leave in Jesus' name. And just like that, the room was filled with a blinding light as Rachel was exorcised and returned to her human form.

Amelia's words hung in the air, tense and charged with emotion. As she finished speaking, the folder flew out of her trembling hands and into Rachel's firm grasp. The priest had stopped his sermon, sensing the building tension in the small chapel. Rachel flipped open the file with a sense of urgency, her eyes darting across the pages in a blur. But they froze when she reached the photo that Amelia had seen earlier. A look of pure anger and determination flashed across her face as she glared at everyone in the room.

"I will put an end to this once and for all. You haven't seen the last of me, Amelia. I will come back for you and everyone else. I will seek revenge for my death no matter what it takes!" Rachel's voice rang out, fierce and unfaltering.

Suddenly, a strong wind whipped through the chapel, causing papers to fly off tables and knocking people off their feet. Daniela felt herself being pulled down to the ground, but then she began to rise again, hovering midair as flames swirled around her body like a protective shield. Liam and others tried to reach her, but were blocked by the intense heat radiating from the flames. Finally, Rachel pulled herself out of Daniela's body with a final show of strength. She grabbed hold of Daniela's locket - her only link to her former host - before disappearing into thin air. The necklace was her lifeline to controlling Daniela's soul within her own body, and until someone could break that connection, Rachel still had power over her victim.

Mindy Cohen stood hesitantly by the door of the abandoned house, her hand poised to turn the handle. The once magnificent structure had fallen into disrepair, with peeling paint and broken windows giving it a forlorn appearance. It had been months since Marve "the Leech," as most people called him, disappeared and defaulted on his mortgage payments. Now, the house was in possession of the bank, and Mindy had been appointed as the realtor in charge. With trepidation, she stepped inside.

The musty smell of neglect hit her immediately, and she wrinkled her nose in disgust. As she closed the door behind her, she heard a strange scratching sound coming from the living room. She cautiously made her way towards the source of the noise, her heart pounding in her chest. Just as she thought she could make out faint breathing behind the wall, something grabbed her throat from behind.

Panic surged through Mindy as an unseen force threw against the wall her. Her vision swam as she tried to focus on what was happening. With horror, she saw Marve's bloated body emerge from a hole in the wall, his eyes a midnight black and his nails elongated into sharp claws.

Before she could fully comprehend what was happening, Marve's face contorted and shifted until it resembled Rachel's - another victim of his possession. In a swift motion, he threw Mindy aside and snatched her wallet and keys from her bag.

As Rachel strutted out of the house with Mindy's possessions in hand, leaving the unconscious realtor behind, Mindy couldn't help but wonder how many more innocent souls would fall prey to Marve's evil intentions.

CHAPTER SEVENTEEN

As Daniela slowly regained consciousness, she was met with darkness and a throbbing headache. She could feel the coldness of the concrete beneath her and the dampness in the air. As she tried to sit up, her surroundings came into view - an impenetrable wall enclosing her in a claustrophobic space. Fear and confusion set in as she struggled to understand how she had become a prisoner in her own body.

The sound of Liam's voice calling out to her from outside pierced through the silence, but she couldn't find the strength to respond. Exhaustion weighed heavy on her body, leaving her feeling helpless and alone.

Despair washed over Daniela as she sat trapped within herself, unable to fight against the thing that controlled her body. She had been struggling against it for so long, yet it seemed to always prevail. She couldn't fathom why this dark entity had chosen her or where she had gone wrong.

In the darkness, Daniela heard the echo of her cousin's voice seeping through the walls. Her heart sank as Amelia confessed to everything - the cult, the control over their bodies, everything. Tears streamed down

Daniela's face as she listened to Amelia's plan to expose the truth and bring justice for all those who had been affected. But how could Daniela help them if she couldn't even escape this prison? If she wanted to make a difference, she needed to find a way back to them first.

Father Thom stood frozen, fixated on the flickering flames that swallowed up Daniela's small and fragile form. Fear crept into his heart as he realized the demon, Rachel, had left her body but still held some kind of control over it. He could only watch helplessly, unable to approach due to the blazing inferno surrounding her.

Liam's voice broke through his thoughts. "What's happening, Father?"

"I do not know," Father Thom confessed gravely. "The entity has departed from Daniela's vessel, yet she remains tethered to it somehow."

Confusion and desperation seeped into Liam's tone. "What do we do now?"

"Hope. And pray." It was all they could do in this dire situation.

Kimbery's eyes darted between Daniela and the priest before settling back on her burning friend. Hope and prayer had been their only solace throughout this ordeal, but Kimbery couldn't find comfort in them anymore. She had reached her emotional limit, worn down by watching her friend suffer.

She studied Daniela for a moment, searching for any sign of her usual faith and strength. But then she remembered - Daniela always wore a rosary, went to confession regularly, and cherished a special locket. Her thoughts came to a halt as she recalled the locket. Without hesitation, she rushed closer to the fiery barrier.

"Liam, did you see if Daniela had her locket on earlier?" she asked urgently.

"Yes," Liam replied with confusion etched onto his face.

"Did you see it when she was moving just now?"

"No...it must have been lost in the chaos."

Realization hit Kimbery like a ton of bricks. "The locket protected her before...maybe it can help us now!" She desperately searched for any way to reach Daniela or get through the fire.

The flames seemed to intensify at her words, as if the demon was aware of their plan. But Kimbery refused to give up. She had faith that the locket would protect Daniela once again - they just needed to find it.

Liam's brow furrowed in confusion as he tried to understand Kimbery's urgent questioning. He had noticed the locket hanging from her neck earlier, but in the midst of a raging fire and their desperate attempts to escape, it seemed like a trivial matter. "Kim, why are you so worried about a locket? We have bigger things to worry about right now," he said exasperatedly.

"It's not there anymore," Kim responded with a grave tone.

Liam was taken aback. What did that have to do with anything? But before he could voice his thoughts, Kim continued. "It may not seem important, but that locket holds significance. Daniela used to always wear it until she lost it in the park. The same park where Rachel's room-mate saw her going."

Father Thom approached them, intrigued by their conversation. "What are you proposing, my child?" he asked Kim gently.

"I'm saying," Kim began hesitantly, "what if Rachel somehow came into contact with Daniela's locket before she was killed?"

The priest's expression grew serious as he considered this possibility. "It is quite possible for a spirit to possess someone through their personal belongings," he confirmed.

Liam shook his head incredulously. "You can't seriously believe that. Are we really entertaining the idea of ghosts here?"

But Kim was adamant. "Think about it, Liam. It makes perfect sense. And poor Daniela can't confirm or deny anything now."

Desperation filled her voice as she turned to the lifeless body on the ground. "Daniela, please hear me. I know you're in there somewhere, fighting against this possession. Don't give up hope, my love. Don't let her win." She paused, tears glistening in her eyes. "This is your body, and we need you to keep fighting."

Her words echoed in the eerie silence of the room. They all knew it was a long shot, but in this desperate situation, they were grasping at any hope they could find. As they waited for a response that may never come, fear and uncertainty hung heavy in the air.

As Daniela lay in the dark prison cell, she could hear Kimbery's voice whispering to her. Despite her weakened state, she pushed herself up and scanned the room for any means of escape. Her eyes landed on a small hole in the wall, barely visible except for the faint light that seeped through from outside. It reminded her of a similar distortion she had discovered on a website linked to the cult that had led her here.

Meanwhile, Liam was surprised by his phone ringing amidst all the chaos. He hesitated before answering, wondering if it was Rachel taunting him again. To his relief, it was Inspector Murray on the other end.

"Detective McGregor?" the voice asked.

Liam responded, "Who wants to know?"

"It's Inspector Murray."

A sense of dread washed over Liam as he braced himself for bad news.

"Yes, what is it?"

"It's about the 911 call we attended a few nights ago. Marve Brittle."

The name sent chills down Liam's spine. This case seemed to be getting worse by the minute.

"What is it?" Liam's heart beats furiously in his chest, a sinking feeling settling in as he waits for Marve's response. Was he involved in this horrific attack too?

"I just got called to his house. Mindy Cohen, the realtor, was attacked and her car was stolen. It all happened at his house." Liam's mind races with possibilities.

"What does this have to do with anything?"

"We found some broken walls here. And what we found inside has everything to do with this case. The skeletal remains of young girls were hidden within the wall. Marve must have fled when he realized we were onto him. Someone saw him speeding away in Mindy's car."

Liam falls silent, trying to process everything. It all seems so inexplicable. He had thought Marve had left town, but now with these disturbing discoveries, he understands why Rachel kept him hidden all this time. Marve was nothing but a mere pawn in her twisted game. But why would a vengeful spirit be driving a car? Where could she possibly be heading?

"Murray, place an ABP on Mindy Cohen's car immediately. We need to find out where she went and who else might have seen or heard anything."

"I'm on it." Murray hangs up and Liam is left alone with his thoughts.

"How much?" he asked gruffly, eyeing her suspiciously.

Rachel's eyes glinted with a sharp intensity as she peered through Marve's vision. The boy stood in her way, but she didn't feel the urge to end his life. He was just an innocent bystander caught up in her plans. But she did need a distraction.

With a flick of her wrist, Rachel directed her power towards the other side of the station where the man's car was parked. A steady stream of gasoline began pouring out, pooling on the ground. A mischievous smirk spread across her lips as she tapped her finger and created a spark that ignited the flammable liquid.

The young man let out a startled yelp as he jumped away from the car, frantically trying to put out the growing flames. As he struggled with the fire, Rachel calmly drove away, confident that no one had seen her orchestrating the chaos. The scent of smoke and burning rubber lingered in the air as she disappeared into the city streets.

"Murray's voice crackled through the phone when Liam answered. "I've got a hit on your ABP," he said urgently.

Liam's heart leapt with hope. "Where is it?"

"A video camera at a local bar just opposite a gas station caught footage of a car speeding away after a freak fire broke out."

"Which direction did the car go?" Liam asked, already reaching for his keys.

"I'll send you a text with the location," Murray said before hanging up.

Liam turned to face the priest and Kimbery, urgency in his eyes. "They think they found her. Father, I need your help to sever the bond between them."

"And what about them?" the priest inquired, gesturing towards Amelia and the others.

"Hopefully, they'll be safe. But we can't risk leaving her with him any longer." Liam's jaw tightened with determination.

"We'll be fine, Father," Amelia spoke up with more bravery than she felt.

Together, they hurried out of the room, their hearts racing with fear and hope intertwined.

Daniela battled with the brick wall, her fingers raw and sore from poking at the small hole. She could feel the weight of time pressing on her as she struggled to widen the opening. The only sound in the desolate room was the tapping of her fingernails against the rough surface.

As she finally managed to squeeze two fingers through, Daniela's heart raced with anticipation. Peering through the hole, she saw rows upon rows of binary code. What kind of twisted prison was she trapped in? Despair threatened to consume her once again, but she refused to give up.

Ignoring the pain in her fingers, Daniela threw herself onto the ground and continued to claw at the wall. A sharp snap echoed through the air and hot white pain shot through her finger. She cried out and cradled her injured hand, a flicker of hope igniting within her.

For the first time since waking up in this nightmare, Daniela felt something other than exhaustion and hopelessness. She felt pain. And that meant she was making progress.

Determined to break free from this digital hell, Daniela attacked the wall with renewed vigor. As she punched and kicked at it, a sliver of light broke through, illuminating the dark room. With each strike, more light flooded in until finally, there was enough for her to see by.

Breathing heavily and covered in sweat, Daniela couldn't help but smile as she noticed one of her heels lying nearby. They must have fallen off during one of her attempts to escape. Grinning triumphantly, she picked up the shoe and continued chipping away at the wall, knowing that freedom was just on the other side. "I'm coming for you," she whispered fiercely into the darkness.

With a fierce determination, Daniela grabbed the shoe and thrust the pointed heel into the crumbling wall. She could hear fabric ripping from the other side and felt a surge of adrenaline as a large chunk of the wall fell to her feet. Kneeling down, she maneuvered her arm through the hole, feeling a sense of hope flood over her. With all her strength, she kicked at the weakened wall, each blow bringing her closer to freedom and redemption.

As she stood up, Daniela could taste the sweet air of freedom, but knew her mission wasn't over yet. Her and Rachel shared a common goal - to put an end to the cruel Cult of Standish and their reign of terror. But while Rachel was willing to resort to murder, Daniela had a different plan in mind.

"I can help you," she said confidently to Rachel, who stood nearby with a determined glint in her eye. "I can read your mind and emotions. Together, we can take them down without stooping to their level."

Rachel's eyes widened in surprise and relief, and together they plotted their next move. They may have had different methods, but they were united in their goal - justice for those who had been hurt by the cult's twisted beliefs. And if it was the last thing she did, Daniela would make sure they succeeded.

Daniela sprinted to the far end of the room, her heart pounding as she took a deep breath. With all her strength, she charged towards the wall, slamming into it repeatedly until finally, with a deafening crack, it gave way beneath her body. The flames that had engulfed her suddenly vanished as she collapsed to the ground with a thud.

Amelia's sharp eyes were the first to notice the abrupt disappearance of the fire. She quickly tapped Kimbery's shoulder, drawing her attention to their fallen companion. Cautiously, they approached Daniela's motionless form, unsure of what to expect. But then, in a miraculous moment, her eyelids fluttered open and shut before fully opening to take in her surroundings.

"Is...is everyone okay?" Daniela asked weakly, still struggling to gain control over her body.

Amelia and Kimbery exchanged disbelieving looks before turning back to face their injured friend. Could it be true? Had Daniela finally regained control after months of being possessed by an unknown entity? Her words only further solidified their hope.

"Amelia...I forgive you," Daniela uttered through trembling lips.

"We'll make them pay for what they've done. To us, our family, this entire town."

Tears welled up in Amelia's eyes as she heard those words from her cousin's mouth. She never meant for this chaos to ensue, but if it meant avenging their loved ones and restoring peace to their hometown, then she was willing to do whatever it takes. And she was grateful for Daniela's forgiveness and determination to fight alongside them once again.

Amelia's heart raced as she watched Daniela frantically explain her plan. "I have to stop Rachel," she said, her voice trembling with fear. "But first, I must retrieve my locket from Cedar Villa before she can possess me again." Kimbery's eyes widened in agreement, a silent affirmation of her previous warnings. The three women knew the danger that awaited them, but they had no choice - Rachel had to be stopped at all costs.

CHAPTER EIGHTEEN

The frigid winter air whipped against Rachel's face as she raced down the highway, her mind consumed with a singular purpose: justice. She would make those cult members pay for all the lives they had destroyed, including her own. Nothing could distract her from this mission, not even the numbing cold seeping into her body.

With determination fueling her, Rachel had made her way up the ranks of the cult, inching ever closer to confronting the two responsible for her death. As she read through the file one last time before reaching their leader, a small part of her couldn't believe that he was truly the mastermind behind it all. But then again, maybe Amelia was just trying to play games with her once more.

No matter, Rachel thought. She would take care of Amelia after dealing with the bigger fish – Marve. His bloated, slovenly appearance disgusted her and she marveled at how such a vile creature could lure in unsuspecting victims. She imagined his building littered with the remains of young girls, their innocence stolen by his twisted desires.

But Rachel wasn't finished yet. Amelia may have been a victim too, but that didn't excuse what she had done. And now it was time for retribution. Rachel's grip tightened on the steering wheel as she mentally prepared herself for what lay ahead. Justice would be served today, no matter what it took.

The night she discovered his dark secret of using and killing innocent girls, her rage consumed her. It was the when she was on the swing porch and he had approached her while she inhabited Daniela. It was a chilling reminder of her own traumatic experience. How could he be worse than the men who had attacked her? At least they were not methodically murdering young women.

As she stood in his home, she never imagined that he would become a pawn in her revenge plot. But now, she relished because he had been imprisoned within the very walls where he had tortured and killed his victims.

"You deserve to suffer," she hissed at him as she saw her own reflection in the mirror. This was the perfect way to take down the leader of the Cult - by using one of his own men against him. She couldn't wait to see the fear in his eyes as she enacted her final plan for retribution.

Father Thom gripped his seatbelt tightly as Liam swerved through traffic, driving like a man possessed. The priest had never seen such reckless driving before, even in all his years of traveling and mission work. Sweat beaded on his forehead as he silently prayed for their safety.

"Can you go any faster?" Liam's colleague had described the suspect's car as a navy blue BMW and they were determined to catch up before it reached its destination.

Liam remained silent, but his white knuckles gripping the steering wheel gave away his determination. He resisted the urge to push down harder on the accelerator, knowing they were already going at dangerously high speeds with only the wailing siren protecting them from getting pulled over by fellow officers.

As they weaved in and out of traffic, Liam couldn't help but think back to five years ago when Amaya was still in his life. It felt like just yesterday, but now it seemed like a distant memory. For the first time since her death, he found himself praying for another woman to enter his life. His heart ached at the thought of her, but right now, he needed to focus on the task at hand and bring this criminal to justice.

As he stood in the empty room, memories of a happier time with Amaya flooded his mind like a tidal wave crashing onto shore. She had been his family, his everything. He could still see her smiling face and feel her warm embrace. But life was cruel and their plans to spend forever together were ripped away from them. Barely three weeks after he proposed, Amaya was involved in a tragic hit-and-run accident that left her comatose.

The search for the driver who had fled the scene was futile and Amaya's chances of survival were slim, according to the doctors. Liam refused to give up hope, believing that God could perform miracles. It wasn't until her accident that he found solace in religion, visiting Amaya's church and praying fervently for her recovery.

For six months, he devoted himself to this new routine, neglecting his work and personal life in the process. But as time went on and everyone else gave up hope, Liam continued to hold onto faith and pray endlessly for a miracle. Even when the doctors urged him to let go and take her off life support, he persisted in his devotion, fasting until food became a foreign concept to his stomach.

But despite his unwavering faith, God had different plans for him. It wasn't until over eight months later that Liam finally accepted defeat and said goodbye to his beloved fiancé. The room echoed with the weight of his heartbreak as he realized that sometimes even the strongest faith cannot overcome fate.

After the death of Amaya, one would have expected Liam's faith to waver. But it only grew stronger. Religion became his refuge in times of despair. He believed that Amaya would have wanted him to stay strong for her. And when he met Daniela, he reminded himself of the same thought - Amaya would have wanted him to move on.

But now, faced with a similar situation, Liam wasn't sure which was worse. With Amaya, there were only two options and he knew the chances of her survival were slim. But with Daniela, he had no idea what to expect. Once again, he found himself at the mercy of God.

With a silent prayer on his lips, Liam begged for Daniela's safe return. He pleaded with God to break the chains of evil that held her captive. He reminded God of his unwavering faith despite the pain and loss he had experienced. He prayed for recompense with Daniela - the one he wanted to start anew with.

But before he could finish his prayers, his phone rang, interrupting his conversation with God. Liam debated ignoring it but realized it could be important. It was Kimbery on the other end.

Before Liam Answered the Call from Kim.

Kimbery's hands gripped the steering wheel tightly, her knuckles white with tension as she drove the police van towards Amelia's house. Daniela sat in the back seat, her eyes darting nervously around the city streets. They had just received a distress call from Amelia, informing them of the group's plan to take refuge at Iris's house until help arrived.

As they deliberated their next move, Daniela couldn't shake off the feeling of dread that hung heavy in the air. She knew that this creature they were facing was powerful and unpredictable. She glanced over at Amelia, who was slumped in her seat, injured and in pain. Kimbery had volunteered to drive, knowing they had no other choice.

It didn't take long for them to find a set of keys for one of the police vans and soon they were speeding towards Iris's apartment. As they approached the building, Daniela could feel her heart racing with fear and anticipation.

"Is that Dani or..." Heath started to asked, his voice trailing off as he looked at Daniela with uncertainty.

"It's me, Heath," Daniela replied wearily. "For now, Rachel has left my body."

Everyone let out a collective sigh of relief, but Daniela knew it was only temporary. She sank into one of the sofas in Iris's living room, exhaustion weighing heavily on her.

Iris rushed into the kitchen to make some herbal tea for Daniela, needing something to distract herself from the overwhelming events of the night. She couldn't believe what she had witnessed - her friend possessed by some dark force.

"Why did we even bring her here?" Iris thought to herself guiltily. But then she scolded herself for such selfish thoughts - how could she abandon her friend in a time of need?

As they all waited anxiously for help to arrive, none of them could predict what would happen next in this dangerous game with the unknown.

The words of Detective Blake echoed in the tense atmosphere as he entered the kitchen with Iris. Fear was palpable, emanating from every person in the room. Even the fearless detective couldn't shake off his own fear, knowing that a brutal killer was among them. As Heath cooed softly to Amelia, tending to her injuries, Kimbery was busy dressing the wounds of Daniela. Maureen remained silent, deep in prayer, until finally turning to ask about Liam's whereabouts.

"Where's Liam?" Her voice trembled with worry for the young man who didn't deserve any of this madness. If something happened to him, Daniela would never forgive herself.

"Rachel has taken over Marve's body and is on the run," Kimbery answered somberly, her eyes flickering with uncertainty.

Maureen turned to Amelia when she heard a faint sound from her. "What did you say, Amelia?"

"She's gone after the leader of the cult," Amelia whispers, confirming everyone's worst fears.

Instantly, Daniela leapt up from the sofa and locked eyes with her cousin. "You know who it is?" she demanded. But Amelia remained silent.

"Amelia?" Daniela pressed, desperation seeping into her tone.

After a moment of hesitation, Amelia finally spoke. "It's..." The name died on her lips as she glanced nervously at Kimbery.

"Just tell us," Daniela urged, sensing the gravity of the situation.

Amelia's hands were shaking as she tried to form words. "I-I can't," she stammered, her voice hysterical.

"Amelia, please speak up!" Heath implored, frustration clear in his tone. "This is a matter of life and death."

But Amelia couldn't bring herself to say it out loud. She knew they wouldn't understand, wouldn't believe her. And if they found out, Rachel would be furious. The constant fear of Rachel's wrath made it nearly impossible for Amelia to betray her trust.

"Do you at least know where she's going next?" Daniela asked, her voice trembling with fear.

Amelia could only stare at the floor, her mind racing with conflicting thoughts and emotions.

"Baby, please," Heath continued, his tone pleading now. "We need your help. More lives are at risk here, including ours. We have to stop her before it's too late."

After a moment of tense silence, Amelia finally spoke. "She's headed to the Real News recording studio," she said quietly.

Kimbery wasted no time in grabbing her phone and calling Liam. Every second counted.

"Please answer," Kimbery whispers to herself as the phone rang. Just when she was about to give up hope, Liam answered.

"Kim?" he said, his tone worried and urgent.

"She's alive! Daniela is alive!"

Liam's question hung in the air, breaking the tense silence that had settled over the group. Daniela could feel their eyes on her, waiting for her answer. She took a deep breath before replied, "Dani. It's Dani." Her voice was shaky but determined.

"Look, we just found out where Rachel might be headed," she continued, feeling a sense of urgency creeping up on her. "It's not a sure thing, but it's a step. She's headed to the Real News TV studios. Find a shortcut and try to get there before her. We'll be there soon."

Kim glanced at Daniela with a sad look and handed her a phone. "Liam wants to speak with you," she said softly.

Despite everything that had happened, Liam still trusted her. Daniela felt a wave of gratitude wash over her as she took the phone and said hello.

"Oh my God! It really is you," Liam's voice came through, filled with relief. "Is she..."

"No, we're still linked. She can come back whenever she wants," Daniela interrupted, trying to keep her emotions in check. "But I'm going to find her and break that link. I can't let her continue to win."

"You're stronger than last time. I have faith in you," Liam reassured her. "Father Thom and I will head straight for the TV station. Let us know when you get here."

After ending the call, Daniela handed the phone back to Kimbery and looked around at her friends and family who had become her support system in this harrowing journey.

In one night, they had gone through unimaginable horrors, but they stood by her unwaveringly. They were the reason she couldn't give up now.

She took another deep breath and knew that she was doing this for them; for everyone she loved.

"Let's go." She said to Kimbery, her voice urgent and determined.

"Go where?" Iris asked, setting the steaming cup of chamomile tea she had brought from the kitchen on the wooden coffee table.

"To Real News studios. Rachel is headed there right now. That's if she hasn't arrived already. Time is of the essence."

Iris felt a flicker of worry in her chest at the urgency in Daniela's voice. She glanced around the cozy living room, taking in the warm glow of sunlight through the windows and the scent of fresh flowers from a vase on the mantle. But Daniela's next words interrupted her thoughts.

"On your own?" Iris quizzed, her eyebrows furrowing with concern.

"No. I'm going with Kimbery and Heath."

"I'll come with you," Iris declared without hesitation. During the time she spent preparing tea in the kitchen, she had felt guilty about her earlier doubts and fears. Friends stuck together through thick and thin, and that was exactly what she intended to do.

"Iris, thank you but I think you're needed here more than with me,"

Daniela replied, placing a comforting hand on Iris' shoulder. "Amelia needs constant attention and so does Detective Blake."

Iris nodded understandingly. She knew Amelia was still recovering from her injuries sustained during their escape from danger. And Detective Blake had also been injured while helping them flee to safety.

"And there's Aunt Maureen," Daniela continued, gesturing towards the elderly woman sitting in a nearby armchair. "I need someone to watch over her and everyone else who isn't coming with us. Please, do this for me. You're the only one here other than Amelia who has knowledge on healing. Amelia is obviously not in a capacity to take care of anyone. That leaves you. I need you, Iris."

Iris could see the desperation in Daniela's eyes and knew she couldn't refuse. The TV station was only a short walk from their current location, but it was still a dangerous journey.

"The TV station is just a few blocks from here," Iris said, her tone cautious. "Be careful out there."

"I will," Daniela promised, determination evident in her voice. "Liam and Father Thom will also be there for backup. And so will Kim and Heath."

But Maureen's soft voice broke through the conversation, pleading with Daniela not to go.

"Daniela, don't go. I beg you," she whispered, a worried expression on her frail face.

"I'm sorry, Aunty. It's the only way," Daniela replied, gentle but unwavering. With one last reassuring look towards Iris, she turned and left with Kimbery and Heath to face whatever awaited them at Real News studios.

The tires of Kimbery's car screeched as she pulled into the studio parking lot. Liam was right behind her, desperately trying to keep up. They had been driving aimlessly for hours, unaware of the correct direction to the station where Rachel was being held. It wasn't until Daniela's urgent call that they realized their mistake and headed towards the navy blue BMW that represented their only hope of finding Rachel.

As soon as Liam stepped out of the car, his eyes caught sight of the BMW and he knew they were close. Daniela rushed towards him, panic etched on her face.

"Liam!" she cried out.

"She's here," he responded, his voice full of determination.

"I can feel her presence," Daniela added, scanning her surroundings with a sense of urgency. In the corner of her eye, she saw Kimbery and Heath step out of their vehicle.

"Can you lead us to her?" Kimbery asked, her voice shaky with anxiety.

"I'll try," Daniela replied, closing her eyes in concentration. She felt a chill run down her spine, a familiar sensation that always accompanied Rachel's presence.

Liam's fingers gripped her arms tightly, but instead of feeling cold, they radiated warmth. It was a strange and powerful connection between them that went beyond mere touch. With her left foot forward, Daniela began to move due east, trusting her instincts to guide them.

But as she walked further in that direction, she could sense that something was off. The chill in her bones lessened with each step, indicating that Rachel was not in this direction after all.

"This isn't right," she stated firmly, turning back on her heels. As she did so, the wind picked up around them, causing a loud whooshing sound to fill their ears.

"That was Heath moving out of your way," Kimbery explained.

"That's why Liam is holding onto me," Daniela realized, grateful for his support. "I don't want to blindly walk into anything with my eyes closed."

As Daniela advanced toward the looming television studio, a palpable tension gripped her chest, each step echoing in sync with the thunderous beats of her heart. The icy tendrils of dread clung tighter to her bones, a spectral grip that seemed to tighten with every passing second. A premonition whispered through her, hinting at the imminent convergence of malevolent forces upon their target – Rachel.

The atmosphere crackled with an otherworldly energy as Liam deftly brandished his police ID, a silent proclamation of authority that brushed aside any skepticism about their unauthorized intrusion. Kimbery's hushed whispers trailed like a haunting melody, detailing the disruption of a live show, the stakes escalating as they closed in on Rachel's elusive sanctuary.

Daniela couldn't shake the magnetic pull drawing her towards the room where Rachel concealed herself, the air pulsating with an urgency that bordered on supernatural compulsion. The weight of the impending confrontation bore down on her, a burden both physical and metaphysical.

Heath's revelation, delivered with an ominous gravity, intensified the gravity of the situation. The notion that Rachel might be inhabiting Marve's body, a puppeteer orchestrating chaos within the confines of the Mayoral Debate broadcast, sent shivers down Daniela's spine.

Without a second thought, Daniela burst into the room, a tempest of determination propelling her forward. Liam and the others surged in her wake, a united front against the encroaching darkness. The clash with security guards echoed like distant thunder, but Liam's swift prowess swiftly dismantled any obstacles in their path.

As Marve, a once-respected figure now tainted by deceit, angrily confronted them, the air crackled with the intensity of impending revelation. "You won't get away with this!" Marve's growl reverberated through the studio, a defiant proclamation against the shadows that sought to envelop him. "I'll expose you for the lying, corrupt scum that you are!"

The stage was set for a spectral showdown, the live broadcast a mere backdrop to the unfolding supernatural drama, where the lines between reality and the macabre blurred into a chilling symphony of deceit and revelation.

Amidst the swirling chaos, the once-orderly debate floor devolved into sheer pandemonium, a nightmarish tableau unfolding with Marve's grotesque transformation. The esteemed Mayor Warren Rex and the impassioned Human Rights activist Abe Thompson stood frozen in a macabre dance of disbelief, their faces mirroring the shock that reverberated through the room. Security personnel, once pillars of order, were violently cast aside like ragdolls by the monstrous appendages that sprouted from Marve's body, each bloated finger a grotesque manifestation of an unholy metamorphosis. The very air quivered with the discordant symphony of the upheaval, punctuated by Marve's voice, a twisted amalgamation of five men's voices compressed into a singular, nightmarish throat.

As Daniela, propelled by a cocktail of fear and determination, rushed towards the unfolding spectacle, she bore witness to Rachel's malevolent plan reaching its zenith. However, a glimmer of triumph danced in

Daniela's eyes as she locked gazes with her former captor, a silent testament to the resilience that had blossomed within her during her
harrowing captivity. The woman Rachel never thought capable of
breaking free was now the harbinger of her unraveling schemes.

"What are you doing, Rachel?" Daniela's voice cut through the tumult, a
desperate plea above the cacophony.

"Making things right," Rachel retorted, her tone unyielding, eyes ablaze
with a determination that bordered on fanaticism. "You weren't
supposed to be here. You were supposed to be... in that prison I put
you in."

Daniela's heart soared with a renewed sense of hope as she witnessed
surprise flicker across Rachel's features. Before another word could
escape her lips, Marve, caught in the throes of disbelief, turned their
way. His contorted features spoke of a realization unfolding in real-time,
a monstrous revelation that mirrored the chaos around them.

In a display of unbridled strength, Marve flung more security personnel
aside as they dared to approach him, his actions a manifestation of the
mayhem that had befallen the once-controlled environment.

"Stop this, Rachel!" Daniela's desperate plea echoed through the
bedlam. "This isn't justice; it's madness! All these people are innocent."

Yet, Rachel, consumed by a relentless crusade for vengeance, met
Daniela's plea with a thundering roar, declared, "No! Not everyone is
innocent. Right here in this room is the man responsible for my execu-
tion. The one who made it possible for those Cult of Standish fanatics
to believe they could sacrifice me for their twisted beliefs."

The audience, caught in the crossfire of revelation and horror, gasped in
collective disbelief. Daniela, relegated to the role of a helpless spectator,
could only watch as the fabric of reason unraveled, spiraling out of
control into a vortex of madness and retribution. The once-coherent
debate had metamorphosed into a macabre spectacle, where the bound-
aries between justice and chaos blurred into a nightmarish tableau of
unforeseen consequences.

"I don't understand what you mean. People care...."

"They don't! They do not. Why has no one bothered to look for all those girls Marve, this man whose body I now inhabit, had built into his walls? Who cared when two young ladies, The Pembroke sisters, went missing on their way back from church? You know what happened to those girls? The Priest, Father Christopher, took one of them for his twisted rituals. The other was just an inconvenience that needed to be taken care of, so he killed her too."

"My GOD!" Daniela exclaimed, her horror and disbelief etched across her face. The chilling tale of the Pembroke sisters had circulated in whispers before she arrived in town. The memory of the disappearances had quickly faded, the town resuming its normal routine with no effort to find the missing girls, no search parties organized.

"Exactly. So what makes me so different? Is it because I, unlike the Pembroke sisters, have the power to avenge my death? Do you want to hear my story? Fine, I'll tell you. A group of men kidnapped me on my way back from a Halloween party. They dragged me deep into the woods and subjected me to unimaginable torture and abuse. I was beaten, molested, and raped by two men until I finally passed out." Rachel's words hung heavily in the air, a weight that the audience couldn't escape.

But Rachel wasn't finished, her voice cutting through the stunned silence. "Just when I thought I had seen it all, they laid me on their sinister slaughter table and ended my life like I was nothing more than an expendable animal."

"Blood of Jesus!" A voice from the audience cries out in shock and disgust.

"All bullshit," another person chimed in angrily. The harsh reality of Rachel's horrific demise was finally laid bare, and it seemed like justice, if it could be served at all, might come too late. The crowd grappled with the revelation, their collective gasps and murmurs forming a dissonant chorus of disbelief. The once-shrouded secrets were exposed, and the town stood at the precipice of reckoning, where the blurred lines of truth and complicity threatened to plunge them into an abyss of darkness.

"Bullshit?" Rachel bellowed, her voice resonating through the room like a thunderous storm. "Is this bullshit?" In a moment of surreal transformation, Marve's visage contorted with rage, his features morphing into hers, a sinister grin spreading across his face. She fixed her penetrating gaze on the audience, then turned to the cameras, her eyes ablaze with fury. "So there you have it, folks at home. The Cult of Standish is real and is being led by my father!"

Daniela's world spun as she grappled with the staggering revelations. "Your... Your father? I don't understand. He did this?"

"Oh, he did this and more," Rachel spat, her words dripping with venom. "In his quest for power, he joined the cult and became their leader. They take orders from him. To 'protect' my identity, he changed my name and refused to acknowledge me as his daughter. I thought it was because of his political aspirations, but I had no idea it was because of his dark, hidden life. He shipped me off to school and forced me into residency. So, dear Daniela, Rachel Chambers is not Rachel Chambers after all. Rachel Chambers is Rachel Chambers Rex."

The weight of the revelation pressed down on Daniela, her knees threatening to buckle beneath her as she struggled to stay upright.

"The Mayor is my father and the mastermind behind the cult," Rachel declared, her voice a volatile mixture of anger and sorrow.

However, as Daniela turned toward where the Mayor had been seated, a sudden emptiness loomed. The entire political spectrum, both Mayor Warren Rex and his opposition, had vanished. Panic surged through her veins, a chilling realization of the depth of corruption that permeated their city. They were now face to face with an insidious force, and the disconcerting truth left them utterly powerless against the tendrils of deceit that ensnared the very core of their existence. The city's façade of normalcy had shattered, revealing a malevolent underbelly that had thrived in the shadows, orchestrating a macabre dance of manipulation and treachery.

CHAPTER NINETEEN

Warren frantically paced his hotel room, unable to believe the events unfolding before him. He had fled from the television station when the man began speaking about the cult of Standish, bringing Abe along to avoid appearing cowardly. But now, as he sat in his hotel room with the television on, he could no longer deny the horrifying truth. His daughter, Rachel, was dead - murdered by the very demons he had once led. In a fit of rage and despair, Warren kicked the wall in front of him, but even the pain in his foot couldn't compare to the agony in his heart.

Years ago, when Warren first joined the cult while working in town with his family still living in Somerset, he had considered this possibility. The priests had toyed with the idea of a Virgin sacrifice and although they had convinced him otherwise Warren always knew it would come down to this. He couldn't risk his daughter becoming a victim, so he changed his name to Warren Rex and moved his family into town under their new identities. However, he never allowed Rachel to change her name or live with them.

She spent most of her childhood in boarding school and when she reached college age, Warren sent her off to a distant residency program.

In public, he ignored her completely, refusing to acknowledge her existence as a way to protect her from the cult's grasp.

But now, as grief consumed him and anger fueled his thoughts, Warren couldn't help but wonder if he could have done more to save his daughter. And as he thought back to all those years of keeping her at arm's length, guilt washed over him like a tidal wave. With tears streaming down his face, he whispered to himself through clenched teeth: "I should have protected her."

He had been living a lie, blinded by his own denial. They had taken her from him, mercilessly snuffing out her light in their never-ending pursuit of control and dominance. And now his daughter, once sweet and innocent, has transformed into a menacing force within society. She speaks of vengeance, driven by a deep-seated desire for retribution against those who wronged her. He knows she is coming for him, and it's only a matter of time before she arrives to exact her revenge.

"Where is he?" Rachel shrieked, her voice carrying through the empty auditorium. "Where is he?" Her eyes darted around frantically, searching for a target for her rage.

"Calm down, Rachel," Daniela pleaded, trying to keep her from spiraling out of control.

"Do not tell me what to do! This is your entire fault! Your fault!" Rachel bellowed, her face contorted with anger as she raised her trembling hands towards Daniela.

As her fingers made contact with Marve's body, Daniela felt a strange sensation in her feet. It was like electricity running through her veins, pushing her off the ground. She heard Liam and the others calling out to her, but their voices were distant and blurred.

The next thing she knew, she was flying through the air and crashing into one of the audience pews. The pain was searing and overwhelming, but she forced herself to open her eyes and take stock of the situation. To her surprise, there were only a few people left in the auditorium. In the blink of an eye, Marve had become a towering figure above her.

But then Daniela heard a voice, calm and commanding amidst the chaos. It was Father Thom, approaching them with his bible held high in one hand. "Be gone, you unclean spirit," he said firmly, his words ringing out with authority. "And stay far away from this creature of God!"

Daniela felt a surge of gratitude as she saw Rachel stumble backwards and fall to the floor. For a moment, it seemed like the ghost possessing Marve had retreated. But then it began to manifest itself again, trying desperately to reach Daniela.

She quickly reached into her pocket and grabbed hold of her rosary, holding it up before her in a protective gesture. With trembling hands, she recited The Lord's Prayer as loudly as she could. The ghost screeched and writhed in agony, unable to bear the holy words.

And then, just as suddenly as it had appeared, the ghost vanished. Daniela's breathing was heavy as she tried to calm herself down, realizing that the danger was not yet over.

"Where is it?" Father Thom asked urgently.

"Gone somewhere else where it has more power," Daniela replied, slowly getting to her feet. "We need to find the mayor before it's too late."

"I just spoke with the news anchor. She said they all ran away when things went awry. But the mayor is still in his hotel room around the block," Kimbery informed them.

"We don't have much time," Daniela said, determination setting in. "Let's hope we can get to him before Rachel does."

Rachel's entire being ignited with a searing anger as she stormed out of the church and appeared at her father's hotel room. She had underestimated the girl - she was much stronger than Rachel anticipated. There had to be a reason for such a drastic change in such a short time, and Rachel couldn't help but blame the detective. The thought gnawed at her, fueling her rage even more.

As she approached her father's room, she could sense his presence inside. Without hesitation, she marched towards the door. Her father was pacing back and forth, looking completely different from when she saw him earlier. In just a few hours, he seemed to have aged years.

Rachel used to love this man, despite his absence in her life. She used to believe his excuses about protecting her, but now she knew the truth - he had been saving her for his own twisted cult.

"H-hello father," Warren stammers as Rachel materialized in front of him.

Her lips curled into an evil smile as he stumbled backwards. He quickly regained his composure and stood up straight, but it was too late - Rachel could see the fear in his eyes.

"Hello father," she mocked, emphasizing the word with venom dripping from her voice. "Your day of reckoning has finally arrived."

Trembling with fear and guilt, Warren approached his daughter Rachel. "Rachel, I swear to you, I had no idea what they did to you. I didn't know you were missing," he pleaded. Rachel's eyes blazed with anger as she faced him. "I thought it was just another innocent girl they decided to kill. What if it was a random girl? Did she not deserve a life?" Warren stutters, trying to explained himself. "I'm not saying that, child. I didn't know it was you they took."

But Rachel wasn't convinced. She knew her father had willingly given her over to the cult for their ritual sacrifice. "You knew they wanted a virgin girl and you gave them the go ahead?!" Her voice rose with each word, until she used her demonic powers to lift him off the ground. "I'm going to enjoy punishing you," she threatened, her eyes glinting with vengeance. Warren begged for mercy, but Rachel wasn't done yet.

"I was your daughter when they took me," she reminded him as she flicked her finger, causing his left knee to snapped with a sickening crunch. He screamed in agony as the pain shot through him, his bone jutting out of a wound. Ignoring his screams, Rachel continued to inflict punishment on him for all the horrors he had allowed her to endure at the hands of the cult. She lifted him again and snapped his right leg, causing another burst of excruciating pain. Satisfied with his suffering, she dropped him to the floor and continued speaking through clenched teeth.

"I was your daughter when they drugged me and beat me...when they raped me...when they dragged me to your slaughter slab...when they plunged a knife into my body." As Warren lay there shaking uncontrollably and crying in pain and remorse, Rachel's final words echoed in his mind.

"I was your daughter, and you failed to protect me."

Warren felt like his chest was imploding, the heat spreading through his body and sweat soaking his clothes. It was as if his blood was boiling inside him. The pain was unbearable, each second feeling like an eternity.

"Please...Rachel," he begged, gasped for breath. "I'm sorry."

"Sorry?" she sneered, her words causing even more tightness in Warren's chest and a surge of anger. "That doesn't mean anything."

Before Rachel could take any further action, Daniela burst into the room, panting and out of breath.

"Don't kill him!" she shouted, fear and desperation in her voice.

But it was too late. In a flash of movement, blood and organs splattered across the room with a sickening sound.

Daniela couldn't hold back the bile rising in her throat as she stared at the gory mess. The mayor, who had been standing there just moments ago, was now nothing but a heap of flesh and bone. His heart lay at Daniela's feet, a reminder of the brutal end he had met.

Tears streaming down her face, Daniela turned to Rachel. "You didn't have to do this."

"There was no other way," Rachel replied coldly.

"But there was!" Daniela cries. "You could have let him face the consequences of his actions. You could have let him suffer the shame and guilt of what he did with his hands. But you took matters into your own hands."

As Daniela stood up to confront Rachel, their eyes locked in a fierce stare. "You are no different from them," she said bitterly. "No matter how much you try to convince yourself otherwise, you are just as cruel and ruthless."

"Don't you dare compare me to them!" Rachel spat back.

"It's over," Daniela continued, her voice shaking with emotion. "Your mission is done. It's time to go back to where you belong. Give me my locket and leave me alone, you evil creature!"

Rachel's expression hardened at the mention of the locket.

"So it was about the locket all along," she said with disgust. "Well, I have news for you, Daniela. The locket is mine now. And I am not leaving without it."

The words cut through the tense silence, Rachel's voice dripping with hatred and malice as she stalked towards Daniela. "You and I are not so different," she sneered, "we are one and the same."

Daniela's spine stiffened as she glared back at her enemy. "We are nothing alike!" she spat.

"Oh, but we are," Rachel taunted, circling closer to Daniela. "Both of us have been hurt by men we loved. We're both victims. And now we are both alone, all alone by ourselves."

"I am not alone," Daniela retorted fiercely. "I may have been hurt, but I have people who love me and have helped me heal. Family and friends who have become family. I am nothing like you."

Rachel's lips curled into a cruel smirk. "Where are these people now when you need them, huh Daniela? Or should I say, Dani?" She mocked.

But before Daniela could respond, the door burst open and Liam, Kimbery, and Father Thom entered. Their eyes widened in horror as they took in the bloody remains of the mayor.

Rachel saw the priest and knew what was coming next. Panic flashed across her face - she was not ready to leave this world yet. Turning to Daniela, she saw that the girl was momentarily distracted as her rosary fell from her grasp.

This was her chance.

With a swift movement, Rachel entered Daniela's body.

"Where is she?" Kimbery cried out in relief.

"Gone," Liam replied with a grim expression. "She got our message."

But just as they thought it was over, a twisted smile stretched across Daniela's face. In a split second, Kimbery was hugging her friend tightly, tears streaming down her face.

But then something strange happened - as the rosary touched Daniela's skin, she suddenly cried out in pain.

"Get away from that creature, Kimbery," Father Thom warned sternly. "That is not your friend!"

But it was too late - Rachel had taken control of Daniela's body once again. And this time, she wasn't going to let anyone stop her.

Kimbery's heart raced as she tried to process the sudden force that lifted her into the air, slamming her against the door with a jarring impact. Each blow felt like a relentless assault, her body yielding to the unseen force. Panic surged through her as she cried out for help, but the face that stared back at her, once belonging to her friend Daniela, now twisted into the sinister visage of Rachel. The surreal transformation unfolded before her disbelieving eyes.

As quickly as it began, Daniela collapsed to the floor, unconscious and seemingly caught in the grip of a malevolent force. The room seemed to pulsate with an otherworldly energy, and Kimbery's vision blurred as darkness threatened to envelop her. The air hung heavy with a sense of impending doom, and Kimbery knew this was only the beginning of something far more sinister than she had ever imagined.

"What... what is happening?" she gasped, her words barely audible over the cacophony of her racing heartbeat. The question lingered in the air, unanswered, as the ominous silence swallowed her surroundings. Darkness closed in, leaving Kimbery suspended in a chilling void, her senses overwhelmed by the unknown. The ominous quiet persisted, offering no solace or explanation, only a foreboding prelude to the unfathomable horrors that lay ahead.

Daniela's eyes flutter open, her body weak and trembling as she regains consciousness. She is back in the prison cell where she was tortured earlier, her mind struggling to piece together the hazy memories. But then she hears a voice that sends chills down her spine.

"And so, here we are," Rachel's cold words echo through the cell.

"Where am I?" Daniela asked, fear and anger simmering beneath the surface.

"This is inside you. You refused to let me take over your soul, and now we are both trapped in your body. How did you become so strong?" Rachel taunts.

"I embraced my weakness and turned it into my strength. And I have something worth fighting for - my friends, my family, Liam," Daniela retorted fiercely.

"You are still the same weakling you were in New York. You never learn," Rachel hisses.

"Give me back my locket and leave, demon!" Daniela commanded with steel in her voice.

"But I'm not finished yet. People must pay for what they did to me," Rachel said with a twisted smile.

"You have caused enough pain. I won't let you hurt anyone else," Daniela declared, her resolve hardening.

"Oh, but I will. Starting with your cousin, Amelia," Rachel threatened, her demonic intentions clear.

Father Thom reverently set his Bible down, retrieving a small, unassuming bottle of holy water from within the folds of his robes. With a practiced hand, he drew the sign of the cross over himself, the two others gathered with him, and finally on Daniela's still form.

His voice rang out with authority and conviction as he recited a powerful prayer, a supplication to the Almighty for mercy and protection. The words flowed smoothly from his tongue, each syllable laced with fervor and determination. As the prayer reached its culmination, Father Thom took a deep breath, the weight of the sacred moment palpable, and then sprinkled the holy water over Daniela's body.

"Daniela!" he called out again, his voice filled with urgency. "I know you can hear me. I need you to fight with us against this evil. Only you have the power to deliver yourself from its grasp. Fight with me!"

His eyes locked onto Daniela's face, a beacon of hope amid the shadows, willing her to respond, to join in the battle for her own salvation. The air grew thick with tension and anticipation as they waited for any sign of life from the young woman lying before them. In that sacred moment, the room held its breath, caught between the realms of the mundane and the supernatural, where the outcome teetered on the precipice of faith and the strength of one woman's resolve.

The priest's voice echoed through the dark, candlelit room as Daniela and Rachel stood face to face. The flickering flames cast dancing shadows, and Rachel's eyes gleamed cold and calculating as she taunted Daniela, holding the locket in her hand like a sinister trophy.

"You can't get rid of me that easily," she sneered, her voice dripping with malevolence. "I have the power now."

Yet, Daniela stood tall, her faith unwavering in the face of the demonic presence before her. "It is not my strength that will overcome you, Rachel," she declared with a resolute gaze. "It is by the grace and spirit of the Lord."

Rachel's response was a chilling laughter, a mirthless cackle that sent shivers down Daniela's spine. "You still cling to this person you serve so blindly," she jeered. "But they cannot save you."

"I know your name. And I have dominion over you," Daniela counters, her voice trembling with determination. "Your name is Rachel, and in the name of the Lord I serve, you have no power over me!"

As Daniela prayed with fervent conviction, the atmosphere shifted. A searing heat radiated through Rachel's body, and she screamed in agony. The locket, once held triumphantly, slipped from her grasp. The demonic grip on Daniela weakened with each uttered word, and Rachel felt herself unraveling, the power slipping away like sand through her fingers. The room resonated with the echoes of the spiritual battle, and as the searing heat intensified, Rachel's defiant laughter turned into tortured wails.

In that sacred moment, the divine prevailed over the demonic, and the room was filled with a profound stillness. Daniela's eyes glowed with a celestial light as she stood unwavering, a vessel of faith and resilience. The shadows recoiled, and Rachel, now diminished and overpowered, crumpled to the ground, her malevolent laughter silenced by the triumphant force of unwavering faith.

Father Thom's eyes widened in shock as he saw Daniela's lips moving. In that moment, the realization struck him—she was fighting the same spiritual battle as he was. She was silently engaging in prayer, a desperate plea for strength and divine protection. He quickly surveyed the others in the room, their eyes closed in profound communion with the spiritual realm. Without hesitation, he joined in, his voice rising above the ethereal chorus, speaking aloud the powerful words of faith.

As Father Thom uttered the sacred verses, he could sense the malevolent presence growing stronger, attempting to physically assail Daniela. But he refused to yield. With every ounce of faith and strength within him, he called upon the holy powers to cast out the encroaching darkness from the innocent soul before him. With a resolute hand, he made the sign of the cross on Daniela's forehead, a symbol of his unwavering dedication to God.

A fierce determination emanated from him as he made another sign of the cross on her chest, willing the demons within to tremble before their Creator. The fear and trembling that afflicted Daniela's body now spread to the demonic entity within her. Each word, each gesture, further empowered Father Thom with the divine strength of the Holy Spirit.

This wasn't just his own battle; it was a battle for the soul of a child of God. With the might of Christ behind him, he would not falter or fail. The power of Christ compelled him onward, breaking through the dark walls that entrapped Daniela's spirit. And then, with one final authoritative command, Father Thom watched as the demon fled from her trembling form, defeated by the overwhelming force of good and light that now radiated brightly within her.

The room, once laden with the oppressive weight of malevolence, now exuded a serene stillness. Father Thom's breath caught as he witnessed the transformative power of faith, a testament to the indomitable strength that could be summoned when one's spirit aligned with the divine.

"Do not resist or delay in your departure from this sacred vessel, for it is graced with the presence of Christ. Do not underestimate my words because of my sins, for it is God Himself who commands you. The sacred mystery of the cross calls to you. The unshakable faith of the holy apostles Peter and Paul, and all the saints, commands you. The powerful blood of the martyrs demands your obedience. The purity and self-control of the confessors demands your respect. The devout prayers of all holy men and women resound in your ears. And ultimately, the profound truths and life-changing mysteries of our Christian faith compel you to obey."

The words echoed in the dimly lit room, each syllable a declaration of unwavering faith and authority. Father Thom's voice, though human, resonated with the divine power behind the sacred rites. The atmosphere quivered with a palpable tension as the spiritual battle raged on, the force of good marshaling against the malevolent entity that had sought refuge within Daniela.

The air seemed charged with a sacred energy, and the demonic presence, confronted by the formidable arsenal of faith, recoiled. The room bore witness to the timeless struggle between light and darkness, where the power of prayer and the divine prevailed over the forces that sought to corrupt and consume.

Rachel let out a blood-curdling scream as the priest fervently performed the exorcism. Daniela's body, now a vessel of divine power, stood upright and moved towards Rachel, chanting prayers and making the sign of the cross frantically. In desperation, Rachel hurled a table at the priest, but he dodged it effortlessly, and it crashed against the door. Lights flickered on and off as Rachel struggled to contain Daniela's soul, which had become powerful beyond belief. Despite her efforts, Daniela closed in on her.

Just as Rachel was about to redirect her forces toward Liam, Daniela seized the moment and grabbed onto her locket. "In the name of Christ, I command you to leave my body!" Rachel yelled, her voice echoing with unwavering faith. "My body is a temple of the Lord, and you are nothing but a mere creature. I command you to flee from this sacred place in the name of our Creator!"

Daniela's words were met with a bone-chilling shriek from within her own body. The lights continued to flicker violently as a strong gust of wind swept through the room, yet the priest and others persisted in their prayers without faltering. The battle between the forces of good and the malevolent entity raged on, each word and gesture infused with the power of divine intervention.

Despite the tempest within the room, the collective strength of faith and prayer held fast, unwavering in the face of darkness. The priest, undeterred, continued the sacred ritual, invoking the power of Christ to cast out the demonic force that had gripped her soul.

In that instant, Rachel fell to the floor and vanished into thin air.

The abrupt disappearance left the room in an eerie stillness. The tumultuous winds subsided, the flickering lights steadied, and the priest and others looked around, their eyes wide with a mixture of relief and astonishment. Daniela, still standing in the aftermath, took a deep breath as if releasing the weight of the supernatural struggle that had just unfolded.

The absence of Rachel's malevolent presence was palpable, and the room, once charged with spiritual tension, gradually settled into a tranquil calm. The priest, guided by the divine, had successfully banished the demonic force that had sought to consume Daniela's soul.

As the silence lingered, the priest uttered a final prayer, his voice a soft hymn of gratitude, thanking the Lord for the victory over the forces of darkness. The others, still processing the surreal events that had unfolded before them, joined in a collective expression of gratitude and relief. The room, once a battleground between the sacred and the profane, now stood as a testament to the resilience of Daniela.

Her proud courage had led her to face the demon head-on, and the room bore witness to the indomitable spirit that had triumphed over malevolence. The flickering candles cast a warm glow, illuminating the faces of those who had stood united in faith, and the air held the lingering echoes of prayers that had pierced through the darkness.

In the aftermath, Daniela stood, a symbol of strength and unwavering resolve. The room, now free from the oppressive weight of the demonic presence, seemed to exhale. The battle had been fought and won, not just by the priest and his sacred rites but by the unyielding courage and faith that Daniela had summoned in the face of unimaginable darkness.

Daniela sat up off the floor, her eyes meeting the gaze of the priest. A cry of "Hallelujah" from the priest called Liam and Kimbery's attention, drawing them to Daniela's side. Their hurried footsteps echoed in the room as they approached.

A strange sensation welled up in Daniela's throat as she attempted to speak. Suddenly, an overwhelming force overcame her, and she began retching uncontrollably. The sound of her vomiting echoed in the room until, finally, she raised her head. In the midst of her expelled anguish lay a shiny metal object—her locket.

"Victory at last," she whispered, her voice carrying the weight of the struggles and triumphs that had unfolded within her. The locket, once a symbol of torment, now lay amidst the remnants of the spiritual battle, a tangible token of the victory she had achieved over the darkness that had sought to consume her.

Liam and Kimbery, witnessing the profound moment, exchanged glances, their expressions a mix of relief and amazement. The room, once filled with the tumultuous energy of the supernatural struggle, now embraced a profound stillness. In that quietude, Daniela clutched the recovered locket in her hand, a physical manifestation of her resilience and the triumph of the light within her soul.

EPILOGUE

The verdant trees disappeared beneath a blanket of snow, the once lively street now quiet and barren. Daniela sat inside the coffee shop, her eyes drawn to the blinding whiteness outside. She took a sip of her hot chocolate, relishing in its warmth as she reflected on how blessed she was to still be alive.

As she set down her cup, memories flooded back from two years ago - a time when she had fought for survival, for her loved ones, against a dangerous cult. It had been a long and grueling battle, but she had emerged victorious in the end.

The winter's chill couldn't overshadow the warmth that radiated within Daniela's heart. She marveled at the transformation of the world outside, a symbolic reflection of the changes within her. The snow-covered landscape bore witness to the trials she had faced and the resilience that had carried her through.

Her mind wandered back to the days when the town of Tisdale had been shrouded in darkness, haunted by the malevolent force of a vengeful spirit. The battle had been fierce, testing her courage and the bonds she shared with those she held dear. Yet, against all odds, they had prevailed.

Daniela's gaze lingered on the pristine snowflakes gently falling outside the coffee shop window. Each flake seemed to carry a tale of its own, a story of survival, redemption, and the enduring strength of the human spirit. The winter scene held a quiet beauty, a stark contrast to the chaos and fear that once gripped her heart.

She could still vividly recall the faces of her friends, the moments of uncertainty, and the confrontations with the darkness that sought to consume them. Yet, here she was, sipping hot chocolate in a cozy coffee shop, surrounded by a world that had moved beyond the shadows of its past.

Daniela's journey had been one of profound transformation. The scars of the battle remained, etched into the fabric of her being, but they were now marks of resilience, reminders of the power she had discovered within herself. The snow outside whispered a silent narrative of renewal, and Daniela embraced it, finding solace in the serenity that had settled over her life.

As the winter afternoon unfolded, Daniela's thoughts shifted to the warmth of the present moment. The coffee shop, adorned with festive decorations, became a haven of peace and reflection. The aroma of freshly brewed coffee mingled with the sweet scent of pastries, creating an atmosphere of comfort.

Daniela smiled, grateful for the simple pleasures that now defined her life. The memories of the tumultuous past were like distant echoes, gradually fading away. She wrapped her hands around the cup, feeling the heat seep into her fingers, and took another sip. The hot chocolate tasted sweeter now, a celebration of survival, of life reclaimed, and of the enduring spirit that had carried her through the darkest of winters.

The whole town had been shocked when news of the cult's existence broke out. Daniela couldn't help but feel grateful that the TV show had shed light on their horrific actions. But moving on with life hadn't been easy - she was afraid of what people would think of her, scared of being used as a vessel again by other evil spirits.

But Father Thom's reassurance and her own resilience had helped her through. And here she was now, sitting in this cozy coffee shop with her husband and daughter by her side, savoring each precious moment together. As the snow continued to fall outside, Daniela couldn't help but feel a sense of peace and gratitude wash over her - for being alive, for overcoming the darkness that once threatened to consume her.

The aftermath of the incident left the small town of Tisdale in a state of shock, but soon life went back to normal for everyone else. For her, however, it was a different story. The stares and whispers followed her every move, some even avoiding her completely, believing she still carried the evil spirit within her.

In the face of judgment and suspicion, Daniela found solace in the unwavering support of her family. Liam stood by her side, a pillar of strength and love. Their daughter, a beacon of innocence and joy, became a constant reminder of the life they had fought so hard to protect.

The cozy coffee shop became a refuge, a place where Daniela could find moments of respite from the judgmental eyes that lingered in Tisdale. Here, amid the warm ambiance and the comforting aroma of brewed coffee, she could simply be herself – a survivor, a mother, and a woman who had faced the darkest of shadows and emerged into the light.

As she watched the snowflakes dance outside, Daniela reflected on the journey that had brought her to this point. The scars of the past were still there, but they no longer defined her. She had reclaimed her life and, in doing so, had become a symbol of resilience for those who knew her true story.

But she didn't care. She had been dealing with the physical and mental aftermath on her own for months now. And as she began to feel suffocated by the judgmental eyes of Tisdale, she knew she needed to face her fears head-on and confront them in New York, where it all began.

Liam had decided to come with her. He left everything behind to support her and help her fight her demons. That's when she realized how much he truly loved her. And when he asked her to marry him months later, there was only one answer that came to mind - a resounding 'yes'.

The decision to return to the place where the nightmare unfolded was not an easy one, but Daniela knew it was a crucial step towards healing. With Liam by her side, the journey became a shared endeavor, a testament to the strength of their bond. As they navigated the familiar streets of New York, each step was a deliberate act of defiance against the shadows that lurked in the corners of her memory.

The proposal, a moment of profound love and commitment, became a beacon of hope in the midst of adversity. Liam's unwavering support spoke volumes, reassuring Daniela that she was not alone in her battle against the haunting echoes of the past. The engagement marked a new chapter, a declaration that their love could withstand the darkest of trials.

The engagement ring on Daniela's finger became a symbol of resilience, a reminder that even in the face of darkness, love could prevail. With every glance at the ring, she found strength and determination to confront the lingering fears that held her captive. The future, once clouded by uncertainty, now held the promise of a life built on love, understanding, and shared triumphs.

They had a small ceremony surrounded by their family and friends, and Daniela couldn't be happier taking on his last name. The intimate gathering was a celebration of love that transcended the elaborate trappings of a grand wedding. It was a testament to the depth of their connection and the genuine joy that radiated from their union.

As they exchanged vows, Daniela felt the weight of the past lifting, replaced by the promise of a future filled with love and unwavering support. The ceremony was not just a union of two souls but a testament to the resilience of the human spirit. Together, they had faced the shadows and emerged stronger, ready to embark on a new chapter as husband and wife.

The resounding 'yes' uttered on that day echoed far beyond the wedding vows. It resonated as a declaration of victory – a triumph over fear, judgment, and the malevolent forces that once sought to devour her spirit. Daniela stood not just as a survivor but as a woman who had reclaimed her narrative and rewritten it with the ink of love and resilience.

She felt grateful for Liam's unwavering love and support as they settled into their new life in New York. He had landed a job with the NYPD while a prestigious advertising agency snatched her up. And with the addition of their son Zen, their happiness seemed complete.

Daniela reflected on how far they had come since the incident, feeling thankful for Liam's unwavering love and support throughout it all.

The others had moved on too, each finding their own success and happiness. Kimbery had landed a big gig in the bustling city of Atlanta, Iris's holistic venture was thriving with loyal clientele, Heath had followed his passion for film and was on his way to becoming the next Spielberg. Amelia had finally completed her grueling nursing program, and her family had traveled back to town to celebrate her graduation.

As Daniela sat in the quiet of her home, she couldn't help but think about how far they had all come since their days at college together. She ran a hand over her growing baby bump, a reminder of the love and support that surrounded her. Suddenly, Liam's voice broke through her thoughts, interrupting her reverie.

"Babe, are you ready?" He stood before her with a bouquet of freshly picked roses, his smiled radiating warmth and love.

Daniela took a deep breath and responded softly, "Yeah, sure."

Liam's eyes sparkled with excitement as he suggested, "The party doesn't start for another hour. We can make one quick stop before heading back home."

But Daniela knew what she needed to do before the festivities began. "No, Liam. I need to do this alone." She gently rose from the table, using him as support as she slowly revealed her rounded baby bump that the table had concealed. "I owe it to her."

Concern etched across his face, Liam protested, "I can't let you go alone. Not with your condition."

But Daniela was determined. With a strength that surprised even herself, she stood tall and declared, "It's just pregnancy, Liam. I can handle it. I faced down a vengeful spirit not long ago." She placed a hand on her stomach, feeling the gentle kicks of her unborn child. "And Zen won't be any trouble at all." A smile tugged at her lips as she thought of the name she had chosen for her daughter. She was grateful for all that she had overcome and the blessings in her life, including this precious new life growing inside her. With a determined stride, she snatched the bouquet from Liam's hands and set off on her own, ready to pay her respects to the one who had helped guide her through it all.

Without waiting for Liam's disapproval, Daniela firmly pulled her coat tighter around her shivering body and stepped out into the chilly night air. The ice under her feet crunched and cracked with each step as they made their way towards their destination. They followed a winding path through the frozen landscape, past twisted trees and darkened bushes, until they reached a small hedge that served as the entrance to the cemetery.

Daniela's breath formed clouds in front of her as she walked down the narrow path, her footsteps echoing off the stone walls of the mausoleums lining either side. She continued on, her feet numbed by the cold but her determination keeping her. It took about five minutes before she finally reached the large mausoleum where she had hidden on that fateful night when she first encountered Rachel.

As she pushed open the heavy doors and stepped inside, a chill ran down Daniela's spine. Memories of that night and all the nights that followed flooded her mind, filling her with a sense of unease. But she shook it off and pressed on, making her way deeper into the heart of the cemetery until she found what she was looking for: Rachel's tombstone.

Standing before it, Daniela's heart ached with sorrow. She mourned not only the tragic loss of a young girl with so much potential but also the cruel fate that had befallen her at the hands of those who sought power and control. The inscription on the tombstone was simple and plain, nothing to convey the bravery and struggles of this young soul. It simply read: Rachel.

With tears in her eyes, Daniela gently placed a bouquet of roses on the grave and traced a cross over it with her finger. "I'm sorry for everything that happened to you," she whispered. "I hope you have found true peace now."

Just as she turned to leave, Daniela felt a gentle breeze brush against her cheek, almost like a kiss. She couldn't help but feel that it was Rachel's way of responding to her words, letting her know that she was at peace at last. With a heavy heart, Daniela walked away from the grave, leaving behind the memories and pain that still haunted her.